THE CICADA PROPHECY

J. R. McLeay

The Cicada Prophecy © 2014 J.R. McLeay

Cover Design © 2015 Damonza

All Rights Reserved

To Tricia — who keeps me young

Contents

One 1
Two 7
Three 15
Four 27
Five 35
Six 43
Seven 57
Eight 61
Nine 65
Ten 69
Eleven 75
Twelve 83
Thirteen 93
Fourteen 107
Fifteen 111
Sixteen 117
Seventeen 125
Eighteen 133
Nineteen 139
Twenty 149
Twenty-one 153
Twenty-two 161
Twenty-three 163

Twenty-four	179
Twenty-five	189
Twenty-six	197
Twenty-seven	205
Twenty-eight	207
Twenty-nine	213
Thirty	221
Thirty-one	231
Thirty-two	233
Thirty-three	239
Thirty-four	245
Thirty-five	251
Thirty-six	259
Thirty-seven	265
Thirty-eight	273
Thirty-nine	279
Forty	287
Forty-one	295
Forty-two	301
Forty-three	311
Forty-four	315
Forty-five	323
Forty-six	329
Forty-seven	333
Forty-eight	335
Forty-nine	339
Fifty	347

Fifty-one	353
Fifty-two	357
Fifty-three	365
Epilogue	371
Acknowledgements	375

Not long ago,

      Two biologists studying the migratory habits of monarch butterflies discovered a group of butterflies that overwinter in the highlands of Mexico lived *six times* as long as their non-migratory cousins. Speculating that the cause of their exceptional longevity was the unique ability to suspend reproductive development by temporarily suppressing juvenile hormones, the researchers were able to artificially reproduce the life-extending effect in the other butterflies by surgically removing their corpora allatum.

Recently,

      Three Americans won the Nobel Prize for Medicine for their discovery that a key enzyme active in childhood is responsible for maintaining the chromosome integrity that controls cell regeneration in humans, and that when this enzyme is switched off after sexual maturity, our chromosomes suddenly begin to shorten—initiating the inexorable process of cellular senescence and adult aging.

Sometime in the future…

One

Even though he had performed the operation hundreds of times before, the Chief of Neurosurgery at Mount Sinai Medical Center hesitated at this crucial moment, with his microdissector poised to slice off yet another child's pituitary.

Here it proudly stood, the so-called *master gland*, the one organ in the human body that charted the destiny of its host, and the surgeon was about to remove it in an unnatural act that would forever change the course of this boy's future.

How ironic, the doctor thought, that nature—or God—would place it here, *so easily accessible to artificial manipulation, and so perfectly separated from the rest of the brain's critical structures.*

It seemed almost too easy to remove the body's definitive organ for regulating growth and aging, then replace it with synthetic hormones designed to mimic these natural effects. He didn't even have to slice open the protective casing of the cranium; the gland could be unobtrusively reached through the nostrils via the natural portal of the sinus cavity, which led directly to the base of the brain.

Funny how only the human mind could figure out how to reconfigure the human brain.

He could see it clearly now, illuminated by the endoscope's bright flashlight, shining in the open cavern of the patient's nasal sella, like a ripe fruit hanging from an apple tree. A tiny pink appendage, no bigger than a pea, connected by a thin stalk to the brain's central processor, the hypothalamus.

"Richard?" The attending anesthesiologist suddenly interrupted the surgeon's thoughts.

"I'm sure you're marveling at the wondrous nature of the human nervous system and your almighty role in its ongoing evolution, but I think there's a patient here who'd prefer you stop playing God for a moment and resume your responsibility as a surgeon!"

There were few people who could talk so candidly to the brilliant and celebrated Dr. Richard Ross, Harvard-educated Ph.D., Professor Emeritus at NYU School of Medicine, and Surgeon-General of the United Nations. But Dr. George 'Mac' McAllister, Chief Anesthesiologist at Mt. Sinai, had been through so many of these life-altering hypophysectomy operations with Dr. Ross that he had earned the surgeon's respect—and friendship.

"I'm just making sure we remove the right part of this lad's brain," Rick joked without looking up. "I have a feeling he might want to keep the important parts."

"Uh huh," Mac replied dubiously, "as if you're the slightest bit uncertain at this particular moment."

The anesthesiologist had a point. The magnetic resonance imaging equipment surrounding the patient's head provided three hundred and sixty degree visibility of the entire lower brain cavity, clearly visible on a bank of monitors mere inches from Rick's keenly scanning eyes. And the tiny flexible penlight snaked carefully up the boy's left nostril into the sphenoidal sinus gave an unmistakably clear and close-up view of the specific organ in question.

"Mac," Rick teased, "I know you've always fantasized about wielding this kind of power in your own hands. You're just ticked about having the lowly job of sedating the patient."

Rick chose his words deliberately, as he knew Mac would bristle at the suggestion he was merely *sedating* the patient. They both knew the business of administering general anesthesia was much more complicated than that. It was critically important for the surgeon to ensure utter relaxation and akinesia of his patient during the operation, for one millimeter of movement at the wrong time would almost certainly mean instant death.

But he also knew his anesthesiologist was smart enough to know when the neurosurgeon was messing with him.

Mac peered across the operating table with mock indignation. "Rick, you know you couldn't perform this operation without me—I'm one of the main reasons for your perfect record."

It was largely true, Rick had to admit. Administering the general anesthetic was one of the riskier elements of the hypophysectomy procedure, as it rendered the patient not only unconscious, but also temporarily incapable of breathing on his own. If the patient were deprived of oxygen for as little as a few minutes, he could experience irreparable brain damage or cardiac arrest. As a result, a breathing tube had to be inserted into the trachea to ensure the lungs and blood supply were sufficiently oxygenated, and the anesthetic team had to closely monitor that his vital signs were stable at all times.

Other surgeons had experienced serious complications from these kinds of procedures, but these two were so disciplined and knew each other so well, they worked together seamlessly as a team and had never lost a patient.

"Are you two just going gab all day, or were you thinking of actually *finishing* this job?" interjected Nurse Benson, who was all business in the operating theater. "I swear—I'm going to report you two someday!"

"For what?" asked Mac. "Wittiest banter in the operating room?"

"Or sexiest duo in scrubs?" added Rick.

"Hey, don't use 'sex' and the two of us in the same sentence, pal."

"I was talking about the lovely head nurse and me, you fool."

"Just get on with it, will you?" Nurse Benson said, rolling her eyes.

Rick knew she was right, and he had no intention of dragging this procedure out. After all, a child's life lay in his hands, and this was deadly serious work. The operating room humor just helped to ease tensions and make the surgery less stressful for everyone involved.

Rick focused the endoscope's light and slowly steadied the laser cutting instrument at the anterior end of the infundibular stalk, as far from the hypothalamus as possible to minimize trauma from the separation of the pituitary, yet still far enough from the pituitary to prevent any spontaneous regrowth. He knew the human body had a remarkable healing capacity and the capability to regenerate severed or damaged body parts. There could be no doubt about the finality of this particular separation of parts. An undetected regrowth of the pituitary at any time in the future could have grave and unexpected results for this juvenile.

With all attending medical personnel prepared for the next step, Rick nevertheless always had to ask.

"Everyone ready?"

"That's what we're here for," replied Dr. Scott, the attending assistant neurosurgeon.

Rick fired a short and tightly focused beam of concentrated laser light and cleanly severed the pituitary from its connecting stalk. Milliseconds later, a clamp applied by Dr. Scott constricted the flow of blood from the severed stem while Rick ejected a small drop of surgical fibrin glue onto its end to close the wound.

Grasping the tiny little gland in a claw at the tip of his operating instrument, Rick slowly and very carefully began to withdraw the equipment from the child's upper sinuses, one side at a time. The exit from, and the entrance into, the delicate depression known as Turk's Saddle, which housed the pituitary gland, was the most dangerous part of the procedure, and he wasn't about to risk jeopardizing another perfect operation now.

Although virtually all the operating equipment was computer controlled and guided by ultra-sensitive joysticks, Rick knew every patient's physical configuration was slightly different and still needed his expert guidance and interpretation of the intricate pathways into and around the cerebral cortex.

Watching very intently through the endoscopic lens, he retracted the razor-sharp equipment just millimeters from the internal carotid artery and optic nerves.

Three hours later in the recovery room, Rick went to see his patient as he slowly awoke from a deep slumber.

This was often the most terrifying part of the operation for every child. Even though the medical team had extensively prepared the young patient for his surgery and reminded him frequently how many others had fully recovered from the procedure, waking up to see if your mind and body will be the same after having a major part of your brain removed was always a little unnerving for an eleven-year-old.

Rick should know—he had been through it himself like everyone else, though the passage of over fifty years had blurred his memories somewhat.

"How's our youngster doing, Jane?" Rick asked, upon seeing the post-op nurse attending to his patient.

Jane smiled when she saw the handsome and distinguished doctor stride into the recovery room.

"All his vital signs are normal, Dr. Ross, and he's sleeping peacefully. Would you like me to wake him for you?"

"Even though I'm sure you'd be a welcome sight for sore eyes," Rick replied, "I'd prefer he sees a familiar face when he comes to. I'd like a couple of minutes alone with him if I may."

The young nurse left the room reluctantly. She admired Dr. Ross, and would have liked to linger with him as he worked his bedside magic; he had many pretty admirers among the hospital staff.

Dr. Ross placed his hand gently on his patient's forehead. The child stirred slowly, and raised his heavy eyelids.

"Good morning Jason—how's my courageous patient?"

"Uh… a little dizzy, Dr. Ross," Jason mumbled, his head still spinning from the lingering effects of the anesthesia.

"You're still a bit sedated while you recover from the operation," Rick nodded assuredly. "It'll go away soon."

"Did you get the little bug?" asked Jason.

Rick smiled. That was their code word for the tiny pod in his brain that would someday make him very sick. Except this bug was a little more insidious than most germs or infections that attacked the body's natural defenses. This one had a universal and destructive intent: to activate the internal clock that would slowly and surely wear down and wear out each and every living cell in his youthful body.

"Yes, we got the little sucker, and it's not going to do you harm any more. But I want you to rest now and let your body regain its strength. In a little while, a very pretty doctor is going to come see you and give you some medication to replace some of the important energy you've lost."

As he stood to leave, Rick took the young patient's hand in his own.

"You're going to be just fine young man, and now that we've got that nasty little devil out of your system, you're going to live a very, very long time."

As he gently shook the youngster's hand upon parting, there was more than just the usual professional confidence in this gesture, for as the young child glanced at Dr. Ross one last time before they separated, he could clearly see the much older doctor's hands looked exactly like his: the same size, and just as youthful, as his own.

Two

Mt. Sinai's newly appointed Chief Endocrinologist, Dr. Jennifer Austin, rested coyly against the open doorframe.

"*Pretty*, hmm—I had no idea you thought of me that way, Dr. Ross," Jennifer remarked.

Rick hadn't noticed the other doctor standing outside the entrance to his patient's room. "Well…you know," he stammered, searching for words that wouldn't betray his quickening pulse, "I was thinking more from the point of view of our impressionable young patient."

Jennifer eyed the neurosurgeon suspiciously. Having recently transferred from Johns Hopkins Hospital, she'd only briefly met Rick in passing, even though their respective functions would require them to work together very closely. Jennifer had of course heard about the legendary Dr. Ross before coming to Mt. Sinai; he was not only the grandson of the scientist who originally broke the code to extended longevity, but also distinguished in his own right for co-developing the current protocols for pituitary/endocrine treatment in connection with the World Health Organization.

Rick was more than twenty years her senior, and roughly her same size. But she could see his excellent bone structure, as evidenced by his relatively broad shoulders and round hip muscles shaping his hospital coat. To top it off, he had a thick shock of wavy blond hair and a strong but perfectly shaped nose. *Very nice*, Jennifer thought, *with that combination of assets, no wonder he has so many admirers.*

"Well then, I suppose I'll just have to be happy making impressions on eleven-year-olds!" she replied flippantly.

Jennifer knew the irony of these words would not be lost on Dr. Ross. Both of them, like everyone else, by virtue of having had their own pituitary glands removed at the same age as their mutual patient, had similarly arrested their physical development at an early stage. Although different people had different levels of intellectual and emotional development depending upon their chronological age, for all intents and purposes, they all *looked* the same age: eleven.

It was Jennifer's job as endocrinologist to see that patients were receiving the correct balance of replacement hormones no longer supplied by the extracted pituitary. This was a delicate and precarious balance. Too much of one kind could tip the body into puberty and trigger the long and slow cellular decline referred to in medical circles as senescence, leading to eventual organ failure and death. An imbalance of another kind could lead to any number of complications, from edema to hyperpigmentation to acromegaly—a condition characterized by grossly oversized hands and feet and grotesque facial features that made the victim look like a Neanderthal.

Maintaining just the right balance of the various types of externally supplied hormones was critically important in not only suppressing the deleterious effects of senescence, but also in keeping all the systems in check so everyone *felt* healthy. It was no easy task replacing what nature endowed, for billions of years of natural evolution had already formed a perfected balanced human design.

For his part, Rick had been looking forward to working more closely with Jennifer since their brief introduction earlier in the week. He had reviewed her credentials prior to her appointment, and she had come very highly recommended by a mutual colleague in Baltimore. First in her class at Johns Hopkins Medical School, and then a distinguished residency at the affiliated hospital. He himself had made the final approval, together with the hospital's Chief of Staff, for her position at Mt. Sinai.

The fact that she turned out to be stunning was a bonus. She had perfect alabaster skin, brown doe eyes, and a gorgeous shade of naturally highlighted auburn hair, pulled back neatly in a bun behind her head.

Rick tried to remain composed. "Speaking of our young patient, have you kept apprised of his status?"

"Of course," Jennifer replied. "I observed the operation from the upper gallery. You have quite a way with words, Dr. Ross, not to mention with those expert hands!"

Rick flushed momentarily, as he recalled his comments about Nurse Benson earlier in the operating room. He'd been so focused on the delicate task before him, he hadn't even noticed who was watching from observation deck.

"Just trying to ease the tension in the operating theater, Dr. Austin."

"I can imagine," smiled Jennifer. "And were you doing the same with that attractive nurse a few minutes ago?"

Damn, thought Rick, *this new endocrinologist has got me in her crosshairs.*

"Of course," he replied, matter-of-factly, "I always try to be amiable with everyone on my team."

"I'll bet—you must have quite a following!"

"Normally, I try to precede my reputation whenever possible. I suppose it didn't work quite so well in this instance?"

"Never fear, Dr. Ross, your reputation is undiminished in my eyes." Jennifer was having fun with her obviously flustered colleague.

"Well in that case, please call me Rick."

"Alright Rick—and I'm officially Jennifer." Jennifer extended her hand, and the two shook firmly.

"I'm actually pleased we crossed paths today, Jennifer," Rick said, beginning to regain his composure. "There was another matter I wanted to discuss with you, besides Jason. Are you familiar with Eva Bronwen's case?"

"Everyone knows Eva, the so-called 'Queen Bee,'" Jennifer remarked.

Eva Bronwen was one of very few adult females specifically bred to carry on the bloodline, by virtue of her mature ovaries and fully-functioning womb. It was a purely voluntary role, for which virtually no one volunteered, since passing through sexual maturity was recognized as a guaranteed death sentence. But Queens were very generously rewarded by the state, and held a kind of unusual celebrity status among the general public. Eva's mother, and generations before them, had carried on the same tradition, so the family was considered 'royalty'. The not-so-flattering appellation of 'Queen Bee' referred to her unique status as sole propagator of the race and her prodigious output of fertilized eggs.

"Did you want me to review her file?" Jennifer asked.

"Yes, she's my personal patient," Rick advised. "I see her from time to time in my midtown office to monitor her general health. She's scheduled for another round of harvesting."

"Would you like me to prepare her next treatment?"

Jennifer knew that in order to maximize the Queen's productivity, she would require a special concentrated course of sex hormone injections at precise intervals in her reproductive cycle to induce the ovaries to produce a plentiful supply of eggs. These would then be fertilized from frozen stores of sperm, after which the embryos would be cryogenically saved for implantation as needed.

"Yes, I think she'll like you very much, Jennifer," said Rick. "But whatever you do, don't bring up the 'Queen Bee' thing; she's very sensitive about that."

"Of course—I'd never want to make her feel uncomfortable."

"Excellent. If you'd like to attend to Jason's immediate needs, I'll get back to you soon with more details on the timing for Eva's treatment."

Rick breathed a sigh of relief. The hypophysectomy operation had been another stellar success, and he felt comfortable placing his special patient Eva Bronwen in the capable hands of Jennifer Austin. Eva had an appointment with him at his private Park Avenue office in a couple of hours, and he decided to soak up some of the Indian summer sunshine by walking the two miles down Fifth Avenue to the south end of Central Park.

Strolling slowly through the Hospital's Guggenheim Pavilion, designed by the renowned architect I.M. Pei, he could feel the bright sunlight cascading through the tall glass ceiling beginning to warm his skin. Normally, Rick would take the rear exit directly into the staff parking area, but today he wanted to feel the energy of the city and walk amongst the people. Anticipating the magnificent view of the lush park across the street from atop the steps of the hospital, he boldly stepped through the front doors of the Pavilion.

Immediately, he regretted his decision. Instead of being greeted by the majestic sight of mature elm and ash trees in autumn bloom, his view was blocked by a throng of demonstrators waving placards and shouting noisily.

Oh great, thought Rick, *not again.* He immediately recognized the familiar slogans painted on the boards above the protesters' heads as belonging to the *Garden of Eden* religious sect. Led by the fervent Calvin James, their mission was nothing less than the return of civilization to the 'natural order of God', whereby men and women were allowed to age gracefully and reproduce in the intended manner.

To make matters worse, the group recognized Rick as the infamous doctor who they saw as championing the charge into the new, unnatural order.

"There he is!" someone yelled. "The evil doctor!"

Oh no, groaned Rick.

Before he could turn around and retreat into the protective sanctity of the Pavilion, the group surrounded him and began chanting boisterously.

"Infidel!" growled a distinct voice from deep in the crowd—a much deeper voice. Rick knew it could only be one person. Turning in the direction of the husky sound, Rick could see a form standing head and shoulders above the mass.

Calvin James was a hulking man who would stand out in any crowd. The only adult male still alive under the age of ninety, Calvin's father had hidden him from the authorities until his son had passed through puberty to protect him from an unwanted removal of his pituitary. Now in his mid-40s, Calvin, like his father before him, was a deeply religious man who took it upon himself to lead a 'divine revolution'.

Fashioning himself as the Second Coming, he looked the part, with long brown hair and an equally long beard. This only compounded his sinister appearance. Muscling his way through his group of juvenile followers, he confronted the neurosurgeon.

Calvin towered over Rick's diminutive frame. "You must stop this affront to God's will!" he bellowed.

Rick knew from previous encounters of this kind that this man was not open to reason. Calvin had long ago been brainwashed by his pious father, and there was simply no room in his belief system for an alternate view, no matter how life-affirming it might be for everyone else. Unlike his juvenile supporters, he had a very finite life, and predictable death, ahead of him. It had been the custom of mankind for millennia to seek answers and comfort in the mystical realm, with the easy promise of an everlasting afterlife. *Why should it be any different for this mortal man?*

Rick wasn't about to engage Calvin and his followers in a confrontation that he could never win. He knew that a security detail would soon be responding to the turn of events on the front steps of the hospital. In the meantime he simply had to keep everybody calm.

"Dr. James," Rick replied, trying to massage Calvin's ego with reference to his doctorate in Divinity. "I'm simply upholding the law, as set out in the Articles of the United Nations, and as determined by the will of the people."

"These are *children* whom you are mutilating!" Calvin sneered, ignoring Rick's statement.

His flock roared in agreement. "Shame! Shame!"

"Sir," Rick replied, "as you know, these actions are taken with the fully informed consent of both the children and their parents." He was simply biding his time, wondering what was keeping the security detail. "Furthermore, we replace all the hormones that are removed."

"Only enough to keep everyone in an *unnatural* state of juvenile development!" Calvin countered.

"*Sin-ner, sin-ner, sin-ner!*" his followers began chanting loudly.

Rick was growing weary. He could only keep the group at bay for so long with this kind of open dialogue.

"Yes," he continued, "but as you know, this allows everyone to live happy, healthy, empowered lives, far beyond what they could otherwise hope for."

"God already enabled everyone to lead full lives—and then to live for eternity in his domain."

Another loud cheer rose from the crowd.

Rick wondered how so many juveniles could fall under Calvin's spell. It was one thing to quietly contemplate one's place in the great scheme of life, and quite another to jump headlong into the uncertain realm of the spiritual world. Just as he was about to consider pushing his way through the crowd, it began to break apart amidst some commotion.

The police had arrived, and with tasers deployed began persuasively motivating everyone to retreat. As the gendarmes cautiously converged on the hulking leader at the middle of the circle, Calvin glared at Rick.

"This is only the beginning, Dr. Ross. God's will be done—I'll see to that."

As Rick continued down the hospital steps with the sound of angry chants ringing in his ears, he couldn't help wonder how one mortal man could hope to change the world.

Three

Eva Bronwen sat impatiently in Dr. Ross's waiting room. Though his private office was beautifully appointed with tasteful Impressionist prints, rich mahogany paneling, and comfortable high-back leather chairs, she felt exposed waiting for her uncharacteristically late doctor. He had never kept her lingering like this before—he'd always greeted her promptly and escorted her into his private office as soon as her arrival was announced.

Other patients were beginning to stream into the office, and Eva could feel many eyes upon her. As the only mature female of reproductive age they had likely seen in person in decades, she was more than a curious oddity. Even though she was widely respected for her role as the reigning matriarch, for most people this was of little personal relevance to them. With every juvenile now fully embracing the promise of indefinite longevity and everlasting youthful vitality, the continued protection of the species seemed relatively inconsequential. She was more a subject of sympathy and intrigue than anything else.

The longer she waited, the more Eva began to feel like some kind of circus attraction, there for the amusement of its patrons. *This was not the way it was supposed to be*, she thought. She was supposed to be admired and uplifted for her selfless act of humanity. She was supposed to be feted and celebrated at every turn. After all, she alone was the savior of the bloodline and the link to the next generation. There were no guarantees that some plague or unforeseen event couldn't wipe out civilization at any moment. The human race literally depended on her and a select group of very few others to ensure its continued viability.

It seemed that with every passing year, the juveniles were growing more and more complacent and confident of their special status. It had been over a hundred years since the first hypophysectomy experiment, and once it was proven to be safe and to indefinitely arrest aging, virtually everyone wanted to drink from the fountain of youth. It was barely an afterthought to encourage some to forego the magic elixir for the benefit of future generations. Now, the only 'generations' referred to in the lexicon were associated with the Queens' own offspring.

At least the United Nations recognized and rewarded her for her role. She and her family were generously compensated with large monthly stipends, ostensibly as payment for their egg production, with even larger payments for every new child carried to term. Plus, she was given a beautiful apartment on the Upper East Side, and an open credit line that allowed her to indulge virtually all of her needs, carte blanche. And of course, she was invited to all the best parties and social gatherings.

But she knew that outside this select circle, there were less flattering perceptions amongst the general population. To the average person, she was little more than a baby-making machine and the occasional object of ridicule. She also knew most people referred to her pejoratively as the *Queen Bee*, and she resented this objectification.

Eva had always hoped that she could somehow raise her standing and esteem among the public to that of a real queen. She wondered why Dr. Ross's secretary hadn't shown her into the examining room instead of asking her to wait in the main lobby with the rest of his patients. *What could be keeping Dr. Ross?* she thought.

At that moment, Rick swept through the front door, looking unusually harried and unkempt.

"I'm sorry for being late," Rick announced, hoping to allay his patients' consternation. "I had an unexpected emergency at the hospital."

He noticed Eva shifting uncomfortably in her chair, and motioned to her immediately. "Eva, I believe you have the first appointment—won't you please join me in my office?"

With great relief, Eva followed Rick into the adjoining room.

"I was getting worried about you, Dr. Ross," she joked as Rick closed the door behind them. "It's not like you to stand me up like this. In your busy waiting room, I was beginning to feel like another exhibit in the medieval collection at the Metropolitan Museum!"

"I'm so sorry Eva, I'll be sure to ask Marie to show you directly into my office if this ever happens again."

"It's alright," Eva smiled. "I suppose I could use a thicker skin anyway." She noticed Rick was looking unusually flustered. "You seem even more high-strung than me today—what's got my normally unflappable doctor so unsettled?"

Ordinarily Rick wouldn't burden his patients with his own troubles, but he had a special relationship with Eva, and he knew that she wouldn't let up until he was fully forthcoming about his delay.

"I just had another little encounter with our mercurial local minister, Calvin James."

Eva knew very well what Dr. Ross meant, having had her own share of run-ins with the Garden of Eden leader. Calvin had confronted her frequently outside her apartment building, imploring her among other things to stop provisioning eggs for the ongoing cloning campaign.

"I think you're being generous referring to him as a minister, Dr. Ross," Eva said. "He's more like a cult leader, if you ask me. At least you're lucky all he wants from you is to stop your operations. I think he has other designs on me."

Rick had long imagined Calvin would desire some kind of union with Eva. On the one hand, it seemed only natural for the two lone adults. Eva was a beautiful, full-figured woman, in her sexual prime at twenty-five years of age. But quite apart from Calvin's potential negative influence over her harvesting role, he was obviously *unstable*—and Rick feared for Eva's security.

"Has he been threatening you?" he asked warily.

"Leering mostly. But it's beginning to feel more like stalking. He caught me last week as I was coming out of Saks, for crying out loud." She scrunched her face in disgust. "And he's more than just a little creepy, with that long curved nose and straggly beard. As much as I sometimes long for a real man in my life, I wouldn't have him if he were the last man on earth."

"Which he very nearly is," Rick joked.

"Don't start with me—I'm serious!"

"I'm sorry Eva. You know we can arrange to step up your security at any time. Would you like me to call my contacts at the State Department?"

In accordance with its obligations under the United Nations Headquarters Agreement, Rick knew Eva officially came under the protection of the United States Department of State Diplomatic Security Service, but to this point she had refused to avail herself of their services.

"No—at least not yet," Eva sighed. "I'm still trying to get out among the people and show that I'm a real person. The last thing I need is to become a recluse in my own building."

"Well, please don't take any unnecessary chances, and do let the authorities know if you feel the slightest bit threatened." Rick decided to shift the discussion onto the main reason for the appointment. "How are you feeling, otherwise?"

"On the whole, pretty good. But I have to admit, I *am* getting tired of these unending fertility treatments and egg donations. Sometimes I wonder how much this mortal body can take."

Rick fully understood Eva's dismay. "I'm sure everybody appreciates how difficult it can be for you, both physically and emotionally. Which is why the state only seeks to harvest eggs from you twice a year."

"I don't even know why it's necessary *that* often," Eva argued. "It's not as if anyone is rushing to have babies any longer. Why *do* we need so many eggs anyway?"

Rick nodded in sympathy. With juveniles having foregone the ability to reproduce naturally, most people had long ago lost their natural coupling instinct. A few people still opted for the cloning option, utilizing the Queen's harvested eggs and surrogate womb, but the cost of carrying a child to term was usually considered too steep for both the donor and the Queen. The harvesting procedure was now considered mostly a prophylactic measure to protect the population as a whole.

"The problem is that human eggs are very difficult to store and keep viable for very long," he explained. "Because it's the largest cell in the human body, the large volume of water within its membrane expands upon freezing and can easily damage its delicate internal structure. Only about two percent of mature oocytes that are cryopreserved and subsequently thawed are in fact successfully fertilized."

"But doesn't the inordinate number of eggs that my fertility treatment produces make up for this low percentage of viable eggs?"

"Well, it's true that the special hormones you take prior to harvesting *do* produce fifteen to twenty eggs, instead of the one normally released in a natural ovulation cycle. But two percent of twenty is still less than one. We are lucky to produce one successful fertilized egg between your two harvestings each year."

"But you told me once that those successfully fertilized embryos are much easier to freeze and store," Eva said, still unconvinced. "Why then do we need even one more of them per year? Hasn't it really boiled down to the fact that we only need one live birth each generation, to ensure at least one child-bearing female is always available to carry on the propagation of the race?"

"Yes," Rick continued patiently, "it's true that multi-celled embryos freeze and store more easily than single-celled eggs; however, the successful pregnancy rate from frozen and thawed embryos is still far lower than with fresh ones. And I'm sure you wouldn't want to subject yourself to more pregnancies than necessary—nor increase the possibility of a miscarriage. Plus, the state would like to build up the bank of potentially viable embryos in the event of an unforeseen calamity."

"Oh great—to make me a full-time baby-making factory?" Eva said, imagining how this would only reinforce the prevailing Queen Bee association.

"Well, I expect not so much for that as to protect against the possibility of your becoming infertile," Rick said, trying to allay Eva's concerns.

"Either way, I'm still just being viewed as little more than a *machine!*"

"Well I assure you Eva, I don't think of you that way—I value your courage and commitment. Plus, you're far too feisty to be considered anything but a full-blooded woman as far as I'm concerned!"

"I'll take that as a compliment, Dr. Ross," Eva replied. "I just wish everyone else could see me the same way; to them I'm just the Queen Bee of their little colony! And the ironic thing is that *real* queen bees live twenty times longer than all the other bees in her hive—yet in my case, the situation is reversed!"

"Yes, that would appear to be true, Eva, though the jury is still out on the ultimate longevity of juveniles. At least you get to enjoy the same level of pampering that a real queen bee does in your particular hive!"

"I suppose I'll have to take solace in that," Eva sighed.

"Which brings us to our current order of business," Rick continued. "I'd like to make an appointment for you to see our new endocrinologist to prepare you for your next round of fertility treatment."

Eva sat up in surprise. She'd had the same endocrinologist for over five years and had grown accustomed to her professional, if somewhat impersonal, engagement style.

"We have a new endocrinologist?"

"Yes, Dr. Evans decided she'd had enough of this high-pressure *capital-of-the-world* lifestyle and wanted to retire to quieter climes. But I think you'll like the new doctor very much. She's intelligent, spirited, and beautiful—just like you. You two should get along famously. Her name is Dr. Jennifer Austin, and she recently transferred from Baltimore. She comes very highly recommended, and I think you'll like her style."

"Beautiful, intelligent, and a great bedside manner—these sound like perfect qualities in a partner for *you*, Dr. Ross. Have we finally found someone who might meet your impossible standards?"

Rick sighed in resignation. "I've got far too many commitments these days to introduce another distraction into my life. Plus, I feel like I'm being besieged by menacing forces from every side, and a pairing of such high-profile public figures would only create a more irresistible target for these zealots.

"Besides, you're changing the subject," Rick said, hoping to get back to the previous topic. "Have you been thinking about the right timing for having a child? As you know, the official plan seeks to maintain at least one female of child-bearing age at all times, and we're nearing the limits of that window for you and your prospective child."

"Yes, of course, I'm familiar with the plan," said Eva, referring to the United Nations' Global Longevity Initiative, establishing the official protocol for protecting and maintaining the population. "I just haven't quite got myself worked up yet to the idea of producing yet another Queen progeny, whom someday I'll have to ask to forego her own eternal youth."

Rick never much liked this part of his job, and he empathized with Eva's situation. It was his duty to advise Eva as her doctor to consider what was best for her overall health and welfare, but it was also expected of him in his role as U.N. Surgeon-General to uphold the charter and encourage each Queen to carry on the tradition.

"You know no one can force you, or your child, to choose one particular path," Rick advised. "You can raise as many children as you wish—or none at all—in whatever manner you choose."

"I know, Dr. Ross, and I appreciate your understanding. But I'm mindful of my duty, and the broader implications for humanity. I have in fact been talking this over with my mother, and we've decided to carry on the family tradition."

Rick reached out to hold Eva's hand. He knew this was a deeply personal decision, as it had been for her mother, and he didn't want her to feel alone.

"Have you thought about how you would like to proceed?"

Eva knew she had many options for producing a baby. She could create a clone by inserting a cell from a chosen live subject, including herself, into one of her own eggs; she could implant an already *fertilized egg* as a viable embryo; or she could pre-select a *sperm sample* from the large sperm bank in frozen storage to fertilize her egg.

Whichever of these methods she chose would require artificial implantation into her womb, after which she would carry the baby to term. The option of producing a baby the old fashioned way was no longer an option for Eva, since virtually all the mature men still living were nearing a hundred years in age, and to the extent any of them could still function sexually, she had no interest in a relationship with a centenarian.

As if reading her mind, Rick interjected. "As you probably know, the cloning option would assure a known healthy female for you."

Eva frowned. "Yes, but it does seem more than a little egotistic to produce another copy of me—or someone familiar to me. And doesn't this limit our genetic diversity moving forward?"

Rick was impressed with Eva's grasp of evolutionary biology, as well as her continuing concern for issues beyond her and her child's welfare. "Well at this point it shouldn't matter too much, since we're only talking about one individual in one generation, amongst a worldwide population of billions. It becomes more significant as this effect is multiplied across successive generations."

"Can we guarantee the sex of the child with in vitro fertilization?" asked Eva, wondering about the second option.

"Yes, we can conduct genetic tests upon the embryo, and only implant a female, if that is your choice," Rick assured. "And we could also give you full historical profiles on potential sperm donors, which would give you some latitude in choosing the likely physical and intellectual traits of your child."

Eva had done a fair bit homework in preparation for this discussion with Dr. Ross. "Yes I know, but to some degree I'm still at the mercy of unknown genetic factors to discover what the effect will be of these recombinant forces in the final shape of my child, am I not?"

Eva continued to surprise Rick with her depth of understanding of the technical aspects of reproductive biology. She had obviously done her homework.

"True, it's not as known an outcome as with cloning, but we can test for many defects in both the embryo and in the emerging fetus. Plus, you should know cloning is not without its own risks. There is a higher chance of miscarriage, and there is the potential for shortened longevity in your child in comparison with artificial insemination."

"How so?" asked Eva.

"As you may remember, our innate longevity is largely a function of the length of time it takes to reach sexual maturity. In general, the longer this takes, the longer any organism lives—there is a direct and consistent relationship in nature. If you were to reproduce a clone, even from one with a late puberty such as yourself, the DNA supplied would only come from that one source, and thus the inbred longevity of the offspring would remain essentially the same as that of the donor.

"On the other hand," Rick continued, "with artificial insemination contributing DNA from the presumably later sexual maturity of *both* contributing parents, this would increase the chance of the offspring having an even later puberty, thus extending his or her lifespan that much more. In this way, you not only have a chance to maximize the potential lifespan of your own child, but also carry forward the extended longevity genes into successive generations."

Eva was now deep in thought. There were many options, and many more implications to consider. "Can I take a little more time to think it over, Dr. Ross? This is a lot to contemplate."

Rick hoped he hadn't overwhelmed Eva with too much information. But the consequences of this decision were simply too important for herself, and ultimately for the evolution of the human species, to be taken lightly.

"Of course, Eva. And please call or see me whenever other concerns arise, or if you need more information. In the meantime, why don't we arrange for you see Dr. Austin at your earliest convenience, so we'll be ready when you are."

"Oh—I almost forgot about that," replied Eva, snapping out of her internal deliberations. "I'm looking forward to meeting this new endocrinologist after everything you've told me about her."

"Well then, how about an appointment next week?" Rick suggested.

Eva checked her schedule. "Can we do next Tuesday at ten a.m.?"

"I'll tell her to expect you," confirmed Rick. "Would you like me to call a car for you? I could have my driver pick you up at the rear exit to the office so you won't have to run the gauntlet of my waiting room again."

"It's alright, Dr. Ross, I'd actually like to walk home and acclimate amongst my subjects," Eva joked, standing to leave. "Thank you again for your time and patience, I'll see you again soon."

"Always a pleasure, Eva. Bye for now."

As Rick escorted Eva from his office, his mind began to wander back to his earlier discussion with Dr. Jennifer Austin, and how he had felt a flood of new emotions after meeting her—emotions he hadn't felt in a long time.

Four

Tian Yin looked out the large picture window on the thirty-ninth floor of the United Nations Secretariat building. From her corner office on the south-west side, she could survey the magnificent skyline of lower Manhattan. It was a beautiful day, and the city was gleaming in the early autumn sunshine. To her right she could see the Chrysler Building, the Rockefeller Center, and the Hudson River shining like a silver ribbon in the mid-afternoon light. To her left, the city stretched languorously across the East River into the boroughs of Brooklyn and Queens. Looking south, the dramatic glass spire of the Freedom Tower soared above the tall rooftops of its stately neighbors, echoing the raised arm of the Statue of Liberty standing proudly in the distance.

For Tian, these icons seemed to reflect the purpose of the United Nations—to promote worldwide peace and security—and in her role as U.N. Secretary-General she frequently liked to peer out over them for comfort and inspiration. As her gaze stretched further beyond, she could see the Atlantic Ocean on the horizon, and she began to think of her homeland far away, on the other side of the world.

Her father had been a Chinese ambassador to the U.N., who met her African-American mother while she was teaching at Columbia University in New York, and together they returned to China upon completion of his posting. Tian had led a privileged life growing up in the senior echelons of Beijing political society during the latter half of the twenty-first century, when globalization forces rapidly shifted the balance of power from west to east. Her distinctive biracial heritage and extensive study at the world's finest educational institutions had brought her to the attention of many powerful leaders, and she quickly rose through the ranks of the diplomatic service.

She seemed the ideal candidate for the position of Secretary-General during its latest vacancy, and after her nomination by the Security Council, she won the appointment with a large majority among the General Assembly. Tian loved the job, and with testosterone-deprived juveniles now holding the positions of power, an unprecedented level of peace and cooperation had swept the nations of the world. The role and stature of the United Nations had risen concomitantly with the rise in world travel and trade, as the final barriers to the free movement of people and goods across national boundaries melted away. The world truly was now a global village, and the United Nations was its primary administrative authority.

The role of the international political body had accordingly shifted from maintaining peace and security to promoting health and prosperity among the world's peoples. The unbridled success of the hypophysectomy program had changed everything. People were living peaceful utopian lives of unparalleled longevity and vigor, and the relative simplicity of the operation had made it possible to grant virtually everyone around the world an opportunity for unlimited youth.

Her only regret was that the scientific breakthrough had been unable to save her beloved parents, or the millions of other mature adults who had passed through puberty before the procedure had gained widespread acceptance. Now it was apparently too late, and it was doubly sad to witness the inevitable aging and passing of everyone's loved ones, when so many others were obviously being spared a similar fate.

A loud buzz from Tian's intercom speaker startled her from her thoughts.

"Yes, Keisha?" she announced to her personal assistant.

"Dr. Ross is here to see you for your two p.m. appointment, Madam Secretary."

"Thank you—please show him in."

Tian had been looking forward to seeing Rick again since they had started working closely on the development of the worldwide protocols for pituitary and endocrine control, and she had some important new issues to discuss with him.

There was a polite double tap on her door.

"Come in, Rick," Tian said as she swung open the ebony door to her chamber. "You know you don't need to knock—my door is always open for you."

"I would never deign to interrupt the important business of our esteemed Secretary-General," Rick said with a wry smile. Tian and Rick had a long-standing friendship and loved nothing more than to dispense with the mutual trappings of decorum each of their positions normally demanded.

"What makes you think any important business ever gets conducted in this ivory tower anyway?" laughed Tian. "You know as well as anyone how hard it can be to get two hundred member states to agree on any meaningful issues!"

"Well yes, but with your good looks and charm, you never seem to have any difficulty."

This wasn't false flattery—there was far more truth than jest to Rick's compliment. Tian had an exotic beauty that transcended borders. Her skin was a flawless shade of golden brown, and she had shimmering jet-black hair cascading down exquisitely carved cheekbones. But she was far more than just a pretty face. Tian spoke seven languages fluently, and had a sharp, incisive intellect. On top of all this, she had an amazing ability to connect with just about anyone from any walk of life and make them want to follow her seemingly to the ends of the earth. Which came in handy every once in a while in her position as the planet's most powerful administrator.

Rick and Tian had a mutual admiration and respect for one another's talents and achievements, and they sincerely enjoyed each other's company. Tian wondered sometimes why they hadn't gotten even closer, but to her dismay, Rick seemed to hold more of a professional than personal interest in her.

"Speaking of charm, Dr. Ross, I see you haven't lost your own flair for making your clients and colleagues feel like the most important person in the world—even me!"

"Ok, let's call a truce," Rick said, finally surrendering the friendly banter. "What's up, you sounded eager to talk about something?"

"Yes, I've had a few troubling issues on my mind. Everything has been going so well with the Global Longevity Initiative, and now that we've got just about every eligible individual signed on for, or having already completed a pituitary removal, it's more important than ever to ensure we manage and control the supplemental hormone supply properly."

"I couldn't agree more," Rick concurred. "What concerns do you have about the present arrangements? They seem to be working like clockwork."

"That's what I'm afraid of," replied Tian. "We're placing the entire provisioning process for everybody's hormone patches in the hands of just one company: Endogen."

"True, but as you recall, we had a good reason for doing this. We wanted to maintain strict control and oversight on the manufacturing and distribution of the patches, since we knew we couldn't afford to have this disrupted at any time. And we felt that by carefully evaluating the most capable organization for doing this, then commissioning it as the exclusive provider, that we could maximize the consistency of supply and minimize the possibility of random error entering into the supply chain."

"Yes, Rick, I remember," continued Tian. "However, the World Health Organization is concerned about being exposed in the event of an unforeseen problem and that we are giving unfair economic advantage to one large pharmaceutical company headquartered here in the United States. They feel there are many other fully capable suppliers having the necessary controls and expertise to assist in this effort."

"I suppose that makes sense," agreed Rick. "What is their proposal?"

"If we were to divide the sourcing of the patches across more organizations, we could ensure a continuing supply while simultaneously spreading the economic advantage from a more diverse supply chain across more member nations," explained Tian. "I wanted to see if you had any reservations before we put the issue before the Assembly."

Rick paused for a moment to consider the proposal. "My only concern is that we are able to ensure the consistency and reliability of the patch formula. As you know, this has been very carefully defined, and even a small variation or disruption could have catastrophic effects. Every hypophysectomized juvenile relies upon these patches to regulate their endocrine balance and maintain health. Right now, this is easy to monitor and control with one local source."

Tian nodded in agreement. "The WHO assures me that with their global resources and reach, they would be able to monitor each of these suppliers in precisely the same way we are currently doing with Endogen. If that's your only concern, may we have your approval as Surgeon-General to proceed?"

"Yes," answered Rick. "I trust your ability to manage the infrastructure and see that all parties are properly aligned."

"I'll issue a statement as soon as we have the details worked out. I appreciate your input, as always."

"That wasn't too difficult," Rick kidded. "Were there any other weighty world issues you wanted to discuss?!"

Tian paused, as her mood suddenly turned more somber.

"No...I suppose not," she said, looking once again outside her window.

It was obvious to Rick that the Secretary-General had something else on her mind. "What is it Tian? You know you can talk to me about anything."

"Well, it's actually...my father," she began slowly. "He's very old and in failing health, and I've been wondering why we've never been able to help mature adults in the same way we've helped juveniles. You'd think there would be something we could do."

Rick nodded soberly. "I'm sorry Tian; if there were anything we could do, believe me, we would be trying. My own grandfather faced this realization when he first discovered the critical role of the pituitary in the aging process. The key is to halt the decline *before* we all reach puberty; after that, the post-adolescent hormone cascade automatically triggers the onset of cellular destruction that is pre-programmed into our genes.

"Unfortunately," Rick continued, "all we can do after that point is try to keep our seniors as healthy as possible within their natural lifespans and make them as comfortable as possible in their declining years. I'd be happy to see your father if you think I can do anything in that regard."

Tian smiled appreciatively. "No, thank you Rick. He's already in capable hands. I suppose I already knew there would be nothing else we could do. It just seems so cruel and unfair, to have two different classes of people living side-by-side in the same generation: aging mortals and ever-young immortals."

"Yes, I've had to grapple with this problem myself—at the hospital, and elsewhere," Rick agreed. "But it's important to keep in mind we don't yet know for sure how long we'll be able to hold back the natural aging mechanisms in juveniles. This hypophysectomy intervention is still a fairly new experiment in the grand evolutionary scheme. It's contrary to the engineered design of our human body, and we can't be certain it won't someday find another unknown path to its natural destination. I think we should be careful about setting too lofty expectations, and using terms like immortal."

Tian paused to consider the weight of Rick's words.

"Yes, I suppose none of us should take this for granted—least of all those holding positions of responsibility for the welfare of so many others. I'll talk to the Director-General of the WHO about tempering its message."

There was momentary silence as Tian was lost in thought once again.

"You know...the funny thing is that this whole pituitary-removal idea might never have come to fruition if the WHO had had its way, so long ago."

"How do you mean?"

"Once your grandfather proved it was possible to retard aging in this manner using chimpanzees as his study subjects, it took a rogue nation's leader to take the first step with humans—in *that* case as you recall, with his own son. None of the other member states would sanction or allow the experiment to be tested with live humans."

"Yes," admitted Rick, "I suppose we have that one not-so-crazy dictator to thank for laying the groundwork for the rest of us—at least in enough time for this generation."

"Indeed," Tian said. "Now, if only you could pick up the gauntlet from your grandfather and see if we could somehow broaden this life-saving idea to those left behind."

Five

The world headquarters of the Endogen Pharmaceutical Corporation sat on a sprawling estate covering over five hundred secluded acres in upstate New Jersey. Hosting over 20,000 employees, the huge complex housed the key manufacturing, research, and administrative functions of the organization. With annual sales of more than $100 billion, the company had grown into the world's largest biotech organization. Although it now offered a wide range of pharmaceutical and health care products for both young and old customers, the primary driver for its large size was the exclusive contract it had won to supply all juveniles' replacement hormone patches. Their "*e*" trademark, etched on every patch worn by every hypophysectomized juvenile in the world, was arguably the single most recognized commercial symbol across the globe.

The top management team was justifiably proud of their ability to secure the U.N. contract, as well as their ability since then to maintain a flawless record of quality control and distribution. None more so than the Chief Executive Officer Roland Jamieson, who had played a key role in the original negotiating process and in convincing the agency of Endogen's suitability for the job. Now, with such a massive network of international resources applied to the task of producing and distributing the patches around the world, he felt comfortable knowing it would be difficult to displace his company as the preferred U.N. supplier.

But in his latest meetings with the Director-General of the World Health Organization and the U.N. Secretary-General, he felt uneasy about the nature of some of their enquiries. Instead of the usual platitudes and self-congratulatory luncheons, they were showing a newfound and inordinate interest in the logistical and financial details of their longstanding arrangement. The questions pertained not only to the typical annual contract price negotiations, which were decidedly one-sided in Endogen's favor given its monopolistic position, but also involved new and unusual concerns about such factors as distribution and manufacturing capacity.

Jamieson couldn't imagine the U.N. would consider upending the terms of their supply agreement, not least because of the displacement it would have upon Endogen's hundreds of thousands of employees around the world, but also because he felt he had built a close rapport with the Secretary-General and that she would never take any drastic action without first consulting him personally. Nonetheless, he thought it prudent to prepare the organization in the event of a sudden or unforeseen change in circumstances, and as such, had ordered a special meeting of his executive committee to discuss the situation.

The meeting was set for eight a.m. sharp in the corporate boardroom, and since Jamieson insisted on strict punctuality, he always showed up at the last appointed second as a show of authority.

"Good morning everyone," he announced, as he strode briskly into the wood-paneled room. Each of his direct reports were dutifully assembled around a huge, glass oblong table. Surrounding them on the walls of the boardroom hung giant original expressionist paintings by various 20th century masters.

"We have a special order of business today, and I wanted your input and recommendations on how we should proceed on a very sensitive matter. As you all know, the company is somewhat beholden to the U.N. under the terms of our exclusive endocrine patch supply contract. We have far too much to lose if this arrangement were to be substantially disrupted in any manner. I would like for us to discuss today how we can best protect the company's interests in the event of a material change in our relationship with the U.N."

"What makes you think these arrangements might change, Roland?" enquired Alan Brache, Endogen Chief Counsel. "We still have the better part of a year remaining in the term of our present contract, and the annual renewals have pretty much been a rubber stamp by the U.N. for several years now."

"I know Alan, and to be honest, I don't have any concrete evidence to suggest this is in jeopardy, other than some odd comments and inquiries from the Director-General and Secretary-General at our last quarterly review."

"What kind of comments?"

"Well, for instance, they were asking how many employees we have committed to the patch supply from our various production and distribution arms around the world," Jamieson said.

"Perhaps they're simply trying to further clarify our costs in preparation for the next round of pricing negotiations?" suggested Joe Bennett, the company's Chief Financial Officer.

"It's possible that's all it is," admitted Jamieson. "But they were also asking about the size and location of each of our plants, and how much is produced at each location. Normally, they don't factor in our capital costs in the pricing formula—as you know, they have traditionally been more concerned about our gross margins."

"Maybe they've finally begun to pay attention to our requests to recognize our fully loaded costs, as we've been imploring them to do for so many years?" mused the CFO.

"I considered that," continued Jamieson. "I just don't see why they would suddenly change their tune after all this time. Plus, they know the majority of these costs have already been substantially depreciated—I think they are more sophisticated in their cost analysis and estimating than we may be giving them credit for."

Jamieson's brow furrowed. "I'm afraid they're getting at something else."

"Do you think they would seriously considering giving the patch contract to another supplier?!" asked Sue Weldon, the Marketing EVP, incredulously.

"I can't imagine that they would take it away from us outright. But they could quite easily parcel out pieces of the supply arrangement to other local area vendors. They may be feeling we're being given unfair competitive advantage and other countries may be taking exception with all of this business going to U.S. interests."

Even though everyone at the table had long known that Endogen was overly reliant on the U.N. contract and unduly concentrated in this market niche, they had become increasingly complacent with their continuing success. None of them had seriously considered the possibility of the company's preferred status changing.

Bruce Ellis, the Production Superintendent, was the first to break the uneasy silence.

"What do you think we should do, Roland?"

Jamieson had been contemplating the ramifications of a U.N. move for some time now and had already conceived a number of countermeasures.

"I think we should find a way to hedge our bets," he stated. "Joe, what can Endogen do to prepare for a worst-case scenario?"

"To be honest Roland, if we were to lose the entire contract, it would decimate our business. Almost half of our revenues, and over two-thirds of our profits, are wrapped up with this single product. Our share price would fall off a cliff overnight."

"That's what I'm afraid of," Jamieson admitted. "You're our finance specialist—what hedging strategies can we take against this?"

"Such a large hit is very difficult to protect against. It's not like when we purchase commodity futures to lock in material supply prices, or take options positions to cover ourselves against currency fluctuations. This order of magnitude would be largely uninsurable."

"There's got to be *something* we can do!" implored Jamieson, banging his fist on the table.

"We could always float a new stock issue to take advantage of our high current share price, and then buy back into the treasury large portions of the outstanding shares after they drop!"

Joe was only half-joking. This was a timeless corporate strategy for taking advantage of transitional share price fluctuations, but such action also sent a strong signal that the company had no better purposes for its capital.

"I don't consider that a viable option," Jamieson replied. "Besides, that would only benefit *some* of our shareholders, and only in the short term. It does nothing to position us to be more competitive, nor focus on carrying on the business as a going concern."

Jamieson was becoming increasingly irritated in his management team's inability to propose workable solutions, and he was far from finished making them think this through.

"Sue," he said, calling once again on his Chief Marketing Officer, "what can we do about diversifying into more product lines?"

"As you know, Roland, we've been trying to do this for some time now. The underlying issue is that juveniles have far fewer health management needs than the rapidly declining adult population base—other than for hormone regulation, of course. Plus, with the FDA and other regulatory agencies requiring extensive longitudinal studies before approving most new health care products, we're probably looking at years before we can introduce any meaningful new products into the marketplace."

"You're all beginning to make this sound impossible!" groaned Jamieson. "Where do we stand with new products in the development pipeline, Nathan?" Nathan Taylor was Endogen's Chief Scientist, in charge of the company's research and development efforts. "How are we coming with the clinical trials for the proposed 'designer' patch?"

"We've been nearing completion on the testing phase for some minor changes in the formula for increased melanocyte production and its effect on improved skin tone," Nathan responded. "We could be ready for production in a few months if we get the required regulatory approvals."

Jamieson recognized a glimmer of hope. "This could be a key differentiating factor for us if the regular patch were to become commoditized by multiple suppliers, don't you think?"

"Unfortunately," Sue interjected, "the market size for that type of product may be limited. Our research suggests skin tone and color is much less of an obsession for the juvenile market than it used to be for the now largely defunct adult market. On the other hand, our focus groups *are* showing an opportunity for a growing interest in specialized patches for boosting sex hormones."

"You mean a type of Viagra patch for juveniles?"

"Nathan's people tell me that it is technically feasible to adjust the levels of sex hormones regulated by the standard patch, to increase or improve sexual interest and function among juveniles." Sue said.

"Yes, *technically*," Nathan quickly jumped in. "But this is a very delicate area, both physiologically and ethically..."

"How do you mean 'ethically'?" interrupted Jamieson.

"I think what Nathan is referring to, Roland," said Sue, "is that a lot of people from the senior generation still think it is immoral for juveniles to be engaging in any kind of sexual activity."

"This debate has been raging since the onset of the pituitary removal program," Bruce interjected. "I for one feel—as do many others—that no one has the right or authority to dictate our individual sexual proclivities. Besides, virtually all of these complaints are coming from a marginal group of aging seniors who have little remaining moral authority or influence. I think for the benefit of the company, and indeed for the betterment of everyone's quality of life, that we should proceed deliberately on this front!"

"I agree," asserted Jamieson. "I think we have to investigate every potential edge we can develop, and put ourselves in a position to be less exposed in the event of forces outside our control. Nathan, I want you and your team to begin stepping up your development efforts on this variation right away, and report back to me weekly on your progress. I'd like us to have some kind of unique new product we can introduce before the current U.N. contract expires.

"Joe, in the interim I also want you to look into whatever means we may have at our disposal—short of buying out our own shareholders—to protect against the financial implications of a serious setback in revenues and profits. I want a report on my desk before the end of this week."

"I'll see what I can come up with, Roland." Joe knew any significant new financing proposal or change in strategic direction would require approval by the Board of Directors. "Will we be presenting any of this to the Board at our upcoming meeting later this month?"

"Hell, no!" admonished Jamieson. "At this point, that is the *last* thing I want to bring to the Board's attention. They'll blow a gasket if we suggest there is the slightest possibility of our losing the U.N. contract. I want this matter to stay in this room for now; even your own people mustn't know. If the market gets wind of even a rumor, all of our stock options will be under water in a nanosecond. Plus, I know many of you have borrowed heavily against your personal collateral to purchase additional shares in the company, and none of us can afford to see this company's shares be taken down. Let's keep this between ourselves for now, and deal with it in a timely and effective manner so it never has to become an issue for anyone else."

    The group sat in sober silence. Everyone was absorbing Jamieson's grave comments and contemplating the potential consequences of failure—in both corporate and personal terms. With a giant blood-red Rothko painting on the adjacent wall hanging over their heads, the executives looked at one another nervously. Everyone knew they couldn't afford to fail.

Six

Thursday was Rick's favorite day of the week. This was the day he taught his Bioethics class at NYU, and he enjoyed the unique intellectual stimulation provided by the academic forum and the opportunity to broaden inquisitive young minds. It was a much anticipated break from the mostly predictable work involved in his general practice and hospital duties. Although the campus environment in Greenwich Village was only a few miles from his uptown offices, it seemed a world apart in attitude. Unlike the frenetic pace of the rest of city, the Village community had a uniquely creative and laid-back flavor, which had long attracted many of the world's greatest artists and intellectuals.

Usually Rick took the subway from his Upper East Side townhouse to the downtown campus; it was a straight run on the Green Line from his 86th Street stop to the Astor Place station. But today he decided to take a cab and seek pre-lecture inspiration in the sights and sounds of the Manhattan streetscape. The route along Fifth Avenue from the upper end of Central Park to its terminus at Washington Square was among the most glorious and uplifting stretches of cosmopolitan real estate anywhere in the world.

After flagging a taxi opposite the Metropolitan Museum, Rick settled in for the twenty minute ride downtown. As the soaring classical columns of the grand museum passed behind, majestic trees framing the park began lining up in perfect formation at the edge of the thoroughfare, like stoic sentinels protecting the public gardens within. In mid-October, the leaves were just starting to turn, and this made the sight all the more magnificent. Rick could see couples walking hand-in-hand along the adjoining carriage path, and others playing with their dogs on the lush carpeted fields beyond.

At the south end of the park, the city's affluent shopping district opened its arms at 59th Street. Dominating the intersection on the south-west corner sat the Plaza Hotel, rising regally above the street in the manner of a grand renaissance chateau. Surrounding the hotel on opposite corners were some of America's most famous retail institutions, including Bergdorf Goodman, Tiffany's, and Cartier. As he scanned to the opposite side of the street, Rick winced as he caught sight of the brassy edifice of the Trump Tower, standing in garish contrast to the old world beauty of its elegant neighbors.

Continuing down the opulent thoroughfare, the taxi came to an abrupt halt at the stoplights beside Rockefeller Center. This was one of the most fascinating intersections in the city for Rick, not least because of the great tradition behind the plaza itself—with its famous skating rink and giant bejeweled tree at Christmas—but also because of its intriguing juxtaposition across from the city's most famous church, St. Patrick's Cathedral.

The massive Neo-Gothic structure, with its ornately carved dual three-hundred-foot spires, was a spectacular architectural tour-de-force, and almost nobody could pass by without stopping at least momentarily to take in its grandeur and beauty. At one time the largest Catholic cathedral in the United States, its scale reminded Rick of the great importance religion once played in the lives of so many people. Now, this magnificent shrine had become almost like another museum along Fifth Avenue—there more for the quiet contemplation of tourists and curious passersby than for the divine inspiration of its rapidly dwindling congregation.

Few juveniles cared any more about the age-old religious traditions passed down by their ancestors. The once great promise and hope of spiritual salvation no longer seemed relevant to a generation of seeming immortals. They believed they would live forever, and felt no need to seek further enlightenment in what they now considered so many ghosts and demons. A few remaining able-bodied seniors dutifully made their weekly pilgrimage to their closest functioning temple of worship every Sabbath to hear the gospel delivered by aging clergymen, occasionally dragging their reluctant juvenile charges in a futile attempt to keep the faith.

As the light turned green and the taxi continued its journey southward toward the university, Rick's thoughts returned briefly to his last conversation with Tian Yin at the U.N. Secretariat building. As Surgeon-General of the United Nations and chief surgeon at Mount Sinai Hospital in charge of the juvenile hypophysectomy program, he often felt conflicted about his primary role enabling this abrupt and seemingly irreversible course of human history. His biology training had instilled a deep appreciation of the simple and powerful force of evolution in the shaping of the human organism, and he often felt uncomfortable interfering with its natural design.

He knew that evolution worked in small incremental steps, with minor variations in physical characteristics from one generation to the next selected and carried forward based on the fitness of each newly evolved organism for its environment. If a particular attribute was more suited to its environment than other another organism's attributes, the stronger and more suited ones were more likely to survive its environment and enable the organism to live long enough to pass along these superior characteristics to its similarly equipped offspring. The cumulative effects of these individual random mutations slowly shaped and evolved each creature to be optimally suited for its environment; this crucible of competitive biological warfare ensured that only the strongest survive. It was difficult to imagine how the recent human intervention in this design could be more intelligent in creating a sustainably equipped version of the human organism.

With fresh inspiration from the drive downtown, Rick strode resolutely into the lecture room at Vanderbilt Hall on the NYU campus. Seated in the large amphitheater were scores of students from various undergraduate and graduate disciplines. Since a new semester had just gotten underway, he was still getting to know his new Bioethics class and had asked everyone to place their names on tent cards in front of their desks so he could address them personally. About half the students were attending from the School of Law, with most of the rest from the School of Medicine. But there was also a scattering of students studying Philosophy and other disciplines, and more than a few who were returning to school after many years, simply to broaden their perspective and stimulate their minds. This was the kind of class Rick preferred, one with the appropriate breadth and depth to promote new learnings and discoveries.

"Good morning everyone," he began. "It's a pleasure to see you all again—I hope you found our first class interesting and enlightening!"

Rick had purposefully made his initial lecture light and entertaining, so as to get everyone engaged as much as possible, and to get to know his students' strengths and sensibilities. But he liked to make them work a little harder in the second lecture.

"Today I'd like for us to talk about the genesis of life, and how the initial design has evolved. It struck me as I was riding downtown this morning, that we live in a very different world than the one envisioned by our forebears. And yet it seems we still have some strong links connecting us. Who can identify some of these connections?"

The assembly stopped to think for a minute. This was one of Rick's favorite moments. The exquisite silence when so many enquiring minds were contemplating the obvious, and not so obvious. Wondering if they should respond with the answer their instructor wanted to hear, or with what they really thought. Of course, Rick knew there was rarely, if ever, a *right* answer.

"Well, I suppose we share some common DNA," replied Ethan, an eager pre-med student sitting in the front row.

Rick smiled. The first, and the quickest, response was rarely the most enlightened. "Yes, that's true Ethan. Biologically, we do share similar traits with our recent ancestors. How about *emotionally*, and *spiritually*—what do we have in common?"

"Emotionally we share a common bond and upbringing," replied Rachel. The philosophy students always seemed to dig a little deeper for inspiration. "Spiritually, many of us share common beliefs and values."

"Such as?" Rick asked.

"Beliefs about how we should comport ourselves, for instance, and our purpose in life," continued Rachel.

Now we're talking, thought Rick.

"And what *is* our purpose?" he asked, as much for his own edification as for the rest of the class.

The room became silent again. This was one of those loaded questions for which everyone—and no one—had an opinion. Some students shifted uneasily in their seats.

Rick decided to change the tone slightly.

"Yeah, that *is* pretty deep for only our second lecture," he said.

The group chuckled softly.

"Let's talk for a minute about those obvious things that make us *different* from prior generations. For one thing, we juveniles seem to think we're going to live forever. Why do others die?"

Gabriel, the graduate medical student, responded. "Everyone who has a mature pituitary eventually dies from the failure of one or other life support organs."

"True enough. And why do these organs eventually fail?" continued Rick.

"Natural senescence—the progressive wasting of the organs as an organism ages." Gabriel was obviously enjoying showing off his technical knowledge.

Okay, if we're going to be clinical, thought Rick, *let's bring it on.* "And what causes this progressive wasting of the tissues?"

"The natural breakdown and decay of the organism's internal cells," interjected Lauren, a biology student.

"Do *all* of the body's cells decay?" asked Rick.

"No, only the somatic cells—*germ* cells continue reproducing indefinitely." Lauren was referring to the body's two main classes of cells: germ cells representing the reproductive functions, and the somatic cells representing the 'body' of the organism.

Rick could see the dialogue was picking up a good cantor.

"And why is it that the somatic cells decay, while the germ cells do not?"

"Germ cells keep dividing throughout the entire life of the organism, while somatic cells have a finite limit to their divisions," Gabriel said.

"Ah yes, the so-called Hayflick limit," replied Rick. For some, it seemed as soon as a condition was officially named, we had conquered the need for further exploration. But Rick's job was to keep everybody thinking. "Why do these particular cells stop replicating when this limit is reached?"

"The telomeres at the end of the chromosomes within somatic cells shorten a little with each division," Gabriel replied. "The cells stop dividing and renewing when the telomeres get too short."

"And why do these telomeres shorten?"

"The soma cells stop producing telomerase in adulthood; this is the enzyme which replenishes the telomeres."

Gabriel sure knew his stuff, Rick thought. *Let's see if we can move the group outside the comfort zone of their biophysiology books.*

"Yet the *germ* cells continue to express sufficient levels of telomerase to maintain the length of their chromosomes indefinitely. Why do these specialized cells apparently not have the same destructive intent as the soma cells?"

The med students looked at one another quizzically. This was a question they had never been asked, nor considered. The rest of the class looked lost. Rick knew he had to get everyone thinking again.

"The germ cells are the ones that produce eggs in females, and sperm in males. Why might the body want to keep these cells productive, at the expense of the body's other cells and structures? What makes these cells so special?"

It was time for the class to think outside the box. Rick could see the wheels spinning in their heads. One of the anthropology students finally raised his hand.

"Yes, Drew?"

"These are the structures that are necessary to ensure the continuation of the species."

"Yes—they represent the natural source of the DNA we mentioned earlier, that links our generations together," Rick continued. "But why do you think nature has evolved to enable these evolutionary agents to outlast their *hosts*?"

Once again, it was the philosopher's turn to suggest an explanation. "Because the ecosystem is in balance," replied Jade, "and if one species were to completely die off, it could set off a chain reaction whereby all species – and life in general – could be in peril of extinction. Most organisms must reproduce to survive."

"That's impressively broad thinking," encouraged Rick. "Let's dig even deeper. Why do you think evolution created this survival instinct in organisms in the first place?"

Now we're getting to the 'meaning of life' questions.

The group quickly reached another impasse, and Rick decided to offer a little help to see if he could get them jump-started once again.

"Is it possible that a living organism's innate impulse to stay alive for another day increases its chances for successful mating and passing on more of its genes to the next generation—thus maintaining the species and preserving the balance of the ecosystem?"

The group looked at Rick with increased interest; he knew he was beginning to stretch the boundaries of their thinking.

"Which brings us back to the purpose of today's discussion: the genesis of life," he continued. "Where did all these life-affirming organisms originally come from?"

The anthropology major stepped in. "Different life forms evolved based on the unique set of environmental conditions that simultaneously evolved over time on earth," said Drew.

"This sounds logical," agreed Rick. "And what caused the earth to evolve this unique set of environmental conditions?"

The med students quickly jumped back into the fray. "Meiotic divisions among germ cells cause random mutations of life forms from one generation to the next," stated Gabriel confidently.

"And non-biological random forces of nature such as asteroid and meteor collisions create new environmental challenges and changes over time," added Drew.

"So, in other words—pure random chance events?" Rick asked rhetorically.

"That's the essence of chaos theory," replied Drew matter-of-factly.

"It makes some sense—but surely we can't boil the meaning of life down to a theory of chaos?" Rick said. "Let's see if we can't continue this line of reasoning one step further. If life as we know it is a product of these random cosmic events, then what created these random events?"

"I suppose we could say the collective forces of the universe, involving time, matter and energy," Rachel interjected.

"And what caused *those* forces to emerge?!" Rick continued.

"Their precursor forms of matter and energy, earlier in time," Drew added.

"And those?"

"*Their* precursors." Drew was drawing upon the intrinsic simplicity of anthropology theory.

"And so it goes: the infinite regress," Rick summarized.

Matt, one of the law students who had been patiently following this line of reasoning, couldn't resist. "So you're suggesting that the source of all living things is simply their immediate precursors—forever back in time?"

Rick was glad to see the law side of the room becoming engaged.

"Matt, do you think there will always be another tomorrow—even if we don't live to see it?"

"I suppose there would be, at least for whatever remains behind..."

"Well, if there will always be another tomorrow, doesn't it go hand-in-hand that there was always a 'yesterday'?" Rick suggested. "If you believe time is infinite looking forward, then by extension it must be infinite looking backward. This is the concept of the infinite regress. Our precursors were begotten by their precursors, and so on, forever back in time—as far as you can imagine." Rick could see the light go on in a few more faces.

"Okay, so we've considered why at least *part* of our bodies is biologically motivated to carry on indefinitely. Let's see if we can understand why the *rest* of it apparently is not!"

The class seemed perplexed. Rick knew they needed another mental primer.

"We've seen that the germ—or sex—cells are exempt and have a kind of 'free pass'—yet all the other cells are apparently programmed to die by eventually halting the replicating process. There's got to be some connection, don't you think?"

Once again, the room was suddenly filled with many cogitating minds. Rick waited a minute before continuing.

"Let's look at some extreme examples of this connection—in pacific salmon for instance. Why do you think they die so soon after mating? We can see them quite literally waste away very quickly after they've fulfilled their biological mandate."

"Well, salmon lay eggs," suggested Jade, "and perhaps their young don't need them to stick around to feed and nurture them like many other species?"

"That's true," confirmed Rick, "the emerging spawn are indeed self-sufficient. And in fact if you look at virtually every other species of life on earth, there is a direct and close correlation between the length of time it takes to reach maturity and the subsequent longevity of the organism. Those that mature quickly lead relatively short lives. Those that mature more slowly live much longer lives. Why do you think that is the case?"

"I would think that the longer the young take to reach maturity, the longer their parents must stay alive to nurture and protect them, until they are able to do so for themselves," suggested Matt.

"Yes, and in fact this connection is clearly borne out in the empirical data," Rick said. "But why do the progenitors—the parents— ultimately have to die?"

Drew had a quick answer. "If all organisms lived forever and could reproduce indefinitely, there would soon be overpopulation and insufficient resources to enable others to survive."

"Okay then, let's follow that train of thought," said Rick, pleased with the way different disciplines were now working together. "If that's true, why must the parents die before their offspring do? Why is it that an organism, once it reaches sexual maturity, begins an inexorable decline toward death—while the next generation of youth stays healthy and vibrant?"

"One could argue that the next generation, by virtue of its having been passed the genes from two strong survivors—which is to say *both* its parents—is more finely evolved and equipped to cope with the ever-changing environmental landscape," surmised Gabriel. "Thus, evolution would seem to favor its survival over its parents."

"Yes—and survive long enough to pass along those better adapted genes to the *following* generation," Rick stated. "In fact, any organism that lived *forever* presumably would reach a point where it was no longer suitably equipped to deal with its ever-changing environment—which of course could have interesting implications for all of us in this room!"

The hall suddenly became silent as the group considered the meaning of Rick's comments.

"*Now* it's getting interesting," he continued, seeing the serious look on the faces of many of his students.

"Let's carry this logic back a little *further* and see if we can find the source of those forces that are both destructive—for the survival of the individual organism, and constructive—for the survival of the species. Evolutionary biologists call this interplay 'antagonistic pleiotropy'."

"Can you explain that, Dr. Ross?" asked Matt.

"This theory says that sexually reproducing species create subtle mutations which are passed from one generation to the next in order to enable the newly emerging phenotypes having the best adapted forms to survive and pass on their genes to the next generation. Once they have satisfied their innate requirement to mate and raise their young, they are no longer needed.

"What I want you to consider is this: where is this mysterious instruction that tells our bodies we are no longer needed?"

"In the genetic codes embedded within the DNA of each species," said a newly emboldened Ethan.

"Fair enough Ethan, but what is the trigger that instructs the young and sexually immature organism to keep growing and remain vibrant—and which also stimulates their subsequent decline and visible aging after sexual maturity? What happens, for instance, to the salmon, physiologically, when they mate?"

"A flood of hormones is released into their system—which impels them to reproduce," said Drew.

"Yes, and apparently also *die* shortly after they have fulfilled their evolutionary imperative," affirmed Rick. "So, if DNA holds the instructions controlling our innate biological lifecycles, and hormones are the messengers, what is the signal that tells these hormones when it is time for them to go to work?"

"The pituitary gland controls most of the body's endocrine functions," said Lauren.

"And what controls the pituitary?"

"The hypothalamus."

"Ah, so all we'd have to do is remove the hypothalamus to stop the body from sending the signal to release the pubertal hormone cascade—which in turn signals our bodies to begin getting out of the way of our offspring!?"

"We *can't* remove the hypothalamus—that's the part of the brain that controls our entire nervous system!" Gabriel exclaimed.

"Well, it certainly wouldn't be much fun if we managed to keep an organism alive indefinitely if it couldn't enjoy its senses!" Rick mused. "What if we merely cut the link between the hypothalamus and the pituitary it controls?"

"Isn't that essentially what we are doing now when we remove the pituitary in juveniles?" asked Jade.

"Exactly. The hypophysectomy procedure severs this link, after which we artificially replace the hormones that would otherwise be supplied by the foregone pituitary."

"But only enough to maintain us at the physiological level of an eleven-year-old," added Lauren.

"Yes. In essence, we're fooling Mother Nature into thinking we're all still waiting for the moment when we'll be able to pass on our DNA to the next generation."

"Or fooling *God*!" intoned an unusually passionate voice from the back of the room.

"Isn't there another *far simpler* possibility—" the student continued, "that all this was simply created by someone greater than us?"

Rick couldn't read the name card of the individual who had replied, but the excitement and tone in the student's voice sounded vaguely familiar, and he knew that if he abided this new line of discussion it was likely to take him far of course.

"Yes, I suppose there is," he replied cautiously. "These are the things we are in this room to consider. However, I sense that will necessitate another long and interesting discussion—why don't we save that for our *next* meeting?"

Rick could see from the student's ardent expression that he wanted to continue the debate, but the meeting time was drawing to a close, and the professor thought this was an opportune time for a break. He decided to try lightening the mood with his closing comments.

"I want to leave you all with a little homework assignment, building on our discussion of today. I'd like to see if you might be able to solve a riddle which has confounded mankind for millennia.

"Which came first," Rick said with a knowing smile, "the chicken, or the egg?"

Seven

Calvin James stood on the pulpit of his church surveying the gathered assembly. His chapel was one of the oldest on the island of Manhattan, and it was showing its age. Its soft brownstone walls were covered in soot and crumbling from years of neglect. Located on a non-descript street in the East Village, the tiny church looked Lilliputian in the shadow of giant skyscrapers looming nearby. Originally christened the Church of the Resurrection by early Dutch settlers in the 17th century, after his split with the Episcopalian order as the church's pastor, Calvin had changed the name to the Garden of Eden. On the front lawn, a colonial graveyard with tilting markers reminded all who entered of the fragility of life, and death. As if to reinforce the connection, Calvin had planted a few apple trees among the gravestones. At this time of year especially, the falling ripe fruit was meant to symbolize man's arrogance and fall from grace in disobedience of God.

Although the Garden of Eden congregation was modest, it made up for its diminutive size in passion. Calvin was a compelling orator, and he could be very effective in building strong conviction for his beliefs among impressionable minds. Most of his assembly was made up of disillusioned juveniles who couldn't—or wouldn't—embrace the nihilistic and hedonistic values of present-day society. Many of them loners or malcontents, they came to Calvin to seek meaning and community they couldn't find elsewhere.

This Sunday, Calvin had prepared a special message for his flock. He had been thinking a great deal about his position in the world, and what meaning he could take from his unique status as one of the world's last adult males. He often likened himself to Adam, the first man, as the one whose shoulders he saw human civilization resting upon. Now, with the unnatural intervention of medical technology creating a new race of überchildren, he saw himself in a similar role as the last hope for the salvation of man.

When everyone was seated, the towering preacher outstretched his arms adorned in ceremonial robes, and a hush fell over the room.

"Friends," Calvin solemnly began his sermon, "we are *all* children of God.

"He created us, in His own image, to share mutual fellowship and love. This is why we are all living and breathing here today, and we have only Him to thank for this gift of life."

Calvin's deep voice resonated within the vaulted chamber and created an eerie echo, as if God himself were agreeing.

"There are those who would have us believe we essentially created *ourselves*—that we simply *evolved* from earlier forms of life. That we originally crawled out of the proverbial swamp as primitive creatures. They would have us believe that all this incredible beauty and complexity that we see around us in the world today is simply the product of some random big bang that happened an unfathomable time ago! *Do you believe this*?!" he admonished loudly.

"No!" came isolated cries from the assembly.

"Of course not!" Calvin affirmed. "There is only one possible explanation for all of this beauty. Something this magnificent could only be created by something *equally* magnificent—the Lord, our creator.

"But the Lord giveth, and the Lord taketh away," he continued solemnly.

This was Calvin's trump card, and he played it often. For millennia, virtually every religion from Christianity to Islam to Hinduism had based its underpinnings on the fear of death and what would be meted out in the afterlife.

"The Bible tells us that God originally created man for eternal life. But when man rebelled against God and ignored His heed, he was punished to die."

Many in the assembly nodded, recalling the story of Adam and Eve eating the forbidden fruit in the Garden of Eden.

"Man, in his selfishness, lost that which was most precious: everlasting life in the dominion of God. And here we find ourselves yet *again*," railed Calvin, his voice rising in intensity, "having forsaken God's plan, arrogantly thinking we can once again create our own design, and live with impunity! Through *self-mutilation* no less—the mutilation of God's *own image*—we try to re-create that which He told us we can no longer have."

The congregation grunted loudly in righteous disapproval.

"Do you think you are going to live forever simply because you allow a doctor to remove a little piece of your anatomy?! God once removed a part from Adam—to create Eve. He did this to enable us to multiply and populate our domain. Yet our very act of self-abasement seeks to deny this God-given facility. We have forsaken our ability to reproduce in the natural manner—*and we have forsaken God Himself!*" Calvin's face grew flushed in moral indignation.

"*Shame!*" came more responses from the creaking pews.

"What will be the consequences?" Calvin asked in a hushed tone, his flock now hanging on his every word. "Can some of us truly live forever? Can we forsake our Creator, and live entirely within ourselves—indefinitely?"

Calvin panned over his congregation as he witnessed many beseeching faces.

"*This is not God's will!*" he bellowed. Calvin's voice was shaking in rage now, and reverberating off the hard stone floor. "God *alone* is omnipotent and omniscient, and we delude ourselves if any of us believes we have the power or the ability to reverse His grand design!"

The congregation was on the edge of their seats. Calvin was their savior, and they were looking for deliverance.

"Let me tell you, my children: life and death are inextricably linked. We cannot have one, without the other. They are *both* essential. In life, we can enjoy the worldly pleasures God meant for us, and in death, we are meant to be reunited with the One who gave us life, and with all of our loved ones. This is God's plan."

"Praise the Lord!" rose scattered cries from the assembly.

As Calvin panned over the assembly, he could see the passion rising among his parishioners.

"*No* one can live in this world forever—we are merely postponing the inevitable. And for those who have forsaken their Creator, they will pay the ultimate *price*. For Hell was created by the Lord as a place of judgment for Satan, and for all those who follow him in their rebellion against God! My friends, we choose our destiny only by embracing God. *What will be your destiny*?!"

"To be with the Lord!" cried a parishioner.

"In the Kingdom of Heaven!!" roared Calvin, turning his head skyward, raising his arms to the rafters.

As the surrounding assembly rose to their feet in collective fervor and their cries of affirmation loudly filled the church, one figure sat quietly alone and motionless near the altar behind Calvin, lost in thought. He couldn't stop thinking about the gauntlet of spooky gravestones he had to walk through every day to enter this chamber. Although he looked very much like all the other juveniles in the church, he was also very different. For he had not yet had his pituitary removed, and there was tremendous pressure borne upon him to resist the life-affirming procedure.

Elias, was Calvin's son.

Eight

Rick felt great. It was the start of a new work week, and things couldn't be going better. Jason had fully recovered from his hypophysectomy operation, Eva seemed to be ready to fulfill her role as Queen, the U.N. master plan was working like clockwork, and the latest class of Bioethics students was providing new inspiration. The only unpleasantness—his recent clash with Calvin James on the front steps of the hospital—had already been forgotten.

But there was something more. He felt different, something he hadn't felt in a long time. He was intrigued, and attracted, by the hospital's new endocrinologist, Jennifer Austin. It wasn't as if Rick suffered from a lack of female companionship. There were all manner of females who flung themselves at him regularly, from the ubiquitous nurses and patients, to some of the most beautiful and sought-after New York socialites. Rick was considered one of the city's most eligible bachelors, and he had everything any woman would want: power, wealth, prestige.

Rick dated often enough, and for the most part enjoyed his social life. He just hadn't met anyone with whom he felt he could build a meaningful long term relationship. But Jennifer was different. Unlike most others, she wasn't deferential or overly awestruck by Rick's position and status. She was her own woman, and wasn't afraid to show it. Rick liked that. Plus, she was damn pretty, and the combination made Rick uncharacteristically unsteady.

This morning, he had some business he wanted to discuss with her, but mostly he just wanted to see her again, so he decided to make an impromptu visit. As he approached her office   in the Annenberg Wing of Mount Sinai Medical Center, he saw her working quietly at her desk.

"Good Morning, Dr. Austin," Rick announced, sticking his head through the half-opened door.

"I thought we'd agreed to be less formal with one another—*Richard*!" Jennifer responded, peering over thin tortoise-shell glasses.

"Oh yeah," replied Rick, momentarily taken aback by Jennifer's sexy librarian look. *She looks even better in glasses,* he thought, *as if that were possible.*

"*Jennifer.* You look...busy. Is this a bad time?"

"No, not at all, I was just reviewing Eva Bronwen's file that you sent me. I see you've made an appointment for tomorrow. Is she ready for a new round of harvesting?"

Rick was a little disappointed that Jennifer wanted to get right down to business. "Physically, she's at the right point in her ovulation cycle," he said, "so the timing seems good to begin the first phase of hormone treatment. Emotionally, however, she's a little fragile."

"How so?"

"A combination of expected fatigue regarding the ongoing hormonal and surgical procedures—as well as some trepidation over the prospect of giving birth."

"She said she's ready for insemination?" Jennifer knew this had to be a difficult decision for Eva.

"No, not yet. But she knows the clock is ticking, and is aware of expectations. I think she'll be ready soon. Anything you can do to lighten her burden on this matter would be greatly appreciated."

"Perhaps she just needs a little more *female* perspective?"

"Yes, I think a female perspective is exactly what the doctor need...ah, ordered," Rick caught himself.

"We *are* talking about the *patient* here, right Dr. Ross?" Jennifer smiled at Rick, slowly taking off her glasses.

"Yes, of course—but who's being *formal* now?!" Rick said, trying to deflect the subject.

"Sorry. *Rick.* Does anyone ever call you Ricky?"

"Not anyone who wants to maintain a continuing working relationship with me."

"Well alright then. It's just that sometimes you seem…adorably cute."

"*Cute?*" replied Rick, feigning indignation. "I'll take dashing, or distinguished, or maybe even ruggedly handsome—but never *cute!*"

"You'd deny me my heartfelt feelings?" Jennifer said, pretending to be hurt.

"Ok, coming from you, I'll take it as a compliment. Let's try to stick with *ruggedly handsome* though, shall we? But before you swell my already oversized ego any more, there was one other little matter I wanted to attend to."

"Really? I can't imagine," Jennifer teased.

"Yes, remember we have that other mutual interest: our young patient, Jason. I see he's responding well to your hormone treatment."

"What the Lord giveth, we taketh away. And replaceth—in a manner of speaking."

"Don't tell me you're another one of those deep spiritual types?" Rick asked, recalling uncomfortable images of Calvin James and his fanatical band of followers.

"No, I was just using an analogy to illustrate the deep spiritual connection between our two roles."

"Yes, it would seem we cannot live without each other!" Rick said, having fun extending the metaphor.

Jennifer was only too happy to play along. "Indeed, my role would be almost *redundant* without you creating so much havoc among juveniles and adults!"

"Hey!"

"Oh come on, I'm just messing with you. That havoc you create is actually quite life-affirming. I wouldn't have it any other way."

"I'm happy to hear you say that, Jennifer. And for my part, I'm glad you're here—to maintain the peace, as it were."

"Yes, we make quite the symbiotic pair, don't we? It seems your job is to stop the flood of hormones, and mine is to control the flow thereafter. Though I dare say my component is the more challenging of the two!"

"What?! I'm the *brain surgeon* here! How much more complicated does it get than that?!"

"Oh *please*! You just snip off a tiny little appendage conveniently hanging inside someone's nostril."

"Like so much mucus?"

"Exactly. Whereas I've got the Herculean task of carefully balancing nine critical and sensitive chemicals throughout the entire life of the patient."

"Well technically, you only need to replace and monitor those chemicals for the first week or two after I do *my* job—then the pharmaceutical company officially takes over. Though I grant you, those are rather important chemicals."

"Darn right! I control the chemicals that regulate everything from your immunity against sickness to your sex drive!"

"So we have *you* to thank for that, do we?!" joked Rick.

"Absolutely. In fact, did you know that the word hormone actually comes from the Greek word *hormon*—which means to stimulate, or excite?"

"I had no idea. Now I see how you have such a stimulating effect on people, Jennifer!"

Nine

It had been a busy week for Tian Yin since her last meeting with Rick at U.N. headquarters. With his blessing, she had been finalizing arrangements to transition the hormone patch supply from the sole authority of Endogen Corporation to a consortium of international companies. The logistics of such a change were extremely complicated, and she had been working closely with the World Health Organization to conduct much of the advance planning.

For the Secretary-General, the most difficult task was managing the anticipated political and economic fallout from the decision. Tian was aware of the full range of stakeholders in the matter, and the potential impact among each group. The first priority was obviously the health and safety of the patch users—the billions of juveniles across the globe who counted on the patch to regulate their essential endocrine balances. But there were also the employees, shareholders, and creditors of the affected companies to consider.

Tian knew that once the decision to change the supply arrangement was made public, there would be an immediate and substantial market reaction, and that billions of dollars of market capitalization and individual wealth would shift overnight. Endogen's shareholders stood to lose the most, but much of this would be offset by a reciprocal gain on the part of the newly awarded companies' shareholders.

For this reason and others, the privacy of the investigation had to be carefully protected, and all parties involved in the preliminary planning were sworn to secrecy. The last thing Tian wanted was a scandal revealing abuse of inside information. Even the appearance of impropriety was unacceptable, and she was mindful of protecting the venerable image of the United Nations.

It was determined that the fairest and safest way to choose the suppliers was through an open bidding process, with at least one official supplier to be chosen from each continent. Upon satisfying the U.N.'s requirements for quality control and scale of operations, each supplier would then be responsible for supplying only that continent's customers, with continuing oversight by the WHO.

Tian had decided to save the bulk of the detailed planning until after the suppliers were chosen, as this would minimize the period of time before an announcement could be made, and reduce the chances of any personal advantage being taken in the intervening interval. She had scheduled a press conference for this morning at U.N. headquarters to announce the program changes.

The press were dutifully assembled in the briefing room, eagerly awaiting Tian's arrival. The Secretary-General rarely held open press conferences like these, and the subject was inevitably important news. At precisely nine o'clock Eastern Standard Time, Tian entered the room and strode briskly to the podium. She appeared luminous as ever, wearing a smartly tailored dark-gray suit with her hair tied in an oriental knot, serving to complement her worldly image.

"Good morning ladies and gentlemen," she began. "Thank you for coming to our little gathering on this rainy Tuesday."

The press corps chuckled politely.

"I have an important announcement to make regarding the ongoing management of our Global Longevity Initiative."

A soft murmur rose from the assembly. The Global Longevity Initiative was of paramount concern to all parties, and this was the first announcement on the subject in a long time.

Tian knew that the wheels of politics and commerce would begin spinning right away, and she wanted to make a pre-emptive strike before rumors started circulating even now. The press conference was being filmed live for broadcast throughout the world, and she knew various financial and information brokers would be reacting to her every comment. She chose her words carefully, but spoke with a deliberate and confident tone.

"The United Nations, in concert with the World Health Organization and the Surgeon-General, has been very mindful of our continuing obligation to assure the health and security of our many constituents around the world. And of course we are all very pleased with the unbridled success of the Global Longevity program. But we are also ever-searching for ways to improve the reliability and the collective economic utility of the program."

Fingers were moving with increasing speed across miniature electronic keyboards, as various members of the gallery reacted to Tian's statements. Conjecture of various kinds had preceded the conference, and no one wanted to be behind the curve in taking first advantage of any new disclosure.

"We believe," continued Tian, "that although the current arrangements are undoubtedly working very well, there is an opportunity to broaden the economic advantage from the current patch supply arrangement to be more inclusive of our many economic and political stakeholders."

A buzz immediately filled the room as many surprised journalists turned to speak with their colleagues, while others began typing furiously into their personal communication devices, passing along instructions and sound-bites to their editors and agents. Some financial brokers got up quickly to leave, to take advantage of the critical information already delivered.

"Please!" announced Tian, eager to complete her statement. "Allow me to finish."

A loud "Shhh!" spread across the room, and the hall quickly fell silent again.

"For this reason, we have decided to allow the process of provisioning juvenile hormone patches to be put open to tender, effective immediately. We will make the bidding terms and conditions available upon the close of this conference, and all eligible parties are encouraged to participate."

"Madam Secretary! Madam Secretary!" Many arms rose with questions immediately begging to be answered.

"I will take questions in a minute, but first I'd like to address some of the obvious concerns. Endogen will continue to fulfill its commitment as exclusive supplier until the current contract expires. We have no wish to interrupt the safe and reliable supply that this organization has provided all of us since the inception of the GLI."

"Will they be allowed to participate in the new tender process?" someone called out.

"Yes, of course," assured Tian, "we anticipate that Endogen will continue to participate in the program, to the extent they qualify and bid competitively. We would like to make this process as painless as possible for all parties. We have no intention of cutting off a reliable supplier and their many thousands of dedicated employees around the world." Tian took a deep breath. "Now, I'd like to take individual questions from the floor—one at a time please."

Almost immediately, a sea of hands shot up from the assembly looking for recognition. Many more people rushed out of the room, intent on looking after more pressing business. Tian knew this would change everything.

So it begins, she thought, as she pointed to her first questioner.

Ten

Eva Bronwen had been looking forward to her appointment this morning with Jennifer Austin. Normally, she dreaded her twice-yearly fertility treatments, but after Rick's illuminating description of her new endocrinologist, she felt a certain affinity for the doctor, and was eager to meet her.

"Good Morning," Eva announced as she approached the reception desk. "I have an appointment with Dr. Austin at ten a.m."

"Yes Ms. Bronwen," the receptionist replied, recognizing the statuesque Queen immediately. "Dr. Austin has been expecting you—please see yourself into her office."

This was a pleasant surprise for Eva. She was expecting another delay in the waiting room as with her prior meeting with Dr. Ross, and she was not looking forward to being scrutinized by another group of curious juveniles. As she entered the office, she saw Dr. Austin working quietly at her desk.

"Ms. Bronwen, it's a pleasure to meet you," Jennifer declared as she quickly rose to greet Eva. "Dr. Ross has told me so much about you!"

"Yes, I'm such a troublemaker—he must have warned you about me!"

"Not at all," laughed Jennifer. "In fact, I think you're one of his favorite patients. He seems to think we'd have a lot in common, so of course I was excited to meet you."

Strangely, though the doctor and patient were not far apart in chronological age, they couldn't *look* more different in terms of their biological age. The full-figured Queen looked every bit a young woman in her prime, whereas Jennifer fit the ubiquitous image of a pre-adolescent juvenile.

"Well if he was referring to your *appearance*, I'll take that as a compliment," replied Eva. "I can see that Dr. Ross wasn't kidding when he mentioned how pretty you are!"

"And you Madam. You're everything I could imagine a beautiful woman would be."

This was no false praise coming from Jennifer; Eva came from good lineage. The Queen had been chosen very carefully, knowing full well she and very few others would be the sole genetic link to future generations. She and her mother had been subjected to a battery of tests to determine they were genetically pure and free of hereditary diseases. There could be no chance of the diminished gene pool passing on serious defective traits, or perhaps even halting the reproductive process.

And of course, it was implicit that the Queen should be intelligent and beautiful, with an ideal body type. Eva had thick natural blond hair, flawless skin, and a model-perfect countenance. In each of the continents across the world, other cultures had chosen their own Queens based on similar cultural preferences—there was also an African, Asian, Indian, Latin, and of course Eva—the Caucasian Queen. It was hoped this plan would preserve both the genetic and cultural diversity of the human race.

"I wonder what *else* we have in common," Eva said, hoping to get to know Jennifer better. "I understand you recently transferred from Baltimore—is that where you grew up?"

"Actually I'm originally from Kentucky," remarked Jennifer self-consciously, imagining how far more worldly the cosmopolitan Queen must be.

"Well, you're certainly a long way from home!" replied Eva graciously. "How are you liking the change of scenery?"

"It's very exciting. There's so much to see and do in New York, but I'm still building relationships and trying to get out more."

"I know how you feel—sometimes I feel like I'm stuck in a fishbowl in this big city!"

"How do you mean?" Jennifer asked, picturing Eva jet-setting around the globe, feted at every turn. "I imagine you'd have all kinds of opportunities to meet the most interesting people, in the most exciting places."

"You mean in my role as the Queen Bee?" joked Eva.

"Well," Jennifer replied, mindful of Rick's earlier warning about Eva's sensitivities on the matter, "I meant inasmuch as your having lots of important connections, and a certain celebrated status…"

"Sometimes celebrity can be a curse, doctor. It's not easy being a young adult in a world dominated by juveniles. Besides, I'm not so sure I'm a celebrity as much as a *curiosity*. I think the elders see me as a bit of a sellout, and the juveniles as a kind of freak."

"I can't imagine," replied Jennifer, beginning to like Eva's unassuming nature. "I'm sure everyone admires your elegance and selfless contribution in this situation. I know I certainly do.

"Please call me Jennifer—since we're going to be spending so much more time together."

"I'd like that, Jennifer. And please call me Eva. I can see why Dr. Ross likes you so much!"

Jennifer was surprised to hear Rick talking about her this way. She felt a certain chemistry between the two of them, but she wasn't sure he felt the same way.

"What makes you think he likes me—we've hardly just met!?"

"It's obvious you've made a tremendous first impression. He was practically gushing about you at our last meeting. Though he pretends disinterest, I can see he feels otherwise!"

"We'll have to see about that," Jennifer said. "So far, he hasn't exactly been storming down my door!"

"Maybe you two should open your doors to one another more often!"

"Good idea," chuckled Jennifer. "How about you, Eva—I understand certain doors may be opening your way, as well?" She was mostly referring to the pending insemination and pregnancy that Rick had mentioned earlier, but also hinting at Eva's relationship status.

"If we're talking about companionship, I don't think I've got a lot to choose from—between geriatrics and juveniles!"

What a shame, thought Jennifer. *It doesn't seem right for this beautiful, sexual woman to spend her whole life as a spinster.*

"There must be *someone* out there for you," she said. "Perhaps we girls simply need to get out and mingle more often?"

"That's a good idea, Jennifer. It might be kind of fun to socialize with some *real* people for a change, instead of all those boring bureaucrats. Plus, if Dr. Ross knew he had some competition for your attention, perhaps he'd be more likely to do something about it!"

"Sounds like fun. How would you like to go out somewhere this weekend?" Jennifer suggested.

"You're on!" Eva said, thrilled to have hit it off with a new friend.

"Of course, you'll have to be the *designated driver*," Jennifer warned. "That is, if you were still planning to start your fertility treatments this week." Both Eva and Jennifer knew alcohol consumption was contraindicated during the harvesting process.

"I'd almost forgotten about that," groaned Eva. "My favorite medical intervention. I don't know why they call me *Queen Bee*; I might as well be *Mother Goose*. Sometimes it feels that all I do is lay golden eggs!"

Jennifer knew this had to be one of the least pleasant aspects of Eva's role as Queen. The donor cycle typically took two to three weeks, and it would mean another round of painful shots and bloating in preparation for the actual egg retrieval. First, Eva would have to inject herself daily with a special drug that would temporarily prevent her ovaries from releasing the usual one egg per month. After about a week, Eva would begin a new cycle of injections of super ovulating fertility drugs that would induce her ovaries to make many more eggs than normal.

Near the middle of this cycle, she would require both ultrasound and daily blood tests to monitor the fluid in her ovarian follicles to see how the eggs were progressing. When the eggs were sufficiently ripe, she would need to take yet another drug to induce ovulation, then each egg would be carefully retrieved one at a time with a special needle inserted directly into her ovaries, under general anesthesia.

The whole process significantly magnified the normal swings in a natural menstrual cycle and wreaked havoc on the patient, both emotionally and physically. All manner of compounded side effects from excess fluid retention, to breast and pelvic tenderness, to headache and fatigue could be expected. Jennifer could well appreciate how this would be an unwelcome procedure for Eva.

"You certainly have a good sense of humor about the whole thing," she remarked. "But now that you mention motherhood, Rick tells me you were getting ready to consider a pregnancy too?"

"I don't think I have much choice," Eva admitted half-heartedly. "I've been told I have to keep the fertility window open."

Jennifer knew exactly what Eva meant. If Eva were to give birth even now, by the time her child reached reproductive age, Eva would be nearing the end of her own fertility lifecycle.

"Yes, I suppose that with about twenty years in a typical reproductive lifecycle to work with, that *would* put a little pressure on you," Jennifer admitted. "If you need someone else to talk this over with sometime, I'd love to help any way I can."

"Thank you Jennifer, I'd like that very much. For now, I guess we'd better get this latest round of harvesting done; then we can talk about implantation. Is my medication ready?"

"Yes, of course. Did you have any questions or concerns about the ongoing process? I mean besides the needles, bloating, headaches, and nausea, of course!"

Jennifer hoped some light-hearted humor might help ease Eva's burden.

"Ha! If only you knew what you're missing—I think that must surely be the best part of being trapped in a juvenile's body. It's not easy being a full-grown woman, let me tell you."

"I imagine there must be advantages both ways," suggested Jennifer. "Why don't we compare notes over drinks this weekend?"

"It's a deal—though it'll be an ironic twist that *I'll* be the one having to drink Shirley Temples, don't you think?!"

Eleven

Roland Jamieson was not looking forward to today's Board meeting. Over the course of twenty-four hours since yesterday's U.N. press conference, pandemonium had broken out at the Endogen corporate headquarters. As Jamieson had feared, the suspected announcement to diversify the juvenile patch distribution across multiple suppliers had caused Endogen's stock price to plummet. The company had lost over forty percent of its market value in a single day of wild trading on world markets. Multiple class action lawsuits had been launched against the company by disgruntled shareholders, arguing that Endogen management had been negligent in not anticipating and hedging against the known risk. The press had a field day exposing the extent of the calamity and assailing management for its ineptitude in managing the affair. Front page news in both the business and mainstream press were calling for Jamieson's head amid headlines screaming *Asleep at the Wheel* and *Foolish Gambit*.

Perhaps most unsettling was the fact that virtually everyone at the corporate campus knew the loss of the exclusive supply agreement would mean mass terminations of thousands of employees, and everywhere Jamieson went he was greeted with angry and accusing looks. To top it off, all day he'd been besieged with calls from alarmed creditors who were hastily trying to arrange meetings with the company's top financial officers to discuss loans whose covenants were now technically in default. It had gotten to the point where he no longer wanted to pick up the phone or leave the relative sanctity of his private office.

But the hastily arranged emergency meeting of the Board of Directors was one meeting Jamieson could not ignore. Normally, the Board met once every three months simply to review and approve proposals put forward by the executive committee and to sign off on quarterly financial statements. Until yesterday, with business going so smoothly, these meetings had become very amicable and accommodating.

Jamieson knew today's gathering was not going to be the typical meeting of the 'old boy' network. For the first time in his corporate life, he sensed his neck was on the line. Further compounding his sense of helplessness had been a recent move to separate the roles of Chief Executive Officer from Chairman of the Board in an effort to project greater shareholder representation and independent governance. Since it was now deemed a conflict of interests to blend these roles under the same individual, Jamieson was no longer able to dictate the agenda and exercise his influence as Chairman over Board activities and oversight. The new Chairman of the Board, Jack Knight, was a hard-nosed old-school administrator whose academic credentials as Dean of the Wharton School of Finance put him squarely at odds with Jamieson's executive sensibilities.

Jamieson waited nervously as the Board members slowly shuffled into the Endogen Boardroom. He greeted them in his normal chummy manner, and they politely returned salutations, but there was no denying the different tone of this meeting. Some helped themselves to refreshments and hors d'oeuvres and quietly made small talk among themselves, but for the most part, they tried to ignore Jamieson altogether. Everyone knew this meeting was going to be contentious, and it was apparent they were already steeling themselves for the unpleasant business ahead.

Assembled around the table were chief executives and directors of some of the largest and most prominent public and private enterprises around the globe—Endogen's Board comprised only the best of the best. Normally Jamieson would be in his element among this high-powered group, but today he found the eerie silence and averted gazes unnerving. Just when he couldn't imagine the tension getting any worse, the Chairman entered the room and quietly took his seat at the head of the table. There were no warm individual greetings and small talk to be made this morning. It was apparent from the scowl on Jack Knight's face that he was going to be all business today.

"Good morning everyone," started the Chairman. "It is obvious that we are meeting today under less than ideal circumstances, to say the least. I think we should all be prepared for a long and sober deliberation of the circumstances and implications surrounding the surprise announcement of the United Nations yesterday morning."

"Was it really a surprise, Jack?" suggested Ted Hiller. Ted was CEO of IntraHealth, the nation's largest Health Management Organization, and had long resented Jamieson's arrogance and domination over the industry. "I mean, couldn't we have seen this coming? It didn't take a rocket scientist to determine that Endogen had an unhealthy concentration and exposure in this area!"

"Exactly," added Andrew Graham, Chief Investment Officer of Occidental Growth Funds, the largest single block shareholder of Endogen stock. "Why didn't top management have a plan for preventing, or at least mitigating this possible turn of events? They must have known the likely impact of such a change. Our fund has been decimated, and many of our individual shareholders have been wiped out overnight."

Oh great, Jamieson thought—*let the blame-calling begin.* He wasn't about to take these accusations lying down.

"*No one* at this table saw this coming," he interjected. "It was never mentioned as a potential threat at prior Board meetings, and you *all* approved the strategic plan for Endogen, as recently as last July."

"No one around this table is responsible for *anticipating* these effects besides you, Roland," replied Andrew. "You are the CEO of this company and it is your primary role to set the direction and manage the risks attendant with the execution of the plan. Our role is simply to monitor your actions and ensure the shareholders' interests are being protected."

"I agree," added Mike Binnington, Managing Partner of New York's pre-eminent law firm, DesLaurier Binnington. "You can't blame any of us for your lack of foresight in this matter. This was entirely an error in judgment on the part of the senior management of this company. You simply dropped the ball here, Roland."

Jamieson panned the room slowly, and was met with many nodding heads. It was apparent that the group was closing ranks on him in a none-too-veiled attempt to protect their own interests. Every person at the table had a fiduciary responsibility to Endogen's shareholders, and no one wanted to admit culpability with the threat of personal legal liability accompanying his position as a director.

"All right, gentlemen, let's not stoop to mudslinging in this room," Jack weighed in. "We are *all* responsible for the interests of this company's shareholders, and we may all be held to account, in one manner or another. I think we should start discussing how we can best mitigate the effects of this catastrophe, and save this organization from even more harm. Although this is a tremendous blow to Endogen, things could still get worse."

"How so, Jack?" asked Phil Friedrich, Managing Partner at ComGroup Consulting. Phil was especially incensed over the matter, given his exclusion by Jamieson over the last few years from Endogen's inner consulting circle. "I can't imagine a worse state of affairs than this. The stock has been crushed, Endogen will likely have to fire more than half its staff, and we all face the real possibility of personal lawsuits in connection with the negligent management and oversight of this company?!"

"At least the organization is still a going concern today," intoned Matt Benson, CEO of Fidelity Bank. "If Endogen's loans are called in, this could seriously impair its liquidity and operating ability. And the company would be hard pressed to recapitalize by floating new shares in the current atmosphere. Roland, what actions have your creditors taken to this point?"

Jamieson was reluctant to admit he had been mostly deferring such calls, or that he had received many ominous messages from the company's largest lenders asking for an immediate meeting to discuss the terms and conditions of outstanding loan arrangements.

"We've received no formal notices as yet, and I am confident we will be able satisfy our ongoing debt obligations for the foreseeable future," he said, trying to sound confident and reassuring, even though he could feel the beads of sweat starting to form on his brow.

"How can you possibly be confident of your ability to meet Endogen's credit requirements when its cost of capital has effectively doubled overnight?" Matt argued. "Surely, this will put the company in breach of its loan covenants, and invoke the calling of many loans?"

"Although technically we may be in default of certain loan agreements," Jamieson said, trying desperately to tread water amidst the turbulent barrage of questions, "I believe as long as we can satisfy our lenders that we are able to continue servicing the debt in accordance with the prescribed payment plans, they will not call any of our debt."

"And how exactly do you propose to do that Roland—" demanded Andrew, "with more than half your revenues obliterated?"

"By systematically downsizing the company in advance of the termination of our patch supply agreement with the U.N., so that our revenues continue to be aligned with expenses." Jamieson could hardly believe he was uttering these words.

"You mean by cutting down this company to a shadow of its former self?!" suggested Jack. "I don't think our shareholders will like that plan very much, no matter how much it may satisfy our creditors in the short term. I think we need to look at some longer-term solutions to rebuild this company's equity and shareholder value. What plans or initiatives do you have in the works to expand into new markets?"

Jamieson hesitated, as he pondered an appropriate response. "As most of you know, the process of gaining regulatory approval for new products is very long and demanding. Most of our initiatives are multi-year proposals that are not likely to begin adding incremental revenue for quite some time after we lose the exclusive supply of Endopatches."

"You've got nothing ready, or even *planned*?!" asked Phil incredulously.

Jamieson could feel his heart pounding in his chest, but fought to maintain his composure.

"Well, we *are* nearing completion on the final testing for a premium patch that would regulate skin tone, but our marketing people tell us the revenue potential for this product is very limited. It would certainly hardly make a dent in the loss of revenues associated with our share of the basic Endopatch."

"So that's it?!" interjected Ted. "All you've got is a puny upgrade for an effect the vast majority of consumers hardly even want or need? I can't believe you put all your eggs in one basket, and didn't even have the foresight to plan ahead for the distinct possibility that you might not have preferred status on the Endopatch indefinitely!"

Jamieson was beginning to feel the sting from the combined press of the directors' questions and accusations. He desperately needed a solution—quickly.

"There *was* one other possibility," he began slowly, his voice breaking slightly, "but I'm not sure it will fly technically, nor be able to gain the necessary regulatory approvals."

"What is it? Don't leave us all hanging out to dry for God's sake!" Mike implored, his fear of personal liability rising by the moment.

"Our Research and Development Group has been working on a new patch that could improve sexual function..."

"How so?" Andrew interrupted, suddenly intrigued. "The Viagra craze has long since passed now that seniors have been replaced with a new generation of juveniles. And I can't speak for the rest of my colleagues, but I don't sense a problem in this area!"

"Yes, of course it's true that juveniles are for the most part sexually functional," Jamieson agreed. "However, with the hormone mix set at prescribed levels to maintain everyone at the physiological level of an eleven-year-old, there is an opportunity of sorts to enhance both the drive and intensity of sexual performance among this segment."

Jamieson could see a few eyebrows raised around the table. He knew he had tweaked their interest—at least temporarily. Perhaps he had found a reprieve, albeit a tenuous one.

"Without affecting the physical maturation status of the individual?" asked Ted, wary of maintaining the precarious endocrine balance that kept everyone locked in a perpetual, but safe, state of pre-pubescence.

"Yes, so my Chief Scientist tells me," replied Jamieson carefully.

"Well, that *could* show some promise!" offered Andrew. "This kind of designer drug could have wide currency and separate Endogen from the other suppliers in this huge market. What is your timeline for development and release?"

"I'm having my Chief Scientist work on this as we speak, and he's promised to provide an accelerated project plan for me next week." Jamieson said, finally beginning to feel some of the tension ebbing.

"I think he should present his findings to this *entire* Board at the first opportunity," Jack ordered. "Roland, I want you to arrange it and notify us as soon as possible. This could be your last opportunity to save more people than you know from an unfortunate demise."

Jamieson understood full well Jack's meaning. But he had far more serious concerns than the possibility of his losing his job as CEO of Endogen. That would be a temporary embarrassment from which he could recover. He knew he had enough connections to land another high-profile academic or professional position fairly quickly. The more critical matter was his *personal* financial liquidity. Not only was his generous allotment of company stock options now firmly under water and unlikely to hold value ever again, he had made the mistake so many other arrogant executives had made in similar situations: he had borrowed aggressively to purchase more stock of the company under his management.

Suddenly—like Endogen itself—he was heavily in debt, with little counter-balancing equity to offset his loans. But *unlike* Endogen, his own personal cash flow would not be sufficient to satisfy these loan requirements. Jamieson knew that it was only a matter of time before his personal bankers called to redeem his debts, and that he would be unable to meet their demands.

Twelve

As he briskly scaled the granite steps leading into Vanderbilt Hall, Rick reflected upon his previous week's Bioethics lecture. The discussion had been lively and stimulating, and not without some surprising twists and turns. Today's lecture was to have a new theme, but there was still some unfinished business from the last meeting and he had prepared himself to go wherever his students wished to take him. He knew that with any Bioethics class, the discussion could lead almost anywhere, and he didn't want to impede his students' creativity by limiting the discussion to just one topic.

Approaching the lecture hall, Rick could hear a loud buzz coming from the charged-up assembly, but the group suddenly fell silent when he stepped into the room.

This should be interesting, he thought.

"Good morning, creative thinkers!" Rick began. "We had a lot of fun last time exploring the profound topic of the meaning and genesis of life, and I hope you found yourselves stretched as much as I was!"

Rick saw many heads in the assembly nodding in affirmation.

"Today, I want us to consider what I hope you'll find to be an equally stimulating subject—*cloning*—and what implications this may have for humanity, when compared to the natural and somewhat old-fashioned way of creating life.

"But first, we have the open matter of our unsolved riddle to address. Who has come up with an answer to the infamous question: Which came first—the chicken, or the egg?"

Matt raised his hand; this week it would be the law contingent to start things off.

"If we accept the notion of the infinite regress put forward last class, then it would appear to be indeterminate.

It's circular reasoning, with no finite starting point," he stated resolutely.

"So it would seem," replied Rick. "So that's *it* then—no one has a solution to this age-old conundrum?"

He slumped his shoulders and sighed, feigning resignation.

"That's a little disappointing!"

"How *could* there be one under those conditions, Dr. Ross?" asked Rachel, the Philosophy major.

"Well I suppose if you limit yourself to thinking of life in its broadest sense, then I guess you're right Rachel. If an organism is simply a product of its progenitors, forever back in time, that would appear to be true." Rick hesitated for dramatic effect. "But when does a chicken *not* resemble its progenitor?"

The room became still.

Silence. Painful, delicious silence, thought Rick. *Is there any better moment, when the anticipation and contemplation of what might follow is more intense?*

After waiting a few moments, it was apparent that he would need to break the group's mental logjam.

"Gabriel, you stated last class that different life forms evolved over time from random meiotic divisions among germ cells, which are passed on to subsequent generations. Doesn't this suggest that each progeny will have different characteristics from its parents?"

"Well…yes, Dr. Ross," the graduate medical student replied tentatively, "but these mutations are normally only minor. The genetic material supplied to the next generation is essentially the same DNA from the mother and father—so a *chicken* would still beget a chicken."

"Yes, that's true," agreed Rick. "The DNA is indeed purely and exclusively supplied by the two parents. However the process of meiosis takes the genetic alleles from both the paternal and maternal germ cells and converts that DNA through a series of divisions and re-combinations into a random *mixture* of that material in the offspring."

Drew, the Anthropology major, looked perplexed. "Wouldn't the same genetic material, albeit mixed up a little, still produce the same *species* in the next generation, Professor Ross?"

"Technically, Drew," Rick continued, "it's the *genes* within the nucleus of each cell that determines the structure and function of the organism. These genes are specific sequences—or strings—of nucleotides found on the chromosomes, which collectively comprise the DNA supplied to the organism. Since these fundamental building blocks, the nucleotides, are constantly being shuffled and randomly re-dealt during the process of meiosis, the resulting order and placement of these strings can change significantly from the originating germ cell of the parent to the resulting gamete cells, which are subsequently passed on to the offspring during sexual reproduction."

"So you're saying these mutations are sufficient to create an entire new life form?!" asked Matt.

"Well it depends, I suppose, on how you define an 'entire new life form,'" Rick explained. "How many of you, for instance, sometimes think your brother or sister is an *entirely new life form*, quite distinct from yourselves?"

A few students chuckled knowingly.

"If you accept that life in all its magnificent forms evolved over time from this amazing process of genetic mutation," Rick continued, "and that land-dwelling creatures may have emerged from the ocean on the putative legs of primordial sea creatures, then how much of a stretch does it take to see that chickens evolved from subtly different forms of life?"

"So you're saying then, Dr. Ross, that the egg came first, and that through the process of meiosis, it created a chicken?" asked Drew.

"Drew," Rick continued, teasing his students for a little longer, "did you know that some species of snake have tiny spurs on their body which are thought to be vestiges of legs from their ancestors? At what specific point would you say the lizard offspring suddenly became a *snake*? Or conversely, at what precise moment did a fish's fins evolve into legs? At some point in this process, another type of creature would have to evolve into a form we would say has now become a chicken."

"But it wouldn't be so much a discrete event, as a series of subtle changes over time, would it, Professor?" asked Rachel.

"Yes, of course. But in each case, the newly mutated egg would *pre*-determine the form of its hatchling."

As he scanned the room, Rick could see a few lights going on among his students, while others were still putting together the pieces. *This looks like a good time to take them to the next stage*, he thought.

"There may not, in fact, be a simple and clear answer here, but it certainly makes for an interesting segue into our next subject of *cloning*," Rick suggested. "At least insofar as asexual reproduction appearing to bypass entirely this powerful evolutionary force of genetic mutation."

"How so?" asked Jade, the other philosophy major in the class.

"Let's have one of our biology students provide us with a brief overview of the cloning process," asked Rick.

Lauren decided to take up the challenge, and raised her hand.

"Yes Lauren?"

"Cloning involves removing the DNA from the nucleus of a living organism's somatic cell, and inserting it into an egg whose DNA has been removed, and then stimulating that egg to develop and produce new young in the normal manner."

"Why then," Rick responded, "must the donor DNA come from a *somatic* cell?"

"Because the other cells," Lauren continued, "the germ cells, only supply *half* the genetic material needed to create a viable new organism. Only the soma cells have both the paternal and maternal sets of forty-six chromosomes, which must be combined to produce offspring. The germ cells only supply one or the other of these halves, and thus require sexual union to combine with the other half."

"In that case, what implications might the process of cloning have on the mutation of life forms from one generation to the next?"

"Cloning produces no change in form between donor and offspring, because they share the exact same set of complete DNA," asserted Gabriel. "The two organisms will be genetically exactly the same."

"And what effect might that have on the survival or longevity of the species?" Rick asked, continuing to probe.

"Since there would be no change in form or function from one generation to the next, the species would never adapt over time with its environment," suggested Drew.

Rick was pleased with how the group was working together once again. "So what might that mean to the ultimate survival of that species?"

"Eventually, the ever-changing environment would create conditions for which the unchanging species would be ill-equipped to manage, and the species would presumably die off," Drew replied.

"Perhaps that's why Mother Nature seems to prefer sexual reproduction over this less exciting asexual form!" replied Rick, with a hint of a grin. "Why then, do you think she makes this preferred process so much *fun*?" he teased.

"By creating the continuous urge to copulate, it has the effect of maximizing the genetic diversity and propagation of the various species," stated Ethan.

"You make it sound so *clinical*, Ethan!" Rick joked.

The assembly erupted into loud, spontaneous laughter.

"It looks like we higher life forms," Rick continued, "who procreate sexually and thus evolve over time to counter any destructive environmental forces, are awarded a two-edged sword. We lead longer lives by more successfully avoiding predation, but we also pay the ultimate price when nature forces us to get out of the way of our better adapted offspring. Lowly *bacteria* on the other hand, who replicate asexually, theoretically can live forever. But because they are poorly adapted for survival, they typically *don't*—so they must reproduce rapidly and prodigiously to compensate."

"Why would nature choose to have *any* species reproduce this way then, Dr. Ross?" asked Lauren.

"That's a very good question, Lauren. But first, let's look at it from a purely selfish perspective," Rick suggested, encouraging the group to switch their line of thinking. "If we humans are among the few organisms that have a *choice* between sexual or asexual reproduction, what effect would a potential parent's cloning have on the longevity and survival of his or her immediate heir?"

"The empirical data shows that cloned organisms normally have shorter lifespans, to the extent that cloning even works in the first place." Gabriel stated.

"How do you mean, Gabriel?"

"Only about five percent of attempted clonal reproductions in higher life forms are successful in producing a viable offspring to term."

Rick continued to be impressed by Gabriel's depth of knowledge of fundamental biology. "*Why* is that, do you think?" he probed. "Why do these cloned organisms seem to have lower survival prospects?"

"Maybe the donor DNA nucleus doesn't properly bond with the egg whose nucleus had been removed," suggested Lauren.

"Or maybe the partly aged DNA from the donor simply starts in the new organism where it left off?" offered Drew.

"Perhaps inherent genetic disorders in the donor cell are carried over, or somehow stimulated when the nucleus is artificially fused into the egg," added Gabriel.

"These are all good possibilities," offered Rick. "Fortunately, we have the capability to perform embryonic screening of the egg to test for and remove defective genetic carriers, so this wouldn't appear to pose too much of a practical problem. And hormonally induced multiple egg harvesting can compensate for the low gestation rate. So it seems we ingenious humans have been able to circumvent many of Nature's built-in barriers to this type of reproduction. But it *is* true that successfully cloned organisms do show signs of diminished longevity, and we still don't know all the reasons why."

A hand rose from the back of the assembly. "Why would we want to mess with a design that has worked so well for so long, anyhow?" a familiar voice asked plaintively. "Perhaps there's *another* reason why it's proven so difficult for man to artificially create life!"

Rick recognized the individual as the one who had introduced the notion of divine creation towards the end of the previous lecture. He had checked the student's file and discovered that Nathan Taylor had a unique and intriguing academic background. As a holder of a Ph.D. in molecular biology, it was unusual for someone at this stage in his professional development to be seeking continuing education in this forum—especially on this subject. Usually, Bioethics was an elective chosen by students in their undergraduate or graduate studies as part of the process of completing their degree in law or medicine. An individual with Nathan's lofty qualifications would normally now be teaching or conducting clinical research to advance his learning.

Although Rick was pleased that Nathan had presented his idea in a more restrained manner this time, he knew from prior experience that the proposed subject could be an explosive one, and he decided to proceed cautiously.

"That's a good point, Nathan," he replied carefully. "Help us understand your point of view. What alternative explanation might you suggest?"

"Simply that 'Mother Nature' has nothing to do with any of this. That *God* created the universe, and everything in it!" Nathan spoke plainly, but Rick could hear the fire in his voice.

"This is indeed an interesting proposition, and one that has had wide currency for many millennia," Rick stated, mindful to remain open and non-judgmental. "How might we reconcile the existence of God with what we have proposed in this room?"

"You can't," replied Nathan matter-of-factly.

Rick decided to give Nathan the benefit of doubt and see where he might go with his argument. "If a Higher Being started everything," he asked, "why couldn't life have evolved *since* then in the manner we have proposed?"

"Because the Bible tells us otherwise."

It was obvious to Rick that Nathan had already made up his mind and was going to resist any alternate theories. Rick knew from prior experience that it would be counter-productive to go head-to-head with anyone who held such strong and passionate opinions. He decided to open the floor for discussion in an attempt to broaden the perspectives and to deflect the confrontation. Unfortunately, he wouldn't have a chance to set the stage, as the class was all-too-eager to jump in.

"What makes you think the Bible is all-knowing?" Gabriel interjected.

"Because it was written by God Himself," Nathan replied.

"How can you know that?"

"Because it is so written."

"Isn't that circular reasoning?" Drew asked.

"There is plentiful evidence to support the Bible's assertions!" Nathan argued even more vigorously.

"Such as?" Gabriel challenged.

"Such as multiple accounts of miracles performed by the Lord."

"How do we know those accounts aren't simply the authors' *interpretations*," Rachel weighed in, "or the interpretations of others from whom those accounts may have been passed down? Much can be lost or embellished in the translation from one person to another over a long period of time. Doesn't the Bible in fact state that it was written by mortal humans—many years after the events so chronicled?"

It was apparent that Rachel had studied her own share of scripture, and Rick was pleased to see the depth of understanding and the level of engagement amongst the group. He decided to let them play this out a little longer.

"It may have been written by mortals," Nathan said, becoming more impassioned and irritated with each counter-argument, "but under the direction of God!"

"So we are led to believe," countered Drew, "by their own words. Doesn't this interpretation really amount to a simple *leap of faith*?"

"A leap of faith that will save everyone who so believes!" exhorted Nathan.

"Save us from *what* exactly," Gabriel said sarcastically, directly challenging Nathan. "We seem to have found a way to give ourselves eternal life, no thanks to your Lord!"

Nathan's eyes lit up. "Your puny efforts to extend life will matter little in the end— when judgment is passed!"

Here we go with the fear-mongering again, thought Rick. *Why must it always boil down to belief purely for the sake of salvation?*

It seemed too convenient an explanation for Rick. Nathan was starting to sound more and more like Calvin James, and Rick wondered if he might in fact be a member of the preacher's flock. He couldn't understand how someone so steeped in the precise science of molecular biology could so quickly dispense with his long training for belief in such a tenuous and simplistic premise. Rick resolved to meet with Nathan after class to better understand his motivations and connections. For now it was time for the professor to step back in to the fray. The lecture was getting out of control, and quickly moving beyond the bounds of both biology and ethics.

"Okay gang, it looks like we have some divergent opinions on this matter and that we're going to have to agree to disagree for the time being. Plus, we're nearing the end of today's meeting, so in preparation for our next lecture two weeks from now, I want each of you to consider another little mind-bending riddle."

As he scanned the room and prepared to present his question, Rick's eyes stopped as they met Nathan's.

"If, as some people believe," he said, "every life has a soul, and every clone is an exact replica of its donor, does that mean that the donor and clone share the same soul?"

Thirteen

Eva appraised herself carefully in her full-length dressing room mirror. She wasn't exactly sure how she should dress for tonight's nightclub excursion with Jennifer. Should she dress demurely, to reflect her matronly image as the anointed Queen? Should she dress more elegantly to reflect her lofty social standing? Or would she dress more provocatively to accent her unique and abundant curves, and reveal to the world what a *real* woman looks like?

What the hell, thought Eva, *why should I be afraid to highlight my natural assets?*

She finally chose a form-fitting, navy-blue dress with a subtle slit up one side to show a little leg, if the mood struck her. A chenille scarf draped loosely around her neck fell softly against her ample bosom, revealing more than a hint of cleavage. Her hair was styled in a bohemian bob, with long corkscrew curls cascading over her creamy skin. Elegant black leather pumps completed the picture—though she doubted many people would be looking that far down tonight.

Eva smiled as she imagined the impact she'd make walking into the nightclub. She was the natural embodiment of fully mature beauty and sensuality, and she knew she would open more than a few eyes tonight. Jennifer had heard of a new place everyone said was the hottest club in town, and Eva was exhilarated as well as a little intimidated about the prospect of mingling among so many juveniles in such an unfamiliar setting.

Her thoughts were suddenly interrupted by the buzzing of her apartment's intercom.

"Hello!" Eva replied, almost tripping as she rushed to press the button on the console.

"There's a Ms. Austin here to see you, Ms. Bronwen," informed the concierge from the main floor lobby of her posh co-op building.

"Yes, I've been expecting her. Please send her up."

"She said she has a cab waiting," the concierge replied.

"Oh, yes, of course—tell her I'll be right down."

Eva had hoped she and Jennifer could chat a bit before heading downtown, but she knew taxis would be in short supply on a rainy Friday evening on the Upper East Side, and she didn't want to flaunt her special privileges by ordering a limousine. With some trepidation, she grabbed her purse and headed out the door.

Jennifer was sitting quietly on a leather sofa in a corner of the marble lobby as Eva stepped out of the elevator on the ground floor. Eva didn't like keeping her new friend waiting, but there was no way around the security rules of her building, which restricted guest access without explicit clearance.

"Hi Jennifer," Eva apologized. "Sorry for the delay."

"No problem, Eva. I'm getting pretty used to these doorman-controlled buildings by now, living in New York."

Jennifer's eyes suddenly widened as she saw Eva moving closer in her revealing dress.

"Wow—you look smashing this evening!"

"You don't think I'm a little overdressed?" Eva was beginning to wonder if she'd chosen wisely. Jennifer was wearing a more subtle ensemble, comprising a pretty oriental blouse over a mid-length charcoal skirt, atop simple but chic flats.

"Not at all," assured Jennifer. "Where we're going tonight, I think most people will be dressed to the nines!"

"Where *are* we going anyway?"

"Let me fill you in on the way—our cab is waiting."

As they exited the building, Eva's doorman held out a large umbrella and escorted them to the waiting car. It was a chilly early autumn evening, and they were happy to take shelter against the rain. As they bundled into the taxi, Jennifer informed the driver of their destination.

"The Hippodrome, please."

"That sounds interesting," remarked Eva. "Where's that?"

"It used to be a revolving restaurant atop the Marriott Marquis hotel that was recently converted into a giant circular nightclub-bar. It just opened, and the girls at work tell me it is the absolute hippest-happening place in town."

"I recognize the location," said Eva. "I used to have the occasional Sunday brunch at that restaurant. Shows you how much I get out—I didn't even know it had been converted into a nightclub!"

"Neither did I," admitted Jennifer. "How are the views from up there?"

"Magnificent. Though I can't say how clear it will be on a dark and drizzly night like this!"

"We'll just have to enjoy the view from *inside* then. Should be lots of good people-watching. Though something tells me *you're* going to be the center of attention tonight!"

Eva scrunched up her nose in protest. "I'm not sure that's exactly what I want on my first unofficial night out in such a long time. Usually I'm escorted to carefully planned and boring official functions like museum openings and theater premiers. I don't know if I'm entirely ready for this kind of experience!"

"Well then, let me be your escort tonight. Besides, how much trouble can we get into forty-eight stories above the street, in the city's fanciest nightclub?!"

Eva smiled nervously, and her gaze shifted to the Manhattan streetscape rushing by her tear-splattered window. Even though it was fairly late on a rainy Friday evening, she could still see plenty of pedestrians walking on the broad sidewalks in the shadow of the streetlamps. Of course, virtually all these people were juveniles, every one of them about the same height—almost a full foot shorter than Eva. It reminded Eva how often she felt like a modern day Gulliver, traveling among the little people of Lilliput.

How true indeed the prophecy, she thought, *that the meek shall inherit the earth.*

Riding up the glass elevator to the roof-top nightclub above Times Square, Eva and Jennifer watched as the flashing billboards at street level fell rapidly away, and the peaks of many surrounding mid-town skyscrapers rose like so many sparkling jewels in the glistening twilight. But when the doors opened on the forty-eighth floor, the two grimaced. The room was packed with club-goers as far as either could see, and a long queue stretched from the elevators to the main entrance door.

"Oh no," groaned Eva, "it'll take us forever to get through this lineup!"

"Let's check at the front door and see what can be done," suggested Jennifer.

As the two worked their way forward to the reception area, Eva noticed many people's attention closely followed their movements. She wasn't sure if they were more concerned about line jumpers or if it was simply that they hadn't seen a young, full-grown woman this close-up before. Either way, she was beginning to feel uncomfortable with so many eyes upon her.

"Excuse me," Jennifer announced as she approached the doorman, "can you give me an idea of the approximate wait time?"

The doorman quickly glanced at Jennifer and then did a double-take as he caught sight of Eva just behind her. His eyes scanned the statuesque beauty carefully and thoroughly—a little too thoroughly for Jennifer's liking. Just as she was about to make a comment, he spoke.

"Are the two of you together?" he asked.

"Yes." replied Jennifer. "This is Eva Bronwen, and I'm her escort."

"Yes, I recognize Ms. Bronwen, of course. There is no need for you to wait in line. We would be pleased to welcome both of you to our establishment at your leisure.

"Enjoy your evening," the doorman said, as he unhinged the clasp and pulled aside the velvet rope.

The two ladies quickly entered the main room.

Some things never change, thought Jennifer. *The beautiful and famous people always get favored status.* Under the circumstances, she wasn't about to complain.

"That was easy," remarked Eva. "Do you always find it so simple to crash the line?!"

"Not quite that easy. I think our doorman fancied you!"

"He was probably just being deferential because he recognized me as the Queen."

"Maybe, but I think that *dress* might have helped a little too! These places always like to fill their establishments with beautiful people, and I think you qualify on many levels."

"You're no slouch yourself, Jennifer," Eva replied. "In fact, I think we make a smashing couple!"

"An *odd* couple perhaps," laughed Jennifer. "Come on, let's see if we can find a table."

As the two moved through the thick crowd, astonished patrons audibly gasped as they caught sight of the tall Queen. Eva towered over the teeming throng, and it was obvious she was being recognized by everyone who saw her. She was thankful the loud music drowned out the comments people were making to one another as they advanced.

"Can you see any open tables?" Jennifer shouted, hoping Eva's height advantage would give her a more commanding view of the room.

"No, it looks like every chair is taken," Eva replied, scanning the room. "Are these places always so busy on a Friday night?"

"I suspect this is busier than most, since it just opened—though it's definitely hopping tonight! Why don't we head to the bar and see if we can find a spot there?"

Jennifer grabbed Eva's hand and led her, somewhat protectively, to the other side of the room. When they reached the counter, she was disappointed to see all the seats were occupied. Nevertheless, the two found an open spot to stand at the corner of the bar.

"Whew," remarked Eva. "I feel like we've just run the gauntlet!"

"More like the *parting of the seas*," said Jennifer. "Did you notice how the crowd separated for us as we made our way through?"

"Maybe they're afraid of me," Eva said, still feeling a little self-conscious. "You have to admit, I do stand out, to say the least. I must look like a bit of an oddity in this place."

"I'm sure they're just marveling at your beauty and grace. It's not every day that a juvenile gets to see what a full grown woman in the prime of her life looks like, up front and personal!"

Jennifer caught the eye of the bartender approaching their end of the counter.

"What can I get you, ladies?" he asked.

"I'll have a Martini, straight up," answered Jennifer.

"I'll have the same, with a twist of lime please," said Eva.

"Coming right up."

"What happened to Shirley Temples?" Jennifer laughed. "I thought you said you were going to take it easy during your fertility treatments?"

"One drink can't hurt me, can it—especially this early in my cycle?" Eva was becoming more conscious of the eyes around the bar upon her once again. Her drink couldn't come fast enough.

A male juvenile on the stool adjacent to Eva recognized her discomfort. "Would you like my seat,

Madam?" he offered, standing up. "Why don't you make yourself more comfortable?"

"Thank you, but please don't feel you have to give it up on my account."

"It's no problem really—I need to stretch my legs for a bit anyway."

"Thank you." Eva was happy to take a seat—not so much to take the weight off her unsteady heels, as to remove herself as the prime focal point of the room by lowering herself to everyone else's height.

The bartender had returned, placing the drinks on the counter in front of Eva and Jennifer. "Here you go, ladies."

"Great—now that we're settled in," Jennifer said, raising her glass, "what do you say we make a toast?"

"Good idea; to what?"

"To new friends—and new experiences!"

"Cheers to that!" Eva replied, taking a generous gulp of her martini. As her focus drifted back to the floor, she was suddenly taken with the degree of intimacy shared by so many people around the room. While some were simply holding hands across their tables, others were kissing and caressing each other in various stages of apparent arousal, while many others were bumping and grinding against one another unashamedly on the dance floor.

"Jennifer, do you mind if I ask you a question?"

"Of course not, Eva. We're here to let our hair down, remember? Ask away!"

"Well, I was wondering as I look around the room, so many people seem to be…hooking up, so to speak. I've often wondered—how does that work? I mean, all these people are essentially locked in eleven-year-old bodies, aren't they? How do they, you know—*get together*—and where does the urge come from? I mean physiologically speaking."

"Yes, I suppose that must seem a bit odd to you, Eva. With your unique hormonal dynamics, you must wonder where these juveniles get all their sexual energy. Actually, everybody receives his or her first natural boost in reproductive hormones around the age of ten—at a stage called gonadarche. Though juveniles are not actually capable of reproduction at this stage since their sex glands are not fully developed, everybody by this time is pretty much otherwise capable of experiencing sex in the normal manner."

"*Capable* and interested are two different things," remarked Eva. "From the look of things in this room, it appears there are a lot of interested people!"

"Ironically," Jennifer continued, "it's the amount of *testosterone* in the bodies of both males and females which regulates everyone's libido. Although these levels may not be as high as yours, especially at certain phases in your cycle, they are more than sufficient at this particular juvenile stage to create both the interest and the ability to engage in sex."

"But aren't these hormones suppressed and controlled after the pituitary is removed?" Eva enquired. "I mean, just how effectively does the skin patch actually replace them, anyhow?"

"There's the rub, so to speak. Unlike the natural pulsative pattern of hormone flows in people who have not had their pituitary removed like yourself, the patch provides a much more steady or constant flow of these same hormones. So their libido levels are normally more controlled, as opposed to the ebbs and surges you may be used to."

"Yes, especially when I'm on these fertility drugs! I don't know exactly what you endocrinologists give me during these treatments, but they do more than just make me produce more eggs!"

"Well, I'm sorry about that, but it can't be avoided. The same drugs that stimulate your ovaries to increase their production of estrogen and progesterone in the middle of your cycle also produce higher levels of the excitement hormone, testosterone."

"I'm not really complaining," Eva hastened to add, "it's just that I don't have the same opportunities that you do to act on my urges."

Just as Jennifer was thinking about how to appropriately reply, the gentleman who had earlier offered his seat to Eva returned to the bar. "Excuse me, ladies, I see you're running a little low—may I buy you another drink?"

"Thank you," replied Jennifer, pleased to have a welcome distraction at such an opportune moment. "I'll have another martini if you're offering.

"I'll have a Virgin Mary," said Eva.

The gentleman looked at Eva inquisitively.

"I'm watching my figure."

"If you don't mind my saying Madam, I think a *lot* of people are watching your figure this evening." He was obviously quite taken with Eva's beauty. "You look magnificent—even more beautiful in real life than on television."

"Thank you, sir." Eva replied, beginning to enjoy this stranger's attention.

"My name's Mike," said the juvenile, extending his hand.

"Well if you've seen me on television, I suppose you know who I am," Eva said, taking Mike's noticeably smaller hand in hers. "I'm Eva, and this is my friend Jennifer."

"Pleased to meet you Jennifer," Mike replied, quickly shifting his focus back to Eva. "You know Eva, I couldn't help noticing that you seemed a little out of your element here this evening."

Eva chuckled. "Yes, I must admit I don't go to these kinds of places very often. I've got to keep up my matronly image, you know!"

"That's not exactly a word I would choose to associate with you, Eva. Besides, you've given this place a little kick in the pants this evening. Perhaps you should get out more often!"

"I think you may be right about that," Eva said, smiling and beginning to feel more comfortable.

Jennifer had been carefully appraising Mike during his exchange with Eva. Although she found him charming and attractive, she was much more interested in him as a potential candidate for Eva. "Tell us about yourself Mike," she interjected. "What do you do?"

"I'm a lawyer."

"A lawyer?" said Eva. "I didn't think people got into trouble anymore!"

"I'm a *corporate* lawyer," laughed Mike. "We try to keep people *out* of trouble—you know, through good contracts, that sort of thing. How about you, Jennifer?" he asked, temporarily diverting his attention from Eva.

"I'm an endocrinologist."

"Ah—so you're the one who helps keep our biological clocks ticking on schedule?!"

"In a manner of speaking, I suppose."

"I make eggs," Eva deadpanned. "Lots and lots of eggs." She paused for dramatic effect. "And every now and then, real people."

"How quaint," kidded Mike, with a knowing smile. "That seems to have become a bit of a lost art. My mother used to say that was the most important job in the world. I would have to say that is even more true today."

"That's very sweet of you," Eva said, beginning to feel an odd attraction to this handsome juvenile. She suddenly found herself at a loss for words. "Um…what do you think of what they've done with this place, Mike?"

"It's beautiful, though you've really got to get on the dance floor to appreciate it. The swirling lightshow coupled with the amazing views out the window—is really quite intoxicating."

"Don't you get *dizzy* from the rotation of the building while you're dancing?" Eva asked.

"Not at all. It's a slow rotation, so you barely notice it. Would you like to give it a try?"

Eva hesitated for a moment. "Thanks Mike, but I don't want to leave my friend right now."

"I understand," Mike said, trying to conceal his disappointment. "I'll give you two a chance to relax. Let me know if you decide to change your mind, Eva. It was a pleasure meeting you both." Slinking away, he melted back into the crowd.

Jennifer looked at Eva in astonishment. "Why didn't you take him up on his offer, Eva?! You don't have to worry about me—I can take care of myself. You should have some fun and let yourself loose!"

"I hardly know the fellow. And you know how self-conscious I am about mixing with juveniles. Besides, how can you even tell how old any of these people really are? Everyone looks eleven! I'd hate to start mixing it up with a *real* eleven year old by mistake—that would be totally creepy!"

"Well *you* of all people should know there have been very few new births or hypophysectomies in recent years. The last major group of juveniles was born over thirty years ago, when the final generation of adult females passed through menopause. Besides, I don't think you have much to worry about with Mike. It still takes more than eleven years to become a lawyer you know! And he seems like a nice enough fellow—well dressed and well spoken. You should go shake your booty!"

Eva shifted uncomfortably in her seat. "Don't you think it's just a little weird for a fully mature woman like me to be even thinking about um...*mixing it up* with under-developed juveniles?"

"It's a brave new world out there, Eva. It seems everyone is hooking up with everyone—and anyone—nowadays. Age and gender don't seem to play the same roles they once did, when people's primary concern was about forming a traditional pair-bond and raising children. Now the act of coupling has become far more of a *social* activity than a biological or reproductive urge."

"Yes, I can see that," remarked Eva, as she noticed various mixed-gender couples touching one another suggestively on the dance floor.

Jennifer looked at Eva directly. "Eva, if you found the right person, don't you think you could share a close and intimate relationship just like anyone else? Besides, it's not that unusual—there are many examples throughout the animal kingdom of females mating with much smaller males."

"What about that whole growing old together thing?" Eva protested. "I don't think that would quite work the same way in my case! Maybe I should just pretend I'm the much larger female tarantula spider, and dispatch my helpless mate after he's done his duty!"

Jennifer had prepared herself for this discussion.

"With most juveniles expecting indefinite longevity, it seems all bets are off with the *til death do us part* idea," She said. "Now it's more about people sharing the moment and losing themselves in the relationship, and not worrying about the future. Plus, to be blunt, with minimal fluid exchange, we don't have to worry so much about disease transmission any more—or in your case, unwanted pregnancy."

"I hadn't really thought of that. It just seems kind of unnatural…"

"If you don't try it, how can you know you won't like it?"

"Are you trying to get me knocked up, doctor?!"

"I'm just trying to make sure you're happy, Eva. You've got so much to offer, and I hate to see you miss out on any part of your potential."

"Well, I can tell you that if we had come here in another two weeks, when those super-ovulating drugs really kick in, I'd probably be ready to take just about anybody home with me!"

"Perhaps we'll have to do just that then!" Jennifer kidded. "In the meantime, why don't you open yourself up to meeting some interesting people, like your new friend Mike?"

It was Eva's turn to look squarely at Jennifer. "You know, if you didn't have first dibs on Dr. Ross, I might have made a run at *him*! You should count yourself lucky you got to him first, you little devil. Speaking of which, when *are* you two going to get together? I can be a match-maker too, you know!"

Jennifer had become so preoccupied with Eva's love life, she'd almost forgotten about her own. Her thoughts suddenly turned to Rick. She had in fact been thinking quite a bit about him recently, having been alternately excited and perplexed.

When was he going to ask me out? she wondered. *He seems interested, but he's not exactly making any passes. Am I going to have to trip over him to make him notice me?!*

As Jennifer contemplated Rick's intentions, she caught sight of Mike approaching the bar once again, this time his gaze firmly fixed on Eva. As she glanced instinctively at Eva, she saw her new friend returning his attention with an equally intense focus—and a hint of a smile.

It seemed there might be a little promise for at least *one* of the girls tonight…

Fourteen

Calvin James sat gloomily in the tiny rectory of his church on 14th Street, ruminating over the developments of the past few weeks and what he'd accomplished in his life. Although he had achieved a measure of success raising attention to the immorality of the hypophysectomy program and had enlisted a number of juveniles to his cause, the impact had been limited primarily to the relatively narrow confines of his own parish district and the local New York City press.

He had failed to raise widespread alarm over the consequences of interfering with God's natural design, and he feared that the world was rapidly losing its moral and spiritual compass. On a purely selfish level, he was more aware every passing day that his small congregation's weekly tithe was barely sufficient to cover the costs of maintaining his crumbling church, let alone his own living expenses, and he felt that he was slowly losing his constituency. As much as it pained him to acknowledge, he knew he was becoming increasingly marginalized under the new secular order, and that to most people in the outside world, he was little more than a pariah.

This had not been his plan. He had seen himself as God's chosen one, literally the last of his kind—standing head and shoulders above the rest of humanity—who, like Moses, would lead the disbelievers and suffering masses out of the wilderness of modern tyranny, back to the light. He was supposed to be the guardian of the faith, a revered spiritual leader, and a role model for humanity. But it had all failed.

Where had he gone wrong? He had faithfully carried God's word and been a loyal servant his entire life. He had sacrificed worldly possessions and resisted the temptations of the flesh—which at times was unbearable, with a cruel allotment of male testosterone naturally coursing through his veins. All this, in the name of upholding and protecting the Lord's faith.

Christ, Calvin implored, looking up for divine guidance, *why have you forsaken me?* Beseeching the heavens, he cried out angrily: *What more do you expect of me?!!*

But Calvin's mind soon shifted back to reality, for there was another critical matter bothering him this Sunday evening. Just as his father had feared for Calvin's safety and protected him from the authorities by spiriting him away prior to their attempt to hypophysectomize the boy, Calvin's own son Elias was nearing the time when he would be expected to undergo the same operation. Although Calvin had done everything in his power to resist the procedure by arguing the matter all the way to the Supreme Court, ultimately it was established that it was a decision left up to the child, after joint consultation with his parents and Family Services.

Calvin knew his son had been brainwashed by the ubiquitous liberal media about the consequences of this decision, and that Elias was becoming increasingly fearful and reticent about foregoing the procedure. Furthermore, although Calvin had tried to keep Elias's current age hidden from public scrutiny by home-schooling him and by exempting him from his tax filing, he knew that his son's birthdate would have been registered at the hospital where Elias was delivered and that somebody was likely keeping track of when he was due for the procedure. In fact, he had been receiving increasingly urgent notices to bring Elias in for a Child Services interview and knew that he wouldn't be able to put them off much longer.

He resolved to take Elias away soon to a place where no one could ever find them—the same place his father had hid him thirty years ago—where he would be able to convince Elias of the righteous path to salvation. But what would this mean in terms of his own legacy? Calvin wasn't sure how much longer it would take for his son to pass through puberty and achieve the safe status of a mature adult. It could be a year, or longer; Elias was only eleven. During their time of hiding, who would attend to his congregation's needs? Who would carry the torch and rail against the infidels to protect God's Kingdom against further attack? He was already losing the battle—how could he save it from crumbling entirely in his absence?

    As he pondered his predicament, Calvin suddenly felt a warmth and peace come over him, for he heard God's reply to his supplications. In a flash of clarity and affirmation, Calvin received his answer. He had a plan—a *grand* plan—one that would have a truly universal impact on his world. In a single act of divine inspiration, Calvin conceived of a way to redesign the world in God's image and lead mankind out of the wilderness.

Fifteen

Rick was eagerly anticipating his meeting with Jennifer Austin this morning. Ostensibly, he had arranged to discuss how things were going with Eva's fertility treatment, but he hadn't seen Jennifer for a week and had to admit he was having trouble concentrating on much else in the interim. Maybe a little face time would quench his preoccupation, or at least help him figure out what to do about this burgeoning interest in his new colleague.

"Hey you!"

Jeesh, Rick thought, half jumping out of his chair. She'd done it again—catching him unprepared in a moment of distraction. He'd hoped that inviting Jennifer to his office for a formal meeting would give him a temporary advantage, or at least permit him to collect himself and put his best foot forward. But here she was again, peering around the door jamb like a playful girl and in one fell swoop, she'd completely disarmed him yet again.

Get a hold of yourself man, he told himself.

"Jennifer! How lovely to see you again. Although you've got to stop surprising me like this—you're making it very difficult for me to maintain my suave, sophisticated image."

"Is that the image you're trying to project with me, Rick?" Jennifer teased. "Did you want me to become another one of your adoring subjects, seduced by your good looks and charm?"

So she wants to play, Rick thought. V*ery well—let's get it on.*

"Well," he said, "I was also hoping to impress you with my big fancy office, with all these certificates and awards."

"Yes—it *is* very large. And I know how important that is to you men." Jennifer proceeded to walk slowly around his room, appraising the various plaques and pictures on the paneled walls, then she stopped at one in particular. "What's this—it looks very *official?*"

"That's a certificate of achievement from the United Nations, on behalf of my work as Surgeon-General with them over the years. Apparently, they seem to think I do important things."

"Well you *do* save all those juveniles from old age and uncertain purgatory with a simple flick of your wrist. Perhaps they should paint a picture of you on the ceiling of the Sistine Chapel next?"

"Blasphemy! Don't you know all neurosurgeons *are* God? You know we're the only ones with the power to reshape the human form. Only *we* have access to the inner sanctum of the cerebral cortex and the mysterious and all-powerful hypothalamus, where we can remove it's agent of destruction, the pituitary!"

"Yes, but do I need to remind you that it was a *woman* whom God personified in his originally removal of man's anatomy—and who was also necessary to populate the world?" Jennifer's eyes narrowed as she came to a photograph beside the U.N. plaque. "Speaking of which—who's the attractive Asian woman you're snuggling up to in this photo?"

"That's our Secretary-General, of course. Don't tell me you haven't followed the meteoric trajectory of one your esteemed colleagues-in-arms?"

Jennifer knew full well who Tian Yin was, and admired her greatly. She just wanted to test Rick's reaction and assess her potential dating competition. "Yes, of course. She's quite pretty, isn't she?"

"Well, I suppose if you go for that smolderingly sexy look." Now it was Rick's turn to make Jennifer squirm. "But I prefer the perky, puckish types—who are less restrained by the diplomatic ties of high office."

"Uh huh." Jennifer wasn't going to bite. Continuing her bemused appraisal of the various artifacts Rick had spread around his room, she stopped at a black-and-white photograph of Rick sitting in a sleek wooden boat with a distinguished older gentleman. "Is this your grandfather?"

"Yes," Rick's tone suddenly turned melancholy, as he moved beside Jennifer to reflect upon one of his favorite images from childhood. That picture was taken more than fifty years ago, at my grandfather's summer cottage in Canada. I loved going for rides with him in that grand old motor yacht. He'd occasionally take me water-skiing behind that beauty, and then we'd sit together in his big Muskoka chairs listening to the lapping of the waves against the dock. This was where we'd talk about the theory of antagonistic pleiotropy, and where he first developed the idea of extended longevity via delayed maturity. I remember having long and fascinating discussions with him about many aspects of biology and evolution. I was only ten or eleven years old in that picture."

"It's funny, you don't look much different now from how you did then," Jennifer remarked. And it was true: even though Rick was chronologically fifty years older—physiologically, his body hadn't aged at all. "If only he could see you now."

"Yes, it would have been nice if he'd lived to see me—and everybody else—benefit in such a profound way from his work. But I carry very fond memories of him, and he continues to be my role model to this day. He'll always be my hero."

Jennifer was struck by this new sensitive side of Rick that she hadn't seen before. His strong family connections made her admire—and desire—him all the more.

"For what it's worth Rick," she offered, "I think he'd be proud to see that you've achieved something just as great."

"Thank you, Jennifer—that's very sweet of you." Rick's eyes met Jennifer's and lingered for many seconds, as they smiled at each other warmly.

"Hey, weren't we supposed to meet today about something important?" Rick said, changing the subject. "I've totally forgotten why I invited you here!"

"Oh yeah." Jennifer's mind had wandered off topic also. "Something about Eva's fertility treatments?"

"Right, Eva. The final piece in the troika. The one who binds everything together and keeps it all from falling apart. I snip off everyone's destructive appendage, you replace the missing hormones to keep them alive, and she ensures we can rebuild the whole system if anything goes wrong. Brilliant! The only problem is that we have to keep *replacing* our very mortal queen. Have you assessed her reproductive fitness?"

Jennifer was a bit sad to have to get back to business so abruptly, but she was eager to discuss Eva's progress, and how well the two of them had bonded.

"She agreed to get started with a new round of treatment last week. As of Tuesday, she's begun taking daily injections of Buserelin—so that suggests a harvesting window around the first of November."

"Good. How did you find her general mood? Did she seem anxious about any of the procedures or next steps?"

"Well she did say something about having to be the Golden Goose laying all those eggs, but at least she's got a pretty good sense of humor about it."

"Yes," Rick laughed. "That's Eva. She's a real trooper! How did you two get along?"

"Marvelously. We hit it off immediately. So well in fact that we decided to go out together and celebrate this past weekend."

"You're kidding?! I knew you two would find some common ground quickly, but not *that* fast! Where did you go?"

"I took her to that new club in Times Square—The Hippodrome. We had a riot! She's fascinating, and a really fun girl."

"Wow. And here I thought Eva was self-conscious about mingling with juveniles. You've obviously been able to bring her out of her shell!"

"She was a little gun-shy about going out to something so far removed from her usual official functions, but she eventually let her hair down and really enjoyed herself. In fact, I think she might have actually found a new boyfriend."

"*What?* A juvenile?! I hadn't thought she—or anyone for that matter—would connect that way. Though I don't suppose why not..."

"Hey, it's a brave new world out there Rick, as I put it to Eva. Everybody's mixing it up with everybody—all bets seem to be off now. Besides, if you think about it, there's really nothing preventing it. It's only natural for people to want to connect and find comfort in the company of someone special—juveniles and adults alike. Plus, it's not as if Eva's got other viable options—all the other adults are nearly a hundred years old!"

"You have a point there. But what about..."

"You're beginning to sound like Eva. What about *what*? It doesn't always have to be about *size* you know—that's so old school! Plus, he's actually older than her, and he's smart, handsome, and a successful lawyer."

"It sounds like *you* were a little taken by him too, Jennifer." Rick was starting to feel vaguely threatened by this new stranger.

"I prefer the strong, silent types—you know, the ones who secretly think they're God's gift to the world," Jennifer said sardonically.

"I see." Rick suddenly felt self-conscious about his previous allusions to God. "I didn't know you were on the market," he said, fishing for an opening.

"If the right one came around, I might be inclined to test the waters," Jennifer replied coyly. "But I'm kind of old fashioned—I expect to be properly courted. Whatever happened to chivalry anyway?"

"Well if you're looking for some sensitive male accompaniment, I'll be happy to offer my services," Rick said, gently extending his hand, bending deferentially at the waist. "Assuming, that is, that I meet your lofty and exacting standards?"

"I suppose you'll do, in a pinch," Jennifer teased, gently squeezing his hand. "At least until the second coming."

Sixteen

It had been less than a week since the U.N. announced its intention to parcel out the production of hormone patches to multiple suppliers, and Roland Jamieson's world had begun to crumble all around him. Endogen's stock price had continued to plummet amid multiple class action lawsuits launched by disgruntled shareholders against both the company and each board member, who bore personal liability in respect of his fiduciary responsibility for management oversight. But these were minor nuisances that Jamieson could put off for years with an army of corporate lawyers using creative blocking tactics in the courts. Of far more immediate concern, three credit rating agencies had recently downgraded Endogen's debt to junk status, which put the organization in technical default of specific loan covenants. This meant that various bondholders could freely redeem billions of dollars in loans—money that Jamieson did not have the capacity to pay out from the company's rapidly depleting working capital. And Endogen's bankers were in no mood to provide bridge loans or extend lines of credit, given the company's deteriorating long-term outlook.

Of even greater concern was the not-so-veiled threat by Jack Knight at last week's Board meeting regarding the security of Jamieson's position as CEO of the company. Jamieson knew that he could be summarily dismissed at a moment's notice, and that the Board would be loath to issue a golden parachute to soften his landing, given the likely outcry from shareholders and regulators alike over his perceived mismanagement of the company's recent affairs. But he wasn't so worried about finding another high-level job elsewhere as he was about the extent of his own personal investment in Endogen and his associated liability. Jamieson had taken full advantage of the company's generous executive share purchase program by taking out large discounted loans to purchase blocks of company stock—most of it at multiples well above its current value. Now his holdings were significantly under water, and he owed many millions more than the value of the underlying collateral.

The only way he could recoup his losses and exert continuing control over Endogen's share price would be to remain in power atop the company's management team and figure out a strategy to rebuild its value. But Jamieson knew he didn't have much time. The Directors on the Board were frothing at the mouth and just waiting for the slightest indication that Jamieson couldn't be counted on to fix the problem. Jack had put him on a short leash and expected a specific and credible action plan for pulling the organization out of this abyss—soon.

The only glimmer of hope was a new product his marketing team indicated might replace their lost sales and potentially put them back in a dominant market position, with a proprietary patch designed to enhance sexual function among juveniles. Jamieson sensed this might be the game-changer he was looking for and he had been leaning on his product development team led by Nathan Taylor to put together an accelerated project plan for bringing the product to market as soon as possible. He had scheduled a meeting this morning with Nathan to discuss the technical specifics and review the preliminary plan.

At the appointed hour, Jamieson heard a quick succession of loud knocks on his office door. Jamieson and Nathan had never had a very amicable relationship during their long mutual tenure at Endogen, and until recently, Jamieson had actually gone out of his way to ignore his Chief Scientist by using his Marketing EVP, Sue Weldon, as a go-between. Even though Nathan held a key role heading the company's five thousand employee Research and Development department, Jamieson had always found him to be too cerebral and volatile to deal with. For his part, Nathan had long resented Jamieson's arrogant and abrasive management style, and felt he'd never been given proper recognition for perfecting the formula and helping to secure the Endopatch contract. Although they tried to avoid each other as much as possible, Jamieson knew that Nathan was simply too knowledgeable and brilliant a resource to lose, and there were times such as now where he needed his unique skills.

"Come in," Jamieson announced from behind his desk.

"Nathan," he motioned upon seeing his Chief Scientist enter, "have a seat. As you remember from our last management meeting, we have some very important business to discuss today. I hope you've got that project plan ready for my review."

"I do. But I'm not sure you're going to like the result." Nathan pushed a large graphical spreadsheet in front of Jamieson.

It was a Gantt Chart, showing brightly colored bars displayed along a horizontal timescale, indicating a projected finish date of two years. *Typical Nathan output*, thought Jamieson. *Arcane, unclear—and overly conservative.*

"What's this? You're saying it's going to take over two years to bring this product to market?!"

"That's actually an accelerated timeline," Nathan replied flatly. "As you know, it usually takes new products at least five years to move through our pipeline from conception to final approval."

"Yes, I *know* that, Nathan," Jamieson retorted, irritated that Nathan was supposing to educate him about a central fact of their business. "But I've spoken with Sue, and she tells me we should be able to position this with our regulators as only a minor enhancement to an existing product rather than a totally new one—which would require minimal testing and approvals."

"That's debatable; I'm not sure the FDA will agree. But either way, the fact remains that we're proposing to make a significant change to the formulation and dosing of a patch used by every juvenile around the world to keep them alive, and we have a responsibility to undertake rigorous testing to ensure it's safe to use."

"Let me and our legal department worry about the feds," Jamieson replied. "The only requirements we need be concerned with at this moment are theirs. If we can convince them that this new patch carries no additional risks compared with the existing patch, and that the only appreciable effects will be a positive ones, we should be able to move this forward very quickly. I just need you to figure out what needs to be changed and by how much, and then work with production to tell me how long it will take to commercialize it."

"This is a very complicated drug, Roland," Nathan said, continuing to resist. "It's not just a simple matter of turning up the dial to happily boost everybody's libido. The formulation comprises a very carefully metered amount of nine essential hormones—from gonadotropins to adrenocorticoids to human growth hormone—each of which controls a critical endocrine function. Plus, there's a separate patch for males and females to control their respective balance of estrogen, progesterone, and testosterone—and this must be precisely adjusted as well. If the balance on any one of these is thrown improperly out of line, any manner of life-threatening complications can result."

Jamieson hated this part of his infrequent conversations with Nathan. As a bio-chemist and Ph.D., Nathan knew the science of endocrinology and pharmacology better than just about anyone, but Jamieson had studied undergraduate biology himself prior to starting with Endogen twenty years ago, and refused to be cowed by Nathan's clinical explanation.

"Look, Nathan, we've already been told by various other experts that this is not only feasible, but that it's a fairly simple process of increasing the dosage of only one of those hormones—testosterone—and that it will take only a minor increase in dosage to yield the desired effect."

"That may be true, but we don't know for sure what *other* possible side effects might occur in connection with a boost to this powerful luteinizing hormone. Too much, and it could cause females to grow hair on their chest, or males to become overly aggressive…"

"Don't be ridiculous, Nathan. We're talking about *juveniles* here, not mature adults. It's all simply a matter of appropriate dosing." Jamieson was losing patience with Nathan. It was time to play his trump card and exercise his authority. "Look—if you don't feel you can do it, I'm sure we can find someone else who can figure it out."

"I *know* how to do it Roland," Nathan backpedaled, not wanting to risk losing control over the critical procedure. "I just think we should be prudent and conduct appropriate trials to make sure it will be safe, and that it doesn't create additional complications…"

Jamieson decided to give Nathan just a little more rope. "How long do you anticipate these trials will take to complete?"

"Effective longitudinal double-blind trials normally take at least a year to determine the short and long term effects. And really, to be doubly safe, we should be conducting preliminary trials with monkeys, so as not to put our initial test group of humans at risk…"

"*Jesus Christ*, Nathan!" Jamieson said, finally losing it. "Give me a fucking break. We're not going to conduct *primate* trials for this thing. It's a simple modification to one simple hormone, for God's sake. And we don't *have* a year to bring this product to market—we've only got a few *months* left before this company could potentially be out of business!"

Both Jamieson and Nathan had reached their breaking point—and Jamieson had just struck a sensitive nerve with his colleague.

"There's no need to be *profane*," Nathan replied coldly. "And I don't appreciate your defiling God's name in my presence."

Nathan also knew he had a degree of leverage he could use over Jamieson. "Fine," he proposed, "I'll move forward on your timetable if you'll put it in writing for the public record that you were fully apprised of the risks for this upgrade, and that I recommended a more restrained and disciplined line of action."

Jamieson could hardly believe Nathan had the nerve to challenge him so directly and threaten him not so subtly.

"The *hell* with that!" he barked. "I'm not going to put myself at the risk of more legal action being taken against me and this company, simply because of your misguided paranoia. This conversation is going to end right here with a simple ultimatum for you and your team. Either make this happen now—and present a workable plan to me by the end of this week—or I'll *fire* your ass and replace you with some other egghead who knows what side his bread is buttered on. Now get the hell out of my office before I change my mind!!"

After Nathan stormed out of his office, Jamieson sat shaking in his chair, trying to settle down from his fit of anger. As much as he was infuriated by Nathan's threats and challenges, he knew that his Chief Scientist was ultimately correct. Under normal circumstances, all of his recommendations would be prudent and standard operating procedure for Endogen. But these weren't normal times—this was a crisis that demanded radical and decisive action. Neither he nor the organization could squander this once-in-a-lifetime opportunity. The *Sexpatch*—Jamieson had already begun to think of it as a new brand—was not only a great idea, it was also one that could quickly re-level the competitive playing field and recoup everyone's investment.

Jamieson knew he couldn't afford to let someone like Nathan disrupt his plans. But he also knew Nathan was smart enough to cover his own ass and make Jamieson the fall-guy should anything go wrong. If the complications from the new patch were serious enough, Jamieson could potentially not only face new *civil* action, but even more serious charges for *criminal* negligence. He knew that he would have to manage Nathan more carefully in order not to provoke him from doing something rash. An apology would likely be necessary, and probably even a compromise on the timetable and testing protocols. Ultimately, however, Jamieson knew something would have to be ready to go public within a couple of months, and to present to the Board sooner, or he and the company would be dead in the water.

    As Jamieson contemplated the full extent of the risks he was facing, he started to tremble once again, but this time for an entirely different reason: *fear*. The personal consequences of failure simply chilled him to the bone. He began to think about what else he might do to save his skin. How could he protect his reputation, and his job? What other potential solutions could there be for pulling Endogen back from the brink? Were there *any* other possibilities for resolving this crisis and reclaiming his fortune? As Jamieson's mind began to go to some dark places, his secretary came in to his office to remind him of a meeting with his central banker.

    God help me, Jamieson muttered.

Seventeen

It was Friday night, and Rick had finally summoned the courage to invite Jennifer out for dinner. He had chosen to take her to one of his favorite restaurants in New York: the Oak Room at the Plaza Hotel. Both the restaurant and the hotel had a glamorous and storied past, hosting celebrities, heads of state, and captains of industry for more than two centuries. Over the last few years, the building and its famous rooms had been neglected and fallen into a state of disrepair, but an extensive renovation was recently undertaken to bring them back to their former grandeur and glory. The hotel had hired one of the city's most celebrated chefs, David Boulud, grandson of the three-starred Michelin chef who originally brought nouvelle French cuisine to America, and Rick was eager to sample the new menu. Plus, the setting for the hotel at the south-east corner of Central Park was one of the most beautiful in the city, and was within walking distance from Rick's and Jennifer's apartments.

Rick had arranged to pick up Jennifer at her place at seven p.m. He decided to use a car service to make their short journey to the Plaza as comfortable as possible. As the car pulled up beside her Park Avenue building on West 77th Street, he paused to take in the magnificent view down the boulevard. Park Avenue was one of the broadest avenues in the city, having been built in the 1800's over the expansive New York and Harlem railroad tracks originating at Grand Central Station. Now paved over in six divided lanes abreast an elegantly landscaped median and framed by tall neo-classical residential buildings running the entire length of the street, the view at its southern terminus was dominated by the stately Helmsley Building, especially beautiful at night lit up in its Art Deco glory, reflecting gilded ramparts and a large copper lantern atop its pyramid-shaped roof. How fitting, Rick thought, that Jennifer would live on one of the city's most beautiful streets.

"I'm here to see Jennifer Austin," Rick announced to the doorman. "My name is Richard Ross." Two minutes later, Jennifer emerged from the adjacent bank of elevators and met Rick with a wide smile.

"My, don't you look distinguished this evening, Dr. Ross," she remarked, carefully appraising his black cashmere topcoat and dark blue Brioni suit.

"And you, Miss Austin, are always a vision of loveliness." Jennifer had chosen a black ruffle-back dress and high-heeled pumps, and was wearing a long gray knit coat with a burgundy jacquard scarf. *Elegant and stylish as always*, thought Rick.

"Well I hope just because we're *dressed* formally tonight doesn't mean we'll have to *act* so formal!"

"Of course not," Rick replied, hopeful this evening would be an opportunity to bring down some of their professional guard and allow the two of them to get to know each other on a more personal level.

"Shall we be on our way?" he said, extending his arm toward the waiting car.

"You ordered a limo? Are we going somewhere important?"

"It's a simple little restaurant, really. I just wanted you to be comfortable. You know those crazy New York City cab drivers. The problem is they get paid by the *distance*, so the faster they cover it and the more miles they put in a day, the more money they make. My driver on the other hand, gets paid by the hour, so he's in less of a hurry to get there."

"Always the rational one, Rick. But it's sweet of you to look after me this way, no matter your motivations."

"I assure you, they're always honorable with you, Jennifer!" Rick smiled, as he opened the passenger door for her.

Minutes later, the car pulled into the circular driveway surrounding the cascading fountain in front of the Plaza Hotel.

"Wow—the *Plaza*!" Jennifer remarked, looking up at the grand edifice of the Renaissance-style chateau. "I have to confess, I've always wanted to experience this quintessential New York City landmark. But I heard it had been converted into a condo?"

"Only part of it. They've kept the hotel operational thankfully, plus all the famous restaurants: the Palm Court, the Champagne Bar, the Oak Room. There's so much history here—they simply couldn't let it all go."

"So which restaurant are you taking me to? I'm on pins and needles!"

"Allow me to escort you." Rick held out his arm for Jennifer, and they ascended the steps leading up to the grand entrance portico.

As they threaded their way through the hotel's posh interior halls, Jennifer couldn't help slowing Rick down periodically to view the photographs of some of the hotel's famous previous guests: Frank Sinatra, Grace Kelly, Winston Churchill. But she stopped abruptly at one framed portrait.

"It's Eloise! I *loved* her, growing up." Eloise was the fictional character in the famous children's book about a precocious little girl who got into so much mischief while staying at the Plaza Hotel.

"Yes, isn't it perfect that the Plaza chose to honor her with her own portrait—at her favorite hotel? It seems all the more fitting to have our first date here, since you're so much like her..."

"Really? Do tell, Dr. Ross!"

"Well, Eloise was independent, and free-spirited like you..."

"And?"

"And clever and cute and saucy like you..."

"Saucy! However do you mean?"

"Let me elaborate over dinner," Rick said, beginning to wonder if he should have started this line of discussion. "I think I need a drink!

As they approached the reception desk of the Oak Room, Rick announced himself to the maître d': "Dr. Ross, for seven-thirty."

"Yes, Dr. Ross—may we take your coats?"

As Rick helped Jennifer off with her overcoat, he noticed for the first time the plunging open back of her dress, revealing her exquisitely carved shoulder blades and tapered waistline, terminating in a subtle ruffle accentuating her indelibly curved backside.

The maitre d' escorted Rick and Jennifer through the magnificent baronial dining room, with its barrel-vaulted ceiling, soaring columns, and Everett Shinn murals—stopping at a corner table next to a lighted fireplace.

"Madam?" he gestured, pulling out a chair facing the room.

"Thank you," Jennifer said, taking her seat. "Rick, this place is lovely—if a bit *rich*."

"Interesting you should use that expression, Jennifer. The Oak Room actually has a long history of hosting the rich and famous. John Jacob Astor, Truman Capote, F. Scott Fitzgerald all ate here; the legendary actor and playwright George Cohan apparently had his own table in this very corner. It began as a gentleman's club—ladies weren't allowed."

"Well times certainly have changed," Jennifer remarked, glancing at many of the restaurant's well-dressed male and female patrons. "I wonder what those luminaries from our past would say if they could see us now?"

"I'm not sure which they'd be more horrified to behold: seeing the place populated with so many ladies—or entirely with juveniles!"

"It's a brave new world, indeed!"

"Speaking of which, one of the reasons I wanted to bring you here is because of their new executive chef. David Boulud—have you heard of him?"

"He specializes in French cuisine, doesn't he? Interesting juxtaposition don't you think, in this very American institution?"

"Yes, you could say it symbolizes the dismantling of society's old boundaries and rules. A 'fusion' of both peoples and cuisine."

"All this symbolism is making me hungry!" Jennifer said, as the waiter arrived and placed the menus in front of them.

"Good evening," the waiter said. "Would you like to start with something to drink?"

"Would you prefer a cocktail, Jennifer, or perhaps Champagne?" Rick asked.

"Champagne is always good!"

Rick scanned the wine list. "How about the Bollinger Grande Année '98? I hear it was a good year."

"I don't know my vintages very well," Jennifer interrupted, "but I thought Champagne needed a few more years to age properly?"

"This one is from *nineteen* ninety-eight."

"Oops! That was a bit before my time. It appears we'll *really* be opening some demons from the past this evening, won't we?"

"It's decided then," Rick said, nodding to the waiter.

As they reviewed the menu to decide on first courses, Rick heard the crackling of the wood burning in the adjacent fireplace and could feel its heat against his skin. Looking across the table at Jennifer reading the menu, he saw the warm light from the fire bathing her skin and the shadows dancing across her striking face.

It had been a wonderful dinner, with Rick and Jennifer sharing long and intimate conversations about their respective childhoods over an exquisite four course meal in their quiet corner of the romantic restaurant. Rick was feeling a closer connection to Jennifer and didn't want the night to end.

"It's a lovely evening," he said as he helped her on with her coat on their way out. "Would you like to walk home through the park?"

"Yes, I'd like that very much, Rick." Jennifer was quickly developing similar feelings for Rick.

As they exited the hotel and walked past the gleaming fountain of Pomona, the Roman goddess of orchards, Rick clasped Jennifer's hand as they walked down the steep steps leading from Grand Army Plaza into the south end of Central Park. For a while, neither said anything to the other, taking in the serene beauty of the park as the winding cobblestone walk wended its way past tranquil ponds and proud monuments, over arched limestone bridges amongst fallen autumn leaves. For Rick, this was the most beautiful season of the year in New York City, especially in Central Park, as the glorious polyglot of color descended upon the dense canopy of trees as they prepared for a new dormant season. After dark, with the moonlight reflecting off the stately bronze statues and glistening flora, it was a sublime retreat from the noisy and hectic pace of the rest of the city.

"Beautiful, isn't it?" Rick said, finally breaking the silence.

"I love this place," Jennifer answered. "So quiet and peaceful. Thank you Rick, for a perfect evening."

"It's still young—let's make this last a bit longer. Can you smell that?" he said, lifting his nose and closing his eyes to sense the air.

Autumn in the park signaled the passing of the season of plenty to a season of privation. The trees had opened their cones and were quickly spreading their seeds before the first frost descended, and the warm earth was giving up its moisture as the cold air condensed fragrant dew on long blades of grass.

"Mmm. Yes, nature. Isn't it divine?"

"A miracle, really. How lucky we were to be at the confluence of the perfect storm that created this masterpiece."

"How do you mean?"

Rick was pensive for a moment.

"I mean, in all the universe, so otherwise cold or boiling, barren and rocky, that we managed to get the climate and biology just right to have created this symphony of symbiotic life."

"Well it can still get a bit chilly on our perfect little planet." Jennifer said, as she pulled up her coat collar and wound her scarf more tightly around her neck. They had emerged at the Inventors' Gate entrance on the east side of the park as it opened onto 5th Avenue.

"Yes, there is a bit of a nip in the air," Rick agreed, wrapping his arm around Jennifer to keep her warm. "Why don't you come to my place for a cup of hot tea? I'm only a few blocks away."

Jennifer paused for only a second. Among other things, she was intrigued to see where Rick lived.

"It *is* a bit of a hike to my place, and I do need to warm up. Maybe just one."

As Rick pulled Jennifer close, they both unconsciously picked up their pace, turning north along the stone wall separating the park from the street. Crossing the light at 78th Street, Rick opened the wrought-iron gate to his townhouse on the east side of the avenue.

Wow, was all Jennifer could think upon seeing the stunning Beaux-Arts townhome. Rising five floors above the street in white-washed limestone, the residence had an impressive façade studded with tall Palladian windows and detailed cornice moldings, topped with three arched dormer windows standing like sentinels behind a balustraded balcony overlooking the park.

Leave it to Rick to stand out from the crowd with his own townhome proudly nestled among all the tall apartment buildings lining the street, Jennifer thought.

Rick placed his key in the carved heavy oak door, and swung it open to reveal a stunning marble foyer.

"It's beautiful," Jennifer said, glad to be out of the cold. "And warm!"

"May I take your coat?" Rick asked.

Rick helped Jennifer off with her overcoat and hung it in the hall closet, then turned around to take her gloves and scarf. As he touched her chilly hands, their eyes met once again—and this time didn't stray. He gently moved forward and kissed her on the lips, and she leaned forward into a full embrace. As their bodies pressed against one another, Rick's hand traced a delicate line down the back of Jennifer's open dress and caressed the small of her back just above the curve of her buttocks.

"I'm not sure I need that hot drink after all," Jennifer remarked as she looked upstairs.

Eighteen

Saturday brought warmer weather and sunny skies over Central Park. The night before had been magical for Rick and Jennifer, culminating with them making love soon after they'd arrived back at his townhouse. Rick decided to make breakfast in the morning, and slipped out of bed quietly at eight a.m. and made his way to the kitchen. Just as he was turning the omelettes in the fry pan, Jennifer emerged with tousled hair, wearing only his dress shirt from last night. He took a moment to admire her shapely bare legs and tight bottom, barely peeking under the rounded tail of his rumpled shirt.

"Mmm—I like that look on you," he said, holding her head softly while kissing her moist lips.

"*Fits* me remarkably well, too," she kidded. "Unlike this *home* of yours—it's gigantic! I could barely find the kitchen."

"Sorry about that—should I have placed signs pointing upstairs?"

"I just followed the aroma. What have you got brewing?"

"I made some fresh coffee, and your omelette will be ready in a minute. Why don't you relax on the terrace? It's a glorious morning."

As Jennifer walked through the double French doors onto the balcony, she gasped as she took in the spectacular view. From the fifth floor of Rick's townhouse, the park across the street unfolded in all its majesty, revealing the bright yellows, reds, and golds of autumn in the blanket of foliage below. The rich palette of color extended into the distance in three directions, bordered by the tall limestone skyscrapers lining the perimeter of the park, creating the illusion of a giant impressionist painting in an elaborately carved antique frame. To the west, she could see the soaring twin towers of the San Remo and El Dorado buildings, to the south the familiar Plaza Hotel rose regally above the canopy of trees, and kitty-corner across the street sat the majestic Metropolitan Museum, stretching four full blocks to the north of Rick's townhouse.

"Boy, this must get old quick, huh?" she remarked, as Rick walked out onto the terrace with their breakfast.

"It's pretty rough, I have to admit. But you know, you get used to it."

"Ha! You can't fool me for a second, Rick. It's obvious you like the finer things in life, and besides, based on your comments last night, I know you've got a special affinity for nature. This must feel like your own personal laboratory at your very feet.

"In a way, it is. Central Park has an incredible diversity of flora and fauna, thanks in large measure to its brilliant designers. There are literally thousands of species of plants and animals in that little green patch within this great big concrete jungle. I almost *tripped* over a wild turkey crossing the road the other day, and there's a large red-tailed hawk nesting on top of that building just a few doors down."

"Well I hope he doesn't get any thoughts about swooping down on us and stealing my breakfast!"

"Not too worry," Rick laughed, "I suspect we juveniles are a little too big a challenge, even for a bird that size."

"Speaking of size, I was examining those interesting miniature trees you've planted over there." Jennifer pointed to a row of neatly arranged potted plants on the stone abutment overlooking the ledge. "They look very mature, and yet they're only a foot tall?"

"Yes, those are *bonsai* trees—one of my hobbies that lets me indulge my passion for biology. These are really my laboratory, as you say, where I can safely experiment with nature, and simultaneously create beautiful works of art."

"What does Bonsai mean?"

"Bonsai is a Japanese expression simply meaning 'tree in a pot'. It's an art form that has been practiced for centuries—since the time of Egyptian pharaohs. Fundamentally, it's a way of cultivating and shaping trees by restricting their growth."

"A bit like juveniles?" Jennifer was intrigued how this related to Rick's other area of expertise.

"Actually, there are some interesting parallels. For one thing, the tree's growth is arrested by carefully clipping off parts of their roots and branches, not unlike the hypophysectomy procedure with juveniles."

"How does that keep the trees so small?"

"The roots dictate the size of the tree—in the same way the pituitary does in humans. The smaller and shorter the roots, the less nutrients it absorbs from the soil and the less food is delivered to the branches. Similarly, by trimming back the ends of the *branches*, the less foliage the tree has to photosynthesize other essential chemicals from the sun and air."

"A bit like restricting *growth hormones* in humans?"

"Exactly."

"Hmm—I can see your attraction to this art. But there's something else I noticed about those trees. Besides being exceptionally small, judging by the coarseness and thickness of their bark, they also appear quite mature?"

"Yes, that's very observant. Actually, they are indeed quite old. Some of those tiny trees at are actually much older than similar species just across the street that stand over a hundred feet tall."

"How does that happen?"

Rick was glad to see Jennifer taking such a keen interest in his hobby, and he was enjoying the opportunity to explain how Bonsai represented a metaphor for present-day juvenile development.

"It involves the same process as with human juveniles. By artificially restricting growth and delaying the development of the tree, it has the effect of extending their lifespan significantly. In fact, there are many similar examples of this occurring in the natural environment."

"How so?" Jennifer asked, happy to indulge Rick's passion for his hobby.

"Well it's a given that with most living things, the slower they develop, the longer they live. Where the environment creates special conditions that restrict that growth, organisms universally live longer. Certain species of fish for instance, that live in very cold or very deep water, live many times longer than their counterparts in shallower and more plentiful parts of the ocean; and certain trees living in limited growing conditions live hundreds of centuries, whereas others may naturally live only a few years."

"What makes them grow so much slower? I assume there's no mad doctor out there cutting back their roots!"

Rick smiled; Jennifer never seemed to miss an opportunity to tease him about his doctor complex.

"True enough, Jennifer—nature does it a different way. Either they restrict the supply of food, sun, or oxygen, and thus cause the organism to grow and mature more slowly; or by lessening the presence of predators, nature allows the organism to take its time 'growing up'. Either way, the delayed maturity of each life form results in much extended lifespans, just as with humans."

"Fascinating." Jennifer was truly intrigued by this unfamiliar aspect of biology.

"How far might nature extend this process?" she asked. "I mean not only for trees and fish, but also for *people*."

"That's the essential question, and conundrum, isn't it?" Rick replied. "There are some fish that live to be well over a hundred years old, and some trees that are almost five *thousand* years old. It remains to be seen just how long we humans might artificially prolong life using this new technique of hypophysectomy and hormone restriction."

"Well, there are a few of us who might say five thousand years is quite enough! That seems like a pretty long time, compared to what we achieved as recently as just a few decades ago."

"Yes, I suppose so. That's part of the reason I like to experiment with these little trees—I'd like to see just how far we can stretch their longevity before we leap to any conclusions regarding the future of higher life forms."

Rick considered for a minute whether he might invite Jennifer to share in the next phase of his research.

"I was actually planning on taking an expedition soon to a place where the oldest known living thing resides—a lonely bristlecone pine tree named Methuselah. Would you like to come with me?"

"Well if it's *that* old, based on your earlier explanation it must be an exceptionally unforgiving place, or one devoid of predators. I can handle the latter, but the former doesn't sound terribly inviting!"

"You're actually right on both counts. It's a barren mountain in the shadow of the Sierra Nevadas—a rather bleak place in terms of climate and topography, but the hike up the mountain should be beautiful. When we get to the top, I assure you, it will be worth the trip. You'll see something magnificent and untouched that has survived natural and human intervention for five millennia, and has stood longer than the pyramids of Giza. Plus, it'll be great exercise, and it'll get our endorphins pumping again."

"How can I resist that kind of invitation? When do we go?"

Nineteen

The past week had been a relatively peaceful one for Calvin James, as he worked quietly on his plan to save Elias from an unwanted hypophysectomy. He had conceived a scheme that would not only foil the authorities in their attempts to mutilate his son, but would also restore God's original design for humanity. The precision of his plan had given him a sense of serenity that he hadn't felt in a long time. Even his last sermon to his Garden of Eden congregation had been toned down, with exhortations to be calm and wait for God's word, Calvin was so sure he would soon lead them out of the wilderness.

As he worked silently in his rectory, a loud series of raps on the entrance door to the church startled him from his thoughts.

Probably another homeless person looking for a handout or respite from the encroaching weather, he thought.

There weren't many beggars still wandering the environs of lower Manhattan, since crime had become virtually non-existent in the last few decades and city resources had been re-directed to caring for the old and infirm. But there were still a few mentally unbalanced people who refused public assistance and wished to maintain their independence by living on the streets. Some were in pretty rough shape, and would call periodically on the few remaining active churches around the city for handouts, and to provide temporary shelter from the elements. Calvin trudged down the long steps from his office to the front door to send the panhandler away. He had no time to deal with miscreants at this moment, for there were far more important matters to address. But as he swung open the heavy wooden doors, he was shocked by the sight that greeted him. A well-dressed female carrying an attaché case was flanked by two serious looking police officers.

"Good day, Dr. James," she announced. "My name is Graciella Rubino, and I'm with the Manhattan Child Services Agency. We've been trying to contact you for some time now to arrange an interview with your son to discuss the hypophysectomy procedure mandated by the United Nations Global Longevity Initiative. We'd like to meet with him now, please."

Damn, Calvin cursed under his breath. He couldn't believe his luck; he was just days from spiriting Elias away where he'd be secure from unwanted intrusion as he passed over the safe threshold of puberty.

Contain yourself, Calvin said to himself. *All you have to do is stall these people for a few more days. Be calm and reasonable—don't give them any reason to take drastic action.*

"Yes of course," Calvin replied in a measured tone, "I'd been planning to bring him in to meet with you soon. We've been busy with his home schooling and preparing for the upcoming holiday season. I could make an appointment with you for some time next week if that's convenient?"

"I'm sorry, sir," the Child Services officer replied. "We cannot accept any further delays. You've had ample opportunity to bring your son in, and regulations require an in-depth interview before every child turns eleven—which our records show is tomorrow. I have a court order to meet with him immediately."

Calvin could feel his blood beginning to boil and the hair on the back of his neck standing on end.

The nerve of these people, thinking they have providence over me and my son. Who the hell do they think they are?

But Calvin also knew that Child Services would ultimately have the final say in this matter—and could back it up with force if necessary. The presence of the police reduced his range of options, and although the two juveniles were far smaller and weaker than him, he knew from previous experience that they would be carrying weapons, and that reinforcements were only a short radio call away. He would have to try and remain calm so as not to set off any alarm bells.

"Fine," Calvin said, "I can collect my son and meet you at your office in twenty minutes. I'll need to tell him what you want, so as not to frighten him."

Calvin simply wanted to shut the door and have a few minutes to think. He might still be able to steal Elias away through a secret passage out the back. At the very least, he wanted to prep his son for the interview in order to resist the procedure. As he began to close the door, the two police officers quickly moved forward withdrawing their billy clubs. Calvin wasn't sure if they meant to use them on him, or simply to wedge them in the door to prevent it from closing.

"We'd like to meet with your son *here*, please," the Child Services agent firmly stated, as one of the officers placed his hand on the door. It was obvious the CSA wasn't going to take any chances losing control over this situation.

"We want him to feel as comfortable as possible," Ms. Rubino continued, "and we'd appreciate your full co-operation. You'll be permitted to observe the process. Please allow us to enter peaceably."

Calvin knew he could overpower the juveniles if he acted quickly enough, but that this would likely just bring more police, who could be waiting around the corner. He couldn't afford to antagonize them any further and risk disrupting his plans. He would have to play along, as much as it pained him to do so—just long enough for Elias and him to make their getaway.

"Alright—but do we really need the *police* to come in also? It will just make my son more uncomfortable. I give you my word that I'll cooperate."

"It's simply protocol sir," replied Ms. Rubino. "The officers will remain at the back of the room while I speak with your son. I'll need thirty to forty minutes alone with him where we can speak freely, so that I may assess his proper state of mind and true wishes. Then you'll be allowed to meet with us together, where we'll make a joint determination regarding next steps."

The more Calvin heard from the Child Services worker, the more he didn't like where this was going. Nonetheless, he felt that if he continued to give the impression of full cooperation that he might be able to delay the CSA from taking immediate action, even if his son were to reveal his true feelings and fears about the hypophysectomy procedure. All he had to do was maintain control and custody of his child for another couple of days; he would give them no other reason to do otherwise.

Calvin gritted his teeth, but managed to force a smile. "Yes madam. I'm happy to cooperate."

He decided to deflect the subject in order to try and reduce the tension.

"Your name," he said, "Graciella—did you know that it means by the Grace of God?"

"Yes, thank you, Dr. James," she replied. The CSA officer had plenty of training for these highly charged situations, and knew it was always best to reach out when an olive branch was offered.

"Yours, I know, is *also* full of great symbolism. The James surname is the name of kings—some scholars believe that Christ himself descended from the James clan. And of course, the great protestant reformer John Calvin laid the foundation for the rise of capitalism and democracy in our society…"

Calvin was growing tired of this calculated and disingenuous game with the Child Services agent. Although it was obvious that Ms. Rubino was well read and had some basic knowledge of religious history, it was just as obvious that she was not a true believer and was purely trying to allay Calvin's feelings—just as he was with her.

"Well I don't claim to be a *king*," Calvin replied hypocritically, "or someone with the profound divinity of Jesus or the influence of John Calvin. I'm just trying to carry the Lord's word and help as many people as I can in this little church within my personal community."

"We *all* need a little guidance and spiritual community at times, Dr. James. Speaking of which—shall we get started? Would you mind bringing Elias to see us? Where might we find a quiet and private place to confer?"

"I think you'll find the rectory a bit cramped," Calvin replied. "It might just be easiest to pull up a couple of chairs on the choir platform over there, near the altar. I could wait in the rear pews or in my upstairs chambers, whichever you prefer."

Miss Rubino appraised the section behind the pulpit where Calvin pointed. It was well lit from large stained glass windows rising above on three sides, and offered some privacy in the form of a thin linen screen used to veil the choir during assembly.

"The choir area will be fine, thank you. If you could bring Elias down and wait by the officers in the rear pews, that would be convenient." The CSA agent apparently wished to take no chances with Calvin getting into trouble under the watchful eye of the attending police.

"Fine—I'll be back in just a moment." Calvin had been feeling increasingly cornered by the situation and could barely breathe. He just needed a few moments alone to clear his head and decide what to do. As he turned to go upstairs, Ms. Rubino interjected.

"Sir, if you wouldn't mind, I'd like the officers to accompany you. It's protocol, once again."

Calvin finally reached his breaking point.

"If *you* don't mind Madam," he said, trying to keep his escalating rage in check, "I'd like to gather my own son without the interference of your officers. This is going to be upsetting enough without him having to be frightened by the appearance of the police. I assure you, I will bring him to you shortly. This is a very small church—it's not as if there's anywhere we can run."

"Fine," Ms. Rubino allowed, after some hesitation. "But please bring him down immediately. We'll give you five minutes."

"I'll return shortly."

As Calvin made his way up the stairs, through the narrow hallways leading to his rectory and to Elias's small bedroom, he pondered his next move. His impulse was to flee, but he knew that even if he managed to get out of the church with Elias, there was a good chance the property was being monitored by the police, and that if they were caught this would only result in them being separated—perhaps for too long. His best bet was to play along and cooperate, while trying to convince his son to be non-committal, at least for a few more days.

Precisely five minutes later, Calvin emerged in the cathedral's central nave with his son.

"Elias, this is Miss Rubino," he said, introducing his son to the Child Services officer. "She'd like to speak with you for a few minutes about some of the things we discussed. Please speak clearly and feel free to express your feelings openly." Calvin looked at the Child Services agent directly. "She won't do anything against your wishes. I'll be waiting by the foyer until you're both finished."

As Calvin slowly withdrew to the opposite end of the cathedral, his eyes met Elias's. He wasn't entirely sure how to read the expression on his son's face, but he knew at this moment that Elias must surely feel as tormented as he was. He knew that Elias revered him, and that he also feared God. He was a clever boy, with strong spiritual convictions—but he was still only a *boy*. Calvin couldn't imagine how anyone at such a tender age could possibly make this kind a life-altering decision. Although he knew the law provided for full and open counsel with Child Services, Calvin also knew where their prejudices lay, and he found it unacceptable that this decision could ultimately be wrested from the rightful parent or legal guardian.

For his part, Elias knew full well how his father felt about the procedure, having been lectured on the subject from the pulpit as well as the dinner table about how accepting the operation amounted to self-mutilation in God's eyes as well as certain banishment to Hell. But he also knew from stolen glances at the newspaper and from surreptitious discussions with fellow parishioners, exactly what the consequences were both ways. He had long agonized about what he would do when the inevitable day came to make this choice. On the one hand, he could embrace the predictable but declining life of a mature adult and expect to live for perhaps eighty more years, with the unclear promise of everlasting life in heaven—or he could abandon his divine duty and lead the virtually assured unlimited life of the ever-young juveniles he saw parade into his father's church week after week. How could he be expected to make this decision? It was an impossible choice—to choose between a finite life devoted to God, or an infinite life devoted to earthly pleasures. Peering up at the altar before him, Elias couldn't take his eyes off the agonized look on Christ's face as he lay on the crucifix, his bloodied hands and feet bound by metal spikes.

Calvin retreated to the rear pews and glared at the two police officers flanking the main door beside him. Although the Child Services agent had positioned Elias on the dais with his back to Calvin so as to avoid eye contact and undue distraction, Calvin could still make out his son's form through the gauzy material of the privacy curtain. The interview seemed to go on forever, and even though it only lasted a little over forty-five minutes, it seemed like an eternity to Calvin. He periodically saw his son's back heaving and spasming, clearly indicating that Elias was sobbing. Many times Calvin simply wanted to race to the pulpit and dash out the side door with his son. The only thing that kept him firmly rooted in his seat was the giant avatar of Christ lying on the cross above the altar. He hoped God would give both him and his son the necessary strength to prevail.

When Ms. Rubino finally emerged from behind the screen and motioned for Calvin to join them, he rushed to the front of the room. Elias was crying, and Ms. Rubino looked very forlorn. He could only imagine what words had been exchanged, and what anguish his son had been through. Surely, he thought, his son had followed his instructions not to reveal his true fears, as Calvin had requested. He was almost afraid to ask the Child Services agent the inevitable question.

"You can see my son is deeply upset and conflicted over this whole matter," he stated. "It's obvious he's in no mood or position at the present time to make a decision on this difficult issue you've put to him. May we be left alone to think this through and give you a definitive answer after he's had a chance to process everything? I'll thank you to leave now, Ms. Rubino."

"I'm sorry, Dr. James," she said, motioning to the police officers quickly catching up. "I can't do that. After carefully assessing your son's concerns and his state of mind, I believe that he is being unduly influenced by you to put off this critical decision, which needs to be made soon. Furthermore, I've heard enough from Elias to believe that he desires this procedure to ensure his continued vitality and longevity. I'm afraid I'm going to have to take him into the temporary custody of Child Services, at least until we can make a final and confident determination as to his wishes."

Calvin's eyes suddenly flashed, and he rose out of his seat so quickly that he sent chairs flying off the raised platform.

"*What?!*" he roared, incredulously. "I'm not going to let you take my son away from me, and defile him against his will!"

He was shaking visibly now, and his face was flushed a deep shade of scarlet red.

"You have no right to be here in the first place, let alone feign to have dominion over this boy's body and destiny. He is *my* child, and a child of *God*—no one else's. I am taking my son now, and I'm asking you to leave this holy chamber before you desecrate it any further. Get out of my church, or by God's will I'll throw you out!!"

As Calvin moved to scoop the quivering and sobbing Elias out of his seat, suddenly he felt an intense pain shoot through his entire body, and he fell to the floor in a fit of convulsions. The police, who had obviously prepared for this circumstance, had shot him with a two highly charged electrified impulses from their taser pistols, each carrying twenty thousand volts. Calvin couldn't move or speak—he was completely incapacitated and in tremendous pain. As the officers quickly moved to bind his hands and feet with nylon tie-straps, he looked on helplessly as his son was led away out the front door.

The last thing Calvin saw was the agonized expression on Elias's face as he looked back at his stricken father writhing on the raised platform under the tortured gaze of Christ looking down from the cross.

Twenty

Eva Bronwen lay draped in a surgical gown on the operating table in room 3R at Mount Sinai Medical Center. It was time to retrieve the eggs which had been developing in her womb with the help of special ovulation-inducing drugs, and although the procedure was by now fairly practiced and straight-forward, the state didn't want to take any chances using anything but the best available facilities to ensure the success of the operation.

Over the previous two weeks, Eva had been administered daily hormone injections designed to stimulate the production of multiple eggs within each ovary and to suppress their normal release. This had produced all manner of escalated symptoms, from severe bloating and weight gain to elevated libido levels. Eva's progress during this time had been closely monitored via regular blood tests and ultrasound scans to assess the development and readiness of her ovarian follicles to harvest the precious eggs. At her last test, it was determined that the follicles were fully ripe and ready for delivery. A special gonadotropin drug was administered to trigger ovulation within thirty-six hours, whereupon a specialist was scheduled to retrieve each tiny egg one at a time, using a long needle inserted directly through her abdomen into her uterus.

Drs. Ross and Austin were also attending to monitor the procedure and to provide emotional support to Eva.

"How's my big girl doing today?" Rick said to Eva as he entered the operating room.

"A lot bigger—and not feeling like much of a *girl*, I'm afraid!" Eva smiled, as she winked at Jennifer following close behind. "I'm glad you only put me through this twice a year—otherwise I'm sure you'd wear this tired old body out in no time!"

"Oh come on," Jennifer teased, "I know the side effects aren't *all* bad! And besides, you're a long way from getting *old*."

"Tell that to my ovaries. I know there's a limited amount of eggs they produce in a lifetime, and based on the number you've pulled out of me so far, I'm surprised I've got any left! Pretty soon, you'll turn me into a dried up old prune."

"Well, I wouldn't say you're becoming a spinster just yet," Rick laughed. "Actually, every female is born with about four million eggs, and you only lose about ten thousand or so every month through regular ovulation—so doing the math, I'd say you've still got quite a few left."

"Where do they all go, anyway?" Eva wondered aloud.

"One or two of them wash out of your system naturally every time you have a period. But you're right about the connection to age, in that many more are lost through the process of follicular atresia every month. That's why it's important to harvest your eggs while you're young."

"Follicular atresia? That's the nicest way so far that you've told me I'm getting old, Dr. Ross! Actually, I was thinking more about where the eggs go that are *retrieved* during these procedures, as opposed to those produced during my normal cycle. You must have an awful lot of them stored away by now?"

"They're kept right here in this hospital, in a secure vault that is carefully controlled to keep them frozen at the just the right temperature."

"Story of my life," Eva sighed. "It looks like no one's ever going to touch my frigid eggs, other than some mysterious lab technician. So much for combining DNA the old fashioned way!"

"I thought you were considering some new possibilities in that area, Eva?" Jennifer said, referring to

Eva's flirtation with a suitor at the Hippodrome two weeks ago.

"Oh, you mean *Mike*? He's a charming enough fellow, and he's certainly showing enough interest in me, but I'm fighting the temptation to take it beyond the platonic level. Which, let me tell you Jennifer, isn't any easier with all these drugs you've given me!"

"Maybe your body's trying to tell you something, Eva?" Rick chimed in. After hearing Jennifer recount their earlier experience at the nightclub, he'd begun to think Eva's recent dating wasn't such a bad idea either.

"*Et tu*, Dr. Ross?" Eva said, noticing Jennifer's hand brush playfully against Rick's smock.

"And since we're on the subject of body language, judging by how close you two are standing to one another, I'm sensing a little extra chemistry somewhere else in this room?"

Rick and Jennifer glanced at each other tentatively.

"I knew it! You two are perfect for each other, and it's high time my GP found someone as smart and sophisticated as Jennifer. I'm thrilled for you both—even if I am a little miffed you chose her over me, Dr. Ross."

"What makes you think…" Jennifer said, shifting unconsciously away from Rick.

"Oh, please! Look at you two. It's written all over your faces—you're smitten. I insist on being invited to the wedding!"

"Whoa! We've only been out to dinner once," Rick interjected. "You might give us a little longer before we start sending out invitations!"

"So how long has it been—two weeks?" Eva ribbed. "When's your second date?"

"Now wait just a second," Rick protested. "This was supposed to be about *you*—you always have a way of turning our conversations around!"

"I'm serious, Dr. Ross," Eva replied, looking suddenly solemn, "I feel like I'm a part of both your lives now, and I don't want you holding something like this back from me."

"We're simply collaborating on some professional initiates." Rick equivocated, realizing he was quickly losing the battle to disguise his true feelings for Jennifer.

"Really?" Eva teased, signaling she wasn't about to submit to the operation until she had what she wanted. "Professional initiatives? What *kind*?!"

"Well, we're going on a little fact-finding trip to the Sierra Nevada mountains this weekend," Jennifer volunteered, barely concealing her excitement.

"What, are you going *skiing*? Isn't it still a bit early in the season for that?"

"Actually, we're going on different type of harvesting mission," Rick replied looking at Jennifer, gently admonishing Jennifer for revealing their new secret. "We're searching for the germinal seed of the oldest tree in the plant kingdom."

"Oh *that* sounds like fun," Eva said. "You'll have to tell me all about it when I come to after the operation."

Quickly seizing the opportunity, Rick motioned to the attending anesthesiologist to turn up the thiopental drip, and Eva instantly fell into a peaceful sleep.

Twenty-one

Rick had been eagerly anticipating his latest Bioethics class all week. The last session on the subject of cloning had been very animated, with more than a few intellectual breakthroughs, but it had finished with another controversial debate over the role of religion and science. Rick had taken his mercurial student Nathan aside after the session ended to enquire about his motivations and discovered he had an excellent knowledge of evolutionary biology, but that he would not reveal where or how he had developed his apparently far stronger spiritual beliefs. Rick resolved to tread lightly on this subject going forward, but to continue gently probing for additional insights into this unusual and mysterious student.

As he entered the lecture hall filled with chatter among the large assembly of students, he scanned the upper row of seats and was disappointed to see Nathan was missing.

Looks like I'll have to inject some of my own controversy to give today's lecture some spark.

"Good morning, esteemed colleagues," Rick announced. "Our last class on the subject of cloning was quite vigorous, don't you think?"

The assembly murmured, remembering the heated discussion with Nathan.

"This week's subject on the link between reproduction and longevity may be slightly less contentious, but hopefully no less interesting. But first, we have the usual matter of trying to resolve our weekly riddle. If you remember, building on our discussion of the relationship between religion and science, I posed the question: If every life has a soul, and every clone is an exact replica of its donor, does that mean that the donor and clone share the same soul? Any takers?"

Gabriel, as usual, was not shy about jumping into the fray. "I thought we established that there's no room for religion in science—or at least that there's no evidence to indicate a divine hand in the evolution of life. In that case, I think we'd have to say that living beings don't have a soul."

"Well, I'm not sure we completely reconciled the co-existence, or exclusivity, of the two," Rick suggested. "But I suppose if you were to outright reject the existence of any divine power or influence, you might conclude that there's no such thing as a 'soul'—at least in the traditional meaning of the word. But what if we were to think of a living thing's soul as that component which goes on living even after it's dead—how might that change our interpretation?"

The group paused and looked at one another quizzically. Rick held up his hands in mock protest.

"Don't tell me you've forgotten about the distinction between mortal and immortal cells from our lecture two weeks ago?! Who remembers which cells never die, and why?"

"The *germ* cells never die," Lauren remembered, "insofar as they are passed on to their offspring in the act of reproduction."

"Right you are, Lauren," Rick said, pleased the group was back on track. "But there's also a distinction in *how* they're passed on, as it pertains to sexual versus asexual reproduction. Why is this important?'

"In the case of *cloning*—which involves asexual reproduction—the offspring receives the same full and unchanged set of genes as that of its parent," Ethan offered.

"So then, if a clone receives the exact same DNA material as that passed down from its progenitor, and those germ cells never age or die, wouldn't that be equivalent to an immortal soul?"

"Only if that clone reproduced asexually and its *offspring* did the same, ad infinitum," concluded Drew. "If the clone didn't do so—or if it died before reproducing—those germ cells would die with it."

"That's very clever, Drew. So in that case, I suppose the only organisms with the closest thing to a soul would be *bacteria* and other simple organisms, who only reproduce asexually!?" Rick was beginning to feel thankful Nathan was absent from today's lecture, after all. "The so-called *higher* life forms, which reproduce sexually, seem to be doomed to finite mortal lives, since no exact replica of them appears to move forward to an afterlife." He paused for dramatic effect. "And yet, as we established in our last lecture, nature has produced a diversity of species that for the most part prefer the sexual form of reproduction. Let's examine this more closely. If nature prefers sexual reproduction, why then does it *punish* us so severely when we practice it?"

"What do you mean, Dr. Ross?" asked a puzzled Jade.

"Well there are ample indications in the natural world that reveal many deleterious associations between reproduction and aging. We've seen how certain species of salmon and octopus wither and die shortly after completing their biological duty. A female *ferret* actually dies of hormone poisoning if it doesn't find a mate once it goes into heat. The poor honeybee drone actually loses his penis immediately after copulating, and literally falls to the earth a broken male. In most species, hormones released after mating, in large or small measure, adversely impact the functioning of the immune system. On this matter, the evidence is universal: the earlier an organism begins reproducing, the more frequently it reproduces, and the larger the size of its brood, the shorter it's life. It appears that in nature, sex kills!"

"And yet it feels so good!" chirped Matt.

The room erupted in spontaneous laughter.

"Ah yes, Matt," Rick replied, "which brings us back to the not-so-golden rule of antagonistic pleiotropy: that which is most beneficial for organisms in the short term, is almost always bad for them in the long term. Though there are some interesting variations and mutations in we humans.

For instance, up until a few years ago, roughly one in eight million persons was born with a condition named Hutchinson-Gilford Progeria syndrome, where the afflicted individual ages ten times as fast as other people, exhibiting all the regular signs of senescence such as shriveling skin and heart disease, as early as two or three years of age. And yet, the one and only part of their body that remains immune to the ravaging effects of old age is the reproductive organs—their genitals remain as pristine and undeveloped as any juvenile's. Why do you think that's the case?"

"Perhaps it's just another instance of nature preserving the germ cells?" intoned Ethan.

"Perhaps." Rick paused, adopting a more serious tone. "Or maybe it's a case of a genetic mutation where these individuals are born incapable of *ever* developing to sexual maturity, and since nature knows they will never fulfill their essential biological function, it acts more quickly than usual to remove them from the competitive gene pool. It appears that Nature, unlike God, doesn't care so much about you as an *individual*—or at least your corporeal soma—it only cares that you pass on your germ."

Rick noticed the facial expressions of many in the assembly change as they considered the implications of this statement. For a few painful seconds, the only sound that could be heard in the lecture hall was that of students shifting nervously in their seats. Finally, one of the students broke the awkward silence.

"What does this mean for of all of *us* then, who have been rendered unable to reproduce in the manner nature intended?" asked Drew.

"Yes, it does sound a bit scary to mess with Mother Nature, doesn't it Drew? It seems inconceivable that in such a relatively short evolutionary time, we might be able to find a way to improve on the natural development of species that billions of years of evolution has selectively perfected."

Rick could see that many students in his class were growing increasingly uncomfortable, and he decided to ease the tension a bit.

"There are, however, a few promising mutations in nature that lend some credence and support to our little experiment. For instance, most insects' lifespans are measured in weeks or months, but the enterprising cicada survives several *years,* because it burrows underground and rests in a state of suspended juvenile development called dauer. When it finally emerges from the ground and becomes sexually mature and active, it survives only for a relatively short six to eight weeks—just long enough for it to mate and lay its eggs. Incredibly, in its brilliance, nature adapted a special genotype of the cicada, aptly named Magicicada, who synchronize their sexual maturity to occur precisely every thirteen or seventeen years—*six times* as long an interval as their non-periodical brethren. Why do you imagine this cohort lives so much longer, and why exactly thirteen or seventeen years?"

"Do the *periodical* cicadas live underground longer as juveniles?" Rachel asked.

"They do indeed—but why precisely thirteen or seventeen years? What's the significance of these regularly repeating numbers for every cohort?"

Silence fell over the room once again. Many students looked at one another, searching for clues. Everyone was stumped—no one could make the connection.

Rick decided to give them a clue. "Who here has studied math? What is unusual—and yet similar—about both of these numbers?"

Everyone thought for a few minutes.

"They're both prime numbers!" Gabriel finally blurted out.

"Yes, and what's unusual about prime numbers, Gabriel?"

"They can only be divided by themselves and the number one—no other numbers."

"So what is the advantage gained from this particular genotype of cicada, collectively emerging and reproducing in these exact frequencies? Think about it."

Rick was having fun stretching—and tormenting—his students.

"Holy cats!" Drew cried. "If that many insects all emerged at once, that infrequently, they would overwhelm their natural predators, who presumably would not have adapted a similar periodical frequency, and this would help ensure more of those cicadas' genes would be sown for future generations!"

"Amazing, isn't it?" Rick remarked. "Talk about intelligent design. And yet—this intelligence isn't applied for the *individual* benefit of the organism, or even for the benefit of any one species. It's simply a random reaction to the competitive forces within nature, designed to reward those organisms best adapted to survive and pass on their genes—yet another example of reproductive fitness, and antagonistic pleiotropy."

Rick was pleased with the progress the students were making, but wanted to give them one more case study to mull over before next week's class.

"We've got time to look at one other example of this issue occurring in nature, before we ponder the ramifications for we uniquely evolved humans. Let's take a closer look at the honeybee, which lives in highly evolved social colonies in three distinct forms: the unlucky male drone, whose only function in its short life is to mate and provide sperm for the queen, the sterile female worker bees, who collect food and protect the colony, and the queen, whose sole function is to produce offspring: *thousands* every day. The drones and the worker bees have a typical lifespan of about one to two months, but the queen lives *fifty* times as long—up to five years! Doesn't this seem in direct opposition to our observation that fecundity is inversely proportional to longevity?"

"Yes—it doesn't make sense," replied Lauren.

Rick was disappointed the group's creative momentum was suddenly ebbing. He knew he would need to give them a break soon to digest the day's learnings.

"Remember to focus on the *collective* as opposed to the individual. What's different about the bee colony, especially as it pertains to *reproduction*, compared to most other species?"

"There's only one reproductive female?" Ethan volunteered.

"Yes, so why might this one female—the queen—outlast all the other bees in the colony, even though it spends all its time doing nothing but producing new young, which appears in conflict with the rule that sex is generally deleterious for individual organisms?"

"It must have a different genetic structure," Gabriel declared.

"Actually, you might be surprised to learn that the queen bee and the other female worker bees share *precisely* the same DNA structure—so their remarkable difference in longevity obviously has nothing to do with their genes. The only thing that causes a queen bee to develop differently from other females in the colony is the way she is *fed*—with a special concoction of royal jelly, a protein-rich secretion emitted from the glands of worker bees. Therefore, her extraordinary longevity has to be an environmental adaptation."

"Perhaps the queen is over-compensating for the lack of other sexually producing females," Rachel mused.

"Or perhaps nature *needs* to keep her alive, until another queen can be produced— otherwise the whole colony would die," Rick suggested. "It seems to always come back to reproduction with Mother Nature. Apparently we humans are not the only ones obsessed with sex."

The group snickered nervously. Rick decided to up the ante and make his students reflect a bit harder before next week's class.

"Which brings us to the end of another lecture—and the riddle to consider for our next session. I'd like you all to ponder this: Since all of us have seemingly been placed in an extended state of suspended juvenile development much like the cicada, but also rendered effectively sterile like the Progeria patient, and since our Queen cannot reproduce as frequently as in the bee colony, what are the possible implications for our particular cohort of humanity?

Twenty-two

Calvin James shifted uncomfortably on his concrete bunk in a holding cell at the 5th police precinct in lower Manhattan. He'd been taken there after the incident yesterday at the Garden of Eden church, where he had threatened the Child Services agent after her disclosure that she was taking Elias into protective custody. Even though Calvin had been bound with handcuffs and dazed by stun guns, it had taken ten juvenile police officers to fully subdue and transport him to the station.

Calvin knew he couldn't be detained for more than twenty-four hours without charge, and he was anticipating a visit by his court-appointed lawyer any minute. He hadn't slept at all overnight, as his mind was racing with all manner of scenarios for retribution. He fully expected to be released after his arraignment before a judge, provided he promised not to act on his threats or commit any other crimes.

His overriding concern now was Elias. His plan to spirit Elias away before he could be administered a hypophysectomy was now almost certainly spoiled, not least because the Child Services agency would be reluctant to disclose his new location, and because he would now be protected behind a phalanx of locked doors and armed guards. His only hope now would be to negotiate a meeting with Elias, where he could try to convince him one last time to resist the operation and save his soul.

But Calvin had other concerns as well. He had carefully crafted a plan that went far beyond saving his son, and it would require his freedom and mobility as well as the ability to communicate freely with his followers, whose assistance he would need to carry out his plan. Since Calvin had no family other than Elias, he placed a call immediately after being taken into custody to the one person he felt he could trust. Although they'd known each other only a few short months, Nathan Taylor had originally come to Calvin in confidence to express his concerns about developments with the Global Longevity Initiative, and the two had subsequently begun to share ideas about how they might fight the program. Of special interest for Calvin was Nathan's unique position of influence as a senior manager at a giant pharmaceutical company, and the fact that he had other resources at his disposal. Nathan could easily post bail in the unlikely event that Calvin was formally charged with a criminal offense, and could act as his proxy if had to spend more time in jail. Unfortunately, the two would now have to be more careful in their collaboration, as Calvin would be under heightened scrutiny and surveillance.

    The events of the last twenty-four hours had only intensified Calvin's rage, and he was now committed to exacting revenge on an even grander scale. His initial plan had been fashioned in incremental steps, but with Nathan's ingenuity and resources he now had the means—and the motivation—to implement his plan on a *global* level. If he couldn't save his son from the forces of evil, Calvin believed he could at least save the next generation of God's children. Pacing excitedly in the narrow confines of his prison dorm while contemplating his next steps, he heard a loud metallic rap on the steel door to his cell.

    "Please step away from the door sir," the armed guard announced with a certain degree of trepidation, "the magistrate is ready to see you."

Twenty-three

The morning sun sparkled across the whitecaps of Santa Monica Bay as Rick and Jennifer drove north along the Pacific Coast Highway toward the Sierra Nevada mountains. They had flown from New York to Los Angeles late Friday afternoon, and had gotten up early Saturday to make the long trek to the Inyo National Forest near the border of California and Nevada, where they hoped to find the world's oldest living tree and harvest its seeds. The six hour drive was scenic and beautiful, and the two marveled at how dramatically the landscape changed as they turned east toward the interior of Owens Valley. The various ecosystems of Central California were a dendrologist's dream, having some of the oldest and most beautiful trees in the world, and Rick reveled in the opportunity to share its bounty with Jennifer.

Crossing over the San Gabriel mountains framing the city of Los Angeles, the palate suddenly shifted from verdant green forests of tall sycamore, maple, and canyon oak, to the flat dusty-red mesa of the Mojave Desert, blanketed with olive-brown creosote bushes and the occasional stunted tree.

"Wow," Jennifer exclaimed, as they crested the mountain range and began their descent into the valley. "Talk about a change of scenery."

"Welcome to the Great Basin of America," Rick declared. "Those mountains we just passed over rise ten thousand feet. The prevailing winds from the Pacific collect the warm, moist air rising off the ocean and condense it into precipitation that falls primarily on the windward side of the range. Very little moisture falls on this side—so little in fact, that none has a chance to accumulate in this watershed and flow back to the sea. Consequently, it's a pretty unforgiving place for most types of flora and fauna."

"Apparently not *all* flora," remarked Jennifer, noticing many stubby little bushes dotting the landscape. "What are all those little brown shrubs? It looks like *they've* at least figured out how to survive here."

"They're creosote bushes, a very interesting little tree indeed. They have the ability to reproduce both sexually and asexually—by dropping branches to the soil, which subsequently take root and form new shrubs, thus avoiding the perils and high mortality of the early seedling stage in this harsh environment. Because the asexually cloned part of the tree shares the same DNA as its parent, many people consider it immortal, and have dubbed it King Clone."

"Does the original tree survive?"

"No, eventually it succumbs to the stress of extreme drought."

"So it's not really immortal then?"

"It depends I suppose, on how you define its meaning," Rick said, recalling the animated discussion on the subject of cloning from his last Bioethics class. "If the new bush is simply a part of the original one, then when the older part dies off, isn't a piece of it still alive? In this sense, for species that reproduce through cloning, any individual is theoretically as old as the species."

"That's a bit too heavy for me this early in the morning," Jennifer laughed. Her eyes caught an unusually shaped tree standing alone amongst the passing brown landscape. "What's the story with that tall cactus? I suspect it has a slightly different survival strategy."

"Actually, that's a type of palm, called a Joshua tree. As we get closer, you'll notice the long bayonet-shaped leaves arranged in dense spiral formations on its arms make it look from a distance like a cactus. It was so-named by early Mormon settlers because it reminded them of the biblical story of Joshua reaching his hands up to the sky in prayer. Its unique adaptation is the ability to germinate under larger nurse plants as a form of protection from the elements and predators, until it's hardy enough to survive on its own."

"It seems nature finds a way to make room for anything that discovers how to adapt to its unique surroundings," Jennifer remarked.

"That's the beauty and the brilliance of it," Rick observed. "And what draws me so far from home."

Jennifer glanced to the northwest and saw the glittering snow-capped peaks of the Sierra Nevada range rising dramatically from the desert floor. "Well it's certainly a long way from the skyscrapers and canyons we're used to in New York!"

"And it's all *natural*—there's nothing man-made up there. Those mountains were formed millions of years ago, long before humans roamed the earth, by colossal tectonic forces as the Pacific plate was forced under the North American plate and drove that chaotic scramble of rocks into the heavens."

Jennifer looked at Rick and smiled. She knew he was excited to explore this new terrain, and she didn't want to deny him an opportunity to share his unique knowledge of its specialized biology and geology.

"Tell me more, wise one. What makes these plates move like that?"

"Most geologists believe it's caused by a kind of convection current that moves the magma in the mantle of the earth. The cooler, denser material at the periphery of the plates solidifies into a hard outer crust that tries to sink, and the hotter, molten material in the core rises, creating circular currents which continually break the crust and create these subductions."

"It sounds a little too *fire and brimstone* for me," Jennifer sighed, as she watched thin slivers of mountain streams cascade down the mountain through the thick green canopy of trees. "I think I'd rather focus on the more tranquil forces of nature, right here on the surface."

"Me too," Rick said, following Jennifer's focus to the lush forest carpeting the steep leeward slopes of the Sierras.

"Don't you just love those majestic trees? California redwoods—*sequoias*—the largest trees in the world."

"Really? It's hard to grasp their scale from this distance."

"Some of those trees are taller than many New York City skyscrapers, rising almost forty stories. There's one tree on the other side of that ridge, named General Sherman, that is more than thirty feet in diameter."

"Is that the tallest tree?"

"He's the heaviest, but not the tallest. That honor belongs to Mendocino, nearer the coast, who is almost a hundred feet taller."

Jennifer couldn't help snickering.

"Why do all these trees have human names?"

"Only the grandest ones," Rick chuckled. "I suppose it's our need to anthropomorphize those things onto which we project our human characteristics and emotions. It mightn't be such a crazy idea though. We do, after all, share this unique habitat together, all the species of life so tightly interwoven and inter-dependent, sharing similar biology and habits. Even our DNA between various species isn't so different."

"What about the infamous missing link?"

"There's not much missing any more. After the human genome was mapped over a hundred years ago, it was discovered that over ninety percent of our genes were the same as those of mice. Even the DNA within the cells of plants and animals appears remarkably similar: the famous double helix that looks like a twisted ladder."

Jennifer was eager to add her own expertise to the equation.

"And the material within those molecules are made from the same four chemical building blocks or nucleotides."

"Yes," Rick mused, "it seems the only thing that separates us from plants and other animals is the way these nucleotides have been randomly sorted from one generation to the next!"

"That, and a few billion years of evolution."

"Yes: the so-called butterfly effect. Small incremental changes, multiplied over long periods of time, allows evolution to create the entirely different shapes and species we see in this little ecosystem called earth."

"One small step for man—one giant leap for mankind?"

"I suppose we should be thankful for that one random permutation long ago that led to our particular branch of the taxonomic tree. Otherwise, we might look like some one-eyed green scaly creatures having this dialogue."

"I don't think I'd be quite as interested in kissing you if you looked like that!"

"I dunno," Rick winked, "Mother Nature has created some pretty powerful impulses to reproduce across every genus."

"You'd better hope I'd be dazzled by your brilliant mind and incisive wit in that case, Rick," Jennifer laughed. "Although now that you mention it, I've often wondered why nature doesn't actually allow different species to cross-pollinate. Doesn't it seem odd that with all of this tremendous variety and all the millions of different types of plants and animals out there—that they only mate with their own kind?"

"Well, it's not as if they never *try*. Those powerful hormones you're responsible for create a mighty potent craving when an animal is under its influence, and I've heard about some pretty unusual coupling attempts!"

"And yet they're never successful in producing viable offspring."

"I suspect it's because if nature allowed it, the pace of evolution would be dramatically altered, with entirely new life forms quickly taking shape that would not have had time to acclimate and adapt to its surroundings, and thus be more likely to die off. Nature seems to favor small incremental changes from one generation to the next in order to allow the organism to thrive in the setting to which it's become accustomed, but also to enable it to slowly adapt to the inevitable changes within the environment."

As Rick continued his drive into the interior, he turned off the main highway just north of Death Valley and headed further east toward some dark mountains.

"Is that where your mythical Methuselah lives?" Jennifer asked. "I can't imagine anything surviving up there. It looks even more forbidding than the desert we just passed through!"

"I assure you," Rick affirmed, "it's still a desert—just a more alpine one. We're heading into the White Mountains, which lie in the immediate rain shadow of the Sierras. These mountains receive less than twelve inches of moisture per year, almost all of which occurs in the winter. The rest of the year, the amount of precipital moisture in the air is about half a *millimeter*—the lowest recorded anywhere on earth."

"I believe that;" Jennifer remarked, "it looks so barren. And also so dark—why do they call them the *white* mountains!?"

"It's certainly not from snow, at least at this time of the year. In fact, it's because of the sun-bleached rock lining their slopes. The geology of these mountains is mostly quartzite sandstone and granite bedrock, which was exposed during the seismic uplift so many years ago. The relative lack of moisture hasn't allowed much life to grow up there, and there is also very little topsoil. So we're essentially looking at a big exposed dark rock. But as we get closer and higher into the mountains, you'll begin to see some white outcroppings, which are patches of dolomite, a type of limestone created under the primordial seas millions of years ago. That's where we're headed."

"What is it about that type of stone that your old tree favors?"

"I suspect it's because dolomite is very low in nutrients, yet retains moisture better than the surrounding sandstone. Consequently, it inhibits growth of less hardy plants, and provides a competition-free zone for our slow-growing friend."

As the car wound its way up the steep mountain, the road gradually became thinner and rougher, changing from a two-lane paved highway, to a gravel road—finally giving way to a dusty path barely wide enough to support their vehicle above the sheer embankments below. Eventually, the track became impassable, and Rick pulled over at the edge of a dense thicket.

"Whew! That was a pretty scary," Jennifer said, breathing a sigh of relief. "I'm surprised the road took us *this* far—there can't be anyone living this high up, and there's obviously no need for logging access. How will we find your tree from here?"

"The grove where Methuselah stands was originally mapped by a curious dendrochronologist named Edmund Schulman way back in the 1950s, but satellite maps now point the way to the site via the nearest roads. I estimate we've still got a good hike of at least two thousand vertical feet ahead of us. You might want to put on your hiking boots and some warm clothing before we head out—it's likely to be pretty chilly near the top."

As Rick and Jennifer began their long ascent toward the timberline, Jennifer noticed the trees gradually becoming thinner, and the groundcover looking more and more sparse. There was virtually no sign of wildlife, and the only sound that could be heard in the cold, thin sub-alpine air was their own heavy breathing, combined with the crunch of their boots on the treacherous rocky soil.

"You weren't kidding about the terrain up here," Jennifer said between deep breaths, as she carefully planted each step for a secure foothold. "This looks more like the surface of the *moon*—it's just a bunch of loose rocks! I thought you said trees needed *soil* to expand their roots and provide necessary nutrients?"

"It depends on what you mean by soil. Let's stop for a little rest and take a closer look at some of these seemingly inhospitable rocks." Rick stooped over and turned over a large stone resting on the ground near a small tree. Jennifer noticed thin ribbons of green running like veins across its crevices.

"That doesn't look like enough food to feed a whole tree!"

"It is if it's a very slow-growing one. Remember, some of these trees live to be thousands of years old—their trunks only grow at the rate of one inch per century. If they put down enough roots with lots of hair-like feeders, they can find just enough food and moisture to thrive. There's a whole community of photo-synthetic bacteria and single-celled organisms like lichen and fungi living under the surface of these rocks."

"Nothing ever goes to waste, huh?"

"In nature, everything is food for something else; eventually, they find each other."

Rick noticed Jennifer's breathing returning to normal.

"Are you ready to continue? We're getting close to the summit."

"Absolutely," Jennifer declared. "I want to meet this character who can survive so long on this kind of diet!"

After continuing up the steep grade a little longer, they approached the crest of a hill and Jennifer suddenly felt a blast of cold air that nearly knocked her off her feet. "Holy smokes!" she had to shout over the roaring wind. "Where did that come from? I can barely *breathe*—and my skin stings!"

"We're two miles above sea level, where the air is increasingly hypoxic," Rick said, as he moved to steady Jennifer. "The thin westerly air is being rapidly funneled up the steep mountainside to this plateau, concentrating its force like a wind tunnel. The heavy winds pick up a lot of microparticles from the rocky sediment on the windward slope, which is pelting against your cold sensitive skin. Why don't you turn in the other direction—I think you'll be a little more comfortable."

"But the view this way is much prettier!" Jennifer said, holding up an outstretched hand in an attempt to block the howling wind while admiring the glorious panoramic view of the frosted Sierra Nevada mountains across the valley below.

"I think you'll find some interesting sights *this* way too," Rick said, pointing to the east. "Come on—let's see if we can find our special tree."

As Jennifer turned around, she faced a gleaming white alpine bowl, dotted with hundreds of scattered trees.

"It's lovely," she said, "but how will we know which one is Methuselah? They all look so similar!"

"We may in fact never find it," Rick admitted. "Dr. Schulman made a point of keeping its location a well-guarded secret. He didn't want any misguided treasure hunters or vandals harming the oldest living thing on earth. But there are some natural clues: look for the thickest trees, having the most exposed deadwood. Hopefully, at the very least we'll find some of his oldest relatives."

"There you go humanizing your trees again," Jennifer chuckled, as she carefully negotiated her way over the thick, white limestone plates scattered like broken tiles on the uneven ground. "So what's the story with *this* particular one?"

"Methuselah was said to be the grandfather of Noah, in the book of Genesis. The bible asserts that he lived for 969 years, and if you carefully follow its chronology, he would have been born while Adam was still alive, around the supposed creation of earth six thousand years ago. Ironically, Methuselah died in the biblical year of the Great Flood that is said to have wiped out most life on earth."

"Where's the irony in that?"

"Don't you see it? God purportedly created the flood to cleanse the earth of non-believers, but he didn't want Methuselah to be killed with the unrighteous. Here is the one place on earth with the least water—and this is the only place where Methuselah's namesake survives!"

"Intriguing. Perhaps he didn't die after all? Maybe this is where he came to escape the flood, and God turned him into a tree to last forever. I can certainly see your fascination with this character." Jennifer turned around a knoll in the hillside and stopped abruptly before a group of gnarled and half-dead trees exposed on a steep, west-facing ridgeline. "Well, if you're looking for more biblical allegories, I think I may have found some of your burning bushes!"

Rick quickly scampered up behind her. "*Yes*," he said excitedly, "these do look promising. The oldest ones will be those getting the most sun, in the driest soil, with the greatest exposure to the wind."

"It still seems counter-intuitive that the trees with the worst growing conditions survive the longest?" Jennifer remarked.

"It's not only trees. *Every* life form survives longer up here than their counterparts at lower elevations who have more abundant food, water, and oxygen. There are also indigenous species of marmot, squirrel, and grouse here that live much longer than their non-alpine relatives—and all of them share the same unique characteristics: later maturity, lower fecundity, and longer hibernation."

"What's the connection?"

"Later maturity is a natural consequence of slower growth. Lower fecundity is a direct response to diminished predation. And longer hibernation is necessary because of the short growing season—which at this elevation is only six weeks over the brief summer."

"They must be getting ready for hibernation *soon* then, I expect!" Jennifer said, as she zipped her windbreaker against the bone-chilling wind. "Judging at least by the plummeting temperature."

"Yes, in fact I hope we're not too late to harvest our seeds. Normally, bristlecone seeds mature in late September, and their cones open in early October."

"We better get a move on then—what exactly are we looking for?"

Rick paused and looked around. There were scores of trees dotting the hillside, spaced roughly twenty feet apart. But he knew the oldest ones would have carved out a little more space for themselves on the slopes most exposed to the wind. All around him were weathered old trees, but he was looking for something different—something special. Surely Methuselah would stand out in some way, he thought. His eyes traced further up the hillside, where he saw a small stand of golden trees with spindly arms shining in the late afternoon sun.

"There!" he pointed. *"That's* what we're looking for!"

As they scrambled up the hard scrappy talus, they came upon a collection of trees that looked more dead than alive. Each tree had been blasted by the heavy winds into a tangle of gnarled and twisted limbs, with barely any sign of vegetation.

"These trees can't really be *alive*, can they?" Jennifer asked incredulously. "There's hardly anything growing on them!"

"That's the beauty—and the secret—of them. They may look more dead than alive, but as long they have any needles growing, I assure you, they are very much alive."

Jennifer examined one more closely. "Why is so much of it dead?"

"Unlike animals, who *replace* cells, plants *add* cells. Consequently, they're always growing—until their size exceeds the ability of the surrounding soil to sustain their need for water and nutrients. But this growth only occurs in one part of the plant called the cambium, an extremely thin layer of meristematic tissue located just under the bark. New cells form on both sides of the cambium each season—those on the inside form the xylem, which conducts water and nutrients up from the roots; those on the outside make up the phloem, which transports sugars, amino acids, and hormones produced in the leaves."

"Not unlike the circulatory and endocrine systems of humans."

"Exactly. As the new cell layers form on the outside, those on the inside become redundant and turn into the dense, hard heartwood of the tree. When the forces of erosion or predation cause parts of the roots to die, so do those parts of the tree above the surface which is fed by those roots. Eventually wind and erosion wears away the dead bark and the underlying sapwood to expose its heartwood. These old guys obviously have a lot of wind and erosion working away at their roots and branches, given the thin porous soil they've found themselves in. Sometimes the only thing sustaining these trees is a thin sliver of bark and healthy sapwood running up one side, supporting a single living branch."

"The ultimate manifestation of Nietzsche's assertion: 'That which doesn't kill me makes me stronger,'" Jennifer mused. "So which one of these tough old buggers do you think might be Methuselah?"

Rick walked through the small, aromatic grove slowly, carefully appraising each tree. He was looking not only at the thickness of its trunk and the density of needles on its branches, but also the porousness of the soil, and the exposure of its roots to the desiccating winds. He knew the oldest and most hardy one would likely stand in the most inhospitable place, showing the most outward sign of wear.

Near the end of the stand, as if bowing in reverence, the grove opened outward revealing a lone tree in a clearing, completely stripped of bark, on slightly higher ground than all the rest. Its exposed wood had been sun-bleached and sand-blasted over the ages to a polished and gleaming caramel color, and it stood defiantly straight in a stout symmetrical pyramid, roughly fifteen feet high. Its branches had been sculpted by the strong westerly winds into a perfect corkscrew spiral, and it appeared to be bereft of any foliage. But as Rick grew closer, he noticed a tuft of green sprouting on its back side.

"This one! This must surely be Methuselah!"

"How can you know?" asked Jennifer. "It's not so different from the others."

"Look at the base of its trunk—it's roughly four feet wide, wouldn't you say?"

"Yes, I suppose…"

"That's considerably thicker than the other ones we've seen so far. And at an average growth rate of one inch per century, that equates almost precisely to the age of the tree determined by Dr. Schulman from his original core sample: five thousand years!"

"But I don't see any sign of *life*—maybe it's completely dead?"

"Look on the leeward side of the tree. See—a good, healthy-looking branch, with *cones*!!"

"You've got to be kidding me. I can't believe this withered old thing has still got the ability to reproduce."

"Remember—plants keep adding cells, instead of replacing them as we humans do. Our internal clocks normally stop replacing cells after we've fulfilled our biological duty to raise young, but as long as these specimens continue to be fed and not succumb to fire, wind, or predation, they're always growing and reproducing. The simple fact that this tree has survived so long means nature wants him to keep producing more hardy plants just like him."

'Speaking of *fire*—how do these trees manage to avoid incineration? They appear defenseless against a lightning strike or a forest fire."

"That's yet another one of their amazing evolutionary adaptations. They are made of an extremely dense, resinous wood that is highly resistant to fire—as well as insects, rot-causing fungus, and bacteria-causing disease. Plus, the rocky limestone groundcover makes it almost impossible for fire to spread from one tree to another. Even the trees' *needles* have adapted an effective fire-fighting strategy: they last up to forty years, four times longer than other pines, so there's rarely any dead ones on the ground to fuel a fire." Rick noticed a thin tendril of smoke rising behind the crest of a hill in the distance.

"I suspect the only danger these hardy old trees have of burning is from people who might chop them down for firewood. Their dry, dense wood would make ideal fuel for woodstoves or fireplaces."

"Who would ever want to live in this God-forsaken place? There's nothing up here but rocks and rodents!"

"Well, you have to admit, the view is pretty spectacular, and it's a great place to come if you want to get away from the hustle and bustle of the city. The air is clean, the sun is shining, and you can actually hear yourself think. I wouldn't mind having a cabin up here myself."

"I'm afraid you'd have to keep these whispering trees and sleepy marmots for company, Rick—it isn't the kind of place I'd want to visit very often." Jennifer noticed the twisted shadows of the gnarled old trees lengthening ominously around her in the late afternoon sun. "I actually find it a little *creepy*—would you mind terribly if we gathered those cones now?"

"Of course. Let's see if we can find a good ripe one."

"What are we looking for, exactly?"

"There should be two different types of cones. The smaller staminate cones are only about a half inch long, and they provide the pollen, or sperm. Most of them will likely have already matured and fallen off the tree. The female ovulate cones are quite a bit larger—roughly three to four inches, with prickly edges. We're looking for one that has its scales opened like a venetian blind. If you look carefully, you should be able to see some wing-shaped seeds on the inside surface of the scales, near the center of the cone."

Jennifer saw a large cone on the underside of the branch and crawled closer. "Yes, I see them. Hard to imagine how the pollen finds its way out of those male cones into these tiny little spaces in the female cones!"

"It's all done by wind, and random chance. As you can see, there's plenty of breeze at these high elevations—and the pollen grains have little air sacs that act like balloons to help keep them afloat before they hit the ground. Plus, the female cones emit a type of fluid that helps to snare the pollen when it lands anywhere near it."

"Not entirely unlike the dance of human copulation. No wonder we're so quick to anthropomorphize them," Jennifer said. "What's the chance that this antediluvian artifact will match his own pollen with the ovulate seeds on the same tree?"

"There's no guarantee that the female seed doesn't mate with pollen drifting over from another tree. But now that you mention it, let's bring some male cones back too, and I'll conduct some DNA tests to see if we got lucky. Plus, just to be safe, I'm going to snip a tiny shoot from the live branch and see if I can graft the buds onto some seedling root stock back home to produce a clone."

"I feel like a *thief* taking anything off this relic," Jennifer said, as she uncomfortably plucked the prickly cone from the protesting branch. "Will he be able to withstand it?"

"Don't worry, the cones would fall off soon enough with or without our help," Rick said, as he carefully placed each harvested item in a ziplock plastic bag, then stowed them in a specially prepared cooler he'd brought to protect them for their long journey back to his New York arboretum. "It's the only way Methuselah can ensure the propagation of his lineage: he's got to find some kind of earthbound source to germinate. And besides—something tells me if he doesn't manage to sow his oats this fall, he'll have plenty more years to keep practicing!"

Twenty-four

The Endogen corporate campus sat shrouded in fog late Saturday evening, as acres of manicured lawns surrounding the estate vented their stored geothermic heat into the cool autumn air. The company's manufacturing operations, operating two shifts a day, seven days per week, ceased operation at precisely eleven p.m., and the parking lot had quickly emptied of all non-essential personnel. All that remained on campus was a small contingent of security guards, who patrolled the grounds and monitored activity in and around the many buildings scattered about the estate. Now the normally busy campus was eerily silent, and almost deserted.

The research and manufacturing operations of Endogen were set back from the gleaming façade of executive offices near the front of the property, in a series of sprawling low-rise buildings covering almost twenty acres. This was where the ubiquitous Endopatches were made, with more than ten thousand employees dedicated to producing nearly a billion patches a day. Every hypophysectomized juvenile on earth wore an Endogen patch that over the course of seven days carefully metered the flow of nine essential hormones normally produced by the now-excised pituitary, after which the patch had to be vigilantly replaced with a new one.

The manufacture and formulation of this product was an exceedingly complicated operation, given that each of its embedded hormones controlled a different metabolic process. Both the quantity and flow of these chemicals had to be precisely controlled in order to ensure the healthy operation of every bodily function. Too much, or too little, of any one chemical element could upset the delicate balance of the endocrine system and lead to immediate and serious complications, or even death.

Mimicking the operation of the pituitary was not an easy job. This incredibly tiny gland, taking direct instructions from the hypothalamus in the lower frontal lobe of the brain next to the cerebellum, regulated everything from hunger and thirst to reproduction and sex drive. Each function was controlled by a separate chemical with a dedicated purpose: growth hormone regulated the pace of cell reproduction; corticotropin controlled glucose utilization and fat metabolism; lipotropin stimulated melanocytes to produce skin pigment; thyrotropin regulated cell metabolism in conjunction with the thyroid; prolactin stimulated milk production and regulated libido; follicle-stimulating hormone controlled egg and sperm production; luteinizing hormone stimulated ovulation in females and testosterone production in males; oxytocin triggered contractions during labor and orgasm; vasopressin regulated water retention and kidney function. All of these essential chemicals were harnessed within a two-inch-square patch of plastic and polymers that reliably and steadily delivered the required dose transdermally through the skin—directly into the bloodstream.

The production of these hormone patches was vertically integrated at Endogen, meaning they produced every component of the product on site. The patch itself was comprised of four components. The external polyethylene backing acted as barrier against intrusion from dust and dirt, while also allowing the skin to breathe by passing moisture and oxygen up from the surface. Directly underneath the backing was the reservoir of synthesized pituitary hormones, in sufficient quantity to last a little over a week. Embedded within the solution was an adhesive composed of acrylic polymers, which held the patch securely to the surface of the skin. A thin microporous vinyl-acetate membrane was placed over the reservoir, to control the flow-through rate of hormones into the sub-dermal capillaries. The final layer was a polyester liner, which protected the product during shipment, and was removed just prior to patch application.

The quantity of hormones in the patch reservoir was measured and metered to deliver just enough of each vital biochemical to maintain every juvenile at the physiological state of a pre-pubescent eleven-year-old, irrespective of their chronological age. The balance and flow of each hormone had long ago been tested and perfected to keep each individual in a healthy and static equilibrium, with only slight variation according to gender. Females received higher doses of estrogen and progesterone, and males were administered slightly higher doses of testosterone. Otherwise, the patch formulations were very similar, and precisely controlled to within six sigma tolerances, meaning the variances of the formula were contained to within six standard deviations of the mean—discrepancies of less than two parts per billion.

Originally, the hormones embedded in the patch were distilled from the ground-up endocrine organs and urine of animals such as pigs and horses, but as the scale of the hypophysectomy program grew worldwide, advances in the field of molecular biology enabled the synthesis of most human hormones from plant sources. The active component of synthesized hormones in the patch was diluted to a concentration of less than one tenth, in a solvent of sugar, amino acids, and other buffers, which were designed to provide the solution with the proper stability, consistency, and pH balance. Also added to the solution in small quantities were glycerine excipients to enhance and accelerate the penetration of the solution through the thick layer of dead epidermal cells on the surface of the skin. A significant surplus of the active ingredient was placed in the reservoir to keep the concentration gradient at the required levels for proper absorption over the course of a full week. Since these active ingredients had low molecular weight, they acted at very low dosages, measured in micrograms per day;

consequently, the cost of the unused drug remaining in the patch at the end of the week was relatively minor.

Of these various patch components, by far the most important and sensitive from a quality control perspective was the composition of drugs in the reservoir. Each of the nine separate hormones had to be precisely measured and mixed in a specified ratio in order to accurately duplicate plasma levels naturally produced by the human body. Similarly, the buffers, excipients, and suspension solvents were measured and blended with the active ingredients in specific quantities at defined temperatures for a specified period of time in order to achieve the necessary consistency and pH balance. The mixing was done in two gigantic stainless steel tanks, each containing over ten thousand gallons of product—one for males, and one for females. Above each of the tanks, in hermetically sealed clean rooms, technicians wearing full-body sterile jumpsuits dispensed each of the necessary ingredients from carefully marked drums into designated feed tubes.

After each batch of solution was mixed, blended, heated, and cooled to the necessary consistency, random samples were taken and measured to ensure all product specifications were within defined tolerances. The solution from each tank was then piped to two separate production lines, where the gelatinous final product was poured and rolled onto long rolls of backing film, followed by the application of the microporous membrane and the protective liner. The four-layer film was then cut into perfect two inch square patches, after which the "*e*" symbol, expiration date, and lot number was stamped onto the backing layer. Finally, the individual patches were sealed in red or blue foil packages to identify gender. Every aspect of the production from start to finish was tightly controlled and monitored to ensure exacting quality standards and to prevent intervention from unauthorized sources.

But on this tranquil Saturday evening, there was one individual in the production facility who didn't belong—someone who had every intention of disrupting the smoothly running and carefully engineered process. He had planned an act of sabotage that would push the shell-shocked company, already teetering close to the edge since the surprise U.N. announcement two weeks ago, over the precipice. He knew the best way to hurt Endogen was to strike the company at its most vital and vulnerable source: by rendering its flagship Endopatch impotent. Although he didn't work in the production department, the employee knew enough about the company's operations to gain access to restricted sites, and he had done his homework very thoroughly. He had studied every possible means for tampering with the patch and carefully chosen the surest approach—one that would not only guarantee maximum disruption of the patch's effects, but would also minimize any chance of connecting him with the crime.

The saboteur knew that Fick's law of diffusion essentially limited his options to three choices. This rule of transdermal fluid dynamics stated that the amount of solution transported through the skin was a function of the total surface area of skin exposed to the active ingredient, the permeability of the drug at the interface with the skin, and the concentration gradient of the solution as it passed through the epidermis. Changing the *size* of the patch was not feasible, not only because it would be immediately noticeable to both the user as well as quality control personnel at the plant, but because it would also necessitate changes to the configuration of the film cutting equipment, which was simply not practical. The second method for disrupting the efficacy of the patch would necessitate changing the *transfer rate* of the drug across the microporous membrane, but this would require changing the production parameters for the porosity of the membrane, which would be equally difficult to accomplish technically.

That left only one practical way to disrupt the patch's effectiveness: changing the composition of hormones in the mix. But this would require access to the clean room where these materials were blended, and that part of the facility was closely monitored twenty-four hours a day behind a series of bio-access coded locked doors that would be virtually impossible to circumvent. At first pass, it appeared to the saboteur to be a hopeless task to tamper with the patch in a large enough scale to meet his goals, especially one that would ensure he couldn't be traced back to the act. After much aborted planning, he finally realized it wasn't necessary to change the quantity of hormones in the patch to disrupt their operation, only the relative *proportion* in the mix. This could be accomplished by adjusting the ratio of each of the nine hormones, or more simply, by changing the *concentration* of these hormones in the blend. Since the concentration of active ingredients in the solution was fixed at a relatively low level—ten percent—it would therefore be fairly easy to throw off the endocrine balance and disrupt the patch user's metabolism simply by changing the amount of *solvent* in the solution.

But how, he thought, could he accomplish this change without gaining access to the clean room, or coercing the technicians pouring the ingredients from the storage drums into the main blending tank? And how could he prevent the subsequent change in formula composition from being detected by the fastidious quality control personnel after completion of the batch? After days of deliberation, it finally struck him: what if he could somehow *trick* the clean room technicians into putting the wrong ingredients into the blending tank? They probably didn't pay much attention to what the contents of each drum looked like; their job was simply to empty the designated material into the feeder chute from the appropriately labeled containers. It was the job of quality control personnel to ensure that the proper ingredients were loaded into the drums, and that the final product emerging from the mixing tanks had the right composition and specifications. This last issue was a more difficult challenge—but not one the right amount of money couldn't fix.

This raised one final dilemma for the saboteur: each batch called for a specified number of drums of each ingredient type, and the clean room technicians undoubtedly kept track of how many of each type of drum were added to the mix. That meant the only way to disrupt the final mix percentage would necessitate *substituting* the drums somehow—or substituting their contents. But this would require opening the tightly-sealed steel drums or moving the five hundred pound containers in such a way that it would not draw the attention of the patrolling guards or video cameras in the room where they were stored. Suddenly, in a flash, it came to him: all he had to do was substitute the *labels* on the drums to accomplish his goal. If he could surreptitiously exchange the labels on some of the solvent containers with one or more of the nine hormone ingredients, this would quickly and dramatically increase the dilution percentage of hormones in the mix—both by adding more hormones and by simultaneously reducing the amount of solvent. And this could be carried out in the far less carefully guarded *storage* room for the drums!

The only question now was how he could get into the storage room without drawing attention, and leave without detection by the security cameras. Fortunately, his position at Endogen afforded him access to this part of the plant for periodic meetings with production personnel, and his presence during normal business hours would not draw suspicion. Over the course of the last week on his passes to and from the area, he had carefully scoped the sight-lines of all security cameras, investigated the patrol patterns in and around the facility, and taken high-resolution photos of the labels on each type of drum. Then he fastidiously reproduced exact replicas of the labels specifying the ingredients contained within each drum, being careful to use the same size, color and texture of paper. In final preparation, after arranging an impromptu meeting with a shipping supervisor earlier in the day, he had placed a thin transparent wedge at the bottom of the rear access door to the storage room to ensure it would be left ajar just enough to break the security lock, so that he wouldn't need to use his access card for entry later that evening.

At precisely twelve midnight, just as the security staff were changing shifts and temporarily suspending patrols, he snapped on skin-colored surgical gloves so as not to leave behind any fingerprints, and silently snuck through the unlocked back door. At this point, even if he were noticed, he could concoct a plausible story about staying late to inspect some records or materials in conjunction with an earlier meeting. The critical matter now was not to be noticed while changing the labels on the drums, and to ensure no cameras picked up his movements after the act was completed. He quickly glanced up to the southwest corner of the storage room ceiling and confirmed that the camera was pointed in the direction of the main access gate. With nobody else in sight, he quickly slipped behind a tall stack of barrels. Trying to breathe slowly and deeply so as not to make any undue noise, all he could hear was the sound of his own heart pounding in his chest.

After taking a few moments to calm down, he slowly set about studying the labels on each of the storage drums. His plan was simply to replace the labels for some of the hormone drums with the labels from the solvent drums. This way, he hoped the loading technicians would unknowingly add more active ingredients to the mix and less inactive ingredients. He had checked which hormones looked most similar to the inert solvents and other buffers used in the mix, and he planned his substitutions so as to minimize any risk of clean room technicians identifying changes during the blending process. He also knew which hormones were the most volatile, and which would be likely to do the most damage. He didn't care who, or how many, people would be harmed—he simply wanted to ensure a widespread and serious reaction. Later in the week, he would ascertain the lot number of the batches produced using these drums in order to avoid using the tainted product himself.

But just as he began gently tearing off the adhesive liner for the first label, he heard the telltale beep of a security door being card-swiped from the opposite side of the room and he quickly scrambled to a dark corner where he crouched low in the shadows. Moments later, he heard the ominous sound of heavy boots on the concrete floor moving toward his location. All types of disastrous scenarios suddenly raced through his mind. Had he been noticed by one of the security cameras? Had he missed its location in one in his previous passes scoping out the room? Had the access door sent an electronic alarm when he opened it earlier? It would be very hard to explain his presence in this part of the room at this time of the day, especially since he was unannounced and had no official business on the docket. More importantly, how would he explain the many loose drum labels he was carrying? He quickly stashed the labels in a narrow space between two drums, and began constructing a tenuous alibi: he had come at the end of the production shift to meet a shipping supervisor and finding him gone, had decided to take an informal inventory of materials before leaving after a long day.

Fortunately, he wouldn't need to test his story. The guard's footsteps moved away from him as quickly as they had come, and began receding into the distance. Apparently, this was simply a routine inspection by the guard—one whose schedule had somehow escaped his earlier scrutiny. After hearing another beep followed by the opening and closing sound of the door, he waited a number of minutes in complete silence. He dared not even breathe, as he strained to listen to ensure no one else was in the room. After peering through a thin opening in the stacked barrels to confirm he was alone, he quickly set back to work. Retrieving the labels he had hastily stored between the barrels, he blew away the rusty dust and smoothed their wrinkled edges against his body. He had brought with him twenty new labels, and although still shaking from the unexpected intrusion, he set about affixing each label on the indicated drums, being careful to ensure the new labels precisely covered up the underlying original ones. His last destructive step, designed to expedite and accelerate the contamination process, was to exchange the labels of three buffer drums with those of the drums containing the permeation-enhancing excipients. There could be no chance that this effort didn't produce the intended consequences—for the saboteur, the stakes were simply too high.

Later that evening, comfortably ensconced in his apartment overlooking the Hudson River, he threw his surgical gloves and shoes in the building's incinerator to remove any chance of tracing his body to the scene. Lying back on his sofa and enjoying the view of the placid harbor, he took a moment to reflect on how well his plan had come to fruition—and how soon its effects would be noticed.

Twenty-five

As he had expected, Calvin was released from jail on his own recognizance after his arraignment before a magistrate on Thursday. Upon consulting with his court-appointed lawyer and pleading not guilty to charges of disturbing the peace and threatening a police officer, the judge was satisfied he was not a flight risk in view of the fact his son was being held in protective custody. Calvin simply had to pledge not to make any attempts to contact Elias other than through official channels, and to reappear for trial at a future date to be determined. Now, three days later, back in the sanctity of his Garden of Eden church, he was preparing to deliver a new sermon—one with a decidedly different tone.

Contrary to his promises before the judge, Calvin had no intention of acquiescing on the hypophysectomy issue, and in fact had resolved to enlist the help of his congregation in stepping up pressure on the authorities. This latest development with Elias amounted to a declaration of war—and now it was personal. He was more determined than ever to use every resource at his disposal to fight the system and return his son and the rest of the world to its natural order. As he watched his congregation obediently stride into his church on Sunday morning like so many bees returning to their hive, he took a minute to survey the teeming assembly. *Now* was the time, he decided, to stir them from their complacency, and mobilize for a new assault against the enemy. He was no longer content to be the apologist for his colony. Calvin believed they were just as guilty of blasphemy as any other juvenile, and that some day they would all pay the same ultimate price for yielding to the narcissistic temptation of immortality. Today, he would show them the error of their ways, and a new path to salvation.

"Children of God—" he began, sweeping his outstretched arms over the assembly, "you have all *sinned*."

Pausing for several seconds to allow his words to sink in, he shifted his penetrating gaze from one surprised congregant to another.

"You have forgotten what it means to serve your master, for you have taken for granted what He has given, and surrendered to those temptations which He expressly forbade.

"How many of you even *know* what it means to sin?" he asked angrily.

Everyone in the assembly knew better than to answer his rhetorical question.

"In his covenant with Moses on the holy temple of Mount Horeb, the Lord laid down the laws by which everyone should live, in the form of the Ten Commandments. Who here can honestly say that he faithfully obeys each of these laws?" Calvin demanded, his voice beginning to rise in intensity.

No one dared utter a sound. Calvin nodded knowingly.

"Apparently, you have forgotten your contract with the Lord—or chosen to ignore it. Today, it has fallen upon me to remind you of these universal laws, and the consequences for disobedience. Listen as I count down these Commandments, and you will see what happens to those who sin.

"Number *Ten*," Calvin boomed, his commanding voice resonating off the arched ceiling as if delivered from an otherworldly source, "thou shalt not covet thy neighbor's goods. Yet how many of you lust after material things you do not possess? One need only witness the surfeit of public advertisements all about this city to see how much greed drives humankind. When God created Adam and Eve, he provided everything they could ever want—a perfect paradise, loving companionship, and a limitless future raising a devoted family—but when they became greedy, they lost their immortality. And so shall you."

Calvin paused once again for dramatic effect as silence filled the chamber.

"*Nine*," he continued, "thou shalt not covet thy neighbor's wife. Not only have you forsaken the sacred institution of marriage, the egregious and widespread popularity of obscene pornography belies your unbridled lust and depravity. God slew Onan for spilling his seed, and so He will strike all others who practice self-abuse."

Some members of the assembly shifted uncomfortably in their pews.

"Number *Eight*." Each intonation grew subtly louder, bouncing off the rafters and echoing throughout the cathedral. "Thou shalt not bear false witness. Is there anyone here who has not lied or concealed something through deceit or secrecy? In the trial of Jesus, many bore false witness against Him, which precipitated his death. Only by confessing your transgressions and asking forgiveness from your Lord or his proxy, can you be cleansed of your shame."

Calvin had consciously expropriated from the Catholic faith the perfect weapon of psychological control over his congregation: requiring confession with their cleric in order to receive forgiveness and absolution. He also knew that by establishing impossible standards of conduct, his followers would always be dependent on their spiritual leader for salvation.

"*Seven*," he resumed. "Thou shalt not steal. Yet you have stolen that which is most precious to your maker. The Lord created mankind in his own perfect image, and by submitting to the mutilation of your body, you are debasing God Himself. You cannot reclaim that which has been taken from you—you can only prevent *others* from the same fate."

Calvin had considered carefully how he would entice his assembly to rise up in a new, brazen attack on the enemy. The setup had begun. He would finish with a call to arms.

"*Six*. Thou shalt not commit adultery. God made Eve from the flesh of Adam, and in so doing signified that forever more man be united to his wife as one. By rejecting the sanctity of marriage and embracing the notion of free love, you have all sinned. In the book of Deuteronomy, we saw that God ordered adulterers be stoned to death. For your indiscriminate behavior, so shall the Lord indiscriminately smite thee."

Calvin carefully appraised his congregation's mood as they sat in stunned silence. Like every effective commander, he knew the best way to build more obedient soldiers was to first strip away their false pretenses.

"*Five*," he railed. "Thou shalt not kill. But you killed a living part of your very *selves* when you guillotined the very organ which gives you life, and which gives others life. The Lord asked you to be fruitful and multiply, but by this act you've willingly surrendered your God-given ability to reproduce. In this way, you've shown you don't need God any more—and soon he will show He no longer needs you."

Calvin could see his parishioners becoming increasingly restless and beginning to stir in their seats. He sensed they were nearing the breaking point.

"*Four!*" he declared, picking up his pace. "Honor thy mother and father. Yet by your selfish act of self-abasement, you've disrespected your parents and sent them into the afterlife without you. You have sought that which was long ago sacrificed to God: everlasting life. Instead, your actions will only separate you from your loved ones, while you suffer eternal damnation in *Hell*."

A few anguished murmurs grew from the assembly.

"*Three*," Calvin continued. "Keep the Sabbath day holy. This means every seventh day you must worship the Lord and refrain from any type of labor. How many of you work from home or operate a business, and stay open on Sunday? This day was meant to be devoted to prayer and relaxation of the mind and body. God accepts no half-measures, and if you want acceptance into His dominion, neither shall you."

"Amen," uttered a few parishioners.

"Number *Two*," he raged, recognizing the critical mass building among his assembly. "Thou shalt not take the name of the Lord your God in vain. You must speak reverentially of the Lord, respect His name, and respect all your oaths to Him. It is not enough to have good intentions—you must *act* in accordance with the Lord's wishes in order to show true respect. This means abiding by all of His Commandments and His instructions. For there is only one *true* and ultimate authority."

"Hallelujah!" many cried form the pews.

Calvin could see the assembly hanging on his every word, begging him for deliverance.

"Which brings us to the *first* and final commandment: I am the Lord thy God, and thou shalt have no other gods before me."

It was no accident that Calvin spoke in the first person for this final directive—he wanted to make it clear that he alone was vested with divine authority and that only *he* could provide legitimate guidance and instruction for his flock.

"Yet you have abandoned your God for worship on the altar of narcissism. Believing that medical science alone can save you, you've revoked your acceptance of the omnipotent power. You forget who made you—and who can *save* you.

Calvin paused for an uncomfortably long moment.

"You have *failed* your God!!" he suddenly thundered, his voice reverberating through the pews, literally shaking his parishioners.

"And unless you take drastic action, *He* will fail you. For your days on this earth are numbered, but your days in the afterlife are not. There is only One who can determine how you will spend them."

As if on cue, one parishioner called out meekly. "Tell us father, what we can do to save ourselves?"

"Yes, yes!" More cries slowly grew from the assembly, until they cascaded into a cacophony—filling the chamber with the collective din of fearful congregants, beseeching their pastor for salvation.

Calvin held up his berobed arms, and immediately a hush fell over the room.

"Do not fear, my children. God wished for you to live forever in His Kingdom, and so shall it be. All He asks is that you lead a righteous life in observance of these commandments, and that you respect His authority. I will take your confessions, and absolution for your sins shall be granted if you pray forgiveness and promise to amend your ways."

Calvin paused.

"But your master needs something *else* from you to demonstrate your contrition and obedience."

"Tell us!" his parishioners cried out. "Tell us, father!!"

For the galvanized congregation, at this moment there was virtually no separation between God in heaven and his earthly avatar standing before them. In their eyes, Calvin *was* God—and they were ready to follow his every commandment.

Calvin knew exactly where he wanted to lead them.

"The serpent beckons once more in our Garden of Eden, and Satan has once again gained the upper hand. One of our very *own* has been taken from us, and he is threatened by the forces of evil. Yes, *Elias* needs your help to save his soul. We need to take him back from the devil—and I need your help. Are you going to stand by and allow another of your brethren be butchered and enslaved by the forces of darkness?!"

"No!" came a united roar from the assembly.

"Elias is pure—he is without sin," someone shouted.

"We will save him!" exclaimed another.

The congregation was standing now, chanting and stomping their feet in unison on the cold stone floor of the shaking chapel.

As Calvin regarded his assembly with pious satisfaction, he caught the eye of another member, standing perfectly still in the side shadows of the transept. A silent nod between them signaled their battle had formally begun.

Twenty-six

Tuesday morning outside the United Nations headquarters on First Avenue was crisp and chilly, as the one hundred and ninety-two flags of its member-nations fluttered noisily in the late autumn breeze. Walking south along the avenue on route to a meeting with Tian Yin, Rick tried to identify each of the ensigns bordering the long strip of international property, starting with Afghanistan at 48th street and ending with Zimbabwe at 42nd street. After recognizing each flag up to Guinea's, he turned east and headed into the main entrance of the compound under the domed General Assembly Hall.

Upon returning from his long weekend exploring the alpine hinterlands of California, Rick felt recharged and ready to face another busy week in the bustling city. But to his surprise, he'd had a message waiting for him from Tian asking if he could meet with her urgently. After their last meeting only a few weeks ago, everything seemed to be going smoothly, and other than some concerns about her ailing father, Tian had sounded fairly upbeat. Rick wondered if she was calling him for medical consultation, or if it had something to do with the scheduled switch to the international outsourcing of hormone patch production.

As he entered the soaring orbital lobby, bright rays of sunlight streamed in from the giant stained glass window on the east wall, designed by Marc Chagall. Titled "Kiss of Peace", the brilliant blue panel reflected various symbols of love and harmony, with the centerpiece depicting a young child kissed by the face of an angel. Crossing the white polished floor of the atrium, Rick stopped briefly to track the movement of the famous Foucault Pendulum, swinging rhythmically on a gold-plated sphere suspended from the seventy-foot ceiling. Providing visual proof that the earth rotates around its axis, the plane of the ball appeared to shift slowly clockwise about eight degrees every hour, as it swung inches above a large orbital ring. Following Newton's first law of motion, the ball itself actually moved in a fixed plane—it was in fact the table *beneath* it that was moving, together with the building attached to the rotating earth.

All is well and proper with the world for another day, Rick affirmed, before headed toward the elevators.

At the thirty-ninth floor, Rick announced himself to Tian's secretary, and she directed him into the Secretary-General's office.

"Good morning, Madame Secretary," he announced, clasping her hand warmly when they met. "You look as lovely as ever."

"It's good to see you again, Rick," Tian said, her eyes lighting up as she kissed her friend on the cheek. "It always seems so long between our meetings."

"Perhaps that's a good sign that everything is working as planned," Rick mused.

"Well, you know how I feel about resting on your laurels," Tian said, referring as much to Rick's continued professional demeanor as to the frequently guarded attitude of her multinational constituents. "Complacency leads to apostasy."

"In my world we have another saying: a rolling stone gathers no moss," Rick affirmed, extending the metaphor with his favorite botanical reference.

"Speaking of which—it looks like *you've* been on the move. You've got some fresh color in your face."

"I just came back from an alpine getaway to a remote region of California. I'm not sure if you're seeing more sunburn or windburn!"

"That sounds like an intriguing place for you to take vacation." Tian said, wondering if the color in Rick's face might also be from some *other* stimulus. "What was the attraction?"

"Mostly, the trip was to conduct some research and collect some new material for my home arboretum. I've cultivated an interest in bonsai over the years, and there was one particular species I wanted to add to my collection."

"I didn't know you were interested in the art of bonsai. Did you know the word originally came from the Chinese word 'pentsai'? In China, trees have long had a spiritual symbolism and were considered to be the link between heaven and earth. For many centuries, it was customary to plant long-lived trees on graves to strengthen the soul of the departed, and to save the body from corruption."

"I didn't know that," Rick admitted. "That's quite fascinating."

"I'd love to see your collection sometime."

"I'll bring one of my special pieces for your office the next time I see you."

"I'd like that," Tian said, disheartened that once again Rick had rejected her advances.

"What's on your mind today?" Rick asked. "Your message had a tone of alarm."

"Actually, I'm becoming concerned by the increase in protests that I've seen around the city pertaining to the Global Longevity Initiative. I'm not sure I like the pattern."

"I wouldn't worry unnecessarily about it, Tian," Rick suggested. "From my experience, these protests seem to be contained to a relatively minor group of religious zealots operating here in Manhattan."

"Normally, I'd agree. But yesterday there was a larger, much more boisterous band set up outside our main entrance, and they wouldn't even let me pass until I called for security. I found it quite disconcerting."

Rick suddenly remembered the second message he'd received upon returning to New York—from Mount Sinai's Chief of Staff.

"Well if it's the same group I've encountered, I think they're fairly harmless. Except for their leader, Calvin James.

He may be especially volatile, in view of the fact that his son is scheduled for a hypophysectomy later this week."

"Yes, he can be frightening at the best of times. Thankfully, I didn't see him this time."

"Are you worried about anything in particular?" Rick asked.

"Well, maybe it's nothing, but I noticed the signs the protestors were carrying and the chants they were shouting were more strident and threatening than usual."

"What did they say?"

"Some of the signs read: *'Our day of reckoning has come!'* and *'We will take back our children!'*"

"That doesn't sound so different from their typical modus operandus," Rick suggested.

"I think it's more a matter of *tone*," Tian said. "It used to be their slogans were more passive and critical, with words like 'Blasphemy' and 'Abomination'. But now they've changed to a more active form—making actual threats."

"I still think they're too small a group for you to worry about. I'm sure the U.N. security forces can keep them in check. There's always going to be a fringe element that objects to any change in the status quo."

"Maybe, but all the same, I wanted you to be more aware of the threat and take appropriate precautions."

"You're not worried about *me*?" Rick asked.

"Well you and I are pretty much the public face of this program. I just think we should be more careful, especially with this unstable lunatic running around. And now he's got all the more reason to lash out. It wasn't so long ago that the world was ruled by testosterone-charged males—I remember what angry men are capable of."

"That's a good point, Tian. I'll put an extra watch at the hospital. In the meantime, it might be prudent to step up security here at the UN as well."

"I'll get on it right away."

"How've you been managing otherwise? How is your father doing?"

"As expected," Tian said sadly. "It's painful to be reminded of the natural cycle of life, with someone so close. Such a terrible thing to see your loved ones withering away, and know they will no longer be with you soon. It reminds one of the fragility of our existence, and how we should never take it for granted. I don't suppose you've made any breakthroughs on arresting or reversing the aging process with adults?"

"I think it's unlikely we'll ever find a way to *reverse* the normal aging process—only arrest it, for juveniles. All we can hope for is to find ways to extend the natural lifespans of individuals, using knowledge and experience gleaned from the natural world."

"Like with your bonsai trees?"

"In a way, yes. We still have a lot to learn from nature. After all, it's had billions of years to practice and perfect its design within its organic laboratory—we've only had a few thousand years or so."

"Well, you keep working on it, Rick—if anyone can figure it out, I'm sure you can."

"I'll keep you in the loop," Rick said, clasping Tian's hands as he stood to leave. "In the meantime, try to keep a wide berth from this unstable cult leader wherever you might encounter him—at least until I've completed his son's hypophysectomy this coming Friday."

"You too—stay safe," Tian said, as she reluctantly let Rick's hands slip away from hers. "I don't want to lose you."

As Rick stepped on the elevator and pressed the button for the main floor of the Secretariat building, he began to think about the operation he was scheduled to perform later this week. The hospital's Chief of Staff had informed him about the circumstances surrounding Elias's forceful removal from his home and the resistance his father had presented in defiance of the authorities. Elias had subsequently been interviewed by psychologists and clearly indicated that he wanted the hypophysectomy procedure, in spite of his father's objections. Rick could only imagine what Calvin must be thinking, but he believed that in such life and death circumstances that the child's health superseded the desires of the parent, much as in prior days when the wishes of children whose parents were on life support were subjugated to the living will of the patient. Walking through the lobby towards the exit, he resolved to take special precautions to protect himself and his charge from any unforeseen backlash. Just as he swung open the doors to the piazza, he was greeted by the loud roar of an angry crowd.

Great, Rick thought, immediately noticing the familiar placards of Calvin's Garden of Eden sect. *This will be the last time I'm taken by surprise by these zealots.*

He briefly considered ducking back into the security of the General Assembly Hall and using a rear exit, but after scanning the crowd and seeing no sign of Calvin, he decided to make a confident show and demonstrate he wouldn't be intimidated.

But the crowd was thicker and more unruly than he recalled last time, and about a third of the way through the thicket, he was recognized.

"Killer!" someone yelled, pointing at him.

"There he is!! The evil doctor!"

"Don't let him through! He's the one butchering our children!"

"Don't let him defile Elias! Stop him!"

Tian wasn't kidding. These guys really do mean business.

Apparently there would be no civil debate or respectful passage today. Rick resolved to get out of there quickly—by any means necessary. As he tried to force his way through the crowd, he was pushed and jostled, almost falling to his feet several times. One juvenile even tried to throw a fist at him. Only his quick reflexes avoided it landing squarely on his jaw.

What the hell is going on? Rick thought. *This isn't normal juvenile behavior—even for Calvin's belligerent sect.*

Redoubling his efforts, he lowered his center of gravity and bulldozed his way through the crowd until he burst through at the top of the flight of stairs. Scrambling down the steps, the group followed him like a swarm of angry hornets. He managed to quickly flag down a cab and jumped in.

As the taxi pulled away from the frenzied crowd and the UN complex quickly faded away in the distance, the last thing he noticed was the iconic sculpture by Fredrik Reutersward, titled 'Non-Violence'. Fashioned in the form of a gun with its barrel tied in a knot, Rick couldn't help wondering if it symbolized a newly polemic phase in an age-old conflict.

Twenty-seven

The dockyards of the Port Elizabeth Marine Terminal in Newark Bay were cloaked in mist Tuesday evening as a lone figure wearing a hooded jersey made his way toward a giant container ship parked at Pier 38, where longshoremen were untying its heavy mooring lines from the iron bollards on the jetty. Stopping at the bottom of the ship's gangway, he paused briefly to exchange a few words with a crewmember, and after furtively passing the sailor a thick envelope, he was quickly motioned onboard. The Panamax-designated vessel, designed to maximize size and capacity for passage through the Panama Canal, was almost a thousand feet long and carried five thousand city-bus-sized steel cargo containers stacked ten stories above the waterline. But the huge freighter would not be passing through the Isthmus of Panama on this trip; its next port of call was Algeciras, Spain—just across the Gibraltar Strait from Morocco.

The ship's manifest listed twenty-four crewmembers, in addition to eighty thousand tons of freight. The unregistered visitor would be holed up in cramped and noisy quarters below deck for the duration of the ten day journey across the Atlantic, carefully hidden from sight from the probing eyes of port authorities and other crewmen. But this stowaway didn't mind his uncomfortable temporary lodging, because very soon he would be relaxing in the sunny, open-air markets of central Morocco, then heading onto his final destination: the isolated resort of Tenerife, in the Canary Islands. He now had enough money to live a quiet life of comfortable leisure, or start up the independent business he'd long dreamed of operating: a charter boat company in the tropics. All that mattered was that he was far from New Jersey, where the law enforcement authorities would soon be looking for him.

As the senior quality control officer at Endogen, he had gone to extraordinary lengths to cover-up the tampering of hormone ingredients yesterday, and he knew that it wouldn't take long before the inevitable consequences of his actions would be making headlines around the world. His complicity in the nefarious act would mean serious repercussions for thousands—potentially millions—of patch users, and all eyes would have been on him to explain how such a significant defect got past his team's rigorous controls. But by the time the breach would be discovered, he would be thousands of miles away, safely ensconced in his newly adopted home country, sheltered from the international outcry and the daily grind of corporate politics. He'd paid a steep price to have his identity changed and his passport doctored, and he spoke enough Spanish to blend in with local population fairly quickly. All that remained for him to make a clean escape was the safe transit of this trans-oceanic freighter, then one final clandestine charter from the mainland to the islands.

Hearing the sound of two powerful tugboats maneuvering into position to nudge the container ship out of port, he propped up his feet for the long voyage to a new life on the other side of the world. As he opened his favorite historical novel about the medieval battle for Christianity in the Mediterranean—*Empires of the Sea*—he felt the lumbering vessel slowly lurch from its quayside berth.

Twenty-eight

After his recent run-in with the Garden of Eden sect at the U.N., Rick had contacted Mount Sinai's Chief of Staff and made arrangements to boost the hospital's security patrols and place their private force on heightened alert. He wasn't exactly sure what Calvin's group was up to, but he didn't like their aggressive new tone, and he wanted to make sure there would be no further escalation of tensions. His biggest concern was that the group might try to disrupt Elias's hypophysectomy operation scheduled for Friday, and Rick hoped the hospital would be able to keep further protests at bay, or at least maintain a secure perimeter around the facility. He believed that once Calvin saw his son was safe and healthy after the procedure was finished, he might finally accept the situation and return to the peaceful practice of his faith.

Now quietly resting at home in his townhouse on Tuesday evening, he decided the best way to unwind after the day's turmoil was to begin work on cultivating the Methuselah seeds that he and Jennifer had collected over the previous weekend. His first step upon returning from California had been to place the harvested items in his refrigerator in order to maintain the temperature and humidity conditions of their native habitat. Like any live organisms, these still viable appendages of the ancient tree had closely adapted to their native surroundings, and any abrupt change in external conditions might prove too great a shock for their sensitive biological systems to continue survival.

The art of bonsai was a painstaking and precarious craft, largely because it involved the replantation and cultivation of delicate organic material from its natural environment to a decidedly unnatural one. Trees normally had a great deal more space to spread their roots and crowns in the wild than they did in the limited confines of a tiny bonsai tray, and once they were transplanted to the artificial environment of an arboretum, they became entirely reliant on their human caretakers rather than the far more familiar patterns and rhythms of their natural ecosystem. Like any other domesticated species, bonsai trees were fully dependent on their horticultural hosts for the provision of food, water, oxygen, and sunlight. To complicate matters further, bonsai enthusiasts went to extraordinary measures to artificially restrict the growth and development of the normally tall and majestic plants, bending them into unnaturally twisted and stunted forms.

The first challenge for any bonsai cultivator was to persuade the captured seeds to germinate. In the natural lifecycle of Rick's harvested specimen, the initial phase of ontogenesis had already begun, when the floating pollen grains made contact with the ovulate seeds in the female cone. With the encouragement of a sticky fluid secreted from a tiny opening near the base of the ovule, the pollen grain spontaneously formed an elongated tube, which penetrated the canal and delivered its sperm to the egg. The subsequent fertilization produced a diploid zygote, after which the incipient embryo went into a period of suspended development over the ensuing long cold winter, awaiting environmental cues to begin germination in the more hospitable spring growing season.

How incredibly similar were the reproduction habits of humans and plants, Rick thought. *We're not so far removed from the rest of nature after all.*

Normally, the fertilized seed would lie dormant for six months or longer in the high elevations of the White Mountains, insulated by its hard coating in the protective shadows of its indigenous limestone rocks. But, as with all aspects of bonsai, there were various methods to accelerate this process through artificial means. The first step was a procedure called *scarification*, whereby the thick seed coat was thinned to make it more permeable to water and air, and to facilitate the release of its enclosed embryo. This would normally be a slow process directed by the natural movement of windswept sand and ice crystals across the barren high Sierra soil, but Rick could simulate and expedite this process by rubbing sandpaper across the seed coat until it became as thin as a sheet of paper.

Once the embryo was ready to plant itself in a hospitable growing medium, all it needed was an environmental cue to signal when it was nearing the time to start growing. In the natural landscape of the Inyo Forest, this would normally be supplied by the warming temperatures of spring, which caused the snow to melt and brought water to the seed. In this case however, Rick would have to replicate these conditions by immersing the newly thinned seed in a jar of distilled water, then storing it in his fridge overnight. Even then, however, the embryonic seed would be reluctant to emerge, since its internal biological clock had pre-programmed an additional period of dormancy, knowing the first snowmelt didn't always mean the end of winter. The final act in preparing the seed for germination was a process called *cold stratification*, where the seed was placed in layers, or strata, of a cool moist growing medium such as peat, to signal it would be safe to sprout in another thirty days or so.

Rick set out to work by first retrieving from his fridge the ziplock bag containing the large ovulate cone, then carefully removing the specimen from the bag. Peering inside the cone through its fanned scales, he could see ten to fifteen ovules still clinging in oval-shaped depressions to the undersides of their individual scales. Knowing the most viable seeds would be the larger ones attached to the scales near the middle of the cone, he reached inside with long needle-nosed pliers, and gently twisted one from side to side by the leading edge of its appended wing. Gradually, the seed and its attached integumen provided some play, until finally it shimmied free. As he performed this delicate operation, Rick's mind wandered again to Calvin and his band of followers. He'd been surprised by the newfound fervor and ferocity of the group he encountered at UN headquarters, and was perplexed by their intent. *What could one man and a small group of renegades ultimately hope to accomplish?*

Returning unsteadily to the task at hand, Rick removed five other large seeds clinging to the interior scales in the center of the cone. He examined each one to ensure there were no cuts or scars, then placed them all in a clear, water-filled bowl. Three of the seeds floated on the surface of the water, and the other three slowly sank to the bottom of the container. Knowing the floaters were likely unfertilized hollow gametophytes, he threw them away. After draining the water from the bowl, he donned surgical gloves and dried the remaining seeds with paper towels. Then he carefully filed down their seed coats with fine sandpaper until he could see the delicate white embryos through the translucent casings, and placed them back in the fridge in a beaker of distilled water.

Tomorrow, he would move the seeds from their baptismal pre-soak into the sterile moist peat bed to complete their embryonic development, then prepare them for final planting. When the seeds sprouted, Rick would send clippings to the genetics lab at Mount Sinai Hospital to see if the collected ovules were pollinated by Methuselah, or by another tree. But even if he were lucky enough to have found a seed self-pollinated by the old patriarch, he knew it wouldn't be a *true* clone, because the genes from the pollen and egg would have intermingled in a different sequence during the natural process of meiotic recombination. The only way to build a true clone of Methuselah would be to unite the fully developed diploid DNA from its collected *shoot* to the rootstock of another plant of the same species. To this end, Rick had conducted an online search of the various nurseries and bonsai clubs in the area to see if they had any bristlecone pine seedlings in good condition, and had picked one up in the afternoon that looked to be about ten to twenty years old. Standing only a few inches tall, it already had developed a craggy overcoat around its trunk, but appeared quite robust and healthy.

His first step in attempting to join the harvested shoot to the purchased seedling's rootstock was to ensure the meristematic ends of each component were properly exposed and bonded. Using a long fork, Rick began to carefully loosen and remove the soil around the base of the seedling, until he could begin to see its roots exposed. Delicately, he took a trowel and worked it around the inside perimeter of the pot to separate the caked-on soil at the edge, as he would a pie crust from its pan. Then he slowly pulled the seedling out of its pot and inspected the soil and roots for signs of root rot or insect infestation. Other than a natural coating of white mycelium fungus, which helped provide necessary water and nutrients to the roots, they appeared healthy and free of infestation. Rick gently shook off the remaining dirt clinging to its hanging appendages, then rinsed the roots under lukewarm water until they were completely bare and whitewashed.

Placing the entire plant on its side on a clean cutting board, he separated the thick central taproot, and cut it off about an inch from the distal end using a sterile surgical scalpel. Then, very slowly and delicately, he cut a tiny "v" shape into the center of the truncated root cap, exposing the fleshy apical meristem on the inside of the stem. Next, he removed the shoot that he and Jennifer had collected from the branch of Methuselah, and cut a tiny inverse v-shape from its clipped end. Rick couldn't help thinking how similar this process was to the cloning procedure with humans, where the DNA from a mature skin cell was inserted into a hollowed out egg cell. Merging the prepared ends of the root and its scion, being careful not to mash them together so firmly as to damage their sensitive meristematic tissue or their outer protective casings, he applied a small drop of organic grafting compound to seal the lesion around its circumference, then wound a thin layer of cellophane tape around the joint to seal in the moisture.

To complete the transformation of his nascent tree, he placed the tiny specimen into a shallow dish of moistened peat moss and crushed limestone, then sprinkled onto the growing medium a small amount of synthetic indoleacetic acid—a plant hormone used to stimulate the growth of the apical stem and facilitate new root generation. To help support the delicate juvenile organism from bending under the force of gravity, he wound a loose ring of electrical wire around the thin stem, and secured it to a sturdy post bolted to the base of the pot. His final act before turning in for the evening was to gently tie a thin insect net around the entire apparatus, then place it in his air conditioned greenhouse on the roof deck.

Let's hope the operation on Friday goes as smoothly as this one, Rick mused, as he turned out the lights and headed to bed.

Twenty-nine

Jennifer had been looking forward to this evening all week. Although she had enjoyed her trip to California with Rick, she'd found him a little too preoccupied with the clinical task of studying and collecting the local flora to satisfy her desire for meaningful bonding time. Tonight, she'd arranged for the two of them to go dancing, where she hoped to have some fun they could *both* enjoy. At nine-thirty p.m. her intercom buzzed, and the doorman announced Rick's arrival at her building.

"Send him up, Joe," Jennifer announced, as she checked herself one last time in the hallway mirror. She was wearing dark skinny jeans over black patent pumps, with a billowy purple and yellow patterned silk blouse. Her softly highlighted auburn hair fell gently over her shoulders, and smoky eye shadow completed her sexy and sophisticated look. Thirty seconds later, she heard two taps on the door.

"Hello, beautiful!" Rick announced, as she swung open the door and he swept her into his arms with a warm, passionate kiss.

"Hello yourself, handsome." Jennifer said, separating herself from his embrace long enough to appraise his attire. Under his unbuttoned overcoat, Rick was wearing navy flat-front trousers with square-toed Ferragamo shoes, and a tightly fitting striped sport shirt that hugged every inch of his well-formed torso.

"Mmm, I'll have some of that, please."

"That can be arranged," Rick said, moving forward and gently pressing his hips against hers, as he ran his fingers through her flowing hair.

"Later, tiger. We've got some dancing to do—remember?"

"Oh yeah. So where are you taking me?"

"That new club downtown where Eva and I went a few weeks ago, called the Hippodrome. Totally cool, and hip. After all that quiet solitude and communing with nature this past weekend, I'm ready to get down and kick up my heels up with some slightly more evolved life forms!"

"I'm up for that!" Rick agreed.

Twenty minutes later, the two emerged from the elevator on the forty-eighth floor of the Times Square Marriott to the booming sound of club music. Working their way to the reception desk, Jennifer announced herself to the concierge, and he motioned them into the main room.

"That was smooth," Rick remarked, noticing the long line. "Do you always get such preferential treatment?"

"I think they believe I'm some kind of VIP, since I arrived here last time with Eva."

"Maybe they just like pretty ladies in their establishment!"

"Come on, you flirt—let's get a drink."

"What would you like?" Rick asked, as they inched up to the bar moments later.

"A Cosmopolitan, please."

"One Cosmo, and one Grey Goose, straight up," Rick said, catching the bartender's attention. Looking around the club, he was impressed by the size and energy of the crowd. "You weren't kidding about this place—it's really hopping tonight."

"Yes, it's a great place to let your hair down after a slow week."

"Was our little hike up the mountain all that horribly boring for you?"

"Well, it was good exercise, and I enjoyed seeing you get excited about finding your old tree. I guess I just don't have quite the same passion for dendrology as you do."

"That's ok," Rick said, handing Jennifer her drink when the bartender returned, "we all have our individual passions."

"Speaking of which—check out the action on the dance floor." Jennifer motioned to the flashing stage, where a large group of excited juveniles were bumping and grinding to the loud beat.

"They're certainly getting their groove on," Rick said. "Shall we join them?"

"Absolutely!"

As Rick and Jennifer pressed their way onto the dance podium and began to move to the music, Jennifer smiled as her eyes met Rick's. He was light on his feet and had a natural rhythm that made him all the more appealing. Unfortunately, she found it difficult to match his steps as she was constantly being bumped and jostled by other dancers moving aggressively on the floor. After the second song ended, Rick could see that Jennifer was growing increasingly distracted, and took her by the hand to an open table where he ordered another round of drinks.

"Is it me, or do they seem a little overly vigorous tonight?" he remarked to Jennifer.

"Yes—and not only on the dance floor," she replied, slowly panning the room. Everywhere she looked, couples in various gender combinations were expressing their physical interest in one another in open and obvious displays of desire. Even more than she remembered in her previous outing with Eva, this time the club-goers were kissing and groping each other with unusual abandon, seemingly uninhibited by the public setting.

"It's been a while since I've been out to a dance club," Rick remarked, "but I don't remember it like this. It's strange, because I had a somewhat similar experience earlier this week outside U.N. headquarters. At the time, I didn't know what to make of it, but now I'm wondering if this might be related."

"You found people kissing and fondling like this on the *street*?" Jennifer exclaimed.

"No, in that case it was a group of protesters, but their behavior was also far more aggressive than usual."

"What do you think is going on?"

"Who knows? Maybe it's just a matter of the young generation continuing to loosen its morals. Or strengthening its *convictions*, depending on which side you look at."

"Maybe we're just getting old!" Jennifer laughed.

"Except we're not getting any older than the rest of these people, remember? At least not physiologically."

"Perhaps we just need to get out more," Jennifer mused.

"Maybe you're right. Do you want to give the dance floor another try?"

"In a minute," Jennifer said, feeling the perspiration beading on her brow. "I'd like to freshen up first."

As she began making her way through the throbbing crowd toward the restrooms, Jennifer couldn't help noticing the way some of the patrons looked at her. Leering, many of them made no pretense about their designs on her—and on her body. Finally lurching into the relative solitude of the ladies room, she was thankful to find a temporary respite from the madness. The restroom was filled with women primping and posturing at the mirror, and she found an open lavatory and closed the door behind her.

Shortly after she sat down on the commode, she heard a rustling sound in the compartment next to her. Trying to mind her own business, she decided she would ask Rick to take her home soon, where the two of them could find a more peaceful setting to enjoy each other's company. Just as she was about to flush the toilet, she heard the unmistakable sound of two people in the amorous act of sexual union, coming from the next stall. Unsure if it was two females, or a male and a female who had snuck into the women's lavatory, their grunting and shuffling noises gradually grew louder and more pronounced. Frozen in shock, she jumped suddenly when the partition shook with a loud bang, as someone shifted violently against the wall. To Jennifer's dismay, the partition soon after began shaking rhythmically, as it was obvious one of the lovers was pounding and thrusting against the other. As their grunting and breathing pitched to a noisy climax, Jennifer flushed her toilet and made a hasty exit from the parlor.

Returning to her table, Rick noticed Jennifer seemed flushed and distracted.

"Are you alright? You seem upset."

"You won't believe what just happened in the restroom."

"Some kind of disturbance?"

"Well, it was *physical* alright—but I think these two were engaged in more *amorous* kind of intercourse."

"You're kidding—right in the restroom?!"

"In the stall next to me. It was unmistakable. They were very noisy, and made no effort to disguise their activity."

"Do you think it was two females, or a male and a female?"

"Judging by the shaking of the partition separating us, and the tone of their voices, I'd say it was the latter."

"Incredible. Everything's really turning upside down, isn't it?"

"*Something's* turning upside down," Jennifer mused. "Can we get out of here Rick? I need some fresh air."

As Rick and Jennifer emerged from the hotel into the chilly November air, Rick turned and held his shaking girlfriend in his arms.

"Rick, you know I'm no prude," Jennifer said, "but that was just crazy. What people choose to do in the privacy of their own homes is fine with me, but this kind of public behavior is unnerving. And it's not really the *sex* that bothers me—that might almost be kind of titillating in any other situation—but a lot of those people upstairs had a crazy *look* about them."

"I know, I was thinking the same thing. I think we should run some lab tests tomorrow to see if we can find out what's going on. It might be nothing, but we can't afford to be unsure."

"I agree," said Jennifer, beginning to warm up. "Can we walk for a bit? I just need to calm down."

"Sure, let's get away from Times Square—this way looks a bit quieter."

Rick and Jennifer turned off Broadway, and headed in the direction of the East Side. For a while, neither said anything as they bundled close to each other in the frigid, late autumn air.

"You know," Rick finally said after a while, "we're not that all that far from the Garden of Eden church. Would you mind if we took a little detour and headed over there for just a minute? I've always wanted to see what that church looks like up close."

"Isn't that where your unpredictable cult leader resides? Why would you want to get any closer than necessary to this lunatic?"

"It's just a feeling I have. His son is scheduled for a hypophysectomy operation tomorrow afternoon. Calvin's been conspicuously silent and absent this entire week—I just wanted to see if there's any sign of activity at his place."

"As long as we don't go inside, or aren't likely to run into him. That's the last bit of additional excitement I need tonight."

"I promise we'll turn around if we see any sight of him."

Jennifer pulled Rick closer. "Are you worried he's planning some kind of intervention prior to the operation?"

"He's definitely capable of it," Rick admitted, "and he's certainly expressed his outrage over the decision to operate. But we've got the hospital on alert, and Calvin's already on probation from an earlier incident. I'm sure he knows he can't stop the procedure and that it would only make life more difficult for himself and his son if he were to attempt any further disturbance."

"Maybe. But in the old days, parents were known to go to extreme lengths to protect their children, and his brand of self-possessed evangelism makes him all the more dangerous. I hope you'll be watching out for him."

"Don't worry, I've already taken every necessary precaution."

As they turned off 2nd Avenue onto a darkened side street, Rick looked up and saw the outline of a tall, thin steeple etched against the inky sky. Although he had researched the location of Calvin's church previously, he recognized it immediately. Just as he imagined, the shadowy Gothic structure stood proudly defiant amongst its sleek and modern contemporaries. Sitting on barely a quarter of an acre, its vaulted roof soared above the two- and three-story facades of its storefront neighbors. But as he got closer, Rick noticed the brickwork was dusty and crumbling, and in obvious need of repair. Four arched stained glass windows flanked each of the two long sides of the nave, and the front entrance was marked by a heavy, double-sided wooden door. Surrounding the perimeter of the property was a black wrought-iron fence topped with spiked finials. Inside the fence, resting in the dark mist amongst bare apple trees, sat many angled and worn tombstones marking the graves of long departed souls.

"This place is totally creepy," intoned Jennifer. "Does Calvin actually *live* here?"

"I believe so," Rick said, looking up to see any sign of habitation. At the rear of the structure on the north wall near the very top, he saw a dull orange light glowing through a tiny window. Just a few feet further above, a faint plume of gray smoke spilled from a chimney. For a split second, Rick thought about knocking on the door to the church and trying to negotiate a truce with the enigmatic cult leader. But Jennifer's trembling arm and his inner voice convinced him otherwise, and the two of them continued walking past the eerie church in silence.

"An apt setting for an anachronistic old relic, don't you think?" Jennifer remarked when they reached the corner. "Can we go home now? I think I've had quite enough of a fright tonight. And besides—you're going to need a good night's rest for another difficult day tomorrow."

"Let's hope not," Rick said, flagging a cab.

As they pulled away from the dark church, Rick looked up at the lonely steeple and couldn't help feeling something was strangely familiar about the place.

Thirty

Shortly after sunrise the next day, a discordant note interrupted the morning melody of an eastern song sparrow outside Mount Sinai Medical Center. As Rick expected, the Garden of Eden protest group had encamped at the front gate, voicing loud objections to Elias's planned surgery and attempting to bar entrance to anyone looking like a hospital worker. It was a larger group than usual, growing increasingly antagonistic as the morning wore on, but the local police were out in force and so far had kept the disturbance under control.

More troubling for Rick was that Calvin was once again missing in action. Normally, under such circumstances, this would be a welcome departure. But today, Rick found his absence highly suspicious and unnerving. He had thought Calvin would want to take a public stand against the operation he considered so immoral and attempt to stoke sympathy for his abused rights as a parent. Rick imagined he might even try to physically disrupt the operation itself; the only thing that would be giving Calvin pause was his recently issued probation. But Rick also knew that wasn't enough to deter sufficiently motivated offenders, and Calvin certainly had plenty of extra motivation to intervene in this case.

With these considerations in mind, Rick had taken extraordinary precautions for this morning's operation. After putting the hospital's security staff on high alert, he'd arranged to have the operating room fortified with reinforced locking glass doors, and requested two guards to protect the entrance during the procedure. If Calvin or any of his followers managed to get past the perimeter, at least they would find it difficult to breach the actual operating theater; Rick simply couldn't afford these kind of distractions during the sensitive and precarious hypophysectomy operation.

After washing up in the scrub room, Rick nodded to the guards as he entered the operating suite, where the surgical team was preparing the patient and Jennifer looked on from the elevated observation deck.

"Good Morning, Elias," Rick announced to his gowned patient lying on the operating table. "I'm Dr. Ross, and I'll be your surgeon today. We've got the best team in the hospital looking after you, so you needn't worry about a thing. Do you have any questions before we begin?"

"Not really," Elias said tentatively, then pausing. "Will it hurt?"

"You won't feel a thing," Rick promised, smiling at the familiar question. "We're going to put you to sleep soon, and when you wake up, you'll be good as new. You might feel a bit weak for a few hours after the operation, but other than that the only thing you'll notice will be a little patch on your stomach." As a gesture of confidence, Rick lifted his gown to show Elias his own patch.

"And that patch is going to keep me alive, and forever young?"

It was obvious that Elias still harbored some lingering doubts from his conversations with his father.

"Yes…at least as long as we know." Rick paused. Although it wasn't really his job to deal with such issues, he nevertheless wanted to hear it directly from Elias before proceeding.

"Are you absolutely sure you're ready to do this?" he asked.

"Yes," Elias didn't hesitate. "I want to stay young, like you and everybody else…as long as you're sure it's safe."

"We've performed thousands of these operations, and you can see how healthy and youthful all of *us* are," Rick said, as he looked at his assembled surgical team.

In a show of support, they all raised their smocks and displayed their patches to Elias.

"Soon," Elias said excitedly, "I'll be just like the rest of you!"

"We'll see you on the other side, son," Rick said as he silently nodded for Mac to initiate the intravenous anesthesia.

As soon as he saw Elias fall off to sleep, Rick quickly moved over to the operating room doors and pushed the newly installed locking bolts into the concrete floor.

"Jesus, Rick," Mac said, surprised by Rick's unusual precautions. "This place is like an armed camp today—are you expecting an insurrection?"

"I hope not, but you've all been briefed about the unique circumstances of this patient. His father is opposed to the operation, and you may have noticed some of his supporters outside the front gate this morning."

"How could we miss them?" Nurse Benson said. "They were pretty aggressive—some of us had to duck in the back entrance to make it in here."

"It appears that hospital security has got the situation under control, but I don't want to take any chances. I'd like to proceed as expeditiously as possible if you don't mind; let's get this job finished before anyone has any opportunity to intervene."

"I'm with you," Mac agreed, struck by Rick's uncharacteristically serious tone.

As Mac proceeded to intubate Elias's lungs, Rick put on a pair of sterile surgical gloves and checked the equipment table to ensure everything was ready. The extensive array of stainless steel instruments glistened under the bright surgical lamps: long flexible endoscopes for providing close-up video of the interior sella structures; nasal specula for spreading and widening the narrow internal passageways; microdissectors and curettes for cutting and scaling tissues; clamps and hypodermic needles for temporarily closing and desensitizing organs; and aspirators and sponges for removing excess blood and other bodily fluids. Most of these instruments connected via attachments with the overhead robotic trolley, whose movement Rick would control using sensitive multi-functional joysticks. Also attached to the trolley was a bank of video screens, which Rick and the other operating personnel would use to monitor every step of the operation.

When Mac gave the 'all clear' sign, Rick attached one of the endoscopes to the trolley, and glided the equipment near Elias's nose.

"Right—let's get started."

Rick carefully began to thread the thin articulated cable holding the illuminated camera and laser dissector up Elias's left nostril using the multi-directional joystick. Toggling the wand delicately between his thumb and forefinger while concentrating on the image displayed by the endoscope on the video monitor, the first obstacle he encountered was the inferior turbinate, a soft flap of tissue controlling airflow into the upper sinuses. Gently pushing the fold aside, Rick could see the sphenoid ostium, looking like the keel on the underside of a boat, marking the base of the sphenoidal sinus cavity. Pressing a small red button on the tip of the joystick, the endoscope emitted a short pulse of ultraviolet laser light, which quickly penetrated the thin layer of cartilage. Peering inside the brightly illuminated cavity, Rick saw the distinct convex shape of the sella turcica—Turk's Saddle—which housed the pituitary. Positioning the microdissector mere millimeters away from the carotid sulcus, the eggshell-thin covering of the interior carotid artery, he proceeded to make a cross-shaped incision on the fleshy protuberance.

How ironic, Rick thought before pulling the folds back to expose the omnipotent gland, *that the gateway to the organ that gives and takes life should be etched with the universal symbol of Christianity.*

The distant chants of Calvin's Garden of Eden group echoing through the halls pulled Rick back to reality, and he quickly handed the computer controls over to his assistant neurosurgeon, Dr. Scott.

"Half way there," Rick exhaled, looking up in the viewing gallery to see Jennifer wink at him. "Now, let's pluck that fruit."

Moving the second microdissector into position at the base of Elias's right nostril, Rick began to repeat the procedure, as he slowly wound the apparatus past the familiar structures on the right side of Elias's nasal cavity, adjusting the joystick ever so slowly and microscopically.

As before, nobody in the room uttered a word.

Just as he reached the entrance to the lateral sphenoid sinus, Rick heard a disturbance from the hall. He heard loud shouts, and in his periphery he saw the two security guards stationed outside the door move quickly in the direction of the noise.

Everybody looked at Rick nervously.

Christ—just what I need at this precise moment, he thought. *We're almost there!*

The sounds grew fainter and more distant, and Rick took this to mean that the security personnel had dissuaded the apparent protestors from advancing any further. Rick looked over at Mac, who quickly nodded for him to proceed. It would only take another few minutes or so to complete the operation.

Returning his attention to the monitors, Rick moved the joystick forward slightly and advanced the microdissector through the right ostium into the narrow passageway flanked by the carotid artery. Just as he was about to move past the primary blood vessel supplying oxygen to the right hemisphere of the brain, he heard the sound of rapidly approaching footsteps coming from the opposite direction of the initial disturbance. Seconds later, he heard a loud crash, as something slammed into the door.

Looking up reflexively, he saw Calvin staring at him through the safety glass with a crazed look, shaking the doors violently, trying to break into the room.

"Let go of my son, you *butcher*!" he screamed through the glass. "You have no right! Give back my child!!"

Fortunately, the locked doors held firm, but Calvin began banging against the glass panels with his fists, causing them to splinter, sending shards flying across the room.

From the observation deck above, Jennifer quickly ran from the room in search of assistance.

Turning his attention momentarily back to the video monitors in an attempt to secure his patient, Rick was horrified by what he saw. A nervous bump of the operating joystick had apparently pushed the microdissector through the narrow covering of the carotid sulcus, rupturing the artery, and Rick could see that it was hemorrhaging violently.

"Mark," he called out to his assistant, "I need a clamp—stat!!"

Dr. Scott, who was controlling the equipment inserted in Elias's left nostril, had already begun to retract a clamp as soon as he saw the severed artery.

"Mac!" Rick quickly motioned to his anesthesiologist. "Stop that man! We can't let him in here. This patient's condition is *critical*—I need to focus all my attention on him."

"What do you want me to do, Rick?" Mac asked, incredulously. "We don't have any weapons in the room other than a few scalpels—and he's twice our size and three times as strong!"

"I don't care what you do—just *stop* him!!"

As Calvin began to break through the glass panel and reach around the inside of the door attempting to unlock it, Mac frantically searched the equipment table for anything he could use to slow down the intruder. Thinking quickly, he picked up a long hypodermic needle from the equipment tray, and jammed it into the intravenous bag hanging from the stand beside Elias's bed. Swiftly pulling back the syringe handle and filling the needle's reservoir with the clear viscous fluid, he moved around the operating table and tentatively approached the door. As Calvin reached out and tried to grab him, Mac carefully timed his thrust and caught Calvin squarely on the forearm, plunging the needle deep into his flesh.

Calvin roared, retracting his arm, while Mac simultaneously moved away from the door defensively. Calvin was still pushing against the door and trying to unhinge it from the inside with wild flailing motions—but his screams and thrashing were rapidly diminishing. Within thirty seconds, he fell away from the door and collapsed on the ground, just as three security guards rushed to the scene.

On the operating table, Rick and Dr. Scott were working furiously to quell the arterial rupture. Dr. Scott had successfully clamped the tear, but Elias's nasal sella had quickly filled with blood and coated the lenses of the endoscopes, blinding the two doctors' line of sight. Rick knew that if the artery were not sealed soon and the blood evacuated, it would put dangerous pressure on Elias's brain and cut off essential oxygen, potentially causing a stroke or death.

"Marg," he shouted to the head nurse, "we need to aspirate—hand me the vacuum!"

Nurse Benson, who had just finished patching the sprouting leak in the I/V bag made by Mac's needle, quickly located the laparoscopic vacuum tube on the equipment tray and passed it to Rick. But first he had to remove the blocking microdissector from Elias's right sinus without the benefit of visual guidance from the occluded endoscopes, and somehow insert the aspirator back into the cavity without further damaging the carotid artery or any of the other sensitive organs. Thankfully, the disturbance at the door was no longer a distraction, since the security personnel had carried the now unconscious Calvin away, and police reinforcements had mobilized in the hall to block access to the operating room from any other potential intruders.

Marshaling all of his concentration, Rick slowly began retracting the equipment from Elias's right sphenoid. Fortunately, his years of experience performing this operation enabled him to conduct the procedure mostly by feel. Closing his eyes, he expertly worked the joysticks, while everyone in the room held their breath. Millimeter by millimeter the long tube slowly began withdrawing from Elias's inner sinus. When the end of the tube finally emerged from his nostril, a torrent of blood gushed out of his nose, and nurse Benson immediately moved into position to place a sponge against the opening to arrest the flow.

"No, Marg," Rick instructed. "Let it flow—it will ease the cranial pressure and make it easier to insert the aspirator."

Quickly disconnecting the microdissector and attaching the aspiration tube in its place, Rick moved the new device back into Elias's right nostril. Knowing that his sightlines into the sellar region would be blocked by the blood still filling the cavities, he placed a superficial nick on the outside of the tube with a scalpel to mark the precise length needed to reach the sphenoid sinus. With precious seconds separating life and death, Rick moved the joystick handles delicately but purposefully, as the tube slowly sank back into Elias's nose.

Nobody uttered a sound while everybody held their breath.

When the mark on the catheter got to the base of Elias's nostril, Rick flicked a switch on the base of the joystick, initiating a loud suction sound. Suddenly, a river of dark red blood spilled out of the tube, as nurse Benson grimly directed the evacuation end into a white sink.

After a few seconds, Rick began to see some spotty images emerge on the monitor from the blood-splattered endoscope, and he could see Dr. Scott's clamp still holding the carotid artery closed.

"What now?" asked Mac, whose attention was once again fully focused on the operation.

"Unfortunately," Rick advised, "we're obviously in no position to complete the operation as planned. The pituitary removal will have to wait—right now we need to figure out how to keep this patient alive for the next few hours—never mind a lifetime. We need to seal that wound quickly and re-oxygenate the right hemisphere before it's too late. The problem is, I'm not sure fibrin glue alone will be sufficient to arrest the flow once the clamp is removed."

Knowing the alternative would mean permanently disfiguring his patient with open-face surgery, Rick could barely utter the words.

"We may need to go in and directly suture the wound with a transfrontal intracranial operation," he said. Looking up to the observation theater, he saw that Jennifer had returned, looking on in shock.

"Jen," he announced, "will you notify the hospital Chief of Staff and ask him to send an emergency standby team down here right away?"

Jennifer nodded and quickly left the viewing room again.

"Alright, Mark," Rick motioned to Dr. Scott as he began to thread another tube up Elias's right nostril. "I'm going to try sealing the wound with fibrin, but be ready to re-clamp if it doesn't hold."

"On my mark," Rick said, taking a deep breath, "I want you to release the clamp. Here we go…"

Thirty-one

Tian Yin woke up in a sweat Saturday morning after a restless night of strange dreams. She'd dreamt she was on a deserted beach on a tropical island, walking alone along the water's edge, with the warm ocean waves lapping over her bare feet. As she peered into the distance, she could see a figure walking toward her—though in the midday haze, she couldn't at first make out who it was. But as they got closer to one another, the familiar face of Dr. Ross came into focus, and he smiled at her. Trying to remain nonchalant, Tian struggled to maintain her leisurely pace, as if this were just another casual encounter with anyone else she might meet on the beach. But her legs betrayed her, and she unconsciously began walking faster. Surprisingly, Rick appeared to be having the same reaction, and as they got closer and closer they increased the speed of their gait—until they virtually ran into each other's arms.

Rick picked Tian up out of the surf in a hearty embrace, kissing her firmly on the lips, and they both fell to the sand in a heat of passion. As Rick's hands explored Tian's body and began to unhinge her bikini top, Tian felt an odd sensation. Rick was cupping and kissing her breasts—*large* breasts—that she hadn't had before. It was a foreign feeling, but she rather liked it, and so, apparently, did Rick. When he then untied her bikini bottom and removed his own trunks, she unconsciously parted her legs in anticipation of the union she had long fantasized about. As Rick positioned himself over her and slowly lowered himself onto her body, she could feel his excitement against her flesh. At the moment he entered her in a passionate flourish, a warm surge of ocean water came up between her legs and enveloped her hips in a moist and sticky pool.

Tian jerked awake, disappointed she was unable to consummate the act in her dream. As she lay on her bed, breathing heavily from the arousal she was still feeling, she began analyzing the vision. *What did it mean?* She already knew that she had a strong visceral attraction to Rick. But why did she have fully developed breasts—and what was the significance of the sticky water? As she closed her eyes and tried to imagine herself back in Rick's embrace, her hand slowly wandered between her legs, where she was still wet with excitement. But it was unusually thick and sticky—unlike anything she'd felt before. And it wasn't just her body—the *sheets* were wet and sticky also.

Sitting up suddenly, Tian wondered what happened. Had she really been this aroused? Turning on the bedside lamp and throwing back the covers, she couldn't believe what she saw: in the middle of her bed, staining her white Egyptian cotton sheets, was a bright red pool of blood. Instantly looking between her legs, she saw where it came from.

At first, she wondered if her bleeding was some kind of psychosomatic reaction to her dream: maybe her vulva had unconsciously bled as if Rick had taken her virginity? Or maybe she had been groping herself while she was asleep, and torn something. Then she looked at her breasts and gasped.

Oh my God! Tian cried out loud, upon seeing the swelling buds and enlarged nipples.

Another possibility instantly entered her mind—an awful, irreversible possibility, which now seemed all too real. Somehow—though Tian couldn't yet possibly imagine *how*—she had crossed during the night over the threshold of puberty and experienced menarche, the unmistakable milestone heralding the transition into adulthood for girls.

But Tian also knew it signaled something far more ominous. The blood in her sheets meant she had suddenly lost her *youth*—and her immortality.

Thirty-two

At eight-thirty Sunday morning, Jennifer's phone bounced loudly on her bedside night table. Reaching over groggily to pick up the vibrating device, she squinted through sleepy eyes at the display. The message was from Mount Sinai's Chief of Staff, Joe Morgan.

Emergency Room swamped. Unusual endocrine disorders. Come in immediately.

"What is it?" asked Rick, who had stayed over after an exhausting forty-eight hours dealing with the aftermath of Elias's interrupted surgery.

"I don't know. Joe says there are an unusual number of cases in the ER this morning, mostly endocrine-related. He wants me to come in as soon as possible."

"That's odd," Rick said, sitting up. "I wonder what's going on—did you have a chance to run some tests on the e-patch?"

"I took some samples in to the lab on Friday morning, then completely forgot about it after the disruption in the OR. But the technicians said they probably wouldn't have the results back until Monday."

"I think we need to see the results as soon as possible; there've been far too many unusual incidents this week."

"Do you think they're connected?"

"They have to be. First the extreme aggressiveness demonstrated by Calvin's sect at the U.N., then the heightened libido on display at the Hippodrome—and now this."

"Let's hope it's not caused by some malfunction of the hormone patch," Jennifer said as she began to get dressed. "We're dependent on these things to keep everything in check—if there's a defect, or it's been tampered with, we could *all* be in trouble."

"Perhaps we should ask our lab techs if they can expedite their analysis and at least give us a preliminary report before tomorrow?"

"Good idea—I'll ask Joe to get on it right away."

Rick nodded, as his focus drifted to the floor.

"Was something else on your mind?" she asked. "You look a little distracted this morning."

"I was just thinking about Friday's operation."

"I know you're upset about what happened, Rick, but it's not your fault. Nobody could have predicted or prevented that calamity. Calvin obviously had the whole thing planned; you did everything humanly possible to protect yourself against it."

"It's not me I'm worried about."

"But you repaired the rupture and stabilized your patient."

"For *now*, but he's still in serious condition. The wound could reopen, or become infected, or a clot could cause an embolism."

"You've done everything you can. You shouldn't beat yourself up too much over this."

"I know," Rick replied, "it's just—I *promised* Elias he was going to be fine. You heard him ask me before we started the operation."

"Rick," Jennifer said, cradling his hand, "*no* one could have anticipated what happened. If anybody's to blame, it's his own father who caused this."

"But the slip…"

"Any other surgeon would have *lost* the patient in that situation," Jennifer interrupted Rick. "You *saved* him—and gave him another chance."

"Maybe," Rick said, returning his focus to the news from the hospital. "Listen—you go ahead to Mount Sinai and look after the emergency cases; I'll be all right. Give me a call when you have a chance, to tell me what you found. And let me know if you need me for anything."

"I will," Jennifer said, kissing Rick gently on the cheek. "See you soon."

When she got to the hospital, the first unusual thing Jennifer noticed was the parking lot. It was filled to capacity, and she had to park four blocks away to find an empty spot on the street.

That's strange for a Sunday, she thought. *Especially this early in the morning.*

Picking up her pace, she walked briskly to the Chief of Staff's office. Joe Morgan hung up the phone as soon as he saw her approaching.

"What's up, Joe? I came as soon as I got your message."

"I'm not sure, Jennifer, but I've never seen the ER this busy, and with cases we haven't seen in a long time."

"Like what?"

"Multiple instances of juvenile menses for one, and nocturnal emissions."

"You're kidding?! That's not supposed to happen."

"Exactly. I was hoping you could make sense of it. But that's not all—there are other issues. Patients have been complaining about unusual swollen glands, edema, and skin lesions…"

"All of this started *today*?"

"Actually, we started noticing some isolated cases as early as Wednesday, but it's been picking up all week. Today was the first day it really got out of control. Can you get down there and try to find out what's going on?"

"I'll head down immediately. But can you do one thing for me before I go?"

"Of course."

"Will you call the forensics lab and ask them for an update on the patch diagnostics they started for me on Friday?"

"You think all of this might be caused by the *e-patches*?!" Joe asked incredulously.

"I don't know," Jennifer replied, "but I also noticed some unusual reactions earlier in the week, and I asked the techs to run some tests as a preventive measure. They said they'd have the results for me tomorrow, but under the circumstances, if you can expedite matters, I think we need to see them as soon as possible."

"I'll call them immediately, and let you know as soon as they have some results."

"Thanks, Joe. I'll report back after I assess the situation in the ER."

As soon as Jennifer got to the Emergency Ward, she knew something was seriously wrong. Just *looking* at the patients in the waiting room, she could see many telltale signs of severe endocrine imbalance. Some patients had bulging eyes, a thyroid disorder indicating periorbital edema, often caused by excessive vasopressin production. Others expressed blotchy pigmentation and acne, indicating lipotropin and testosterone imbalances. A few even exhibited pronounced brow and jawbones, an extremely rare condition caused by overdoses of growth hormones. But mostly, everybody just looked—*older*. Male juveniles had darkening hair on their upper lip, and some females were beginning to show bulges in unusual places. In previous years, many of these symptoms had been associated with various pituitary disorders such as tumors, but all of these patients had long ago had their pituitary removed.

"Thank heavens you're here, Dr. Austin," said the admitting nurse on duty when she saw Jennifer. "I have no idea how to process these patients. Our normal triage procedure doesn't reference these kinds of symptoms. Where do I begin?"

Jennifer scanned the waiting room, trying to sort and filter the cases by severity, but she wasn't sure either. Since nobody appeared in imminent danger, she would simply have to process them in the order they presented themselves. Then she saw a pretty female hunched in a corner of the room wearing dark glasses, and recognized her from a photograph in Rick's office.

"I'll start with her."

Thirty-three

By Monday morning, the press had discovered the extent of the escalating hormone problem and gone public with the story, amid sensational front-page headlines proclaiming *Thousands Afflicted with Mystery Disease*, *Epidemic of Sudden Maturities,* and *Hormone Disorder Causes Freak Deformities*. Many more juveniles had experienced their first period or wet dream, and quickly rushed to their doctor or the closest hospital in a confused state of shock and bewilderment. Others were experiencing more serious symptoms of severe hormone imbalance, such as goiter, pancreatitis, and hyperadrenocorticism, displaying obvious outward signs of excessively puffy faces, neck lumps, or jaundice. Everybody was panicking, and hospital emergency rooms around the country were overflowing with hysterical patients demanding immediate treatment.

At Mount Sinai Medical Center, the Chief of Staff called an emergency meeting with Rick and Jennifer to discuss the situation. At eight a.m., the three sat down in Joe Morgan's office.

"Thanks for coming on such short notice," Joe began. "I'm sure by now you've both read the morning headlines."

"Pretty hard to miss," Rick said. "All the front-line media outlets seem to have picked it up. If we haven't already reached capacity, this will surely make it all the more difficult to treat everyone."

"Exactly. But I think even more critical than the palliative issue is how we *stop* this thing. I've gotten the results back from the lab, and I think you'll be interested to see what they've found."

"Were the patches out of spec?" Jennifer asked.

"That's an understatement. There were massive overdoses of the active ingredient found in the pouches."

"Which ones?—there's nine hormones in the mix."

"They've isolated at least six so far. Growth hormone, lipotropin, testosterone, estrogen, thyrotropin, vasopressin…"

"You're kidding?!" Jennifer exclaimed. "How can that happen? These things are supposed to be tightly controlled and checked at the manufacturer. There's never been any discrepancy like this before."

"How much *were* the overages, exactly?" Rick interjected.

"Oddly," Joe advised, "it wasn't the total quantity in the reservoir that was out of line—only the proportions. The technicians found significantly less buffers than specified, but much higher concentrations of the active ingredients. Normally the ratio of active to inactive ingredients is about one tenth—in this instance it was two to one."

"Buffers to hormones?" Jennifer asked.

"The other way around."

"Oh my god," Jennifer moaned, immediately recognizing the severity of the situation, "no wonder we're seeing such severe reactions. If that level of infusion continues, we'll be seeing much more critical complications soon—not to mention many likely deaths!"

"I don't get it," Rick said, with a confused look on his face. "Even with *that* level of hormone imbalance, I'm not sure we should be seeing this degree of reaction. The patch has an embedded filter, which is supposed to modulate the quantity of medication delivered to the skin."

"That's the *other* surprise," Joe said. "The lab also found inordinately high levels of *excipients* in the mix, which accelerates the transfer rate."

"*Christ*," Rick exclaimed.

"Exactly," Joe replied. "It now seems obvious that someone has tampered with the patches. But we don't know how many, or which ones. *Anybody* could be at risk—including each of us."

The three doctors glanced at each another uncomfortably.

"On the way into the meeting today," Rick quickly interjected, 'I called my contacts at the Centers for Disease Control to see how widespread this is. They consolidate incident reports from all around the country for this sort of thing. So far, they've catalogued just under ten thousand cases of endocrine poisoning."

"That's an awful lot," Jennifer observed, "but that still seems relatively small, given the hundreds of millions who wear the same patch. Maybe not *every* patch is contaminated?"

"Let's hope so," Rick nodded. "Joe—did the lab by any chance send you any of the patches they tested?"

"Yes, but.."

"May I see them?"

Joe handed Rick a specimen jar filled with an assortment of pink and blue plastic patches, and Rick immediately took some out and began inspecting their inside surfaces.

"What are you looking for, Rick?" asked Jennifer.

"Lot numbers. Endogen stamps all of their patches with unique lot numbers for every batch they process…and I can see that all of these patches are stamped with the same number. That seems to indicate—at least so far—that this contamination is limited to only one batch."

Joe immediately moved his hand to his lower abdomen and rubbed his patch.

"I know what you're thinking, Joe," Jennifer said. "But if any of us were wearing patches from the same contaminated lot, we surely would have felt or noticed something by now. It appears that the three of us got lucky."

"We don't know how much longer that will last," Rick noted. "Nor how many *more* people might be exposed to this batch—now, or in the near future."

"What do you think we should do, Rick?" Joe asked. The Chief of Staff was speaking more now as a worried patch user, than as Rick's nominal boss. He knew Rick had far more experience and knowledge with these types of issues, and that as Surgeon-General of the World Health Organization, Rick's authority vastly exceeded his own when it came to epidemiological matters.

"First, we should notify Endogen immediately about our findings, so they can try to locate the source of the contamination and stop production of any more defective patches. They should also be able to tell us where they've shipped the batches from this particular lot, so we can try to recall the defective ones before they cause any more damage. I'm going to ask the Director of Communications at the WHO to issue a press release warning anyone who's wearing a patch bearing these numbers to replace it immediately with one carrying a different stamp. We should also notify the *police*, since it is apparent this was the work of someone with criminal intent."

"What do you recommend we do about the *existing* cases?" Joe asked. "What can we do for those who are already affected?"

Rick turned to Jennifer.

"Assuming the other patches with different lot numbers are okay," she said, "we should be able to quickly stop the symptoms from getting any *worse* by returning the dosages to normal. If *all* the patches are affected, we'll have to administer the hormones intravenously—though I can't imagine how we'd deal with that many cases in such short order from our limited stores of supplementary hormones."

"What about those who've already experienced menarche and spermarche?" Joe added. "Can that be *reversed*?"

This time it was Jennifer who looked to Rick for clarification.

"If you're referring to the issue of arrested development and its connection to aging—this is a situation without precedent. It's hard to say if we can reset their biological clocks. Elsewhere in the natural world, once sexual maturity has been attained, there's never been any going back. We'll just have to see if their mature bodies accept the lower juvenile doses."

"At the very least, this is going to be a public relations disaster," Joe noted. "Everyone's come to expect a certain equilibrium and the notion of indefinite youth. I shudder to think how the affected individuals will take the news if we can't reverse these effects. Especially if this spreads beyond the U.S."

"I agree," Rick said, standing to leave. "I'm going to make enquiries about that right away. Joe, will you notify the appropriate people at Endogen about what we've found, and also call the police to begin an investigation? I'll contact the UN Secretary-General to discuss the global implications and see what she wants to do."

Jennifer suddenly reached out and grasped Rick's arm.

"Rick, before you go," she said, "there's something else you should know…"

Thirty-four

Roland Jamieson was working quietly in his office when his personal intercom line lit up at eleven-thirty Monday morning.

"What is it, Kristen?" he announced distractedly to his secretary.

"There's a Director Inzucchi from the FBI here to see you. He wants to meet with you immediately."

Jamieson had been expecting this call since receiving a message from the Chief of Staff at Mount Sinai Medical Center two hours ago, when he was informed they had found massive hormone overdoses in Endogen patches, and that they were notifying the authorities. Soon after, he had scrambled his senior staff to discuss how the company should respond.

If he had previously thought things couldn't get much worse at Endogen, he was now almost wishing for a return to the relative peace of two weeks ago. The media had built the escalating epidemic into the most sensational story in decades, and had begun to link the catastrophic symptoms with the likely influence of a defective e-patch. Class-action lawsuits were already being filed by the hundreds, with the cumulative liability vastly exceeding the net asset value of the company. The company's stock, previously hovering around two dollars, was now trading in unprecedented volume on the New York Stock Exchange for mere pennies. And every Director of the company was being served with new civil suits for breach of conduct and fiduciary duty.

But the CEO knew it could get worse—much worse. If Endogen and its officers were found to be negligent in the manufacture and testing of the e-patch, he and others could be found criminally liable for manslaughter or criminal neglect. Jamieson might be able to delay the FBI for a few hours, or even a couple of days, but he knew they could easily secure a warrant and that his best defense would be full cooperation.

"Have him wait a few minutes," he paged his secretary back. "I'm going to ask Bruce and Alan to join us."

Jamieson knew his Production Superintendent would be better able to answer many of the questions the police were likely to ask, and that his Chief Counsel could provide valuable guidance on what had to be disclosed. Picking up his handset, he quickly dialed his two lieutenants. Five minutes later, Jamieson's secretary ushered two plain-clothed federal agents into his office, where the three executives were calmly waiting.

"Mr. Jamieson?" the more senior of the two FBI agents began, as he shook Jamieson's extended hand. "I'm Assistant Director Inzucchi of the New York district office of the Federal Bureau of Investigation, and this is Special Agent Sanchez. We have some questions concerning troubling new developments uncovered this morning regarding your company's hormone patches."

"Yes, of course," Jamieson said, trying to appear relaxed. "I've asked our company's head of production, Bruce Ellis, to join us, since he should be able to furnish you with more details. And this is my Chief Counsel, Alan Brache."

After the five shook hands, the two police officers sat down, and each pulled out a pen and black journal.

"Mr. Jamieson," Director Inzucchi began, "I understand you've been made aware of the serious discrepancy in the chemical formulation of your patches. How long have you known about this defect?"

"I just found out this morning, when I received a call from Mount Sinai Medical Center. Of course, we immediately conducted our own tests to substantiate the findings."

"Do your findings corroborate those of the hospital?"

"Essentially, yes."

"As I'm sure you know, this is a very serious matter, in light of the many severe health conditions that have been experienced over the last few days."

"We don't know for certain that the patch discrepancy is causing all of these problems," Alan Brache quickly asserted.

"Sir," Director Inzucchi stated impatiently, "all of the patients that have been examined for these disorders were found to be wearing these defective patches."

"*Everybody's* wearing our patches," Jamieson replied, "—but only a relatively small percentage seems to be affected."

"If you call several hundred thousand people suffering serious hormone poisoning a small percentage," Inzucchi said dryly.

"All of the affected individuals," Agent Sanchez added, leafing through his notes, "were found to be wearing a patch with the same lot number, Lot BZ834776. Given that others with different lot numbers have so far not been affected, this would appear to provide conclusive evidence that the defective patches are the cause of this problem."

"We agree it is a serious issue," Jamieson backpedalled. "But it seems to have been corrected. As Agent Sanchez points out, the problem appears to be isolated to a single batch."

"When did you produce that batch?" Director Inzucchi asked.

"We've checked our records," Bruce Ellis advised. "All of those patches were produced last Monday morning."

"How many patches bearing this lot number were produced in that batch?"

"About three hundred million."

Jamieson saw the look of surprise on the two agents' faces.

"How many of these have been *shipped*?!" Inzucchi asked.

"All of them," Bruce said. "We run a just-in-time shop, where each of our twice-daily production runs is shipped out within four hours of packaging and crating, in order to maintain freshness and ensure sufficient global supply of the product."

"Do you have records of where all of this product was delivered? We'll need to coordinate with the necessary agencies to recall these defective patches in order to minimize any further occurrences."

"Yes, but basically it's shipped all around the globe. Pharmacies typically only carry two days' worth of supply, so we ship our product daily to local distribution hubs in every country, in order to ensure fresh supply is on hand at all times."

"Right," Director Inzucchi intoned. "You'll need to advise the FDA and WHO about those shipments. Our primary concern here today is how this discrepancy found its way into your system. Who has access to the ingredients placed in the patch?"

Bruce checked with both Jamieson and Alan, and they nodded their assent to proceed . "The primary ingredients are added from a secure mix room staffed with only two people at a time."

"But you run two shifts a day?"

"Yes…so taking into account our seven-days-a-week production schedule and personal vacations, this means we have six clean room mixers."

"We'll need to talk with each of them."

"We can arrange that," Jamieson offered, "but I can't imagine you'll find any wrongdoing by these operators, since not only do they receive intensive training, but they all know every batch is carefully checked for discrepancies—so any attempted tampering of the product would be quickly exposed."

"Who supplies and manufactures the ingredients added in the mix room?" asked Agent Sanchez.

"We produce all of the ingredients in-house—in this facility," Bruce replied.

"How many people are involved in that process?"

"Thousands, but each ingredient is carefully tested to ensure proper consistency and quality before being sealed into steel drums."

"Who else has access to the drums before they are used in the mix room?"

"They're stored in a secure storage facility adjacent to the mixing chamber—but we've found no evidence that those drums were opened or tampered with."

"We'll need to conduct our *own* investigation," Director Inzucchi declared. "You'll need to provide our forensic team access to those drums, and to each of the other locations."

"Of course," Jamieson said, glancing uneasily at Alan. "We'll provide full cooperation. Just let us know what you need."

"What I don't understand," Inzucchi continued, "is how such a huge discrepancy could get *out* of your factory, let alone *in* to it. Don't you have sophisticated quality control equipment and procedures to find this sort of thing before it gets out the door?"

"Yes, of course we do—and we're currently undertaking an intensive internal audit of that department to find out where and how that happened."

"Who's in charge of the quality control operation? And why didn't you invite him to this meeting?"

"Unfortunately, I've been unable to locate him," Jamieson said. "He hasn't shown up to work since last Tuesday, and we haven't been able to reach him."

Inzucchi scribbled something quickly in his notepad. "We're going to need all the particulars for that employee. In the meantime, I'd like you to provide Special Agent Sanchez with a tour of each of the areas you've referenced today, and access to all of the relevant personnel. There's going to be quite a few more investigators showing up here over the next few days. We're treating this as a crime scene, so you're going to have to cease production in the specified areas until we can finish our investigation."

"How long will you need?!" asked Jamieson, sounding alarmed. "We can't shut down for too long—we need to maintain a constant supply of patches to keep everyone supplied with the essential medication."

"You said every pharmacy around the world has two days' supply on hand, right? We'll be done here before then."

Director Inzucchi turned to Special Agent Sanchez. "Sanchez, please keep me abreast of what else you find here today. I'm going to get our forensics team scrubbing the clean room and storage area immediately."

As the two police officers stood to leave and shook hands with each executive, Director Inzucchi paused to look into the eyes of each of the three men—particularly Jamieson and Bruce Ellis. He had over twenty-five years' experience reading the faces of criminals from all walks of life, and he was looking for the slightest twitch or sign of nervousness that might indicate either one was hiding any material facts. He knew that both were highly motivated not only to protect the interests of their employer—but also their own hides.

Neither betrayed any sign of nervous tension. For Director Inzucchi, that was a problem.

Thirty-five

When Rick returned to his office after the meeting with Mount Sinai's Chief of Staff, he had a message waiting for him from Tian Yin. He could hear the anxiety in her voice, but he noticed something else in her tone—it sounded strangely deeper, and more mature.

Calling back immediately, she picked up on the second ring.

"Tian, it's Rick. I just got your message."

"Rick—thank heavens you called," Tian replied in a strangely disembodied voice. "So much has happened in the last couple of days. Have you been following the latest news?"

"Yes, I've been scrambling all morning to collect more information, and there are some key details I wanted to discuss with you."

"I've arranged a special meeting for one o'clock with the Director-General of the World Health Organization—can it wait 'til then?"

Rick considered telling Tian what he'd discovered about the bad batch of Endogen patches, but based on Jennifer's report of her condition, he decided it would be best to discuss the particulars when he saw her personally.

"Yes, of course—I'll see you then."

Three hours later, when his cab pulled up in front the Secretariat Building, Rick was relieved to see no sign of protestors—only the familiar sculpture of Reutersward's twisted gun, standing vigil over the eerily silent courtyard. But he knew it was only a matter of time before a new group of angry citizens descended on the square, demanding answers—and restitution. The utopian lifestyle the state had created for every juvenile had cultivated a sense of entitlement that he knew would not easily be surrendered.

Making his way once again past the gently swinging Foucault Pendulum in the public lobby, he was reminded of the powerful connection between the forces of biology and physics. Perhaps, he thought, it was too much to expect humankind could repudiate the laws of nature that had guided the cycle of life for millennia. He knew Tian would likely have some strong opinions on this subject today, and that she would need some delicate counseling in view of the recent developments in her own life.

When he got to the top floor and Tian rose to greet him in the Secretary-General's office, Rick was shocked by how much she had changed. Noticeably taller than when he last saw her, she seemed to tower over the diminutive Director-General standing next to her. Even more obvious were her newly proportioned curves, as her swelling hips and bosom formed a distinct hourglass shape in her now overly tight skirt and blouse.

Standing awkwardly in half-profile in a failing effort to disguise her newly budding form, she quickly dispensed with introductory salutations before retreating behind the sanctity of her large executive desk.

"Rick, you remember Dr. Sanjeet Singh?" she began.

Rick had met the Director-General only a few weeks ago, when the World Health Assembly elected India's Minister of Health as the new head of the WHO.

"Yes, of course. It's good to see you again, Dr. Singh. Though it's unfortunate we have to meet again so soon, under such extraordinary circumstances."

"Indeed," Dr. Singh sighed, "it seems my appointment will begin with a trial by fire."

"Sadly, yes," Tian remarked. "I called you both here today to get your opinions on how we should address this hormone…" she paused to search for the best choice of words, "*disequilibrium* that we've witnessed over the last few days, which became public today. Obviously, it will require an immediate response and a coordinated international effort."

"I've already begun a number of initiatives to investigate the cause and possible containment of the problem," Rick said, trying his best to sound reassuring.

"Could you fill us in on what you know?"

"Our testing lab at Mount Sinai confirmed the Endogen patch has a number of ingredients that are significantly out of spec, and we've determined it's limited to one batch of patches that were produced last Monday."

"I *suspected* there was something wrong with the patches," Tian said, her hand immediately drifting down to her abdomen. "Is there any way of identifying which ones are bad?"

Rick handed Tian a hand-scribbled note across her desk.

"Yes—we've identified they are all marked with this lot number."

"Endogen also called my office this morning to advise us of the discrepancy," Dr. Singh added. "Our Director of Communications is in the process of issuing a Stage Six alert, advising all juveniles to check their patches and replace those bearing the defective lot numbers with new patches. I've also notified our regional offices to begin removing and recalling the defective patches from inventory, in cooperation with Endogen's local distributors."

"Unfortunately," Rick advised, "that's not going to make much of a difference now. All these defective patches are now nearing expiration, which means most will have already been replaced in the normal course of weekly turnover. It looks like the damage has already been done. The good news is that all subsequent patch production appears to be fine."

"What does that mean for those who've *already* been affected?" Tian asked as she quietly peeled back the adhesive on the patch underneath her blouse.

"Many of the less severe symptoms of hormone overdose such as edema, hypermelanosis, and acne can be quickly reversed—but others may take longer to adjust. We've never experienced anything like this before, so to some degree we're just going to have to see what happens when everyone's endocrine levels are returned to normal."

Dr. Singh then asked the question they both suspected was foremost on Tian's mind. "Do you think those who've been affected will respond to the lower levels of hormone infusion?"

"That really is the essential issue now. It remains to be seen if the more mature bodies of those who've been affected will return to homeostasis with the prior juvenile hormone levels, or if it will be necessary to boost their hormone infusions to meet the new demands..."

"How can so much change and maturity happen in only a week?!" Tian interjected, finding it increasingly difficult to contain her mounting anger.

Rick knew the extraordinary levels of hormones that Tian had been subjected to over the last week were also making her unusually testy and volatile.

"Unfortunately," he continued, "the hormone levels in these particular patches was so extreme—more than ten times normal—that it was equivalent to receiving *ten weeks* of adolescent doses, which historically has been more than enough to push juveniles past puberty."

"How could this have happened?" Tian cried, surrendering any remaining pretense of objectivity and throwing her now-crumpled patch in the wastebasket in disgust. "We *both* reviewed and approved the quality control procedures at Endogen when we qualified them as our primary producer years ago!"

"It appears," Rick replied softly, trying to calm Tian's nerves, "that this may have been the work of one or two disgruntled employees working alone or in tandem, whom the FBI are now trying to find. But I understand that Endogen is working on new, more stringent controls as we speak to prevent this kind of problem happening again."

"That won't help them much in the next round of *bidding*," Tian said bitterly. "This should virtually eliminate any chance of them qualifying as one of the new suppliers." She paused for a moment to calm down. "It's too bad we didn't start this redistribution initiative sooner—we might have avoided this catastrophe."

"Maybe—but I think wherever there are sufficiently motivated people, there will almost always be a way to circumvent protocols and security procedures."

"What kind of person would possibly want to risk this kind of harm to so many people, anyhow?" wondered Dr. Singh. "And how could they have been certain they or their loves ones wouldn't be affected?"

"That's what the FBI is trying to figure out," Rick said. "It's probably some kind of fringe group or loner, holding a grudge."

"Like our friend at the Garden of Eden church?" Tian suggested. "I hope the FBI starts with him."

"Calvin certainly *would* appear to be a motivated party. The good news is he's already behind bars, which will expedite his questioning. We'll have to see if or how he's connected with this."

"Is there anything else you think we can do to contain the situation," Dr. Singh asked Rick, "to prevent it from happening again?"

"I think we've done pretty much everything we can at this point, beyond the issuance of a press release informing everybody what's happening, and what they need to do to minimize further damage. We should advise those who have experienced unusual symptoms in the last week to see a qualified medical practitioner immediately, and of course to replace their patch. As Tian mentioned, we will probably also have to review and strengthen the qualification standards and manufacturing protocols for future suppliers, not to mention those currently in place at Endogen. And we should be prepared for further questions and fallout from those who've already been affected—especially if they don't return to their prior equilibrium."

"Sanjeet," Tian asked, beginning to refocus her thoughts after her earlier outburst, "has the WHO been keeping track of the total number of hormone poisoning cases around the world?"

"Yes—it's already well into the hundreds of thousands, though we've had some trouble keeping up with the accelerating reports coming in today. It's hard to say how many of these might simply be an over-reaction from the press coverage."

"It shouldn't be difficult to identify valid concerns with a simple blood test," Tian said, remembering the sample Dr. Austin had taken from her during her visit to the hospital yesterday.

"I think we should expect these numbers will rise even *higher*," Rick suggested. "It's my understanding that the single defective batch produced three hundred *million* patches, and with these levels of overdose, I would imagine just about everybody wearing one of those patches will be affected in one way or another."

"Do you think we might see more serious complications than those already reported?" Tian asked, becoming newly concerned about her own health.

"Hopefully, the rapid return to normal hormone levels from the re-application of good patches will bring everybody back to proper homeostasis. But it's possible those who've experienced thyroid or pancreatic dysfunction could develop more serious complications, such as diabetes or Grave's Disease."

"I was thinking," Dr. Singh added, "it might be a good idea to mobilize temporary walk-in clinics, especially in remote regions, to manage the higher expected caseloads, and to offer specialized treatment for those most seriously affected. That way, at least we can take some of the pressure off local hospitals."

"Yes—that would be extremely helpful," Rick said. "The sooner we can make that happen, the better."

"I agree," intoned Tian. "Alright then. We seem to have a workable plan for dealing with this crisis, at least in the short term. Let's just see what happens when all the defective patches are replaced. Sanjeet, please keep me apprised as you get more information about the numbers affected, and regarding your progress setting up the local clinics. Rick—can you stay behind for a few more minutes to discuss another matter?"

Dr. Singh stood abruptly, taking his signal to leave. "Thank you, Madam-Secretary, I'll be sure to let you know as soon as I have any new information to report."

Tian waited a few moments for the Director-General to let himself out and close the door behind him.

"Rick, there was something else I wanted to ask you about personally. As you've probably noticed..."—she paused as her throat choked with emotion—"...I was one of the unlucky ones wearing the defective patch this week."

Rick didn't think it would be useful to mention that he knew she'd already been treated, and that Jennifer had advised him of her condition.

"I've seen a specialist at your hospital," she continued, "who was very clear about my condition. But I wanted to ask you something she couldn't answer."

"Yes, of course Tian."

"When I look at myself in the mirror...I see somebody I don't recognize. I never thought such an image could be so unsettling—or *grotesque*. But the worst thing is, I've had my first..."

"Yes, I know," Rick said, as he moved closer to comfort Tian. "And I assure you, you're as beautiful as ever."

"But...my period?"

257

"Let's just see how your body responds to the new round of hormone therapy," Rick replied, unsure for the first time of his own words. "Maybe in this case, one period doesn't truly signal menarche. The human body is an amazingly adaptive organism…"

"You mean—" Tian asked plaintively, "this doesn't have to be a *death sentence*?"

"Let's not talk like that. We're going to do everything in our power to make this better. If you want, I can act as your personal physician in this matter. I brought you a supply of good patches to start with. If there's a way to turn this around, we'll find it together."

"Thank you Rick," Tian said, as she wrapped her arms around Rick's neck and pressed her breasts against him. "I always knew I could count on you."

Thirty-six

In the four days since Elias's aborted hypophysectomy operation, his condition had stabilized, but he remained in the Intensive Care Unit of Mount Sinai Medical Center under close observation. From all appearances, the emergency closure of his carotid artery in the midst of Calvin's attempted intervention had been successful, and subsequent brain scans showed the wound to be healing normally. Now it was simply a matter of time for the arterial lining to repair itself behind the temporary patch of fibrin glue.

The healing process would take a number of weeks to complete. After the surgical hemorrhage was plugged, Elias's white blood cells had rushed to the area, engulfing and destroying any germs introduced through the open wound. Subsequently, clotting enzymes activated by the torn blood vessel mobilized sticky platelet cells which were dispatched to the site and clumped together to help plug the opening; this plug would form a scab and be reabsorbed into the body. Eventually, fibroblasts would begin to gather at the site to produce collagen, which would gradually heal the wound with natural connective tissue.

Although Elias was stable, he was still not out of danger. If part of the fibrin glue or the blood clot were to break off before the healing was complete, it could quickly travel through his bloodstream and become lodged in an artery, cutting off circulation and causing brain damage or cardiac arrest. Fortunately, post-operative cognitive tests with Elias had indicated the temporary stoppage of blood and oxygen to his brain was not long enough to cause any loss of mental acuity. He was now sleeping quietly in his hospital bed, with tiny electrodes attached to his chest monitoring his heart rate and the oxygen saturation of his blood.

Shortly after eleven a.m. on Tuesday morning, Elias's body suddenly jerked, and he woke up with a start. Almost immediately, his breathing became labored, and the normally regular oscillations of his heart rate pattern on the cardiac monitor beside his bed began dancing wildly. Fifty feet away, a loud alarm went off at the ICU nursing station. Jane was the nurse on duty and looked up from her charting responsibilities to view the monitor providing a live feed from Elias's room, and instantly leapt to her feet. She immediately recognized the signs of a cardiopulmonary emergency: the rapidly spiking EKG pattern and plummeting blood oxygen levels meant her patient was receiving insufficient oxygen to the heart and lungs, and would soon be in danger of cardiac arrest. Instantly picking up her phone, she dialed the emergency extension and gave the operator the bare essential facts: code name, the hospital unit, and the room number. Then she rushed to Elias's suite to initiate emergency life support procedures.

When she entered the room, Elias was sitting up clutching his chest and gasping for breath.

"It *hurts*—" he cried between gulps for air, "my *chest* hurts! And I can't *breathe*!!"

Following standard protocol, Jane immediately initiated an emergency assessment.

"Were you eating, or did you choke on anything?" she quickly asked.

Elias shook his head quickly from side to side.

From her years of experience providing critical care support to geriatric patients on the ICU, Jane had seen this condition before. She reached into a sideboard beside the bed and pulled out a high-flow oxygen mask, then immediately connected the long transparent tube to an outlet in the wall. Placing the mask snugly over Elias's nose and mouth, she dialed up the flowmeter to ten liters per minute.

"This should help," she stated, while ratcheting up Elias's bed to support his body. "Try to lean back and breathe deeply—the doctor will be here soon."

In his elevated state of shock, Elias was only barely aware of the loud announcement over the hospital's public address system.

"Code Blue," the announcer called. "Respond immediately to Unit IC-2A. Repeat. Code Blue—Unit IC-2A."

While she waited for the emergency response team, Jane tried to comfort her patient, but his rapidly deteriorating condition belied her gentle caresses and forced smile. Elias was beginning to cough raspily, and the spastic expansion and contraction of his abdomen indicated he was laboring to oxygenate his lungs. Unfortunately, Jane knew there was little else she could do for him until authorized personnel arrived on the scene.

Where is the EMT team?! she agonized.

Although it was only a few more seconds, it seemed like an eternity before Dr. Boyd, the ICU resident doctor, rushed into the room with two other nurses, one of whom was rolling a medical cart carrying a defibrillator, IV supply box, and an AmbuBag.

"Status?" Dr. Boyd curtly ordered.

"Heart rate 145, respiration 35, pulse oxymetry 85%—all rapidly deteriorating." Jane answered.

"Is his airway clear?"

"From what I can tell, yes."

Dr. Boyd pulled a tongue depressor out of his pocket and tilted Elias's head back. By now, Elias was hacking and wheezing, and his eyes were wide as saucers with fright. Dr. Boyd quickly placed the wooden stick on the back of Elias's tongue and looked down his throat with a lighted laryngoscope.

"Prepare a syringe with five thousand units Heparin—stat!" he ordered.

After confirming an unobstructed airway, Dr. Boyd knew there was only one other explanation for Elias's alarming symptoms—he had experienced a massive pulmonary embolism, with a large blood clot lodged in the major artery leading from the heart to the lungs. If the clot were not removed soon, Elias would be unable to deliver oxygen to his lungs or his heart, which would lead to imminent cardiac arrest.

As Jane quickly plunged a sterile syringe into a bottle of the prescribed anti-coagulant and filled it to the indicated level, Elias began thrashing wildly on his bed in respiratory distress. With the three nurses helping to hold Elias down, Dr. Boyd drove the needle into Elias's arm and emptied the contents into his bloodstream.

"He's turning blue!" another nurse shouted.

"Prepare for CPR," Dr. Boyd announced.

"No!!" Rick shouted, suddenly appearing in the doorway. He had rushed to Elias's room as soon as he received the emergency page. A quick scan of the monitors above the bed confirmed his grim diagnosis: the tall, peaked P waves in a tightly bunched S1-Q3-T3 pattern clearly indicated Elias was suffering from Cor Pulmonale: acute distress in the right ventricle, from which the pulmonary artery descended. Elias's lungs were quickly filling with blood, and Rick knew that the normally prescribed chest compressions and electrical defibrillation associated with cardiopulmonary resuscitation would only aggravate the condition.

"The only way to save the patient now is to remove the embolus," he said, quickly pushing the less experienced doctor aside.

"Jane—bring me a pigtail catheter right away. I'm going to attempt a percutaneous thrombectomy."

Having assisted doctors with these kinds of procedures previously, Jane knew this was a complicated operation which involved threading a thin guide wire with a coiled tip through Elias's femoral artery into the base of his heart, where the surgeon would attempt to scrape away the occluding tissue mass.

"Shall I prepare the OR?" she asked.

"There's no time," Rick declared, seeing Elias starting to cough up blood. "We need to do it right now!"

Thirty-seven

Calvin James lay on his cold damp bunk at the Manhattan Detention Complex, where he'd been moved two days ago after being denied bail at his latest arraignment hearing. Nicknamed 'The Tombs', the city-block sized structure had been built in the mid-nineteenth century over a boggy swamp in the Bowery, after which the massive complex soon began to sink into the fetid ground, creating a festering dungeon where thousands of prisoners abjectly awaited word of their fate or were sentenced to hang. Over the years, the facility had housed such notorious inmates as Mark David Chapman, Carlo 'Don Capo' Gambini, and the infamous hedge fund swindler, Bernie Madoff. Now thoroughly modernized, the nearly empty nine hundred bed jailhouse echoed with the ghosts of its long departed souls.

Calvin looked up at the dull gray concrete ceiling of his cell and contemplated his next step. Although his attempted interruption of Elias's surgery had been repelled by hospital security forces, he had accomplished his primary goal of stopping the operation and at least temporarily preventing the removal of his son's pituitary. During Elias's recovery from surgery, he planned to launch a new legal challenge to the state's plan to supersede his parental authority over Elias's health. In consideration of his current situation, although he had seriously violated the provisions of his earlier release from custody, Calvin believed his latest offense would not be deemed sufficiently grievous to keep him behind bars for long. Even if he were sentenced to a short jail term, he was confident he'd be able to continue directing his subversive campaign from the inside, since he still had many unfinished plans to carry out.

As a sinister smile gradually developed on his thin lips, he heard the sound of a key rattle in his cell door.

"Mr. James," the prison guard improperly addressed him as he swung open the heavy metal door, "there's an officer here to see you from the FBI. You'll have to come with us to the interview room."

As two juvenile guards escorted him down a long hall, Calvin felt the need to correct the ill-informed correctional officer.

"It's *Doctor* James, if you don't mind—I'd appreciate you accord me the proper respect while I'm under temporary detention."

When Calvin arrived at the sterile interview room, he saw a single polished steel table with two metal chairs, surrounded by four walls embedded with smoky glass panels. In one chair sat a serious looking individual wearing a dark gray suit. The two guards closed the door behind him and retreated to sentry positions in the adjacent hall.

"Dr. James," the seated juvenile declared when he saw Calvin enter the room. "I'm Special Agent Sanchez from the Federal Bureau of Investigation, and I'm here to ask you a few questions. Please make yourself comfortable."

"Whatever would the FBI want with me?" Calvin asked, looking surprised. "Does your agency have jurisdiction over the incident at the hospital?"

"We're not interested in that matter—that is a concern for the local police. I'm here regarding a matter of interstate commerce and industrial sabotage."

"I can't imagine how I could help you with that," Calvin replied. "I have no involvement in any of that business."

As a consequence of his confinement over the last few days, Calvin was genuinely unaware of the recent news concerning the hormone outbreak and the suspicion of patch tampering.

"Perhaps not," continued the agent, "nonetheless, because of your past actions speaking out against the Global Longevity Initiative and your continuing interference in its related activities, you are a prime suspect."

"I have no idea what you're talking about. I've only exercised my civil rights in respect of peaceful protest, in defense of my own rights and those of my constituency."

The FBI agent eyed Calvin carefully for any sign of nervousness.

"Until recently, you mean," he said. "Your forced intrusion at Mount Sinai could hardly be termed a peaceful protest."

"Like you said, that's a matter for the local police," Calvin replied dismissively. "It doesn't concern you."

Agent Sanchez could feel his blood pressure starting to rise. Apparently, he had misjudged Dr. James—this was not going to be an easy interview subject.

"Yes," he continued. "Except as it pertains to your possible motivation for this other, more serious, crime."

"What is it exactly, Agent Sanchez, that you wish to ask me?" Calvin said, feigning irritation. "Perhaps you should stop dancing around the issue, and get right to the point."

Calvin was actually quite interested to hear the latest news and get an update on recent external developments, even if it came from this adversarial source.

"Where were you on the evening of Saturday, November twelve?" Agent Sanchez demanded.

Calvin paused for a moment, unsure whether to reply.

"Where I *usually* am at that time of the week," he finally replied. "In my personal rectory at the Garden of Eden church, where I reside."

"Were you with anyone who can attest to your activities and whereabouts on that evening?"

"Normally, I would have been spending a quiet evening with my son—but as you may already know, he was viciously removed from his home by the Child Services Agency earlier that week."

Calvin stared at Agent Sanchez with cold, blank eyes.

"Yes, I'm aware he's been relocated," Agent Sanchez replied. "And there was no one *else* you saw, or met with, that evening?"

"No—I was quietly preparing my sermon for the following day's address."

Agent Sanchez paused for a moment to review his notes.

"Do you know anyone who works at the Endogen headquarters in New Jersey?"

Calvin smiled, as the purpose of Agent Sanchez' investigation was now becoming apparent—and he had no intention of providing information that might incriminate any of his followers.

"Not directly," he replied, "but I have a large congregation at my church, and Endogen is a very large company. There's a good chance that some members of my assembly may in fact work there."

"I see." Agent Sanchez scribbled some notes on his note pad. "What kind of interaction do you have, exactly, with your congregants beyond the delivery of your weekly sermon?"

Calvin was beginning to enjoy this little battle of wits with his opponent, for he knew that Agent Sanchez would not be able to connect him to any wrongdoing at Endogen, and he was happy to continue playing this game while misdirecting the FBI agent as much as possible.

"I take their periodic confessions as their spiritual counselor of course, and offer additional personal guidance and counseling as requested."

"Who did you specifically see for any direct consultations in the week leading up to the tenth?"

"I have hundreds of members in my congregation who need frequent spiritual guidance and support. I do not keep track of the names and addresses of everyone who comes to see me in times of need."

Agent Sanchez peered into Calvin's eyes for any sign of subterfuge, or any nervous twitch that might belie his true knowledge and motivations.

"Have any of your followers confided in you that they had planned or undertaken any illegal activities pertaining to Endogen's operations?"

"They have not," Calvin replied flatly. "But even if anyone *had*, I would not be at liberty to share that information with you, as their confessions are a sacred and private covenant between themselves and their pastor."

"We could subpoena you," Agent Sanchez threatened, "where you would be required to disclose such information under oath."

Calvin's face suddenly filled with blood as he lost his cool.

"Are you *kidding* me? Under *oath*?! What do you and the rest of your security apparatus know about oaths?" he railed, staring directly at the dark glass windows behind Agent Sanchez, knowing full well others were observing the interview. "There is only *one* valid oath that I, and the rest of my brethren, are duty-bound to follow, and that is our oath to *God in heaven*—to follow His commandments, and His will. There is no other valid law!"

Agent Sanchez saw that he was starting to get under Calvin's skin, and decided to press the advantage in an attempt to make him crack and possibly reveal some relevant information.

"There are also the laws of *men*, sir," he replied firmly, "that must still be respected in order to live in a civilized society. And may I remind you, these are laws that are also *enforced* by men—with serious consequences. We are *all* duty-bound by these laws."

"Perhaps lesser men—or *boys*," Calvin mocked, looking again directly into Agent Sanchez's eyes. "Those in the service of God know a higher power. I'm not afraid of the laws of men, as you call them. They have only led to the desecration of this society, and there is only *one* Judgment Day that everybody must reckon with. And that will happen after you and I, and everyone else in this world, *dies*—which you surely will."

Sanchez decided to ignore the veiled threat, and attempted to calm Calvin down in a last ditch attempt to extract some useful information.

"I respect your right to practice your beliefs, sir, and only ask that you respect my duty to protect those under my jurisdiction as well. If you would be kind enough to answer just one last question before I leave—have you noticed anyone *missing* from your weekly sermons since the evening in question? We are specifically looking for someone who abandoned his job last Monday."

Calvin took a minute to settle down before he replied.

"I've only been able to conduct one sermon since then, because of my incarceration. But I assure you, my assemblies are *always* full. My congregation is very devoted—they always pay their respect on the Sabbath."

"I'm sure they are, Dr. James," Agent Sanchez said, finally giving up. "I'm sure they are a *very* devoted following."

As Calvin smiled smugly at the FBI agent, the two guards suddenly entered the room and stopped about ten feet back of the table. Looking very nervous, their hands hovered close to the holstered taser pistols by their sides.

"I'm sorry to inform you, Mr. James," the first one again erroneously addressed Calvin. "We've just been advised that there was an emergency at the hospital—your son has passed away."

Calvin's smile quickly faded from his lips, and the color drained from his face. Everything in the room suddenly seemed to fade away, and he became lost in his thoughts, anguishing over the loss of his son.

Then, just as abruptly, he became filled with rage as he slowly rose from his chair.

"Sir," Calvin could hear one of the guards vaguely utter in his subconscious, "we need to take you back to your cell now. Please come with us…"

As Calvin clenched his fists and the veins began to visibly rise in his neck, the two guards slowly withdrew their tasers and all three officers nervously stepped back a few paces, awaiting their captive's next move.

Thirty-eight

Joe Morgan sat in his executive office at Mount Sinai Medical Center reviewing the hospital's operations reports for the week and shifted uncomfortably in his chair. In his role as Chief of Staff, one of his primary responsibilities was monitoring and controlling the key performance measures for a range of patient and staff services. Every day he received electronic summaries showing updates and changes in vital statistics relating to patient inflows and outflows, average wait times, treatment time, length of stay, capacity utilization, and the number of NYDs—an indication that the evaluating doctor had not yet diagnosed the cause of the patient's presenting problem.

Over the course of the week, he had seen steady increases in the number of Emergency Room admittances, as well as average wait and treatment times. Starting slowly at the beginning of the week, the rate of increase had escalated dramatically, becoming a torrent by Friday morning. Perhaps most disturbing for the Chief of Staff was the high proportion of NYDs and the capacity utilization figure for the hospital. As was the case the previous week when the ER was swamped in response to the tainted patch, hospital beds and staff were once again stretched to the limit. Joe had anticipated a temporary increase in hospital activity as a consequence of the patch error, but he had expected the number and severity of cases to diminish as affected users quickly changed over to the correct juvenile doses. With a degree of foreboding and alarm, he had called another meeting with his two endocrinology experts, Drs. Ross and Austin, to discuss the situation and try to establish appropriate containment measures.

At ten a.m., he heard a tap on his open door and looked up.

"Rick, Jennifer," he acknowledged, seeing the two doctors, "please come in. I've been reviewing the daily ops reports, and wanted to discuss the unsettling trend in admittances and NYDs that I've noticed accumulating through the week. We're overstretching capacity once again, and I was hoping one or both of you might have some insights on what's causing all this, and what we should do about it."

"Yes, I've noticed it too Joe," Jennifer replied. "I've been spending more and more of my time this week treating walk-ins in, and I don't like what I see."

"What have you been seeing? Aren't the tainted patch users responding positively to the proper juvenile doses?"

"That seems to be the problem—most of them are not. Although many of their previous symptoms have abated, we're seeing a raft of new, more troubling symptoms."

"I can't imagine anything worse than what we saw earlier in the week and over this past weekend. What are the primary diagnoses?"

"We're still conducting tests to confirm a variety of causes, but the bulk of the cases appear to be complications of hypothyroidism and Addison's Disease."

"But those are diseases related to *in*sufficient hormone production. I don't understand—why would we be seeing that? Aren't all the previously affected individuals now wearing good patches?"

"Yes, which is all the more troubling."

"Have we tested the new patches to ensure they have the right hormone levels? Maybe we've got another instance of tampering?"

"I've been sending random samples down to our lab for evaluation throughout the week," Jennifer stated, "and they assure me that all the patch hormones are within specified parameters. There have been no further anomalies."

"What do you think is going on, then? Is it possible that the previously affected individuals have not yet returned to juvenile homeostasis, or that they need different dosages?"

"I'm afraid it's looking more and more like that is precisely the case, Joe," Rick weighed in. "I've consulted my contacts at the CDC and WHO, and they indicated they're seeing exactly what we're experiencing here at Mount Sinai—all across the country and around the globe."

"Jesus," Joe exclaimed, alarmed by the growing scale of the problem. "What do you recommend we do now—what are our options?"

Rick looked at Joe grimly.

"Unfortunately, I don't think we should continue the present course of treatment using juvenile doses. The symptoms appear to be escalating in severity. It seems obvious now that the mature bodies of those previously exposed to the tainted patches have higher hormone requirements, and if they continue under these current deficit levels, we will see progressively deteriorating symptoms associated with hypothyroidism—starting with hypoglycemia, then anemia, eventually leading to diabetic ketoacidosis."

"That's fatal!"

"Exactly. We're obviously going to have to examine an alternative course of action. I think we're going to have to begin applying mature doses to try to reverse the decline and bring them back into stasis."

"But that will mean…" Joe said, barely able to utter the words, "they'll all permanently become—*adults*?"

"Yes," Rick replied, "hopefully healthy adults."

Joe stared at Rick and Jennifer blankly for a few moments, as he contemplated the implications of this news.

"There's no way we've got enough supplies of adult hormones on hand to treat everybody. Or the ability to restock our pharmacy through current sources."

"I know," Rick said. "We'll have to begin ramping up production of new hormone patches in mature doses for those who've been affected. I've already put in a call to the Secretary-General to begin the provisioning process."

"For *everyone*?" Joe asked, incredulously.

"Unfortunately, I don't see any other way."

"Do you think they'll *accept* this—knowing what it means?"

Rick knew exactly what Joe meant. "I don't think they have any other choice. It boils down to the choice between dying quickly, versus the expectation of a full and healthy mature lifespan."

"Well, the stuff is *really* going to hit the fan now," Joe declared, slumping back in his chair. "I'd hate to be in the shoes of an Endogen executive when this comes out. The affected people will be breaking down their doors, looking for heads to roll."

"It's unfortunate, but they are largely to blame for all this," Rick mused. "Endogen should have had tighter controls on their production process. This latest development will only speed up the outsourcing of production to other suppliers."

"Have the police made any progress on finding the primary culprit?" Jennifer enquired.

"From what I know, not yet," Rick said. "But it's only a matter of time. There are seven billion highly motivated people wanting to find the perpetrator—and very few people who had the motivation to commit the crime."

"I assume they're looking closely at that cult leader who caused such a disturbance here at the hospital last week," Joe stated. "There's not much doubt he has both the ability and motivation to do this sort of thing."

"Maybe—we'll just have to wait until the FBI has finished their investigation."

"At least he's in a place where he can't cause any more trouble for a while," Jennifer added, knowing Calvin had been remanded into custody.

"For now, yes. But I understand he's being released temporarily to attend Elias's service tomorrow."

"You're kidding!" Jennifer exclaimed. "I can't believe they're letting him out!"

"He'll be under close guard—they couldn't very well not let him attend his own son's funeral."

"I hope you'll be staying as far away from there as possible," Jennifer said, immediately concerned for Rick's safety.

"Actually, I intend to pay my respects. Especially since I feel partly responsible for what happened."

"Surely you know there's nothing more you could have done, Rick," Joe interjected. "The autopsy confirmed the cause of death as a pulmonary embolism, which could not have been prevented. You did everything you could to save him. This unfortunate event was entirely his father's doing."

"I agree, Jennifer added. "I hope they charge him with *murder* and put him away for a very long time!"

"Something tells me this won't be the last we'll see of Dr. James," Rick replied. "He's shown himself to be a very determined and resourceful adversary."

"Well, at least be careful tomorrow, Rick," Joe said. "We certainly don't want to generate any more friction between the two of you—who knows what else this character is capable of."

"Don't worry, I'll be staying in the shadows. I have no intention of engaging Calvin any more than absolutely necessary. With luck, he won't even see me."

Thirty-nine

Saturday morning was brisk and chilly as Rick drove over the Brooklyn Bridge at the end of a long, slow-moving funeral procession. The sun was shining brightly, and on the bay below he could see the tiny billowing sails of sleek white sloops contrasted against the broad blue expanse of New York's harbor. Passing under the soaring arch of the bridge's west tower, Rick marveled at the beauty and engineering simplicity of the mile-long viaduct. Built more than two centuries ago to accommodate horse-drawn traffic, it was once the longest suspension bridge in the world and the tallest man-made structure in the western hemisphere. While many of its newer iron-and-concrete-clad neighbors sat crumbling and decaying, the Brooklyn Bridge's prescient designer, John Roebling, choose to build his out of hardy granite and galvanized steel cables, which showed no sign of wear and tear, and easily bore the weight of thousands of tons of modern vehicles. Equally impressive was the simple and graceful beauty of the design. Approaching the twin gothic arches framing the massive tower on the Brooklyn side of the bridge, the interlocking latticework of cables looked to Rick like an elegant spider's web of simplicity and strength. Taking the BQE expressway exit off the bridge, Rick nodded a silent tribute to another scientist who took his principal cues from nature.

Elias's funeral was to take place in Green-Wood Cemetery, one of the oldest and grandest burial grounds in the United States, located next to Prospect Park in Brooklyn Heights. The spectacular grounds overlooking New York Bay comprised almost five hundred acres of rolling hills and dales, with a blanket of mature trees providing shelter for thousands of species of birds and other wildlife. When it opened in 1838, it was a popular respite for harried city dwellers, inspiring the subsequent development of other preeminent outdoor public spaces, including Manhattan's

Central Park. Along with its seasonal gaggle of Canadian geese and American black ducks, masked raccoons roamed the shadows at night with the many fireflies which lit up the sky like so many elusive spirits. Among its famous permanent denizens were such titans of industry, art, and politics as Leonard Bernstine, Louis Comfort Tiffany, Jean-Michael Basquiat, Samuel Morse, and Theodore and Alice Roosevelt.

  As the long line of cars approached the main entrance gate at 5th Avenue and 25th Street, Rick slowed to behold the astonishing edifice. Modeled after Pere Lachaise, the famous eighteen-century Paris cemetery, the intricate facade looked like a cross between Paris' Church of Notre Dame and the Temple of the Sagrada Familia in Barcelona, Spain. Carved out of solid red sandstone in the Gothic Revival style, its soaring triple spires and religious friezes evoked the grandeur and excess of medieval art and religious practice. The inscription above the main portico read "The dead shall be raised", with the sculptural relief showing dramatic scenes of grieving and resurrection, reflecting the spiritual promise of rebirth. Near the top of the tower, a large copper bell sounded the arrival of the funeral procession, where a nesting flock of wild monk parakeets—descended from a single mating pair who escaped from a shipping container on route to South America via JFK airport—squawked their disapproval.

  Only here, Rick thought, *at this surreal interface between nature and architecture, could one find such an incongruous sight.*

  Continuing behind the wall into the quiet solitude of the park, Rick caught up with the funeral train as it moved to the right, passing a small byzantinesque chapel set in a quiet dale at the edge of a lily pond. Not much bigger than many of the stately mausoleums belonging to the wealthy families buried on the grounds, its central dome and four rounded turrets looked like a miniature version of Christ Church

Cathedral in Oxford, England. Rarely used any longer for funeral services, it sat as a lonely sentinel over the tombs and crypts stretching far off into the distance.

As the procession slowly wound its way through the narrow serpentine paths leading into the necropolis, Rick was astonished at the beauty of the surrounding landscape. With trees and shrubs of every imaginable variety providing natural context for the graceful statuary and magnificent monuments, it reminded him of an immaculately groomed and palatial sculpture garden. Wild azaleas, dogwoods, and smoke brush sat juxtaposed with stately Victorian mausoleums in a harmonious interplay of nature and art. Most of the leaves had fallen from the deciduous trees at this late stage of the fall season, and the colorful dusting of discarded foliage created the impression of a rich ornamental carpet amongst the sculpted tombs. In springtime, Rick pictured it with the fallen petals from the hundreds of cherry trees on the estate, covering the ground like pink snow.

The slow-moving funeral procession afforded Rick a first-hand opportunity to take in the sights and sounds of the park. Many of the mausoleums and monuments were architectural masterpieces, and each had a story to tell. Resting between two giant blue cedars lay the tomb of the wealthy nineteenth century tobacconist John Anderson, accused of murdering his pregnant mistress. Designed in the Greek post-and-lintel style, its triangular pediment roof supported by four Ionic fluted columns called to mind the majestic Parthenon in ancient Athens. On the opposite side of the twisting lane at the end of a long granite stairway, lay the mausoleum of Imre Kiralfy, a Hungarian Jewish immigrant who produced many successful American Broadway shows at the turn of the century. Built in the classical Roman style, surrounded on all four sides by tall polished Corinthian columns, it sat majestically next to a large yellow elm tree. Further up the road next to a sleepy willow, stood the gaudy Egyptian pyramid-shaped tomb of the minor American composer Albert Ross Parsons, replete with reclining sphinx guarding its heavy copper doors. As if in silent protest, the simple bronze bust of Horace Greeley, founder of the New York Tribune, looked on disapprovingly atop a small granite pediment set amidst nearby craggy pine trees.

    As the funeral procession continued its labyrinthine journey through the park, Rick gasped as he rounded a bend and glimpsed the imposing Neo-classical mausoleum of John MacKay, standing next to a majestic Japanese maple. The massive, tiered granite tomb, topped with a heavy Celtic cross, was larger than many New York City brownstones. No stranger to ostentatious displays of wealth during his day, MacKay, one of the richest Americans of the nineteenth century who discovered the largest silver deposit on the North American continent, had outfitted his tomb with electric heat and illumination.

    But the largest tomb in Green-Wood cemetery belonged to Stephen Whitney, a prominent Manhattan Protestant and cotton speculator, who had his very own chapel built on the grounds. The magnificent eight-sided Gothic structure, surrounded by rhododendron, ivy, and ornamental trees, was equipped with a bench and table for contemplative visitors. Not far away, on the crest of a hill at the highest point in the park, stood The Civil War Soldiers' Monument, a thirty-five-foot-tall soaring granite column guarded by four stoic soldiers, whose bronze effigies were fashioned from melted Confederate army cannons. The adjacent statue of Minerva, the Roman goddess of battle, standing with her outstretched arm saluting the Statue of Liberty across New York Bay, commemorated the Revolutionary War Battle of Long Island, fought on the site in August, 1776.

    The procession finally slowed to a stop near a hillock overlooking the bay, where Rick saw the funeral party beginning to assemble under a large weeping beech tree, next to a small casket resting over an open hole in the ground. Stepping out of his car, he pulled up the collar of his heavy overcoat as much for protection against the biting wind as to conceal his identity, then found an inconspicuous spot under the tall tree's pendulous branches, near the back of the assembly. The group was larger than he expected, and he was thankful that it allowed him to blend in amongst the crowd, especially since he noticed Calvin glance suspiciously in his direction as he approached the party. There was a conspicuously large complement of uniformed police standing a respectful distance back, to which Rick unconsciously edged closer. He recognized many people in the assembly as members of Calvin's congregation, who he'd seen demonstrating many times outside the hospital and at U.N. headquarters. Scanning the crowd quickly, he recognized another familiar face: Nathan Taylor from his Bioethics class, who was standing next to a grim-faced Calvin James on the front row.

  At the head of the open grave stood a lone juvenile wearing long pastoral vestments, whom Rick did not recognize. It was strange to see someone other than Calvin preparing to give the benediction, but of course Rick knew Calvin's freedoms would be tightly restricted under his present house arrest. The police were obviously not going to take any more unnecessary chances with this powerful and unpredictable individual temporarily unshackled.

  When everybody was fully assembled, the pastor began his homily.

  "Dearly beloved, we are gathered here today to lay to rest to another Christian soul on these hallowed grounds…"

  As the pastor paused to allow reflection, Rick could hear the wind whistling through the tall tombstones surrounding the gravesite.

  "Though Elias's life was taken from us prematurely," the minister continued, "he now moves to a world of everlasting peace and blessed fulfillment—in God's domain."

Rick thought he caught a few hostile glances looking his way, and he pulled his collar up higher while inching closer to the relative safety of the police contingent.

"Let us pray now for our lost brother," the pastor continued, "that his soul be delivered to the Lord—where he may be protected forever more in the Kingdom of Heaven."

Many heads in the congregation bowed .

"Lord Jesus, who died for our sins, forgive the transgressions of our brother Elias, and grant that he may rise up so that he may bathe in your light and know the glory of God, for we know that only *you* hold the key to everlasting life."

As the minister continued his invocation, Rick's gaze stretched off to the serenity of the bucolic harbor below, where the distant skyscrapers of lower Manhattan echoed the tall granite obelisks dotting the cemetery's hillside. Catching sight of a distinctive brown tombstone resting nearby, he noticed the prominent inscription and bronze portrait of D. M. Bennett, the famous American freethinker. Inspired by Thomas Paine, Bennett became America's most passionate and prolific critic of religion in the nineteenth century. Often persecuted for his outspoken views in which he advocated birth control, labor reform, women's rights, and taxation of church property, he was eventually arrested and jailed for publishing 'obscene' material. His epitaph read: "Here lies the defender of liberty, and its martyr; the enemy of superstition, and of ignorance, its mother." Rick wondered how Calvin would feel to find his son buried so close to the prominent libertarian. In the background, he was vaguely following the pastor's continuing speech.

"We now commit Elias's body to the earth, for we are dust, and unto dust we shall return. Receive him now, Lord, into the kingdom of the saints, so that he may be with you—forever and ever."

Suddenly, a thundering explosion wrenched Rick away from his thoughts, and he instinctively clasped his hands protectively over his ringing ears. A large pall of black smoke swiftly rose from the vicinity of Elias's casket, and people began running in every direction. The smoke was so thick Rick could barely breathe; he quickly pulled a handkerchief from his pocket and held it over his mouth to help filter out the hacking fumes. The police were trying to rush toward the source of the blast, but the stampede of mourners impeded their progress for many long seconds.

When the smoke finally began to clear, Rick could see that Calvin had disappeared into the hazy fog.

Forty

Tian Yin felt nauseous as she pressed the elevator button for the executive offices on the top floor of the United Nations Secretariat building. Rick had requested another urgent meeting with her to discuss the latest developments regarding the patch irregularity, and the earliest she could clear her schedule was Saturday afternoon. She had been busy planning for the annual reception ball honoring the five Queens to be held this evening at Lincoln Center, and together with her responsibilities for coordinating the WHO's response to the earlier patch tampering issue, she'd barely had a chance to eat or sleep all week.

Although Rick had only indirectly mentioned what he wished to discuss at today's meeting, Tian already knew the reconfigured juvenile patch was not working as planned. The breadth and severity of her symptoms—fatigue, nausea, muscle cramps, extreme thirst, unusual sensitivity to cold, and frequent urination—indicated that her body was not properly adjusting to the prior doses of juvenile hormones. Even more troubling were the *external* signs of escalating imbalance: her hair was beginning to thin, and she was developing unsightly brown spots on her skin. She had tried to cover them with makeup, but it was becoming harder and harder to conceal to the outside world that her body was deteriorating. Tian hadn't felt the need to consult with a doctor to get a proper diagnosis—the daily updates from Dr. Singh confirmed that similar problems were being experienced by juveniles all around the world, in roughly the same proportion as had been reported from the previous patch anomaly. It was obvious to Tian that the re-application of previous juvenile doses simply was not having the desired effect for those unfortunate individuals who had been exposed to the tampered patch.

As she opened her office's heavy door on the thirty-ninth floor and walked slowly toward her desk, she paused at the window to gaze at the city spread out below. The late November weather was chillier than usual, and she could see fog rising off the East River, as the surface water on the estuary evaporated into the colder ambient air. The natural north-south alignment of the city's broad avenues drew her focus to the tip of Manhattan Island and the harbor beyond, and she began to think once again about her ill father, wondering if this was how it felt to grow old.

A soft tap on the door interrupted her meditation, and she swung around to see Rick pausing tentatively in the entranceway.

"Rick," Tian smiled, "please come in. It's good to see you again."

Rick had prepared himself for how Tian would look today, but he was still taken aback by how tired and worn she appeared. Still as tall and erect as earlier in the week, her skin nevertheless looked dull and pallid, and she had dark circles under her eyes.

"Hello Tian," he said, forcing a smile, holding her cold hand while he kissed her gently on the side of the cheek. "Sorry to interrupt your weekend plans, but there's been some unsettling developments since we last met, and it simply couldn't wait. I'm afraid the recalibrated patch isn't having the hoped-for effect—there've been a number of complications."

"Yes, I know," Tian replied resignedly. "Unfortunately, I've experienced them firsthand. Plus, Sanjeet has been keeping me apprised with field reports from the regional offices. It seems our improvised clinics have been overrun with all manner of new hormone-related problems. I wondered why you didn't invite him also to today's meeting?"

"I've been staying in touch with him," Rick affirmed, "and we've corroborated the latest findings. I wanted to see you personally about a couple of other matters."

"Okay, but you'd better give me your assessment of the hormone problem first—though I really don't think I need a doctor to figure it out."

Rick paused for a moment as he pondered how to delicately deliver the bad news. "All the blood tests are indicating a variety of diseases associated with panhypopituitarism."

"I don't understand—how can any of this be caused by a *pituitary* condition? All juveniles—even the healthy ones—have long since had their pituitary removed."

"It's simply a catch-all term from the pre-GLI days. It means insufficient hormone production, which is normally controlled by the pituitary."

"But I thought the patch error had been fixed? Aren't we—*they*—now receiving the proper prior doses?"

Tian was obviously struggling to separate her own condition from those of her constituents.

"Yes, but for whatever reason, it appears to be insufficient to meet the metabolic needs of those who were previously exposed to the increased doses." Rick was finding it difficult to continue addressing Tian in the third person to describe the impact. "It seems their bodies have established a new set point, which is demanding more mature—or at least *adolescent*—doses."

Tian looked at Rick quizzically. "It just doesn't make sense—we were only exposed for a week at most." She was no longer making any effort to maintain the illusion of separation.

"How could such a short exposure have caused an irreversible change in our metabolism?"

"I'm not entirely sure, to be honest. It's likely some kind of cellular, or genetic, response. It's as if everyone affected passed through adolescence—and their bodies refuse to go back. In any event, the symptoms and the assays all point to a clear diagnosis. The problem is growing more severe by the day, so we need to make a change."

"What do you propose?" Tian asked.

Rick hesitated awkwardly. "I don't think there's any other choice: we're going to have to convert all of the affected people over to adult doses."

Tian's heart sank. "Which means all of us are going to be converted into adults—*permanently*?"

"It appears there's no other way. We're working against powerful *genetic* forces now—not simply chemical ones."

Rick addressed Tian directly to be as clear as possible. "Your body is demanding, and needing, adult doses to survive."

"Shouldn't we give the current plan a little longer to see if it takes?" she pleaded, trying not to sound desperate. "The implications are simply too grave if we make this wholesale leap right away."

"The implications are far direr if we stay the present course. We are seeing the early signs of diabetes and Addison's Disease. If these conditions aren't treated soon with proper hormone replacement, the next step will be severe dehydration, convulsions, myxemic coma, and ultimately *death*, as toxins build up in the body from insufficiently metabolized fatty acids."

Tian suddenly became conscious of the chronic dryness in her mouth, and was reminded of her increasing need to urinate.

"Are you sure this will definitely cure these problems?"

"It certainly will stop these specific set of symptoms associated with insufficient hormone production. But we're in uncharted territory here, and I think we're all going to need to be careful about making unconditional promises during this transition."

Tian knew that Rick was referring none-too-subtly to her continuing duties as UN Secretary-General.

"Which brings up another issue," she said, temporarily regaining her composure. "How will we be able to provision the new adult doses of hormones for the millions of affected individuals? Very few of the older adults currently require hormone therapy, by virtue of their functioning pituitaries. How will we find sufficient quantities of these mature hormones in the required doses, in such short order?"

Rick had already considered this and had prepared his recommendations.

"We'll have to produce a new patch configured for adults, using the existing stock of synthetic hormones already produced and available at Endogen—which was the other reason I wanted to see you today. We'll need to begin ramping up production immediately, and also send out another worldwide advisory to ensure everyone who was previously affected changes over immediately to the new patch."

"But we're still not finished qualifying the new vendors!" Tian protested. "Can we trust Endogen to turn this around so quickly? And how will they know the right amount of hormones to include in the patch?"

"I've got our best endocrinologists working on the formulations as we speak. We should be ready to go by early next week. Then it will simply be a matter of adjusting the concentration levels of the existing hormones in the new adult patch."

"So that's it, then," Tian said, slumping back in her chair. "We're simply going to have to accept this new social taxonomy: juveniles, mature adults, and now: newly emerging adolescents. I'm not sure everyone's ready for this—least of all *me*."

Rick leaned forward and held Tian's hands. "I know this is going to be difficult for a lot of people. If you feel you need to take some time off to process all of this and rebuild your strength, I'm sure everybody will understand. Sanjeet can coordinate things in your absence, plus with the existing WHO infrastructure in place…"

"Hey—don't count me out already!" Tian sat up suddenly. "I'm not prepared to go gently into the good night just yet!"

Rick smiled. He knew Tian would have no intention of slowing down. "Does that mean you'll be attending tonight's Gala at Lincoln Center?"

"Well, I *am* the Master of Ceremonies, and that's a role I suspect Sanjeet might not be so eager to jump into." Tian wondered why Rick had never asked to escort her to any of these annual events, and instead always showed up on the arm of another beautiful woman. "Will I see you there?"

"Of course. I never miss a chance to mingle with such eminent and attractive people—including you of course, Madam Secretary. Plus, I've got to keep an eye on my special patient, Eva, to make sure she doesn't do anything that might compromise her role as Queen."

"Yes—especially now that that role appears even more important than ever. After all that's happened these past couple of weeks, it's entirely possible we may need the Queens to save us all from self-destruction. Let's hope this latest turn of events will be the last disruption in our grand plan."

"I wouldn't count anything out," Rick replied tersely. "Nature has a way of throwing surprises at us and disrupting the equilibrium from time to time."

"*Culling the herd*, you mean?" Tian said, referring to the agricultural practice of removing sick or weak animals from the population, but also alluding to the recent maturing of juveniles.

"No," Rick stammered. "You know what I mean." He saw Tian smiling at him, and realized she was just teasing him. "We might want to avoid references like that in our official communiqués by the way."

Tian's smile began to fade as she swiveled her chair and gazed once again outside her window.

"It looks like you'll be outliving me after all, Rick," she said, looking away. "Perhaps I'll be joining my father in the next world sooner than expected…"

Rick hesitated, as he choose his words carefully. He imagined this was the kind of discussion people had with loved ones when they first learned of their pending mortality.

"Tian, there's no reason why you can't live a long, full life—just like he has. Nobody guaranteed that the rest of us would live forever anyway. These recent developments just prove how shaky this whole arrangement is. Besides, you're still young and beautiful, and you've got the whole world literally in your hands. Keep your chin up—we still need you."

"Well," she said, swinging her chair around swiftly, "if this new plan of yours would just clear up my skin and give me back my full head of hair again, that will be a good start. I don't suppose you brought an advance sample of your magic potion with you today, did you, doctor? I could use a little rejuvenation before tonight's special event."

"It's a little more complicated than that, I'm afraid," Rick smiled. "But soon—very soon—we should have you as good as new."

"The new, more *mature*, me, you mean?"

"Hey," Rick said, trying to lighten Tian's mood. "Talk to the Queens tonight about what it's like to be a woman in the prime of her life. I think they'll tell you it's not so bad."

"I might just do that." Tian looked at her watch, mindful of the evening's upcoming event. "Was there something else? You said there was a couple of things you wanted to discuss."

"Yes," Rick said, suddenly recalling the extraordinary events from earlier this morning. "It's probably nothing you need to worry about, but I wanted you to know that Calvin James escaped custody earlier today."

"You're kidding?!" Tian exclaimed. "How did he get out? I thought he was locked up?"

"Unfortunately, he escaped while attending his son's funeral this morning. Quite the Houdini act—I saw the whole thing."

"You were there?! What happened?"

"Essentially, it was one big diversionary tactic. I'll tell you all about it over dinner tonight if you want all the gory details. Am I at the head table again with you?"

"Of course," Tian said, disappointed that Rick hadn't taken her earlier hint for an escort. "You're still our go-to man in this crazy mixed-up plan. In fact, I have a feeling you'll be the center of attention as much this evening as will be our official guests of honor."

"Wonderful," Rick replied, "just what I need right now. Anyway, I just wanted you to keep your head up and alert your people to keep an eye out for this character."

"You don't think he'd be foolish enough to attempt another act of sabotage so soon after his escape, do you? I imagine he'd want to get as far away from here as possible right now."

"You never know with Calvin. He's certainly demonstrated his willingness to stick his finger in where it doesn't belong many times before. Plus, he's undoubtedly got an even bigger chip on his shoulder, now that his son has died. I just don't want you to take any unnecessary risks, since he's previously targeted both of us."

"Well at least he's pretty easy to identify—he doesn't exactly blend in with the crowd. I'll alert our security people here at the U.N. and arrange for tighter security at tonight's Gala, just in case. Thanks for looking out for me, Rick."

"Always, Madam Secretary," Rick said, rising to give Tian a kiss on the cheek. "See you again in a few hours."

Forty-one

Assistant Director Allesandro Inzucchi sat at his desk on the nineteenth floor of the FBI regional headquarters at 26 Federal Plaza in lower Manhattan, reviewing the file for the Endogen investigation. He'd had over thirty men assigned to the case, headed by Special Agent Sanchez, including forensic specialists in chemistry, toxicology, serology, computer systems, audio-video technology, and fingerprint and DNA analysis—and there were still precious few leads. By the end of the week, he had begun to lose patience with the lack of progress. Millions of people were still suffering from the after-effects of contamination from the tampered patches, and his political bosses in Washington were demanding immediate answers. Although his team had already put in many extra hours on the case, Inzucchi let it be known that he expected them to work through the weekend until they found something. At noon Saturday, he called in Agent Sanchez for an update.

Hearing a tap on his glass office door, he answered without looking up.

"Come in," he demanded.

"You called, sir?" Agent Sanchez said, standing tentatively in the doorway.

"Sit down, Sanchez. I want a full update on what you've uncovered in the Endogen investigation so far. I'm getting heat from the Director, and he wants some answers—fast."

"We've made some progress," Sanchez replied tentatively. "I'm hoping we'll have some suspects soon."

"What have you got specifically?"

"Fibers and DNA."

"Excellent. Have you traced them?"

"Not yet. We haven't sufficiently narrowed the pool of suspects."

"Where did you find the evidence—in the mix room?"

"No, those guys were spotless. We've got twenty-four hour video of their movements, and we found no evidence of any change in their routine."

"What, then?" Inzucchi asked, growing impatient. "Where did you find the fibers and DNA?"

"In the storage room for the raw materials and on the labels for the empty drums. We found the previous labels had been overlaid with counterfeit ones. But it looks like the perp got sloppy—we found woolen fibers and saliva spatters on some of the fake labels, and similar ones on the storage room floor."

"Have you run it through CODIS?"

CODIS, the Combined DNA Index System, was the FBI's aggregated database of DNA profiles collected at federal, state, and local crime laboratories across the United States.

"No match. It's obviously someone without a criminal past."

"What about the fibers? What type of material was it?"

"Fine wool, dyed dark blue. Our fabric specialist says it's likely from a business suit—an expensive one."

"Just as I thought," Inzucchi said. "An inside job. Can we match it to anyone working at Endogen?"

"That's the problem. There's over twenty thousand employees working at that site—and Legal won't let us run everybody through for sampling."

"If the fabric is from a business suit, don't we just need to focus on white collar employees?"

"That's still almost ten thousand people—this is their head office. As you know, we've got to have just cause to conduct a search, or demand samples."

"How many employees wear an expensive dark blue suit?!" asked Inzucchi, growing increasingly exasperated. "Can't we narrow it down any further?"

"Unfortunately, blue is still the predominant color in the business world, and I think we'd be on pretty tenuous ground singling people out based on their clothing designer."

"What about the DNA sample?"

"Not much help. The profile comes up white male."

"Great—that ought to narrow it down," Inzucchi said sarcastically, knowing full well over half of Endogen's employees fit that profile. "Let's focus on *motive* then."

Director Inzucchi had been reading the news reports of Calvin James's various acts of civil unrest with interest for some time.

"What about that church pastor who's been demonstrating against the GLI? I understand he was arrested recently for a disturbance at the hospital—the local police would have taken his DNA when they arrested him."

"Already checked," Sanchez affirmed. "It didn't match our sample. And he claims to have no involvement in the Endogen matter."

"Of course not," Inzucchi said, plopping his feet on his desk. "What about his followers—I understand many of them have also been quite active in protesting against the U.N. initiative. Do any of them have connections at Endogen?"

"We secured a warrant to search Dr. James's church records, and we cross-referenced three members of his congregation who work at Endogen. But they all came up clean on the DNA testing."

"And the Director of Quality Control, who quit so soon after the tampering?"

"No connection to the Garden of Eden church, as far as we can tell."

"Any progress on his whereabouts?"

"None. The doorman at his apartment has reported no sightings in the last couple of weeks, and there's been no activity in either his phone or email accounts since he disappeared."

"What about his bank records and credit cards?"

"He withdrew all the funds from his bank and investment accounts a couple of days before he disappeared, amounting to a little over a hundred thousand dollars, and he's not used his credit cards since Tuesday."

"Any suspicious transactions on the cards *before* then?"

"None."

"Did you check airline and shipping records to see if anyone matching his description left the country recently?"

"Yes—nothing on the official record."

"What about Interpol—have they got anything on this guy?"

"Nothing. Wherever he is, he's covered his tracks very carefully."

"He's obviously somebody with means," Inzucchi declared, "or he's getting a lot of help. Somebody of his stature wouldn't last for long on a hundred grand without access to credit."

"Unless he got a payoff for turning a blind eye," Sanchez suggested.

Director Inzucchi nodded, as he mulled Sanchez's theory. "And the video cameras in the storage room—I suppose they came up blank too?"

"Unfortunately, yes."

"Isn't access to that room tightly restricted—how did the saboteur get in there?"

"There are three access points: a main loading door, an inside door leading to the operations area, and an outside emergency exit door."

"Are they not all monitored?"

"The main loading door was monitored by a fixed cam, the inside door can only be opened with an authorized employee access card, and the other door was equipped with an emergency alarm."

"*And...?*" Inzucchi asked impatiently, looking Agent Sanchez directly in the eye.

"Neither the videotape nor the access records show any unauthorized access. We believe the perpetrator likely disabled the emergency exit, then propped the door open to gain entrance from the outside."

"It *had* to be an inside job then," Inzucchi stated. "Who else would have intimate knowledge of the security system and be able to disarm it from the inside?"

"It would seem so," Sanchez offered.

"So all we're left with is a mysterious white male wearing a dark blue suit—and a missing employee?"

"So far."

"Christ, that's not a hell of a lot. The Director isn't going to be pleased with this. We're going to have to find some stronger leads, or one or both of our heads will be on the block. I want you to start interviewing every suit in that place who has access to, or knowledge of, that part of the business—I don't care if you have to question every Goddamn employee! Get on it," Inzucchi said, "and report back to me daily."

"Yes sir," Agent Sanchez replied, backing slowly out of the Director's office.

Forty-two

Eva Bronwen peered from her limousine's window as it slowed to a stop under the dramatic cantilevered projection of Alice Tully Hall. The jutting overhang protruded several meters beyond the edge of the glass façade of the building, supporting three stories of seemingly weightless exhibition space extending the entire length of the block at Broadway and 65th Street. In anticipation of the gala event at Lincoln Center, a large crowd of curious onlookers had formed behind police barricades lining the sidewalks opposite the hall, and the staccato burst of camera flashbulbs from the assembled press illuminated the recessed courtyard on Saturday evening in a frenzy of strobe-like pulses.

Eva and the other Queens were the guests of honor at the annual United Nations Tribute Gala at Lincoln Center, an exclusive event that attracted the city's most famous and powerful celebrities. She watched as familiar dignitaries and entertainers emerged one by one from the caravan of polished black Mercedes to a fusillade of flashes, before heading down the red-carpeted stairway leading into the giant atrium lobby. Politicians and other U.N. notables received a polite response from the crowd, and popular entertainers, many of whom would be performing later in the evening in the Starr Theater, elicited enthusiastic hollers and requests for autographs, but by far the greatest attention was focused on the Queens.

Perhaps it was the fact that few ordinary citizens ever saw the reclusive adult females in person, or that they stood a full head taller than most other persons attending the ceremony, but Eva suspected the newly acquired reverence was because many of the onlookers suddenly recognized, with the surprising turn of events in the past couple of weeks, that the Queens held a special and critical role in preserving the legacy of the human race. Whatever the reason, whenever they emerged from their limousines—all the more eye-catching in their long silk taffeta dresses and glittering diamond crowns—a spontaneous and hearty round of applause rose from the assembled throng.

"Don't worry, Eva," Mike said, noticing her glance up at the large abutment looming over her head, "it won't fall on you."

"I'm not concerned so much about that," Eva said to her escort, "as all this commotion. It's a much bigger crowd than in previous years, and a lot more press. I still haven't gotten entirely comfortable at these events, with all the special attention."

"You'll be fine—you look absolutely stunning this evening. Soak it up, I'll protect you from the paparazzi."

Eva smiled at her companion. She'd grown closer to Mike over the course of the last few weeks, and was glad to have somebody familiar to distract her from the constant glare of publicity.

"I feel ridiculous wearing this pretentious crown," she said, adjusting the scratchy headpiece in her perfectly coiffed hair.

"It's only for this special event. You can take it off in a couple of hours, but I must say—I think it rather becomes you."

Eva was about to protest when somebody opened the car door from the outside and extended a white-gloved hand into the limousine.

"May I assist you, madam?" the curb-side porter asked.

Eva took the attendant's hand and carefully stepped onto the red carpet as Mike followed behind. Suddenly, a burst of flashbulbs erupted in her face, and various members of the press called for her to pose for the cameras. Grasping Mike's arm tightly, she smiled politely, while rising applause grew from the gallery.

"Funny how it takes a crisis to be appreciated," she murmured to Mike as she descended the stairs, trying not to trip over her gown.

When she entered the busy atrium lobby, Eva noticed the Gala attendees were loosely clustered in packs around each of the Queens. Strange, she thought, how nobody gave her and the others much mind except at these infrequent official functions. Nevertheless, she had to admit that she occasionally enjoyed being treated like a queen, and she resolved to enjoy the evening as best she could.

"I'll have one of those!" she chirped, as a waiter approached with tall glasses of Champagne on a silver platter.

Taking a quick sip, she noticed Rick and Jennifer on the far side of the room, making their way toward her.

"Eva," Rick said as he approached, "you look smashing, as always. It looks like your new Endocrinologist has been taking good care of you."

"It must be that magic elixir she's been giving me," Eva replied, smiling at Jennifer. "It certainly has had a stimulating effect!"

Rick looked at Eva's companion awkwardly.

"Excuse me," Eva said. "This is my escort for the evening, Mike Binnington. You remember Mike, of course, Jennifer."

"Yes," Jennifer replied, "it's good to see you again, Mike. I'm happy to see that Eva hasn't been *entirely* rejecting your advances!"

"She's been a perfect lady—befitting a queen," Mike answered, looking at Eva warmly. "It's my supreme honor to accompany her tonight."

"Pleased to meet you, Mike," Rick said, extending his hand. "Though I admit I'm a little jealous I wasn't asked to be Eva's date for this event."

"I knew you had someone *else* in mind this year, doctor," she said, winking at Jennifer. "And I couldn't be happier for you both."

"To fellowship and fraternity!" Jennifer said, raising her glass.

"Cheers to that!" Eva agreed.

"Good evening, Majesty." Eva turned in the direction of an unfamiliar voice, and almost dropped her glass. She recognized Tian Yin immediately from the many official functions they'd attended together previously, but this time Tian looked very different—and not at all well. It was immediately obvious to Eva that Tian had been one of the unfortunate recent victims of the tampered patch, for she had grown several inches taller since they'd last met—and both her voice and her figure had matured appreciably. Even more alarming were the appearance of mottled brown splotches on Tian's usually impeccable skin, which Eva could make out under the heavy application of makeup.

Eva had been keeping carefully abreast of the daily press reports concerning the effects of the tampered patch and she knew that almost five percent of the general population had been affected, but she hadn't expected the Secretary-General of the U.N. to be one of its casualties. From her own experience taking concentrated doses of hormones, she felt a certain degree of empathy with the Secretary-General—though she knew that Tian's case was a more serious matter, with far more wide-reaching implications.

"Madam Secretary," she said, pretending not to notice the change in Tian's appearance, "how lovely to see you again."

In an effort to break the tension, Eva turned to introduce the others in her group.

"May I introduce my friend, Mike Binnington? You know Dr. Ross, of course. And this is Dr. Jennifer Austin."

Tian quickly recognized Jennifer as the doctor who had treated her at Mount Sinai after her initial reaction to the defective patch. She also noticed that she was standing intimately close Rick.

So this is the woman who's been stealing Rick's attention, she thought. *What a coincidence—though she is very pretty.*

A softly tinkling bell thankfully broke the awkwardness, and Tian signaled that it was time to enter the adjacent reception hall, where they were to be seated for a formal dinner. Tian led the party to the large round head table, where the other four Queens were already being seated with their guests, along with the Mayor and his wife. As they took their seats, Tian coordinated the introduction of all the guests, and everybody immediately resumed their polite chatter.

The hall was arranged in a long rectangular shape, with scores of sumptuously decorated white-linen-covered dining tables looking like bejeweled daisies on the rich green broadloom. Each place setting was adorned with an abundance of polished dinner- and silver-ware, plus crystal wine goblets of different shapes and sizes. The guests were seated according to rank and importance, with the guests of honor and the Secretary-General seated at the head table, followed by ambassadors and other high-ranking political figures in near proximity, then presenters and entertainers who were to perform later in the evening, and lastly by corporate executives and other wealthy patrons, who had paid thousands of dollars a plate for the privilege of attending, seated at the rear.

The menu, handwritten on a feathered linen place card in the middle of each diner's gold-embossed charger plate, listed a sumptuous seven course meal with dishes originating from around the world. Starting with a Russian caviar canapé appetizer, followed by Spanish tomato gazpacho soup, then Italian arugula salad with baby beets and pistachios, potato-crusted Chilean sea bass, Japanese Kobe bacon-wrapped filet mignon, and Madagascar chocolate mousse with Rwanda Coffee ice cream—the meal finished with an assortment of American and European cheeses, accompanied with twenty-year-old vintage Port wine. After every serving, waiters dressed in crisply pressed tuxedos dutifully removed the used plates and refilled empty wine glasses.

When everyone had completed the main course and their dinner plates were removed in preparation for dessert, two waiters arrived at the head table and began pouring Champagne from opposite sides. Rick thought it was odd that their uniforms looked a bit rumpled and that they didn't open the wine bottles at the table as was normal etiquette, but he didn't think it was his place to criticize this minor breach of protocol, especially since he knew Tian had more than enough on her mind than to deal with such trivial issues. When the waiters had finished their round of the table, requiring two magnum bottles to fill everyone's glass, Tian raised her flute in a toast.

"Although we will be officially honoring our guests of honor with presentations and entertainment when we transfer to the Starr Theater in a few minutes—" she began, "I'd like to make an unofficial toast to our *five leading ladies*, whose grace and elegance have been a beacon of hope for civilization and for all the people of this world. Here's to our Queens!"

Everyone immediately raised their glasses, and took a hearty sip of Champagne.

"That's a little different," the Asian Queen remarked, looking inquisitively at her champagne glass, "—a rather odd buttery taste."

"Yes," the Latin Queen said. "Almost nutty."

"Like almonds," agreed the Indian Queen.

Rick pulled the unfinished bottle of Champagne from the icy water in the silver-plated bucket the waiter had provided at table-side to keep it cool, and looked at the label.

"Dom Perignon, vintage 2102," he said, "Normally, it's quite dry and crisp-tasting."

Suddenly, he noticed the Asian Queen breathing irregularly, and her skin became flushed.

"What is it Madam?" Rick asked, alarmed. "Are you all right?"

Two seats to the left, the African Queen suddenly clutched her stomach and took a sharp breath. Within seconds, four of the Queens were shaking violently in their chairs and gasping for air. Rick flew to his feet immediately and went to the side of the Asian Queen's chair, followed soon after by Jennifer, who attended to the African Queen. Rick looked into the Queen's eyes and noticed her pupils were severely dilated, then he placed his finger over the carotid artery on the side of her heavily perspiring neck and felt her heart rate racing at over one hundred and fifty beats per minute. Looking up at Jennifer for confirmation, they quickly nodded at one another.

"They've been poisoned!!" Rick announced, catching the attention of a passing waiter. "Do you have Syrup of Ipecac in your kitchen?" he asked, referring to the tonic commonly used to induce vomiting.

"Syrup of wha…" the waiter bumbled.

"Call 911," Rick interrupted. "Get an ambulance here—immediately!" Then, taking a moment to consider the magnitude of the situation, he added: "Make that *five* ambulances!!"

As the waiter ran off, many of the guests in the room rose from their seats and began approaching the head table in a state of alarm.

"Mike," Rick said, quickly looking up, "help me move the Queens onto the floor. We may need to resuscitate them—they're not receiving enough oxygen!"

By now Rick recognized the telltale signs of cyanide poisoning: acute shortness of breath, tachycardia, and flushed, deep-red skin—all indications that the delivery of oxygen was being blocked to the body's cells. The almond-tasting Champagne that the Queens had mentioned earlier confirmed it. He knew if they didn't receive first aid soon, there would be nothing more he could do for them. There was only one known antidote for cyanide poisoning: amyl nitrite, administered by an inhaler, followed by intravenous injections of sodium nitrite and sodium thiosulfate. Only the collective effect of these combined medicines could release the poison's death grip on the oxygen molecules struggling to replenish the Queens' rapidly dying cells.

But as Mike and Rick moved into position, the Queens suddenly began foaming at the mouth, and then one-by-one, slumped over on their place settings—completely motionless. Grimly, Rick and Jennifer quickly checked their pulses and confirmed that their hearts had indeed stopped.

Suddenly remembering *Eva*, Rick looked up and was surprised to see her sitting perfectly erect in her seat, ashen-faced and shell-shocked, but still very much alive.

"Eva!" he cried, dispensing with any formalities. "Are you all right?!"

"I—I feel a little nauseous," she volunteered tentatively, "but otherwise I think I'm okay."

"We need to get you to a hospital—this has obviously been a targeted attack on the Queens. We may need to pump your stomach. Come with me!"

Without waiting for a reply, Rick took Eva's arm and quickly led her to the street entrance, where he could hear the distinctive wail of emergency vehicles rapidly approaching. Within seconds, an ambulance pulled to a stop on the Broadway side of the building, and Rick motioned to the attendant as its rear doors swung open.

"This woman may have been poisoned!" he said to the emergency medical technician as the driver quickly joined them at the rear of the vehicle. "I need you to take her to the nearest hospital immediately." Looking at Eva, he added: "I'm coming with you."

"Rick," Eva replied softly. "It's alright—I'm okay. Obviously I didn't receive the same poison as the others, otherwise I'd be feeling a lot worse than I am. I'm just sick to my stomach from fright. There's no room in here anyway," she said, looking around the tightly packed patient compartment. "I'm sure these gentlemen can take care of me on the way to the hospital. Why don't you follow me in a cab, if you feel it's absolutely necessary?"

"Alright," Rick said, taking a few seconds to calm down and assess the situation. "I suppose that does make the most sense. Which hospital will you be taking her too?" he asked the driver, wanting to be absolutely certain of the address in case he lost them on route.

"St. Luke's/Roosevelt," the driver replied. "It's only seven blocks south."

"Fine, I'll meet you there. Tell the attending physician to check for signs of cyanide food poisoning, and to perform a stomach evacuation if there's any doubt."

The ambulance attendant nodded, then helped Eva onto the bed in the rear of the ambulance and shut the doors. Immediately, the siren began wailing and the ambulance pulled into heavy traffic and was gone before Rick could flag a taxi coming from the opposite direction.

Across town, many miles away on the upper east side of Central Park, a mysterious figure in a white lab coat closed the door as he exited the Cryogenics Lab of Mount Sinai Medical Center, then briskly walked toward to the hospital's main exit. In his hands, he clasped an object about the size of cell phone. As he emerged from the main doors and began his descent of the stairs leading onto Fifth Avenue, he pressed a red button on the device—and an enormous explosion emanated from the bowels of the hospital. Soon after, alarmed and frightened patients and staff began streaming out of the exit, as thick white smoke poured from the open portal.

With a smug smile, the furtive figure crossed the avenue at 98th Street, and disappeared into the park.

Forty-three

When Rick arrived with Jennifer at St. Luke's/Roosevelt Hospital a few minutes after the ambulance carrying Eva had departed Alice Tully Hall, he immediately went to the Emergency Department nursing desk to enquire about Eva's status.

"I'm Doctor Ross," he said, flashing his Mount Sinai identification badge. "I'm here to see Eva Bronwen—can you tell me to which room she's been taken?"

The attending nurse looked at Rick blankly. "How do you spell her name?"

"Bronwen: b-r-o-n-w-e-n. Please hurry—it's urgent."

The nurse typed in the name on her computer, then looked up. "I'm sorry, Dr. Ross, no one by that name has been admitted to our hospital."

"What?!" Rick replied incredulously. "That's *impossible*—the ambulance left minutes before I did, and it would have had much quicker access on route. There's no chance I could have gotten here before they did.

"Have you received a call from EMS?" he asked, knowing it was standard protocol for the attending paramedic to advise the incoming hospital of the patient's condition and the estimated time of arrival.

"No sir, I'm afraid not. Are you sure this is the hospital they were coming to?"

"Yes—absolutely." Rick looked over at Jennifer quizzically, and she nodded. Jennifer had arrived at curbside before the ambulance departed, and clearly remembered the closing conversation with the ambulance attendant.

"Do you have the number for central ambulance dispatch?" Rick quickly asked the nurse.

She checked a thick Rolodex beside her phone, then jotted a number down and handed it across the desk. Rick pulled his mobile phone from his pocket, and dialed the number.

"Yes, this is Dr. Ross," he said, as soon as the operator picked up on the other end. "I'm the attending physician for Eva Bronwen. She was just picked up by an ambulance at Lincoln Center a few minutes ago, but the receiving hospital has no record of her transit. Do you have information as to where she's been taken?"

There was a pause on the line while the operator checked her files.

"We received an emergency call to send five ambulances to that location twenty minutes ago," the operator replied, "but our records indicate that nobody was picked up. The paramedics who arrived on the scene found four DOAs, who have been referred to the Office of the Chief Medical Examiner. We have no record of any other transportation to or from this location in the last few hours."

"Are you certain?! Do you handle all EMS service in the city?"

"Yes—all authorized emergency services are dispatched through this central switchboard."

Rick hung up the phone and looked at Jennifer with a stunned expression.

"What is it?" she asked. "What did they say?"

"They can't find her anywhere in their system. There was no ambulance dispatch record of her pickup at that location."

"You're kidding?!" Jennifer exclaimed. "What do you think we should do?"

Rick thought for a moment, then suddenly looked up at Jennifer with alarm.

Picking up his phone again, he dialed 911.

"Yes, I'd like to report a missing person," he said. "I have reason to believe the Queen has been kidnapped, in connection with the recent multiple murders at Lincoln Center. My name is Dr. Richard Ross. Could you put out an all-points-bulletin for a suspicious red ambulance in the mid-town area, and have the police contact me at this number as soon as possible?"

Rick hung up the phone and looked at Jennifer. Neither one said a thing.

Forty-four

Late Sunday morning, Rick sat on his private terrace in a woolen sweater reading The New York Times, while a pot of fresh coffee brewed in the kitchen. He'd had an exhausting evening staying up late providing details to the police about Eva's disappearance, and he was struggling to put together all the seemingly disconnected events of the past few weeks. First, the juvenile hormone patch had been secretly tampered with, leading to potentially disastrous consequences for millions of juveniles, then four of the Queens were murdered on the same evening as Eva's kidnapping, and now, he had just read in the morning paper that the worldwide supply of human eggs had been destroyed in a carefully orchestrated simultaneous attack on the five official storage banks located around the globe.

How could this all happen so quickly, and so easily? he thought. The Global Longevity Initiative had been brilliantly conceived, and meticulously planned and safeguarded: one carefully selected global supplier of juvenile hormone patches; five supposedly renewable queens; and decade's worth of future egg supply carefully stored in secure cryobanks on five separate continents. Everybody thought the plan was foolproof and indestructible. But here it was, systematically falling apart, and within a thread of imploding completely. The one remaining link holding it all together—the last surviving queen—had been snatched from the relative safety of her protective cocoon, with no apparent means for replacing her and her indispensable supply of life-giving eggs. The recent tampering incident had demonstrated the fragility behind the central premise of the GLI—that it was possible to provide eternal health and longevity for the world's juveniles by artificially suspending their physical development—because it showed that even the slightest interruption could potentially decimate the entire human population.

What now? Rick thought. What would become of the human race? Three hundred million juveniles had to go on an untested regimen of adult hormones to save their lives—but for how long? It was all so new and unpredictable; Rick had an uneasy feeling about what lay ahead. And the *rest* of the world's juveniles, who were still ostensibly 'safe' on their previous fixed doses of juvenile hormones—what would become of them? Could they someday awaken like so many dormant Cicadas, only to find they'd suddenly matured, with a short time to live? What would happen then? The entire human race, the most advanced civilization known to inhabit the universe, would disappear, possibly never to reemerge. It had taken billions of years of natural selection and random mutations to craft the human organism—what were the chances it could happen again? And what of all the *artifacts* and advances created by intelligent life over the course of man's relatively short sojourn on earth? By the time nature could evolve another advanced life form of equivalent capacity, the geo-physical forces of erosion and entropy would likely have buried or obliterated everything we'd worked so hard to build and create.

The prospect was simply too painful for Rick to consider, and leaning back in his chaise lounge chair he closed the paper, contemplating the next steps. Looking up beyond the rooftops of the city's skyscrapers, he could see soft, white cumulus clouds slowly tracing across the pale blue sky.

The forces of nature, he pondered, were immutable, and inexorably moving. In the greater scheme of things, whatever would happen, the tiny powers of man would be helpless to prevent. *Maybe we're just insignificant specks in a grand design after all*, he thought. *No more special than the lowly roundworm, or primitive bacteria.* Maybe this was the natural and inevitable course of man, along with every other organism and random collection of molecules in the universe—destined to meld and grow into bright and impressive stars and satellites, only to eventually collapse and disappear into a black hole under the weight of their own hubris.

As Rick mused over the meaning of life and the attendant forces of the universe, he was interrupted by the sound of his doorbell ringing five floors below. *Who could this be at this early hour?* he wondered. He didn't have any appointments, and it was a bit early for deliveries. Plus, he'd told Jennifer that he hoped to sleep in today and have a bit of personal time to collect his thoughts. As he headed toward the stairs, he glanced toward his rooftop greenhouse and made a mental note to check the condition of his bonsai trees on the way back up.

Under normal circumstances, he wouldn't think twice before opening his front door, but in view of the violent and unprecedented events of the past few weeks, he decided it was prudent this morning to look through the view hole first. Peering through the tiny convex lens, he could see an unfamiliar juvenile male wearing a crisp dark suit. Checking the periphery to ensure he was alone, Rick swung open the door.

"May I help you?" he asked.

"I'm Special Agent Luis Sanchez with the Federal Bureau of Investigation," the visitor replied, flashing his identification badge. "I've been assigned to investigate the disappearance of Eva Bronwen, and I understand you may have some relevant information in the matter. I was hoping you might have a few minutes to share what you know with us."

"Yes, of course," Rick said tentatively, "but I already gave a full statement to the police last night."

"I'm aware of that," Agent Sanchez continued. "But the case has been transferred to our jurisdiction, since it appears to be a kidnapping. I wanted to go over the details and see if you know anything else that could be helpful in locating her. May I come in?"

"Yes," Rick said, as he motioned to the left side of the foyer. "Please come into my sitting room. May I get you something to drink—perhaps a coffee?"

"That would be fine, thank you. I'll take it black, please."

"I'll be right back," Rick said, as he quickly ascended the stairs to his kitchen, where he poured two cups of coffee from the brewing pot. When he returned to the sitting room, he found Agent Sanchez studying the many pictures and photographs Rick had hanging on his wall, showing him with prominent public officials and dignitaries.

"You seem to have known Ms. Bronwen very well," Agent Sanchez commented, as Rick handed him his cup.

"She was...*is*...my patient," Rick said, catching himself. "I've known her since she was a child. She's a very special woman."

"Yes, so I understand," Agent Sanchez said, looking a little too long for Rick's comfort at a picture of Eva in a long, tight-fitting ball gown, standing beside Rick at last year's U.N. Gala. "All the more reason we need to find her before something else happens."

"I couldn't agree more," Rick replied, beginning to grow impatient. "How can I help you specifically, Agent Sanchez?"

"Do you remember any distinguishing features of the ambulance that picked up Ms. Bronwen last night? Perhaps a partial license plate, or a vehicle identification number?"

"As I mentioned to the officer last night, I was far too focused on getting Eva to the hospital as quickly as possible and advising the EMT of her condition, to notice any of that. All I know is that it was the standard red and white colors of the New York City ambulance service."

Agent Sanchez took out his black notepad and began making some notes. "And the ambulance attendants—did you recognize them from anywhere?"

"I'm afraid not—though I did help the police artist develop a preliminary sketch of each of them."

"Yes, we've been given those. Did they act at all suspicious—" Agent Sanchez continued, "anything for instance that might suggest they might not be qualified paramedics or EMTs?"

"Not that I could tell; they seemed to be wearing an official uniform. But I didn't engage them in a very technical discussion, because Ms. Bronwen didn't appear to be in imminent danger or having undue distress."

"I understand you took a taxi to the hospital immediately after the ambulance departed. Were you able to follow them?"

"No, the ambulance disappeared beyond the stoplight by the time I was able to flag a cab."

"Did you see in which direction it headed?"

"South, towards St. Luke's/Roosevelt Hospital, where the EMTs said they were taking her."

"Of course it never arrived there," Agent Sanchez announced dryly.

"No," Rick replied, growing increasingly irritated with the tone of Agent Sanchez's questioning.

"Do you know of anybody who would want to harm the Queen?" Sanchez asked, suddenly referring to Eva in the formal sense.

"No, everybody I know admires and respects her tremendously. She has, after all, made a tremendous sacrifice to protect the continuity of our people."

"For *juveniles*, yes," Sanchez remarked. "But for *adults*, I suspect she's viewed as just another mature woman—albeit one with special privileges."

"She's the only fully grown woman left on the face of the earth who's still capable of reproducing—and producing eggs," Rick replied testily.

"Yes, and who could stand to benefit from that?"

"It appears," Rick said, referring to the morning headlines he'd just read concerning the cryobank explosions, "certain people are in a hurry to *eliminate* the supply of eggs, rather than protect them."

"So now Ms. Bronwen is the lone source of eggs, stored or otherwise?" Agent Sanchez asked.

"That appears to be the case, yes."

"What do you know about *Calvin James*?" Sanchez said, suddenly shifting the focus of his examination. "As an adult male, would *he* not be interested in her reproductive abilities? It seems a little too co-incidental that he escaped from custody around the same time as these suspicious events."

"Yes—I was thinking the same thing."

"I understand you have a history with him?"

"I'd hardly call it a *history*," Rick contended. "We had a few run-ins while he and his band of followers were demonstrating outside my hospital and at the U.N., where I frequently attend official meetings."

"How long have you known him?"

"I've known *of* him for roughly ten years," Rick clarified. "Ever since he took over leadership of the Garden of Eden church from his deceased father, and he became more active in protesting against the GLI."

"You've had *no* other contact with him?" Agent Sanchez asked.

"Other than incidental contact when he tried to disrupt his son's surgery and when I attended Elias's funeral yesterday—none."

Agent Sanchez had checked Rick's file and was aware of the recent incident at the hospital and the subsequent funeral.

"Do you have any idea where he might be right now?"

"I only know of the location of his church, on the lower east side."

"Yes, we've been monitoring that location since last evening, and there's been no sign of activity."

"If he's involved in any of this," Rick said, "I can't imagine he'd be foolish enough to return to such an obvious place."

Agent Sanchez appraised Rick warily.

"Do you know any of his followers, or anyone in his congregation?"

"Only one, Nathan Taylor, who is a student in the Bio-ethics class I teach at NYU."

Sanchez recognized the name as one of the individuals he had identified from Calvin's church who worked at Endogen.

"How did you establish his connection with Calvin James?"

"I saw him standing beside Dr. James at the funeral yesterday."

Agent Sanchez scribbled something again in his notepad. "Has he acted suspiciously with you at any time?"

"Other than being unusually passionate in his defense of the theory of intelligent design—I'd have to say no."

"Intelligent design?" Agent Sanchez asked, obviously not schooled in matters of spiritual philosophy.

"The theory that all of earth's bio-diversity was created by an intelligent higher power."

"I see," Agent Sanchez replied. "Did he ever make reference to the role of the *Queen* in any of this?"

"Only indirectly," Rick replied, intrigued why the FBI agent was taking such a high degree of interest in Nathan suddenly. "In connection with our classroom discussions of cloning, and the reproduction of the species."

"And what was his position on that?"

"He was adamantly opposed to the idea of cloning, and believed that all creatures should not be artificially constrained from reproducing in the natural manner."

"So he was also opposed to pituitary removal and artificial hormone control by means of the patch?"

"Yes, of course—anything that conflicted with his worldview, as he believed God had designed it."

Agent Sanchez suddenly closed his notebook, and slowly rose from his chair.

"If you see or hear anything else you feel might help us in this matter, please give me a call," he said, handing Rick his card. "We'll be giving this matter our greatest attention over the next few days. Please also let us know if you'll be travelling out of town anytime in the next few weeks. Thank you for your time this morning, Dr. Ross."

Agent Sanchez shook Rick's hand, then Rick showed him to the door and closed it gently behind him.

So the chase begins, Rick thought.

Forty-five

Throughout the last week of November, there was little further news about Eva's disappearance, and Rick grew increasingly concerned for her safety. He couldn't imagine why anyone would want to harm or kidnap her, but he had an uneasy feeling that her disappearance was somehow connected with the recent sabotage and destruction of eggs from the world's cryobanks, and with Calvin's escape. He had long feared the two adults might someday form a union, but he never imagined it would take the form of a forced abduction. As he sat in his Mount Sinai office overlooking the capacious foyer of the Guggenheim Pavilion, agonizing over where Eva might have been taken and what additional unpleasantness could be in store for her, he heard a soft tap on his door.

"Penny for your thoughts?" Jennifer asked, peering at him through the open doorframe. Rick had been unusually distant and detached from Jennifer the last few days, and she hoped an impromptu visit might get him to open up a little. Plus, she was in need of a consult on another matter that was rapidly consuming her attention.

"Hey babe," Rick said, looking up sheepishly. "Sorry I've been so preoccupied this week. There's been a lot going on, and I've just needed a little time to sort things out."

"I totally understand, Rick. You've had a lot to deal with. I just wondered if you wanted to talk. You know I worry that you sometimes put too much pressure on yourself by holding everything in."

"I know—my so-called *caveman complex*," Rick chuckled, referring to Jennifer's pet name for his habit of retreating from social interaction to solve his problems. "It's just that I've been racking my brain trying to figure out why anybody would want to kidnap Eva, and what all this has to do with the assassination of the other Queens and with the destruction of the egg supply."

"It seems apparent they're linked," Jennifer said, taking a seat on the other side of Rick's desk. "Could it be that somebody is trying to corner the supply of human eggs in some kind of sick plot to profit from it?"

"I wish it were that benign—if I can use such a term to describe four murders and a state kidnapping. But I fear Calvin is somehow wrapped up in all this, and I think he has other designs on Eva. I can't believe how stupid I was for not insisting on stepping up security for her."

"I don't think *anyone* could have stopped this crime," Jennifer said, trying to reassure Rick. "It was clearly planned well ahead of time—and if Calvin organized it, he obviously had a lot of help."

"Just like at his son's funeral. That was also carefully staged, in full view of the police. The guy's obviously got a lot of…"

"Resources?"

"I was gonna say something else. And that's what worries me the most. The testosterone raging in his system hasn't had an outlet for such a long time, and Eva must present a tempting target. Who knows what short- and long-term intentions he has with her."

"I'm sure the police are doing everything in their power to find her," Jennifer replied. "He can't possibly get very far—they both stand out too much. Eventually, somebody's got to see one of them. Besides, Eva's a strong woman—I think she'll find a way to keep it together until they're found."

"I hope you're right," Rick sighed. "Anyway, I've been so self-absorbed in my own troubles, I haven't given you much attention. I know you've been busy this week as well—how has the transition to the adult patch been going?"

"Actually, that was the other reason I wanted to see you. There've been a number of worrisome developments."

"More problems with the patch? I thought we'd gotten Endogen fully configured for production with the new formulation earlier in the week?"

"We did—they've been producing the adult patch to the newly defined specifications since Monday."

"What else could go wrong? The adoption rate should have been fairly immediate, given the urgency of the WHO advisory and the mobilization of the worldwide distribution network."

"All of that's been seamless," Jennifer replied. "The problem's been entirely to do with the *reaction* to the new patch."

"What are you seeing?"

"It's early of course—only a few days—but the symptoms have not been improving. If anything, they've been getting *worse*."

"That doesn't make sense," Rick remarked. "The previous problems were associated with *under*-production of required hormones. Hasn't that been corrected with the new formulation based on *adult* specifications?"

"Yes, but now these individuals are beginning to exhibit adult problems—*advanced* adult problems."

"In what way?" Rick asked, growing increasingly alarmed by Jennifer's news.

"We've been seeing accelerating ER visits throughout the week from the adult patch wearers exhibiting everything from arthritis, hypertension, cataracts—even early signs of cancer."

"Those are all aging diseases!"

"Exactly."

"All this in a matter of days?"

"Apparently," Jennifer replied. "I was hoping you might be able to shed some light on all this. It's very irregular, and extremely worrisome. I'm not even quite sure how to treat these cases. We could use conventional therapies like drugs and surgery to treat the symptoms, but at this rate we'll soon be over-reaching our resources—plus it won't help to stop the surge of cases we're expecting from the millions of affected individuals who still haven't reported. What do you think is going on, Rick?"

"I was afraid something like this might happen," Rick said, massaging his aching forehead. "We've been holding back the floodgates for so long, I feared if we reopened the window of adolescence, there might be an extreme reaction."

"Even though we're setting their hormone infusions at the more moderate levels of young adults?" Jennifer asked.

"It might not make a difference," Rick replied. "Their bodies have recognized they've passed into sexual maturity, and now they've begun the irreversible process of natural senescence."

"But why at such an accelerated pace?"

"That's the million-dollar question. In other species, when certain phenotypes have had their development naturally or artificially suspended, they've often experienced an advanced or accelerated aging process after maturity."

Jennifer was familiar with the theory of antagonistic pleiotropy, and remembered the classic examples referenced in her pre-med biology courses. "You mean like cicada, or the C. elegans roundworm?"

"Yes. But there could be other mechanisms at work. In Hutchinson-Gilford Syndrome for instance, a genetic mutation stimulates accelerated aging shortly after birth."

Jennifer stared at Rick quietly while she processed his comments, then drew a sudden breath.

"Do you think the suppression of hormones in juveniles might have somehow created an inherent genetic mutation in everybody?"

"I don't know. But I think it would be prudent to take some cell cultures and begin DNA profiling on the affected individuals immediately. Hopefully, we can pinpoint the source of the defect, and see if there's some kind of antidote or counter-measure that can be developed."

Jennifer paused to consider the ramifications of Rick's assessment.

"You know that Joe's going to be all over this," she said, anticipating the hospital Chief of Staff's reaction.

"I'm afraid we've got far more important things to worry about now than simple matters pertaining to hospital administration. We can't afford to let this get any further out of hand; we've got to get some answers—soon. If we were to lose this cohort of adolescents, with no other tangible means of reproduction available, our civilization could be on the razor's edge of extinction."

Jennifer looked at Rick as the blood slowly drained from her face. She knew exactly what he meant, but she also knew there was nobody more qualified to address this critical issue than her colleague and new companion.

"I'll notify Joe and get on the DNA profiling immediately," she said, getting up to leave. "In the meantime, please let me know if you hear anything about Eva."

"I will," Rick said, as he stood to see Jennifer to the door. "The way things are going, we may need her now more than anyone thought possible."

Forty-six

Eva stared blankly at the back door of a gray panel van as it bounced over a bumpy dirt road, while she shifted uncomfortably on the bare steel floor of the windowless cargo compartment. She'd been on the road for many days, and although she had no idea where she was or where she was being taken, she estimated the vehicle had traveled hundreds of miles from New York since the night of her abduction at Lincoln Center. After speeding away in the ambulance, her abductors had taken her to a deserted rail yard and quickly transferred her to the unmarked van, where she was unceremoniously handcuffed to the carriage assembly on the underside of the front passenger seat, while the ambulance driver and attendant were replaced with two new drivers. Eva thought it was strange that neither had made any effort to hide their identities from her; whoever they were and whatever their purpose, it was apparent they had no intention of returning her to normal society anytime soon.

Although she had repeatedly implored her abductors to reveal what they wanted with her, they had remained stone-faced and silent during most of the trip—stopping only periodically to allow her to attend to her biological needs or to throw her cheap snack food from the front seat, which she would awkwardly nibble with her one untethered hand. Wherever they were taking her, Eva noticed they were very careful to avoid detection, because whenever they made necessary stops, it was always on a quiet stretch of country road where there was no sign of human habitation. After carefully checking to ensure the way was clear, the two would escort her into the adjacent woods at gunpoint, and make only a halfhearted attempt to turn away while she relieved herself. Eva was at least thankful the long gown she was still wearing from the ball afforded a modicum of modesty, as it covered most of her lower body while she squatted over the fetid soil.

How far the exalted Queen has fallen, Eva thought to herself. She now wished she'd accepted Rick's offer to accompany her to the hospital in the ambulance—though she couldn't imagine how he would have anticipated this elaborate subterfuge and prevented the gang from executing their malicious plan. As she drifted off to sleep on the hard steel floor, she tried not to think of the other Queens gasping their final breaths around the table at the U.N. gala, and how they painfully fell victim one-by-one to cyanide poisoning.

    A few hours later, Eva woke to the sound of the van skidding to a stop on a gravel road, where the two juveniles got out of the vehicle and closed the doors behind them. Soon after, she could hear them in a muffled conversation some distance from the van, and she strained to listen. She couldn't make out what they were saying, but she thought she heard the voice of a third person—someone with a very different sounding tone. The timber of his voice was much deeper, and it had a strange lilt to it—like someone who was accustomed to speaking to others in an authoritative or pedantic manner. After a few minutes, she heard the sound of another vehicle's doors opening and closing, then it started up and drove away.

    As Eva held her breath, she could hear a set of footsteps moving toward the van on the crunchy gravel, but this time it sounded like only one set of feet. As the driver's door swung open and Eva looked up over her shoulder to see who it was, she gasped in horror. Filling the open space of the doorframe, she saw the sneering mask of Calvin James.

    "Good afternoon, your majesty," he snickered, smiling menacingly at Eva. "It's nice to see you again. Though I'd hoped we'd meet again under more accommodating circumstances."

    "Wha…what do you want with me?" Eva could barely get the words out of her choked up throat.

"Why, I'm *saving* you of course," Calvin replied, as he stepped into the driver's seat and closed the door behind him. "From those self-righteous barbarians who've been using and debasing you for so long."

"I don't *need* any saving," Eva snapped, "least of all from *you*. Why can't you just leave me alone?!"

"You weren't meant to be alone, my lady. You're a national treasure—one who's been neglected and abused for far too long. God has other intentions for you."

"I'm *not* alone," Eva argued, suddenly conscious of the lopsided bargaining position she found herself in. "I have a rich life—and many people who love me. I don't need anyone or any *authority* telling me what's right for me!"

"You mean like the U.N. authority that's been extracting eggs from you to support their grandiose plan—or people who love you like that juvenile who escorted you to the Ball? How could he ever satisfy you? I hope you weren't thinking of developing any kind of serious relationship with him? That's not only unnatural, it's *blasphemous*. God didn't intend for children and adults to commingle in that way."

"Leave Mike out of this! He's simply a good friend and confidant. What have you done to him?"

"I bet he is," Calvin sneered. "But you needn't worry about him, Eva. It's only *you* I want."

"What could you possibly want with me? We have nothing in common—you *repulse* me!"

"You'll see what I want with you soon enough, my dear," Calvin said, as he looked lasciviously at Eva's bare, splayed legs in the back of the van. "I'm going to show you how to be a *real* queen, and how to properly serve your dominion. We're embarking on a mutual journey that will change the course of mankind forever. You and I will begin a new testament to God's will, and lead the path for a new civilization."

"You'll never bend me to your—or your *God's*—will," Eva seethed, as she tried in vain to shake herself free of her shackles. "And you'll never get away with this; the whole world is looking for you."

"Where I'm taking you, no one will think to go or follow." Calvin reached into a bag on the passenger seat, and threw a blanket at Eva's feet. "It will be just you and me—in our own secret Eden."

As Eva felt an encroaching chill, she wrapped the prickly blanket around her and curled up in a ball on the cold, dank floor.

Forty-seven

Tian Yin woke up Sunday morning feeling very odd. Throughout the week, she'd seen increasing signs that her body was not responding well to the newly formulated adult patch, and she'd grown increasingly concerned. It had begun with subtle signs such as vague new aches in her muscles and joints, and small spider veins on her lower extremities. But her hair was continuing to thin, and she had recently developed an irritating ringing sound in her ears. Two days ago, she'd had to buy reading glasses to counter her rapidly deteriorating eyesight. But this morning she felt markedly worse.

As she rubbed her painful, swollen fingers and strained to lift herself out of bed, she shuffled to the washroom where she relieved herself once again, only two hours after her last mid-sleep interruption. When she was finished, she flushed the toilet and moved to the sink to wash her hands. Looking up groggily at the mirror above the basin, she could barely make out her own image. Reaching for the reading glasses she'd left at the side of the commode, she awkwardly placed them over the bridge of her nose and looked up.

Immediately, she took a step back and shrieked in horror. The image in front of her was one she no longer recognized—it was that of an old and haggard woman. Scarcely believing her eyes, she tentatively stepped forward to take a closer look. As she moved to within inches of the mirror, she gasped as she observed the telltale signs of advanced aging: the once taught and plump skin on her youthful face was now sallow and lined with deep ridges and wrinkles running from the edge of her graying hairline to the hanging folds on her neck.

Staring abjectly at the sickly stranger in the glass, Tian saw a lone tear slowly streaming down her cheek. For she knew at this moment, that her life's work had been hopelessly sabotaged, and that suddenly, everything had changed.

Forty-eight

By the first week of December, a panic had begun to sweep across the globe as millions of adolescents wearing the adult patch were seeing irrefutable evidence that something had gone horribly wrong with the plan to return them to normal stasis. Hospitals around the world were inundated with shocked and terrified adolescents presenting a variety of symptoms associated with rapid aging—from arthritis to osteoporosis, hypertension, cataracts, and cancers of the reproductive organs. Even more distressing for the victims were the obvious *outward* signs that their bodies were swiftly declining: deepening wrinkles, proliferating age spots, and rapidly graying hair. For many, this rude awakening represented a blunt reminder of an immutable fact of life they'd long since discounted: their own mortality.

No one had expected this kind of reaction to the adult patch, least of all the previously happy and complacent juveniles. Although most of the newly configured patch users had come to terms with the fact that they would no longer return to their previous juvenile state, they had grudgingly accepted the probability that they would still live the long healthy lives of normal adults. But the surprising turn of events of the last week had quickly transformed their attitude. No longer docile adolescents looking to their nominal juvenile masters for treatment and care, they were now angry and volatile young adults, increasingly frustrated with the perplexed responses and unclear diagnoses provided by their junior caretakers.

In the last couple of days, bands of furious adolescents had begun to assemble outside the U.N. building on First Avenue and at Endogen headquarters in New Jersey looking for answers—and for someone to blame. With the crowds growing increasingly agitated and aggressive by the hour, large regiments of police in riot gear had been dispatched to each location to try to keep the protestors at bay. But by

Monday morning, the situation was getting out of control, as swarms of outraged adolescents converged on the two institutions symbolizing their fall.

At One Endogen Place, on the normally quiet grounds of Endogen headquarters in suburban New Jersey, Roland Jamieson looked down upon the assembled mass of protestors swarming outside the main entrance gate to the executive tower from the relative safety of his office on the twentieth floor. Even from his lofty perspective, he could hear the crowd's angry chants through the thick double pane windows and see the slogans scrawled on their waving placards.

"Murderers!" they shouted.

"Endogen must pay!" others screamed.

Their brightly painted banners, hand-scrawled in bold colors on makeshift cardboard panels, looked to Jamieson like fallen autumn leaves shifting on a moving tide as it crashed against the rocky shoreline—rising and ebbing against the countervailing force of riot police valiantly trying to push it back.

"Criminal negligence!" read one of the waving posters.

"String up the CEO!" said another.

As Jamieson watched the angry crowd vigorously pumping their placards and pressing toward the front doors, another aquatic metaphor came to mind: that of the annual spawning ritual of the sockeye salmon. The adult salmon, similarly pumped up on hormones, were also singularly focused on reaching their target destination—in their case, to release and fertilize eggs at their spawning ground for the next generation. The mad tapestry of colored banners amongst the surging crowd reminded Jamieson of the telltale spotted orange and red colors of dying salmon.

As he watched the crowd converge in a tighter pack and slowly begin to penetrate the line of police in riot gear, he could see the determined adolescents begin to stream through the barricade of clear plexiglass shields, like packs of single-minded salmon breaching the downstream current of a narrowed river pass. It was now obvious that, like their highly evolved eukaryotic cousins, this cohort would not be barred from their ultimate purpose.

Jamieson looked on in an oddly detached manner for a few more seconds, then quietly turned and calmly walked past his frightened secretary, who had also been listening to the alarming developments outside. Without saying a word, he made his way to the nearest exit in the hallway, where he briskly ascended a flight of stairs and opened a heavy steel door leading to the roof. Waiting on a raised helipad on the flat roof deck was a sleek executive helicopter with slowly turning rotor blades, painted in rich blue Endogen colors and emblazoned with a large yellow "*e*" logo on the side door.

Nodding to the pilot, Jamieson climbed in as the rotors rapidly spun up to full speed, then the copter lifted off and banked steeply away from the angry, chanting crowd below.

Forty-nine

On Monday afternoon, Joe Morgan called an emergency meeting with Rick and Jennifer to discuss the latest developments with the rapid aging situation. If he thought he had a logistical and medical nightmare on his hands two weeks ago when the defective juvenile patch was first identified, this turn of events concerning the adult patch was far more serious. His emergency room had been overrun with angry and frightened adolescents demanding instant treatment, many of whom were threatening doctors and nurses who didn't attend to them immediately. Instead of the relatively docile group of individuals who had previously submitted peacefully to treatment from their juvenile caretakers, the new group was a hostile band of aggressively aging adolescents, desperately seeking a cure. But this time there was little hope for salvation or a return to health. Everyone knew that the obvious and extreme signs of accelerated aging signaled something far more ominous, and that they were rapidly running out of options.

In an effort to manage the volatile situation, Joe had tried to step up hospital security with local police reinforcements, but he was told they were too busy dealing with other protests and random acts of violence around the city. It was now obvious to Joe that the only way he or anyone else could hope to put a stop to the rapidly deteriorating situation was to discover the cause of the rapid aging problem, and hope that a cure could be found quickly. At Rick and Jennifer's request, he had authorized genetic tests on the latest batch of patients, and today he was looking forward to their findings. When the two doctors presented themselves at his door at the appointed hour, he motioned for them to come in.

"I didn't think this situation could get any *worse*," he began, "but we're now in the midst of a bigger crisis than I ever imagined. And it's no longer primarily a logistical problem; it's become an out-of-control *epidemic*. I've literally got people breaking down our doors demanding to be treated and cured. I was hoping one or both of you might have some answers for me."

"I'm afraid it's even more serious than we previously thought, Joe," Rick replied with a grim expression. "The tests have come back, and they don't look good."

"What did the DNA profile show?"

What had once taken decades and hundreds of millions of dollars to accomplish—a complete genetic map of the human genome—could now be completed using state-of-the-art technology in mere hours. Advanced electron microscopes, using beams of electrons instead of traditional lenses and normal wavelengths of light, were capable of magnifying culture specimens collected from patients up to one million times, and could actually see individual atoms. Using special enzymes harvested from common bacteria to cut and segment the deoxyribonucleic acid compounds found within every living human cell, advanced computers sequenced the complex strings of material into a personalized 'map' of six billion letters, which could then be compared to the normal chromosomal patterns of healthy individuals.

"We've isolated a mutation in the LMNA gene which produces the lamin-a protein," Rick answered.

"What does that mean?" Joe replied, not nearly as well versed in the science of human genetics or molecular biology as Rick.

"Unfortunately, this protein is an essential chemical that provides the structural scaffolding to hold the nucleus of every cell together. It's the same kind of mutation observed in patients with Hutchinson-Gilford Progeria syndrome."

"My god," Joe replied, recognizing the disease that afflicted some young children, causing irreversible rapid aging soon after birth.

"And the *cell cultures,*" he asked, referring to the other test the doctors had ordered,"—do they corroborate your findings?"

"Unfortunately, yes," Jennifer interjected, pushing two electron micrographs across the desk toward Joe. "In this EM you can see more than fifty percent of the adolescent's nuclear membranes are misshapen—compared to less than *one* percent in the corresponding picture of a healthy juvenile. I'm afraid it's true; somehow the defective patch—or the adult patch—stimulated a mutation of this gene which provides the building blocks for healthy and normal cell regeneration."

"What percentage of the new adult patch wearers have presented with this condition?" Joe asked, hoping the mutation was simply an aberration limited to just a few victims.

"*All* of them," Rick replied.

"Jeezus," Joe exclaimed, finally recognizing the full scale of the disaster. He knew full well that if this condition weren't corrected, it effectively meant a near-term death sentence for more than three hundred million people across the globe.

"What can we do?" he asked.

"Unfortunately, nothing at the present time," Rick stated flatly. "After decades of trying, scientists still haven't found a way to reverse the genetic damage in Progeria patients, and I fear this will be a similar situation. Plus, in this case, we've got even less time to find a cure. With Progeria victims, the normal lifespan is about thirteen years, but this group of adolescents appears to be aging *ten* times as fast. I think their lives will be measured in months, or maybe even weeks, at this pace."

"We'll never be able to provide adequate care for this many affected people with our existing facilities," Joe protested. "What do you propose we do?!"

Rick and Jennifer looked at each other, already knowing the answer.

"We can only provide palliative care now," Jennifer responded. "At this point, it's probably the morgue and funeral homes that should be concerned with overwhelming demand for their services. We can provide pain medication of course, but many of these individuals may be better off being cared for at home or in hospice, since there is very little we can do for them now."

"Nothing?! Joe implored, still not ready to believe his world-renowned hospital was helpless to treat so many critically ill patients. "We're not even going to try finding a cure?!"

"I've sent samples down to the National Institutes of Health in Bethesda," Rick replied, "where the best clinical minds in the country will be working on this. But I wouldn't hold out much hope. Much as cancer does, this bug has now burrowed deep into the genetic infrastructure of every adolescent, and taken root in virtually every cell in their bodies. Unfortunately, some kind of lethal biochemical signal seems to have been triggered, and there now appears to be no way of stopping it. We may have fooled a little too much with mother nature, and now she's bent on removing this damaged cohort from the population."

"What are the implications of this for the GLI?" Joe asked, suddenly thinking once again of his own health. "Do you think the *rest* of the juvenile population is at risk?!"

"That remains to be seen," Rick suggested. "Maybe this is just a freak reaction to certain individuals being pulled out of juvenile stasis, and their genetic clock is catching up for lost time. I've got a meeting with the Secretary-General and Director-General of the WHO later today, and we'll have to make some tough decisions—but it likely won't amount to much more than a new advisory for those already affected. We can only hope the rest of humanity will be spared the capricious judgment of a force greater than us."

As Rick stood to leave, Jennifer peered over at him sadly, knowing he was heading into an even more uncomfortable meeting, where he would come face-to-face with the personal consequences of this horrible disease with his terminally ill friend and colleague, Tian Yin.

Six hours later, in the dimming light of the late autumn afternoon, Rick walked south along the East River waterfront after his meeting with Tian Yin and Sanjeet Singh, trying to clear his head. As he feared, the meeting at U.N. headquarters had been awkward and uncomfortable. Tian had not accepted the news about the genetic mutation and his prognosis well, but even more disconcerting was how much worse Tian looked. Rick had steeled himself for how she might appear, but he was completely unprepared for what he saw. Since the Lincoln Center event ten days ago, she seemed to have aged many years, and perhaps even more disturbing for Rick, she appeared to have given up all hope, now seemingly going through the motions in her duties at the U.N., resigned to her grim fate.

Rick had tried to lighten her spirits by mentioning how he and other top researchers would be doing everything in their power to find a cure for the genetic anomaly, but they both knew the prospects were dim for any kind of antidote. By the close of the meeting, the three had simply agreed to put out another Stage Six WHO advisory, and to encourage member-states to provide additional public funding for the expected increased palliative care needs of adolescents over the ensuing weeks. To make matters worse, Rick had already begun to hear rumors from his other contacts at the U.N. that the Security Council had started a preliminary search for a replacement Secretary-General, as they didn't expect Tian to be useful in her present capacity much longer.

As he bundled up against the cold December wind sweeping across the river and headed south toward the Williamsburg Bridge on the lower east side, his thoughts turned once again toward Eva. It had been almost a week and a half since she disappeared, and he was growing increasingly concerned for her safety. There had been no further word on her whereabouts, nor any kind of ransom demand from her abductors. His repeated calls to Special Agent Sanchez at the FBI had only gotten delayed messages indicating little progress, but reminding Rick to call if he saw or heard anything new. Rick had no idea where Eva might have been taken, but he was now certain Calvin was involved. Although he knew Calvin would never be foolish enough to take Eva to his Garden of Eden church in the East Village under the watchful eye of the local police and FBI, for some reason Rick turned west and began to make his way toward the little church on 14th Street anyways.

As he approached the dark cathedral silhouetted against the moonlit sky, he reflexively looked up at the tall steeple topped with its weathervane-like cross, hoping it might somehow point to where Calvin was hiding. Looking through the mist created by his steamy breath condensing in the chilly evening air, he saw the familiar profile of the church's chimney stack rising above the roofline where he'd previously seen a light shining in Calvin's rectory window. Although there was no sign of activity anywhere to be seen on or about the property, somehow the sight of the chimney triggered a subconscious memory for Rick. As he stopped and peered pensively at the crumbling structure, trying to remember what significance it might hold and how it could be connected to Eva's disappearance, he suddenly remembered something that was missing from his last visit here three weeks ago. That night, when he had stopped by after his nightclub excursion with Jennifer and seen a light in Calvin's rectory, he'd noticed something *else*—there had been smoke coming from the chimney, obviously from a fire Calvin had burning in his fireplace on that similarly cold autumn evening.

Somehow, this image triggered a visceral memory for Rick, and his eyes suddenly widened as he remembered the distinctive scent of the smoke wafting down to street level when he had entered the cab to go uptown. Quickly reaching into his coat pocket for his cell phone, he punched in Agent Sanchez's number. Suddenly, he knew where Calvin had taken Eva.

Fifty

On Tuesday morning, FBI Special Agent Luis Sanchez sifted through the wreckage of overturned office furniture and broken glass on the twentieth floor of the Endogen headquarters building in Somerset, New Jersey. After the police line protecting the main entrance to the executive tower was breached during yesterday's siege, hordes of angry protestors flowed into the building bent on retaliation and destruction. No artifact or symbol of corporate power was spared, and many of the trapped employees were subsequently terrorized by the frenzied mob. Some of the support staff who remained behind to defend the building after most of the executives escaped through hidden exits had been threatened and physically accosted by incensed adolescents looking for anyone to blame.

Although the police had quickly responded to the uprising with armed reinforcements and were ultimately able to disperse the crowds using tasers and tear gas, it was not before the rampaging adolescents had vented their anger and frustration on the human and material symbols of their misfortune. Like a neutron bomb, it seemed as though they had gone through the entire building and left nothing unturned. The giant Endogen glass logo hanging in the lobby had been smashed to pieces, and expensive works of art in the corporate boardroom had been pulled down from the walls and shredded until barely recognizable. Roland Jamieson's office, clearly marked with his Chief Executive Officer title on the outside door and his nameplate on his desk, had been uniquely singled out, with his personal effects smashed and strewn across the floor, and the large picture window overlooking the courtyard shattered.

The local police were now combing through the building looking for fingerprints and other evidence, interviewing support staff in an effort to identify those responsible for the assaults. But Special Agent Sanchez was here today on a different mission; he had little concern for the relatively minor acts of vandalism committed by the rioting adolescents—his only interest was in finding new evidence that might help solve the disappearance of Eva Bronwen and discover who was involved with the tampering of the juvenile patch. Assistant Director Inzucchi was growing increasingly displeased with his lack of progress, and the latest uprisings had only intensified pressure from Washington to solve the cases soon.

So far, Agent Sanchez had very few leads in either case. Although the New York City police had found the stolen ambulance used to kidnap the Queen from Lincoln Center, FBI analysts were unable to find any fingerprints they could trace through their criminal database. On the night of the Gala, the police had found two waiters bound and gagged in a storage room behind the kitchen, but no progress had been made finding their replacements who had stripped them of their clothes and poured the poisoned Champagne. And even though an all-points bulletin had been issued to report any sightings of Calvin James or Eva, neither of the two adults had been seen since their disappearance two Saturdays ago. Last night, in a hopeful turn, Sanchez had received a call from Dr. Ross, who believed she'd been taken to a remote mountain deep in the California interior, but Sanchez thought his evidence was too flimsy to take seriously.

On the matter of the Endogen case, some more promising leads had been uncovered fairly early in the investigation, but since then Sanchez and his team had hit a brick wall. There had been no progress finding the missing quality control manager who fled shortly after the tampering incident, despite a worldwide Interpol alert and search. It was widely believed he'd left the country with some kind of payoff from the ringleaders, but there was still no sign of the main saboteur or his accomplices. The one concrete piece of evidence that Sanchez had been able to uncover—fiber samples and human saliva on the replacement labels of the contaminated drums—had also led to a dead end; he'd been unable to narrow the field of suspects sufficiently to begin testing and cross-referencing samples with the collected evidence.

In an effort to open some new leads and uncover any useful additional information, Sanchez had decided to meet with Endogen's embattled CEO once more to see if the chief executive could provide any clues, given his unique knowledge and understanding of the giant organization.

As Sanchez stepped over the splintered threshold to Jamieson's office, he saw the CEO in his shirtsleeves looking pensively outside the broken window.

"Quite a *mess*, isn't it?" Sanchez said, announcing his arrival.

Jamieson swung around, surprised to see Special Agent Sanchez among the regular police investigating the break-in.

"Yes—who would have thought it would come to all this?" he said, looking about his ransacked office.

"Amazing what a little extra testosterone will do." Sanchez sniffed, referring none-too-subtly to Endogen's loose oversight of the tampering incident.

"I'm surprised to see you here, Agent Sanchez," Jamieson replied, choosing to ignore the crack. "I wouldn't have thought you'd have anything to do with these protests and the break-in; I thought you were primarily investigating the patch tampering incident?"

"I still am. This break-in concerns me only insofar as it might be connected to the missing Queen or the tampering case."

"So you haven't made any progress in uncovering the perpetrator in the tampering case, then?"

"Not really," Sanchez replied, not yet willing to divulge the limited information he'd unearthed so far. "I was hoping you might be able to help me with some of that today."

"I've already told you everything I know. We've given the FBI our full cooperation and access to every part of the organization."

"Yes, unfortunately it's revealed very little so far."

"Perhaps you'll never find the saboteur," Jamieson suggested, with a little dig of his own. "He appears to have cleverly covered his tracks."

"Not entirely. We *have* discovered how he accomplished the tampering."

"Oh really?" Jamieson suddenly seemed interested. "How?"

"Somebody got into the storage room for the bulk materials containers and switched the labels on the vital ingredients." Sanchez said, revealing only part of what he knew.

"How ingenious," Jamieson replied. "Have you got any idea as to who it might be?"

"Not really—I was hoping you might be able to shed some light on that."

"I wouldn't have any idea. Sorry, that whole side of the business hasn't really been a priority."

"So it would seem," Agent Sanchez said dryly. "What about your quality control manager who disappeared so suddenly after the tampering affair. Do you have any idea where he might have gone?"

"I wouldn't have a clue. I barely knew the person. He reported in through the Production Superintendent, three levels below me in the organization."

Sanchez eyed Jamieson suspiciously, surprised by his alleged ignorance of this key part of the business—one he seemed to show much more knowledge about in his previous interview. He decided to look around Jamieson's office for any sign of anything unusually out of place.

"Do you mind if I take a few minutes to look around your office?"

"No, of course not. Though I can't imagine why you'd want to look *here*. Shouldn't you be digging around more in the Production and Operations side of the business?"

"We've already *done* that," Sanchez said, growing increasingly irritated by Jamieson's patronizing attitude. "It's possible someone from your group of attackers yesterday might have left some incriminating evidence."

"Knock yourself out," Jamieson replied, shaking his head at the futility of Agent Sanchez's search.

As Agent Sanchez slowly moved about Jamieson's office, using his highly trained eye to inspect any and every artifact that might provide any germane clue to his investigation, he stopped behind Jamieson's desk, where he noticed a blue suit jacket loosely draped over the scuffed leather chair.

"Is that your jacket?"

"Yes—why?"

"It seems a bit dirty," Agent Sanchez said, noticing a small brown discoloration on the front lapel.

"Really?" Jamieson said, picking it up and holding it to the light from the window. "It must be from the protestors who looted my office yesterday. I left it on my chair when I saw them break through the front door and suddenly had to leave. I suppose I'll have to get it dry-cleaned."

"Do you mind if I take a sample for our records?"

"I suppose not," Jamieson replied suspiciously. "Though I can't see what any of this could possibly have to do with the tampering incident, or the Queen's abduction."

"Let *us* worry about that," Sanchez said icily, as he took a swab of the fabric and placed the specimen in a clear plastic bag.

"Thank you for your time today, Mr. Jamieson," he said, as he suddenly turned to leave. "We'll be in touch."

As Jamieson watched the FBI agent walk smartly out of his office, he retrieved the suit jacket draped over his office chair and inspected the lapel. Somehow, the minor discoloration had escaped his earlier scrutiny. Shaking his head in dismay, he walked into his personal washroom and began vigorously blotting it with a moist towel.

Fifty-one

At LaGuardia airport on the edge of Flushing Bay, Rick and Jennifer waited in the departure lounge of American Airlines for their early morning flight to Los Angeles. After he was rebuffed by Special Agent Sanchez concerning his assertion that Eva had been taken by Calvin to a cabin in the White Mountains, Rick immediately notified Jennifer to tell her he was planning to go there himself the following morning. Jennifer had tried vigorously to dissuade him, believing it was far too dangerous to confront Calvin by himself, but recognizing that Rick couldn't be convinced to let the matter stand with the police, she eventually insisted on coming with him. Grudgingly, the two agreed they would have a greater chance of success working together, if indeed they did find Eva with Calvin.

"You realize this is a crazy idea, don't you?" Jennifer said as they headed toward the departure gate after hearing their boarding call.

"*Somebody's* got to save Eva," Rick flatly intoned, "The feds seem to have more important concerns on their hands."

"Well you have to admit, it's a pretty tenuous link you've suggested."

"I don't think so at all—what are the chances that this same unusual resinous wood odor would be found anywhere else on earth, besides the one remote place where it naturally grows?"

"How can you be absolutely certain it was from the same wood?! I'm sure a lot of pine trees smell alike."

"These ones had a unique aroma, remember? It was from their special resin that makes them so fire resistant."

Jennifer had to admit the old growth bristlecone trees in the Inyo Forest had a uniquely strong scent, unlike anything she'd smelled before.

"Well maybe some logging company harvested a few trees from the region," she argued, not quite ready to concede the point, "recognizing they produce such a nice aromatic fuel?"

"You sound just like the skeptical FBI agent. Besides, these particular trees are far too small and inaccessible for loggers to be interested in harvesting firewood."

"Maybe Calvin likes to hike the Sierras too," Jennifer said, beginning to realize the futility of her argument, "and simply brought back some souvenirs to remind him of the fresh air?"

"What—as checked baggage on his return flight?!" Rick said, as he stowed their bags in the overhead storage bins. "Come on Jennifer, *now* who's stretching?"

"Okay," Jennifer conceded, taking her seat beside Rick, "so what if he *is* there? Who's to say he's got *Eva*? Maybe he's just gone somewhere to lie low and avoid jail time for the incident with Elias."

"Calvin knew full well that wouldn't be a serious enough offense to keep him behind bars for long. He obviously orchestrated his escape for some grander purpose. The assassination of the Queens, the destruction of the egg supply, then the kidnapping of Eva—it's got his hands all over it."

"Why *there* though? It's an awfully inhospitable place to hole up."

"If you think about it, it's the perfect place to hide, precisely for that reason. It's one of the few places on this continent where you can be almost guaranteed no one's going to stumble across them."

"But how could they possibly *survive* up there?! You said yourself: there are very few food sources, and surely there's no power supply that far from any built-up area."

"Remember the grouse and marmots? And there's easily enough wind or solar energy at the top of the mountain to power a small cabin. As long as he's got a rifle or some kind of makeshift animal trap, I'm sure he can find enough food to feed two people."

"Great, so we're going up against a crazed armed man in his fortified cabin on top of the most inhospitable mountain, in the height of winter—completely unarmed?!"

"Yes," Rick smiled, "but we'll have at least one advantage: the element of surprise."

"That makes me feel *so* much more comfortable." Jennifer scoffed.

"Hey, you can still back out," Rick offered. "I didn't want to put you at risk in this venture anyway."

"Are you kidding?!" Jennifer exclaimed. "I made that mistake before, when I let you go to Elias's funeral alone. You could have gotten yourself killed then too. I'm not letting you anywhere near this lunatic by yourself again, if I can help it. Besides, at least I can provide some kind of diversion to give you a fighting chance."

"Yes, you *can* be very distracting when you set your mind to it," Rick kidded, as the two buckled their belts before takeoff. "I hope you remembered to pack your heavy woolens and parka—it's going to be a lot colder on top of the mountain this time."

As Jennifer heard the roar of the aircraft's engines and felt the jet accelerate rapidly off the runway, she looked out her window at the skyline of mid-town Manhattan falling away, and tried not to imagine what horrors Eva might be facing while she awaited her improbable rescue.

Fifty-two

Eva peered out the window of her tiny cabin at the bleak and lonely landscape stretching off to the horizon. For as far as she could see, there was nothing but an empty canvas of cold white snow, dotted with the odd stunted evergreen tree. She had been brought to this isolated hut in the mountains three days ago, with little indication of Calvin's intentions or how long he planned to keep her. But shortly after, it became horribly clear exactly what he wanted, when he forced himself upon the Queen and sexually assaulted her repeatedly.

She initially struggled to resist his advances, but this only served to inflame Calvin's passion. Amidst her continuing resistance, he eventually tied her to his rattling old bed and had his way with her. Her screams for help were only met with malevolent laughter, for Calvin knew there was no one to hear them for hundreds of miles. In a fit of desperation, she'd tried to run away one night when he was preoccupied in the lavatory, but the crusty, foot-deep snow exhausted her within a short distance of the cabin. After calmly strapping on snowshoes, Calvin quickly overtook her and dragged the shivering and sobbing Queen back to his shack.

Now Eva could foresee no escape from her personal hell. Even if she managed to steal away from Calvin while he was sleeping, she wouldn't get far in the sub-freezing alpine temperatures, since he had locked all their warm clothes in a footlocker under the bed. All she had to wear was the flimsy silk ball gown she'd worn at the Gala and a thin cotton negligee Calvin had given her, which barely covered her upper body. Besides, she wouldn't even know in which direction to head, since she had absolutely no idea of her location, or how far it was to any sign of civilization.

Eva knew she had nowhere to run, sequestered in this tiny one-room cabin on a remote wilderness hillside. As

Calvin stoked a fire in the wood stove behind her, she looked up at the twinkling stars in the moonlit sky and imagined herself back in New York City, where she and Mike danced under the sparkling lights of the Hippodrome with everyone looking on in awe. How much she longed to be back among the people from which she once felt so alienated. Only now, after spending just a few days with her volatile contemporary, so viciously driven by powerful hormonal impulses, could she see the inherent value of a world populated exclusively by peace-loving and thoroughly rational juveniles.

"There's no one out there to save you, my queen," Calvin said, as he suddenly came up behind Eva and placed his soot-covered hand around her waist. "It's just you and me in this perfect paradise, where no one will ever find us."

"I'm not your queen, you filthy animal," Eva said, as she recoiled from Calvin's embrace. "And I never will be!"

"With time I'm sure you'll come to feel differently," Calvin replied calmly, pulling her back against his rigid body. "We were *meant* to be together, like Adam and Eve—the first man and woman. Except in our case, we're the *last* ones."

Eva could feel Calvin's excitement rising as he pressed himself firmly against her backside.

"But not for long—" he continued, "you and I are going to rebuild the human race the way God meant it to be."

The thought of Calvin violating her again sickened Eva. His foul breath on her neck and his greasy hair falling on her bosom was more revolting than anything she could have imagined. The only way she'd found to get through the ordeal was to imagine what she would do to him when she had an opportunity to inflict her revenge.

"You're *insane*," she said, seething with contempt. "You think you can actually start your own race of people in this inhospitable place? The rest of the world will eventually find you—and I will *never* bear you any children!"

"Oh, you *will*, my lady," Calvin said, his voice rising in intensity, "and we will surely repopulate the earth. For we are the only two people left who have the means to do so. You will bend to God's will—and to my desire—as it is written in the book of Genesis."

"So *you're* the one who killed the Queens," Eva replied, trying to distract Calvin from his lascivious thoughts. "I should have known. Only a deranged lunatic like you could be so cruel and heartless."

Calvin moved his gritty hand further under Eva's nightgown. "Yes, Eva—I wanted you all to myself. And now with the other Queens gone, there can be no dilution of the race that only *we* will create."

"Aren't you forgetting something?" Eva said, wrenching herself temporarily free. "What about all the stored *eggs*? New queens can be created from them at any time."

Calvin smiled at Eva's ignorance, as he pulled her closer.

"My devoted disciples have taken care of that. They destroyed all the eggs the night of your kidnapping."

Eva looked at Calvin incredulously.

"That's impossible! Those eggs are stored in secure cryobanks all over the world."

"How naive, my sweet sheltered Queen. How hard do you think it is to put on a hospital uniform and steal somebody's security pass? My people did their homework—it was far easier than you can imagine."

Eva began to piece together the seemingly disconnected events of the last few weeks.

"Just like the tampering of the juvenile *patch*?" she asked, wondering how deep Calvin's plan went. "Do you have any idea how many millions of people you've harmed and potentially condemned to death from your selfish act of vandalism?"

"I had nothing to do with that—though that too would have been easy for me, since one of my lieutenants is highly placed within the Endogen corporation. Of course, I'm not at all unhappy about that turn of events. I've been warning for years that this juvenile longevity plan was doomed from the start. But don't worry about your unfortunate friends—they'll soon be going to a better place. All they have to do is repent and ask God's forgiveness—which they will do in due course, because *everybody* wants to be immortal."

Calvin threw his head back and cackled loudly.

"You *beast*!!" Eva screamed, trying to twist out of Calvin's arms. "If you and your God were so righteous, you wouldn't *kill* people in order to demand their loyalty."

"Life and death is the way of the world, my dear," Calvin said, tightening his grip around Eva's midsection. "We simply need to accept that—and enjoy life's ephemeral pleasures to the fullest."

As Calvin leaned in to kiss Eva's neck, his soiled hand clutched her bare breast under her nightgown.

"I'll *kill* myself before I let you take me again, you pig!" Eva screamed, as she flexed her lower leg behind her and found Calvin's testicles with her heel.

Calvin bent over and winced, but managed to maintain his grip on Eva.

"I like your fire and fortitude, Eva," he panted, violently swinging Eva around and ripping open her negligee. "Our children will have strong bodies and strong minds. Just what they'll need to take over the world."

As Calvin began unbuttoning his pants and dragging Eva toward the bed, he stopped abruptly when he heard a strange scratching sound coming from the small window by the lavatory. Cocking his head for a moment, he strained to listen to the curious noise. Deciding it was just a loose branch scraping against the side of the cabin from the force of the howling wind outside, he resumed his advance toward the bed. But when the strange noise was followed up by an unusual clicking pattern, he temporarily dropped his grip on Eva and moved toward the rear of the cabin to investigate.

Precisely at the moment he turned away, Eva noticed a small flashing light coming from the window on the opposite side of the cabin. Moving tentatively towards the strange glow, she suddenly noticed Jennifer's face through the foggy pane, motioning frantically just outside the glass. Catching her breath, she quickly glanced over at Calvin, who was still peering through the lavatory window at the rear of the cabin to see if he could ascertain the source of the earlier sound. Hurriedly darting her eyes back to Jennifer, Eva saw her pointing to the door with one hand while making an unlatching motion with the other. Instantly recognizing Jennifer's meaning, she moved to the front door where she quickly unlatched the heavy wooden beam that blocked the door's forward entry.

Just as she lifted the plank, Calvin swung around and realized he'd been intentionally distracted. As he lunged across the floor, the door swiftly swung open, and he saw Rick standing on the threshold, illuminated by the cabin's gaslight streaming out into the pitch darkness. For a few seconds, neither said a thing, as they quietly appraised each other through the open doorframe. Suddenly, Eva made a motion to escape, but Calvin grabbed her arm and threw her violently back against the wood stove. The hulking cult leader now stood defiantly between Eva and Rick, glaring at his nemesis. Noticing some movement in the shadows behind Rick, Calvin shifted position to see who else was with him, and Jennifer emerged from beside the cabin to join her boyfriend.

Calvin stared at the two juveniles inquisitively for a moment, then a large sneer slowly formed on his long, bearded face.

"Don't tell me you two came up here *alone*, Dr. Ross?" he chortled. "Let me guess—no one else would believe you when you told them Eva had been taken to some lonely mountaintop in the California wilderness? Did you really think you and your girlfriend would be able to take me single-handedly?! I think it's finally time I taught *you* a fundamental biology lesson, and show you who the alpha male is in this environment."

As Calvin clenched his fists and began moving menacingly toward Rick, Jennifer suddenly lunged in front and thrust a small aerosol can toward Calvin's face with her outstretched arms. She pressed the actuator button on top of the can frantically, but nothing came out—the freezing temperatures had apparently jammed the mechanism.

Calvin paused briefly, as if momentarily threatened by the improvised weapon, then let out a sinister laugh.

"Is that the only weapon you brought to this engagement?!" he sneered. "How pathetic. Haven't you two learned by now? The hand of God will never be vanquished."

As Calvin resumed his advance toward the open door, Rick looked around and saw a snowshoe resting just inside the door frame. Pushing Jennifer behind him, he quickly picked it up and held it threateningly over his head like a baseball bat.

Do you think you're going to stop me with a *shoe*?" Calvin mocked, pausing only briefly. "After I beat you senseless with that thing, I'm going to make you watch while I have my way with both of your women. Then you'll see what it really means to be a man."

In a burst of speed, Calvin lunged toward Rick and flicked the snowshoe out of his hand, as if batting a fly. Grabbing Rick fully around the neck with one giant hand, he struck Jennifer with the other as she rushed forward protectively, instantly knocking her unconscious.

"Prepare to meet your *maker*, Dr. Ross!" Calvin seethed, as he tightened his grip around Rick's neck. "Your time, as everyone's must in due course, has finally come. You've only a few seconds left to ask for God's grace, so you'd better do so quickly."

As Calvin pressed his thumbs against Rick's trachea and began to cut off the air supply to his lungs, Rick kicked and flailed, attempting to strike Calvin in the shins—but this only heightened the cult leader's rage. Lifting the much smaller juvenile off the floor with outstretched arms, Calvin began shaking and squeezing Rick until he turned blue in the face. Just as he was about to lose consciousness, Rick suddenly saw Calvin's eyes fly wide open and he heard him utter an unearthly bellow, as he loosened his grip around Rick's throat and dropped him to the ground. Gasping for air, Rick looked up and saw Calvin slowly topple over him through the open door, landing face down in the cold, hard snow just beyond the threshold.

    Embedded deeply in Calvin's back, directly between his shoulder blades, was a still smoldering fireplace poker, shimmering in the cold, dense moonlight. Glancing behind him, Rick saw Eva—shaken and furious—standing over Calvin with dark, soot-covered hands.

Fifty-three

The morning after his return from California, Rick placed an electronic tablet displaying the front page of The New York Times on his kitchen table, where Jennifer was sipping her morning coffee. Prominently displayed on the front page was a large picture of the two of them beside Eva, as they triumphantly emerged from the jetway upon their return to LaGuardia airport. Boldface headlines trumpeted the resolution of the Endogen tampering case and the Queens' assassination, as new information uncovered by the FBI in its ongoing investigation and by Eva during her week-long captivity in the White Mountains spilled out the sordid details.

Almost lost among the celebratory headlines was a shorter story further down the page detailing the deteriorating condition and rising death toll among the world's rapidly aging adolescents, and a much smaller picture of Tian Yin. Looking thin and drawn, she was announcing at a U.N. press conference the results of the juvenile patch tender process—and her resignation as Secretary-General.

Concurrent with the licensing of five newly authorized vendors, Endogen's contract was being canceled amid revelations that it's CEO, Roland Jamieson, had been found to be the ringleader in the tampering of its e-patches. His accomplice, Endogen's quality control manager, was apprehended by FBI agents on a yacht off the coast of the Canary Islands, after Jamieson revealed his plans to start a charter boat company and Interpol traced the owner of the newly registered vessel to a deceased individual whose identity the manager had assumed.

Eva's exposé of Calvin's organization structure and the plans he shared with her at the cabin had led the FBI back to Nathan Taylor, who eventually confessed his and various other Garden of Eden church members' complicity in the planning and execution of the Queen's kidnapping, the destruction of the egg supply, and the assassination of the other Queens' at the Lincoln Center Gala. Eva, Rick, and Jennifer had been treated for minor bruises and concussions after their return from Calvin's cabin, but all three were issued a clean bill of health and were resting comfortably after their mountain ordeal. Now all that remained to be resolved was the critical matter of the rapidly aging adolescents.

"The conquering heroes return, huh?" Jennifer commented upon seeing the picture on the front page.

"So it appears."

"Crazy, isn't it," she remarked, reading the lead headline about Jamieson's arrest. "Who would have thought Endogen's CEO was behind the patch tampering? What was he thinking?!"

"Obviously, he wasn't thinking very clearly. Desperate men are driven to desperate measures."

"All because of the prospect of losing the U.N. contract?!"

"Not entirely. That set in motion an unfortunate sequence of events that led to the pummeling of his company's stock, and he was so heavily invested and leveraged that he apparently saw no other way out of his personal financial predicament."

"But how did he stand to gain from driving his own company to financial ruin? And how did he manage to hide his actions from the financial authorities?"

"He was very clever. Instead of directly shorting the company's stock, which would have immediately raised the attention of securities regulators on the New York Stock Exchange, he purchased put options on the more obscure Chicago Board Options Exchange, and hid his ownership of these positions in a complex nest of numbered companies."

"Put options?" Jennifer asked.

"It's a security which provides the owner the right to sell the underlying stock of a company—in this case,

Endogen—at one fixed price, and profit when he buys it back at a much lower price. It allows the holder to magnify the gains he would normally get from shorting the stock, by investing far less capital up front and assuming a much bigger stake in the downward fall of the shares. He would have made out quite handily had he not been caught."

"Except they always get caught," Jennifer mused, "—just like Calvin. Unfortunately, he paid a far higher price for his misadventure."

"He did. Although he might have gotten away with his plan too, at least for a while, if we hadn't gotten lucky."

"Yes," Jennifer admitted sheepishly, "it turns out you were right about the connection between the burning wood scent at Calvin's church and the source of that wood in the forest atop the White Mountains. But how did you know he had a cabin up there?"

"I didn't. It was just a gut feeling, and I decided to run with it. The FBI certainly wasn't getting any closer to finding her—and we had nothing to lose."

"Except our *lives*. We came pretty close to losing those!"

"Yes," Rick admitted, "I suppose we got a bit lucky there too."

"What were you thinking going up there without any weapons or backup?" Jennifer teased, not wanting to pass up an opportunity to rib Rick one last time. "I told you it was a crazy idea!"

"Well, if you remember, I initially intended to see if we could simply confirm Eva's location, then call in the police when we had irrefutable evidence. It wasn't until I saw Calvin intending to rape Eva, that we had to act quickly."

"It certainly went down pretty fast after that," Jennifer remarked. "I still think it's a miracle we all survived. It seemed for a moment like that cult leader truly was possessed by a supernatural power!"

"He certainly overpowered us easily enough," Rick admitted. "I think even if your mace can had worked properly, it mightn't have been enough to stop him in time. Where did you get that stuff anyhow?"

Rick knew there was no longer any reason for juveniles to carry protection against violent offenders, and consequently few stores carried the product due to the extremely rare instance of these kinds of offenses.

"It was actually *bear repellent*. I picked it up at a mountaineering shop at the airport when you went to the restroom. I wanted to have a backup plan in case we got into any trouble."

"It certainly did get us into trouble—it almost got you killed!"

"I was trying to save your fanny, remember?" Jennifer chided. "Thank heavens for Eva—I think she's the real hero in all this. How's she doing anyway?"

"She's still a little shell-shocked from the incident and experiencing some post-traumatic stress from Calvin's treatment of her, but she's glad it's finally over."

"Unfortunately, it's not yet over for the millions of aging adolescents," Jennifer said, scanning the other story on the front page of the paper. "What will become of them, and of the Global Longevity Initiative, now that all the eggs have been destroyed?"

"We'll just have to begin rebuilding the protective stores of eggs using our one remaining Queen, assuming Eva is still up to the task. Conceivably, we could replace the other queens by using her newly harvested eggs to create new mature females, assuming the will is still there to do so. As for the future of the GLI, we'll just have to hope that another random ecological intervention doesn't throw us out of equilibrium."

"Or human intervention," Jennifer said, referring to the tampering incident.

"Or *divine* intervention," Rick suggested, recalling Calvin's final invocation to him at the cabin.

"Let's hope all that intelligent design nonsense finally fades from public discourse, now that its chief proponent has perished."

"Well there's no denying that the design of this sophisticated ecosystem is indeed *intelligent*—even if it's simply from the invisible hand of evolution, systematically weeding out less intelligent or capable organisms not as well equipped to compete in the ever-changing landscape. Either way, it all comes back to the notion of chaos theory: small unpredictable changes in the static environment lead to extraordinary changes and mutations in that environment over time—over which we have little control."

"What about those unfortunate individuals who weren't so lucky to escape this latest disturbance—what will become of the rapidly aging adolescents?"

"I'm afraid there's no hope for them now," Rick said, offering his grim prognosis. "The genetic anomaly is thoroughly embedded on a cellular level and impossible to remove now. As horrible as it sounds, it's nature's cruel way of culling the herd. The sick and non-reproductive ones are simply getting in the way of the survival of the fittest—it's an inevitable fact of the natural environment. We can only trust that nature is once again doing what's best for the whole."

"Another example of your rule of antagonistic pleiotropy?"

"Yes—unfortunately, what's good for the individual is usually bad for the whole species. And vice versa."

Rick glanced down at the picture of Tian peering sadly out from the front cover of the newspaper.

"Except in this case, we're talking about individuals we know and love."

Epilogue

On a cold February afternoon, Rick stood on a knoll on the south edge of Green-wood Cemetery overlooking New York harbor. Not far from Elias's burial site rested the simple headstone marking the fresh grave of Tian Yin, who had just been buried in a grand ceremony attended by hundreds of dignitaries. Tian had specifically requested to be buried in her newly adopted country, in a location with a view across the ocean to her homeland. It was a clear day, and Rick could see for miles across the sun-dappled bay, past the majestic Statue of Liberty raising her arm as if in salute, to the horizon shimmering in the afternoon sun. He thought it was a fitting resting place for the luminous leader who had so elegantly bridged the two worlds. The epitaph on her tombstone simply read:

> *Tian Yin, 2060-2110.*
> *Somewhere between heaven and earth lies the promise of rebirth, for the acts of this life lay the seeds for the next.*

The mourners had long since left the burial site, but Rick lingered afterward until the cemetery workers had covered the grave with fresh soil, because he wanted to give Tian something he had long ago promised her. Bending down, he took a small glass jar from the pocket of his overcoat, and carefully removed a tiny seedling. As large fluffy snowflakes began to fall from the bright sky, he planted his newly sprouted Methuselah seedling in the loose dry soil in the shadow of Tian's headstone. Kneeling over her grave, he paused for a moment to say goodbye to his dear friend, then gently patted the earth around the tiny green shoot.

As he stood to leave, he felt the pager in his pocket vibrating. Squinting to read the display in the bright sunlight, he saw it was a message from Eva.

Just discovered I'm pregnant. Have decided to keep the baby—it's a girl! E.

Rick smiled as he headed toward the ancient Gothic spires of the cemetery's exit gate.

So the cycle continues. Perhaps Tian said it best: all that is guaranteed in this world is that in death, lay the eternal seeds for renewal.

Independent authors such as myself depend upon your readership and feedback to continue our passion for writing. If you enjoyed this book, please share your review on my Amazon book page at:

getbook.at/cp

Like, share, post, and follow me at:

https://www.facebook.com/thecicadaprophecy

https://twitter.com/jrmcleay

www.jrmcleay.com

Watch for my next medical thriller, **The Medusa Miracle**, to be released exclusively on Amazon in the next few months!

Acknowledgements

The initial germ for this novel was planted more than thirty years ago when my best friend in college threw the gauntlet with his graduation gift to me, a book titled 'Conquest of Death'. This book suggested that within our lifetimes, advances in biology and medicine would find a way to reverse the aging process and ultimately 'conquer death'. At the time it seemed pretty far-fetched, but tremendous strides in biochemistry have been made in recent years, and we are now beginning to understand the mechanism of aging at the molecular level and seeing the potential to arrest the cause of life-threatening diseases and perhaps aging itself. To Richard Ross, who suggested with youthful bullishness 'if anyone can do it, you can'—you are the inspiration for the protagonist in this story, and my role model for achieving ethical excellence in everything we do.

The medical science underlying the central hypothesis in this book, that hormones activated when we pass through puberty send chemical signals which slow and ultimately restrict the cellular replication process that keeps our tissues healthy, is a synthesis of many theories previously developed in this area of study. In this respect, I have stood on the shoulders of giants trying to gain new insights into the potential applications and learnings from the field of biogerontology. Most notable of course is the work of Charles Darwin, whose seminal study 'On the Origin of Species' and his development of the theory of evolution is the foundation upon which all of modern biology rests; but also George C. Williams, whose book 'Sex and Evolution' revealed the intrinsic trade-off between traits that help our survival in early life and diminish our survival in later life.

My interest in this subject—and the specific challenge of investigating why organisms die—was stoked by my professional experience as a root cause facilitator in industry. One propitious day, a particular client, Scott Boggs, challenged me to apply my process to a difficult health problem, and this began my passionate pursuit of ever-widening and more complex investigations of health issues heretofore unsolved. Eventually this led to the ultimate biomedical conundrum: why do we age and die? Of course, this story presents only one hypothesis, albeit one grounded in real medical science and much empirical study, but this hypothesis could not have been formulated without the extensive training and fundamental root cause analysis experience I received during my many years as a consultant and associate with Kepner-Tregoe.

I would also like to thank those who reviewed my initial manuscript and provided invaluable feedback. Graciela Barrera graciously offered to read my first draft (which was all the more challenging during her first pregnancy), and gave me positive feedback to continue developing my story. Kelly Kreth gave critical and constructive feedback on my writing style, with many suggestions for story improvement and potential titles. And of course Mom, Dad, and my son Britton gave supportive feedback that this story had potential—thanks for your continued encouragement. Finally, special thanks to Dr. Silvio Inzucchi, Professor of Medicine at Yale University, my providential seatmate on the Acela Express between Washington DC and New York City, who generously offered his special expertise on the subject of endocrinology and who edited my story notes concerning the hypophysectomy surgical procedure.

This book is dedicated to those technicians and scientists on the leading edge of biogerontology research, whose exciting and emerging discoveries in this field are driving the race to solving mankind's greatest medical quest—the conquest of death in our lifetime.

Printed in Great Britain
by Amazon.co.uk, Ltd.,
Marston Gate.